My Way to You

By J. Glassburn

J. Glassburn

Acknowledgments

Getting to this point in my life has always been *the* dream. Ever since I was a young teen, it's been my passion to write stories, and it was always the goal to write and publish my own novel. However, *life happened,* and my personal ambitions were placed on the back burner. Now, at thirty-one years old, I'm so excited to introduce my first novel to you all.

My first thank you is to YOU, my readers. Thank you so much for picking up my book! I appreciate your support, and I sincerely hope you enjoy my novel. Just know that I'm sending you a virtual hug, and I'm only a message away. If you want to connect, feel free to reach out to me! I would love to hear from my readers.

I also want to thank my other half, my husband, Shayne Glassburn. Shayne, thank you for being my sounding board and for never getting tired of hearing me talk about my characters and this crazy dream of mine. Your encouragement and guidance during this whole process has meant the absolute world to me. From the day that I confided in you about this many moons ago, you have always encouraged me to write down the stories that bounced around in my head. I can't say thank you enough for always being by my side and pushing me to fulfill this dream of mine. Thank you so much for being my safe space and my person. I love you from the bottom of my heart.

To my mother, Rhonda Pannier, thank you for being my other person. Your continuing encouragement for me to go after this means so much to me. Thank you for being my (other) number one fan and for always believing in me. This last year was rough for me, but you always picked up the phone and gave me the guidance and love I needed. Writing this book means so much to me, and I know I wouldn't have gone for it, if it wasn't for your continuing encouragement. Love you!

I also want to give a shout out to my other parents who also have supported me in this crazy dream of mine. Thank you to my dad, Robert Palmer, stepmom Stacy Palmer, and stepdad Keith Pannier. Your love means so much! I know I come up with some crazy off the wall ideas, but each one of you always listens to me, and I can't thank you all enough for it! I love you all so much!

And now my siblings... Thank you guys so much for listening to me go on and on about this! Nicole Bowers, Ryan Palmer, Kyle Pannier, Cesselie Pannier, Ethan Palmer. You guys mean the world to me, and your support during this process has been wonderful. Nikki and Cess, thank you for encouraging me the most during all of this. Your feedback has meant the world to me, and you both gave me amazing input. I appreciate you both so much and love that you two aren't just my sisters, but my best friends.

I need to make a special shout out to my brother, Ryan Palmer. Have you seen my cover? It's beautiful and perfect and it's all thanks to him. Thank you, Ryan, for working on this for me. I know it was rough for a little bit there, but just know that it means so much to me that you created my first cover. It's stunning, and your artistic talent blows my mind every day. I will always be grateful that you went on this journey with me!

To my Grandma Pat, mother-in-law Tonya Tidaback, and my Glassburn family, (you all know who you are!) thank you so much for just being there and believing in me! I love you all!

Now to my children, Remmy and Emma. Seriously, they make this parenting thing easy. They are the best kiddos I could have ever asked for. They are sweet and kind and for being two littles, they were understanding when I told them I had to work on

J. Glassburn

my book. Remmy and Emma, I love you both so much! I'm truly blessed to be your mom!

To my Beta Readers and my Editor, thank you so much for taking the time to read and edit my book. Your thoughts, opinions, and advice meant everything to me. You all gave me such great feedback, and I know editing my book was no easy task. You all have helped me blossom my novel into something great, and I could have never done it without you!

I am so blessed to have the support system that I have. Thank you all so much for being *you*, and for being the light for me this last year.

I hope you enjoy *My Way To You*.

Love,

J. Glassburn

J. Glassburn

Copyright © 2022 Jessica Glassburn

All rights reserved.

ISBN- 9798353508298

Dedication

This book is dedicated to the man that has loved me unconditionally.

I love you, Shayne.

J. Glassburn

My Way to You

Chapter 1- *Abby*

If I could be granted one freebie in life that had zero consequence, I would use it today to kick Michael Carter straight in his microscopic balls. Is it childish? Of course. Rational? Not at all. Would it make me feel *so* much better right now?

Abso-fucking-lutely.

I would give just about anything to be able to stand up from my small office cubicle, march right over to him, stare straight into his cold, heartless eyes, and kick him right in his sacred jewels. Then, when the asshole would fall to the ground in complete and utter agony, I'd laugh loudly—like a deranged psychopath.

If I have to sit here one more minute, I may do just that.

I knew as soon as I walked into work this morning, and saw Michael's office door firmly closed, that today was going to be an incredibly long day. My eyes have been trained to look there as soon as I walk into the office; if the door was open, it would be a decent day. If it was closed, I was going to want to smash my face repeatedly on my desk. I knew what the 'closed office door' meant. I wasn't stupid, even though Michael apparently thought I was.

My morning so far consisted of sitting at my desk, doing actual work for a solid twenty minutes, and pretending to be busying myself with imaginary work that I simply don't have for the remainder of the time. *Seriously*. It's snail pace kind of slow right now. If that's not bad enough, I also get to sit back and watch the

Michael and Hallie show. My blood boils every time I hear her heels clatter on the vinyl office floor, and it takes everything in me to stay rooted in my chair.

I heard the heels before my eyes found her. I slowly breathed in and out and reminded myself that I do not look good in orange. Without wanting to, my eyes glanced up over my cubicle. Today, the fashionista wore a very tight black dress that looked like it belonged at cocktail hour, rather than the workplace. Her short platinum blonde hair was down and full of tiny spirals around her face with not one single hair out of place. She had bright red lipstick painted on her lips, yet her eyes were covered by thick black sunglasses. I felt the urge to call out to her, *"Hey dumbass, you're inside,"* but because I'm a damn professional and this was *my* workplace, not hers, I refrained. The last thing I wanted on this mundane Thursday was to be the cause of wildfire gossip.

She walked down the hallway as if she was a damn runway model. Poised as ever, she clutched her leather briefcase to her side confidently, swaying her hips. She glanced around the office, flashing my co-workers her bright teeth and dazzling billboard smile. I waited for the inevitable Miss America wave and sure enough, she delivered. Some co-workers waved back enthusiastically, but most just nodded in greeting. I refused to wave or make any kind of eye contact with her. I'm rather an impulsive kind of woman, maybe slightly insane, and know that the only way I would acknowledge her is with my middle finger.

Her name was Hallie Weston, and she's the top Real Estate Agent in our county. She lets us all know it, too. *"Oh, you don't know who I am? I'm Hallie Weston! I may look familiar to you, my billboards are all over this damn city. I'm #1 Real Estate Agent here, don't you know."* At first when you meet Hallie, you find her charm mesmerizing and her brown eyes enchanting. During our first introduction, she went out of her way to include me into the conversation, lightly touching my arm when she laughed, and acted as if we were the best of friends. Soon, I came to the realization though that behind that pretty smile was a lioness ready to pounce. Little did I know during our first encounter, that her next victim was *me*. The way she shook my hand and told me that I was just *'so darn cute'* and *'I've heard that you're a wonderful Processor, you should be so proud!'* should have been my first clue that she was fake as her tits, but at the time, it wasn't in my nature to judge anyone so harshly.

It's in my nature now though. I despised the woman with every ounce of my being.

I'm woman enough to admit that the real reason why I do not like Hallie is because she's a gorgeous human being, and I'm nowhere close to her league. I'm not generally a jealous person, but with her, I can't stop myself. She's confident, has a body that would be deemed perfection, a flawless, symmetrical face, to die for glossy hair, and the most perfect, bronzed skin tone. If all of that didn't make her sound perfect, she's also slaying it in the Real Estate industry. I wish I could say that she's a beauty with no brains, but that would be a lie, and if there's one thing that I despised most in this world, it's lying. She's been nominated as the Top Women's Real Estate Agent for a second year in a row in Florida and speaks at several *Women's Success* conferences a year.

Then there's me. The rocking body I used to have has been gone since the day I peed on a stick. I own, but do not wear, fancy nice dress clothes. Nowadays, I opt for a more practical look. Today for example, I'm rocking awesome black capri dress pants with my old lady black sandals which are very worn down. I'm wearing a plain, gray cotton t-shirt with what I believe has a Cheeto stain on my right boob from my earlier purge session. I'm not exactly dressed to impress today, but what can I say—*laundry day.* I have no makeup on my face today because it's freakin' Florida and it will just melt off anyway and then there's my *hair.* My long, once luscious brunette hair is pulled up from the nape of my neck with my favorite black alligator clip. Again, because it's Florida and it's hotter than balls out there today.

I know my look is not sexy or even remotely cute, but I'm always just so *damn tired*. I'm legitimately running on fumes, and I have been this way probably for the last few years. I'm having to jump over constant obstacles, and the hurdles get larger each day. If it wasn't for caffeine to get me through my days, I'd be a waste of space. Even the thought of trying to get myself 'dolled up' in the morning with a cute outfit, nice hair, and makeup *exhausts* me. I start my day at the crack of dawn with the quickest shower known to mankind, followed by making my family breakfast. My husband requests an omelet to start his day and my son prefers the classic chocolate chip pancake. Then there's me, who chooses an apple because I don't have to cook it. After I get breakfast ready, I gear up for battle and face my biggest morning challenge: get my oh so stubborn child out of bed. It's a workout that requires my full attention, and I must be somewhat caffeinated before I start the daunting task.

Even though that boy makes me want to reach for the Advil bottle every morning, he's my world, and I wouldn't give up those exhausting mornings for anything. Once he wakes up a little bit, eats a little food, drinks a little milk, he's approachable and full of hugs, kisses, and "*I love you, Mommy's*". He may be part of the reason why I'm slowly losing my sanity, but his happiness, wants, and needs always go first to me. They always will, too, because he's my Remmy.

It would be a hell of a lot easier if I had support from my husband. I would probably fall down on my knees in happy tears if he offered just one time to take Remmy to school, or make breakfast, or do just one item on my extremely long list. Unfortunately, my husband in all of his glory tells me that he can't be *bothered* with those mundane tasks and that maybe I should prioritize my time a little better.

That's what I need to master, *time management skills*. It couldn't possibly be that maybe what I need is just a little help.

My husband spends his days working out in the morning, followed by a run, eating the breakfast I prepare for him, and then he leaves for his eight to five job. Some days he goes golfing instead of work right away. He says it's *'schmoozing'*, but I call it bullshit. After work, he goes out with his clients or partners and doesn't come home until the sun is down, leaving me to do *everything*.

What a wonderful life he lives.

Speaking of the devil, *my husband,* Michael, finally opened his office door. Yeah...the Michael Carter that has the tiny balls that I want to kick, is my husband. I'm such a lucky lady.

Working with your spouse is no easy task. One out of ten do *not* recommend it, especially when your husband has problems controlling his eyes and dick. I used to watch him flirt with countless women during my typical eight-hour work day, but due to how painfully slow we are right now, I'm working reduced hours. At first when my boss pulled me in and told me of the news, I was distraught. I loved my schedule, making my own money, and separating myself a little from home, but after a week into the new schedule, I felt lighter and even relieved. It was nice being away from that place and Michael's shenanigans, but I still missed the busy office atmosphere.

"Hallie, it's good to see you! Let's talk, shall we?" My eyes glanced towards Michael's booming voice, and I felt my body start to cringe as he pulled her into the enclosed office. Truthfully, he sounded like a douche when he talked that way.

"Hallie, it's so good to see you," I whisper mock into my computer screen. *"Let's talk, shall we?"* Idiot.

As soon as the oak door clicked shut, I fought the urge to start gagging. Does he really think that I'm completely oblivious to what he's doing in there? The whole office knows, for crying out loud. Even as the door clicked, my fellow co-workers' eyes flitted over to me for the briefest moments, disapproving scowls etched into their faces. It was insanely embarrassing, knowing that your fallen relationship was widely known throughout the office. You would think one would be more subtle with their affair, but I never said Michael was bright.

I didn't have concrete proof of his actions; I've never witnessed Hallie straddling him, but I've always been taught to trust your gut feeling and my gut screamed that Michael was cheating. The red flags started to pop at me a few months ago, but I ignored them. I couldn't accept it because how could my husband cheat on me, after everything I've done for him? It was getting harder by the day to ignore it when it was right in front of my face. For one thing, I always knew when Hallie would be stopping by the office because Michael would have the blinds and office door tightly shut, especially when generally he had an open-door policy.

Right on cue, my Instant Messenger pinged at me, and I quickly accepted the flashing message. It was Carol, a fellow Processor, that sat a few cubbies down.

"Seriously?" she wrote. I shook my head and started to type back.

"Seriously..." I typed back.

We know better than to write more because the Big Man is always watching and the last thing I wanted was to be pulled into HR's office for speaking ill of their top Loan Originator. It wouldn't matter that Michael was my husband; they would fire me in a heartbeat just to prove a point. They had a Zero Tolerance policy for bullying, as they should, but it still made me wonder what their policy was for screwing Realtors for deals? Probably frowned upon.

I glanced at my empty email Inbox and decided that it was time for me to call it a day. Sitting here with nothing to do except watch Michael's office door, did not seem enjoyable to me. I went through the process of clocking out and shutting my computer down. I gave Carol a knowing look as I grabbed my purse from the nearby hook. Her lips pursed into a frown, her soft brown eyes full of distress for me.

Carol was the absolute sweetest lady I've ever met, and she was my lunch buddy. She's voiced her opinions to me numerous times about my husband whenever I gave in and vented to her. I didn't do this often, but I knew I could trust her.

"Divorce him, he's an asshat," is her usual argument with me, but I always reply with the same thing. Yes, he is an asshat, but he's my husband, and the father of my son. I remind her that it's my job to take care of them and we don't have any proof that he's actually screwing her. The last time I said this to her, Carol covered my hands with hers on the table and whispered, "But sweetheart, who's taking care of you?"

No one, Carol. I'm not even taking care of myself.

Hallie's shrill laugh came from the office door, and I felt my face pucker in distaste. I groaned. *Out loud.* My co-workers glanced over at me, and they gave me sympathetic looks, which only intensified the anger bubbling underneath my skin. This was just plain sad. *Pathetic.* I didn't need or want their sympathy. What I needed was to know what in the world could possibly be *that* funny?

Images of the two of them in there, caressing and touching each other, spread through my mind vividly and my stomach lurched in response. I needed to get the hell out of here before I barged in there and made a fool out of myself. I glanced over at Carol and her sad eyes. I gave her the best smile I could manage, a little shrug and blew her a kiss. I walked as fast as I could on wobbly legs, knowing that the entire office was watching me as I left.

As soon as I escaped, I let out a sigh of relief and breathed in the hot, humid air. I leaned back on the brick building, my eyes closed as I let the Florida sunshine blast my face, reveling in the warmth it provided.

"Everything will be okay," I whispered to myself, with a firm nod. No one was dying and it wasn't the end of the world, but it felt as if it was the end of *my* world. I didn't know how to fight against it.

I cleared my throat, trying to get the lump that appeared to leave, but it was lodged in there, nice and tight. I forced myself to move my legs and I weaved in between the cars in the staff parking lot. My black SUV remained in the spot that I left it, number fifteen. I unlocked the door swiftly and slid into the leather interior. The stagnant heated air blasted me as beads of sweat started to protrude on the nape of my neck. I turned the car on, rolled down the windows, and popped the sunroof open to let out the cruel air. With another exasperated sigh, I collapsed into the back of my seat.

"He's having an affair," I said out loud. It was time to come to terms with this fully; my husband of six years was screwing other women. I couldn't even recall the last time that *we* had sex. Each time I tried, he turned me down, and eventually I quit trying. It wasn't like I didn't want to, because I did; the vibrator just wasn't cutting it anymore, but Michael always had an excuse. He was too tired, or he wasn't feeling well. Most of the time, it was well past dark when he would come home anyway, and I would already be fast asleep. It was just easier that way, to be asleep when he came home, because if I happened to wait up for him, we'd end up arguing for another few hours, and I would end up crying myself to sleep.

Just as I was about ready to fasten my seatbelt and head home, I heard my phone buzz within my purse. I unzipped the top of the bag and dug through the many contents within, until my fingers grasped the smooth plastic. I pulled it out eagerly and glanced down to see my mother's smiling face flashing on the screen.

"Hi Mom," I said. I cleared my throat and tried to take a deep breath so she wouldn't hear the frustration and sadness that was evident in my tone.

"Hi Abs!" I closed my eyes and listened to her warm, sweet voice, letting her voice soothe me. I would give anything to be able to see her in person today, but with her states away, it wasn't possible. My heart longed to be with her though. I missed her, but today was the first day in a long time that I actually felt that I needed her.

"How are you? How is your day going?" I asked. The hard lump started to throb in my throat as I fought back the tears brimming my eyes. I always felt that my mother had some kind of sixth sense when I needed her. I blinked rapidly, willing the tears not to spill. I didn't want my mom to know how unhappy I've become as of more recently. As far as she knew, I was happy here in Florida.

"It's going good, sweetheart. I am currently knee deep in cake flour and sugar." She let out her welcoming laugh and I quickly wiped a tear that escaped. "The town is having a bake sale in the square tomorrow to raise money to replace the play equipment at the park. I'm making my chocolate cake, peanut butter pie, and my Reese's cake. I hope it all turns out, it's a little humid here today."

"I'm sure it will. Sounds delicious. I wish I was there to help," I replied.

"Oh, I wish you were here, too, Abs. Your dad and I are missing you and Remmy something fierce. How are you both?"

"We're good. Today is Remmy's last day of school. I'm going to pick him up soon and then I thought he and I would spend the evening in the pool."

"Aw, that sounds like so much fun. I know you both will enjoy yourselves." Mom paused for a moment and continued slowly. "How is Michael doing?" Her added question seemed forced, but as usual, I didn't comment on it. I paused, too, because I didn't know what the hell to say to her. *He's terrific, Mom, probably balls deep in a Real Estate Agent right now.*

"He's fine, he's working a lot," I managed to say.

My parents never really did like Michael. Their forced conversations and stiff posture when he was around, told me all that I needed to know. They also didn't like it when we both decided to put down roots in Florida. Florida is approximately a 19-hour drive from my small hometown of Carrington, Illinois. In Michael's defense, I have always loved Florida. I fell in love with the sunny state, the palm trees, and the beach. I was always a 'sun person' and the sunshine always put me in a good mood, even on the worst of days. I did miss my parents though; I missed seeing my mom whenever I wanted to, and going out to lunch with my dad. We FaceTimed and talked quite a bit though, but it wasn't the same. It's hard to make memories over video chats.

"Well, that's good. I hope business is doing well for him. How's work for you?"

"Slow," I answered with a sigh. "The market is not all that great right now and we've seen a decline in just the last few weeks. They reduced my hours for now, which is fine with me. Extra time with Remmy."

"Well, I know you enjoy working. I hope it picks up, but in the meantime, enjoy that time with Remmy! They grow up so fast," Mom said, with a sigh. "You know, maybe this is a good time to come visit us?" Mom's voice chirped. "It would be great to see you both. Your dad and I want to come visit you, too. Maybe you can visit here first, and then we'll come visit you before Remmy starts school again in the fall? You can stay as long as you want, and I can get your room ready and the guest room ready for Remmy."

My heart faltered at her excitement. I would love to go home and visit with her, but I knew deep in my heart that if I visited, it would be like putting a stake right through my marriage. Our marriage was already so rocky, what would happen if I went for a long visit, nineteen hours away? I know full well that there's no way in hell Michael would come. He'll bring up some bullshit excuse about his job and how he couldn't take a vacation right now. No, I had to try to focus on my marriage and my own little family. I had to get things back on track here first, but I wasn't going to tell Mom that.

"We would love to come and visit, Mom. Let me look at our calendar later and I'll let you know if we can make it work."

"Okay, sweetheart, you just let me know so I can get the rooms ready. Are you doing okay, Abs? You sound a little down." *There it is.*

"I'm okay, Mom." It was a lie of course. I was a hypocrite for doing so; after all, I hated lying.

From the corner of my eye, I noticed the office door spring open and two people emerge from the office. Hallie was first, walking with a little pep in her step and to my displeasure, my husband was following right along. Hallie pranced in front of him while Michael's eyes were trained right on her ass. *Bastard.* My insides lurched from seeing the two of them unexpectedly and I felt myself lean down in my seat as I peered at them.

Hallie spun around and gave Michael a bright smile. My windows were still down, so I could hear what they were saying clear as day. My mom was prattling away on the other end of the phone, but I tuned her out so I could hear better.

"I can't believe I get the pleasure of having you treat me to lunch *and* drinks later," Hallie said with a flirtatious smile. Her voice was full of sugary sweetness, and it made me want to hurl. "I feel like a lucky lady. Where will we be going?"

Michael beamed back at her, and I felt my entire body fall. The anger and jealousy that zipped through me dissipated; his eyes held such adoration for Hallie, and I couldn't for the life of me remember when Michael last looked at me that way, let alone smiled.

"Abs, you there?" Mom said on the other line; her voice started to grow concerned. My eyes darted from the happy couple and back to my steering wheel.

"Yeah, I'm here, sorry Mom. But listen, I gotta run to the store and pick some stuff up for dinner. I'll call you later, okay? I love you. Tell Dad that I love him, too. Good luck with your baking."

Mom hesitated, but finally said, "I love you, too, Abby. Call me later when you have time."

I quickly agreed and hung up the call, tossing the phone from hand to hand. Even though I wanted to dart right on out of here, I sat there for a second longer, letting my attention drift over to them. They were walking to Hallie's car, her flashy red Camaro, but to my surprise, Michael didn't get in the passenger seat. Instead, he slid into the driver's side. My eyebrows puckered as she handed over her keys casually, as if she's done that so many times before. I bit down on my bottom lip as the tears filled my eyes again.

Yes, he was having an affair with Hallie.

"Fuck you, Michael Carter," I said out loud. "*Fuck you.*"

Sawyer

"Class, I hope you enjoy your summer! To my student athletes, remember to check the summer calendar for gym hours. Take advantage of the schedule. Reach out to me with any questions that you may have. I'm leading the summer sessions, so I better see some of you there. That includes you, Jerry," I said, just as the last bell of the year buzzed through the school.

Most of the class was already storming out of the door, eager to start their summer vacation. If I had the choice, I'd be running like hell after them. I was definitely ready; some of these kids did me in this year with their cocky remarks or pissy attitudes. Teenagers were rough.

I watched the students file out one by one, with the exception of my student Sammy. Sammy was slow at packing his things up today, when generally, he was the first one out the door. His head was down, a frown etched on his face and my teacher radar came in full force. Even throughout class, I could tell something was up with him. We played a game of Jeopardy today, and Sammy didn't raise his hand once. Instead, he doodled idly in his notebook which wasn't typical of him. He was smart, quick witted, and always the first to raise his hand.

"Ready for the summer, Sam the Man?" I asked. I started collecting my own things up on my desk; my classroom was already packed up and in the back of my truck. I did this in haste during my lunch hour.

"Yes, sir," he responded firmly.

"You alright, bud?" I asked. "Anything you want to talk about?"

I've always been vocal with my kids that my door was always open; whether it was school related or not, they knew I would give them a listening ear.

"I'm okay, Mr. Gibson. Thank you," he said politely. I nodded to him, not wanting to push the conversation. If he wanted to talk, he'd let me know, but still, I couldn't help but eye him as he packed up his things.

"You're welcome."

Sammy lingered a moment longer in my classroom, his feet slowly shuffling. I watched as he turned towards the door, and then abruptly turned and stopped.

"Actually, sir, there is something I'd like to talk about," he said. He licked his lips, his eyes averting my gaze. I nodded and leaned on the edge of my desk.

"Sure, what's up?" I answered him.

"I've been thinking… and well, sir, I really want to get off the bench next year."

My eyes widened a little bit at his confession and my heart sank a little in my chest. *This was going to be that kind of talk.* He was a great kid; hard worker, nice, polite, straight-A student, but athletics from a coach's perspective were not one of his talents. He was tall and lean, but with those tall legs came with incoordination and he just never got the hang of it the last few years.

"I just want to make the most of my junior year," he admitted sheepishly. He looked down at his feet, kicking at an imaginary object in front of him.

"I understand that, Sammy," I told him honestly. I folded my arms across my chest. "You're a wonderful student and you should be damn proud of yourself for your accomplishments the last few years." I paused, collecting my train of thought. "As for sports next year, the best way to get off that bench is to bust your ass. I've been there, kid, it's hard." I didn't add that sports always just came to me, and it was easier for me to play ball then focus in a classroom.

"Here's the summer calendar," I told him, grabbing the bright orange piece of paper from my desk. "I encourage you to take advantage of it. You don't have to do all of it, but just some of it will help. We have a ton of weight room activities, running days, and then in July, the camps will start to gear up for the next year." Sammy's eyes averted my gaze as he grabbed the paper from my hand, and he remained silent. "Do you think you could participate?"

"I want to, sir. That's the problem…" he began with a sigh. "But, I have to work this summer."

"Have to, or want to?" I asked.

"Have to," he replied with a shrug. "My dad took off on me and my mom last month. I need to work this summer and help her pay the bills."

The tear in my heart that was stitched years ago started to throb as I looked at Sammy. His confession crushed me as a wave of memories flitted back to me. Not so long ago, I, too, felt the exact same way, but my experience was different than Sammy's. My father didn't have a choice when he left; he was cold-heartedly robbed of that choice.

"You're a good kid," I told him softly. "Your mom is lucky to have you."

"No, Mr. Gibson, I'm lucky to have her," Sammy said proudly. He stood taller at his words and my heart nearly crushed in my chest.

"My mom took a second job as a waitress at the bakery in town. She's busting her ass trying to make this work for me. Excuse my language, sir, but she is. She's the best Mom I could have ever asked for."

My throat tightened at his words and more of my own high school memories started to pour in. I remembered the pained feeling of watching my own mother step up and break herself in two just for me. I begged her to let me get a job and help, but she always refused and told me my future was too bright and that it wasn't my job to take care of her.

"Let's talk about this more," I told him carefully. "Do you have a job lined up already?"

"I started a mowing business, so most of the time I'll be mowing for neighbors. I'll also be cleaning gutters, you know, that kind of thing. I have next week already booked up with people," he added with a shrug.

"That's a great start," I told him. I've always been an emotional bastard, and my eyes started to swim at his confession. I cleared my throat. "How about this?" I took the summer schedule from his hand and on the back of the paper, I wrote down my cell phone number with a nearby Sharpie.

"Take a look at this calendar and see what you can do. If you can make some of it, great, if not, text or call me and I'll do what I can to help. I have the key to the gym and will let you in any time that you want to get a workout in. Hell, most of the time, I'm already there myself. I'll help you as much as I can to achieve your goals, if that's something you want. But don't burn yourself out, Sammy. Your mental health is far more important." I patted his shoulder and stood up from the desk, turning away from him.

"You're a great kid, Sammy. Don't forget that," I told him sincerely. "If you're interested, I'm on the town baseball board. Come by the field this weekend and I may have some work for you."

Sammy's eyes brightened and he nodded eagerly. "Thank you, sir."

"You're welcome, kid. Enjoy your summer. You're only young once. Have some fun, too." I clapped him on the back. With a little more confidence than before, he slung his bag over his shoulder and this time, returned my smile.

I tried to busy myself with cleaning up my desk, but my mind kept going back to Sammy. I tried to fight the anger that started to seep in and used my old techniques to try to cool down, but Sammy's sad expression kept flashing in my mind. I sat down on my desk chair and breathed in and out slowly. It wasn't right what Sammy was going through. What kind of father just leaves their wife and teenage son? A father shouldn't leave their kid unless they have to. *Like mine,* I thought. I didn't know the circumstance behind it all. I know there's two sides to a story, but it all made perfect sense to me now from Sammy's recent behavior. The smiling, giddy kid just wasn't there the last few weeks and now knowing why, my heart shattered for him.

I sighed, knowing there was nothing more that I could do for the poor kid right now. Getting myself worked up wouldn't help the situation, but the deep wound I had for my own dad started to prickle in my chest from the flood of memories. Flashes of my mom's grief poured through my mind: her sobbing on the kitchen floor, to the mornings that she was too weak to get out of bed, to the way her face looked so blank when I tried to talk to her at dinner that I hastily made for her. I didn't respond to the loss the same way she did. I was the angry one who used my fists as my weapon. It took my mother getting a phone call from the Principal to shake her out of her grief; she was a ball of fire picking me up from school that day. All I could remember doing was watching her, seeing real emotion on her face, and I felt relieved that she was coming back to me.

I shook my head, forcing the dark memories to subside. I couldn't dwell on those memories for too long; it hurt too much to think about, and I refused to start my summer break with a therapy session. As I threw the last of my belongings into my cardboard box, I quickly vowed that I would do everything in my power this summer to help out Sammy and his mom. They were good people, Sammy was a great kid, and he deserved better. I grabbed my leather laptop bag, slung it over my shoulder, and grabbed the box before leaving my classroom. I walked to the classroom door, turned around one last time to look at the bare room and smiled.

"That's a wrap," I whispered, flicking off the lights.

I turned out of my classroom, and started to walk down the empty hallway, when I heard someone calling my name from behind.

"Sawyer!"

I froze, clenching my teeth. *Shit.* I knew that voice. I strongly considered just booking it down the hallway but knew that would be rude. With a small sigh, I turned around.

"Holy shit," I whispered, jumping in my step. Miss Edeen was standing right behind me, when I expected her to be further down the hall. I didn't even hear her footsteps approach. She's always had a way of sneaking towards me. "Hi," I said, forcing a smile on my face.

Miss Edeen was our school's librarian. She was just hired last school year when the former one retired. Even though our previous librarian was ridiculously crabby from all her years dealing with students, I still missed her. At least she didn't ask me out every other day.

"Hi!" Miss Edeen beamed. Her blonde, bouncing curls surrounded her face as she talked. Today, she wore a bright pink lipstick that did not do her any favors. Her eyelids were covered with a thick blue shimmer eyeshadow. I forced my face to remain neutral as she annoyingly chomped on her gum.

"Aren't you just so excited for summer break? I know I am," Miss Edeen cooed. I nodded politely.

"Yes, I am. Looking forward to it. You have a good summer," I told her, nodding quickly to her. I turned around and did my best to walk away from her, but she was quick to follow. *Go away, Miss Edeen,* I thought.

"Any big summer plans?" she asked. Her sickly-sweet perfume clouded me, and I tried my best not to breathe through my nose.

"Not really," I replied. My first mistake. I should have lied right away.

"Any plans tonight? How fun would it be if we met for a drink? We haven't had the chance yet, you know," she said, letting out her loud cackle. God, this woman annoyed me to no end.

"As entertaining as that could be, I do have plans," I told her. I waved at our secretary as she gave me an all-knowing grin. I winked at her and watched the blush flush her cheeks as I walked through the Commons.

"Oh, phooey," Miss Edeen said, pretending to pout. Seriously, someone should tell her that pouting as an adult, especially on her, is not attractive in the slightest. "Well, you have my number," she said, forcing a smile on her face. I tried to walk faster to get away from her. "Call me if you change your mind. You know, Sawyer, I would really just *love* to get to know you a little better. You know, *outside* of work." I wanted to fall down and die.

Better late than never to address this. I was one hundred and ten percent over her flirtatious innuendos this last year. You'd think she'd get the hint after a dozen or so rejections, but she still keeps coming at me and I was tired of dodging her in the halls.

"Actually, Miss Edeen, can I be candid with you?" I asked. Her eyes lit up and she flashed me a bright smile. I almost decided to turn around and leave. I continued, choosing my words carefully. "I've been thinking about…your invitations and as much as I appreciate them, we shouldn't go down that path. We are co-workers and I think it would be best to keep things professional between us." I watched her face fall, and it nearly crushed me, so I quickly added, "I would hate to lose your friendship."

"Oh," Miss Edeen said in a clipped tone. She looked away from me, the hope draining from her pointed face. I sighed and tried to rectify her disappointment, without leading her on further.

"Thank you, though," I added lamely. I always hated turning down women. The guilt always ate at me when I watched their faces fall.

"I appreciate your candor, Mr. Gibson," Miss Edeen said, her nose in the air. I sighed and gave her the best smile I could.

"You have a lovely summer, Miss Edeen." I gave her a curt nod, turned, and bee lined for the front door before she could ask anything else from me.

Once I made it safely to my truck, I turned on the engine and listened as it roared to life. I was still driving the same old, beat up, green Chevy pick up I had as a teen. I've had it repaired more times than I could count, but the memories in this old thing were worth every penny.

I pulled out of the school parking lot, feeling the rush of freedom hit me as I rolled my windows down. Days filled with doing whatever the hell I wanted were finally here and I was ready to kick it off right. My summer was already jammed packed, but I preferred it that way. It kept my mind busy, and I preferred to be out in the public, rather than home alone.

I drove through my small hometown of Carrington, Illinois, waving at each person as I passed. It was a small populated town, with just over a thousand people. The people here were kind and were always willing to lend a helping hand to their fellow neighbors, but they could be nosy as hell. That's the only disadvantage of living here; everyone knows everyone else's business and the gossip around here spreads like wildfire.

I've had my fair share of rumors about me around this damn town. I was either a womanizer or I was gay, which if you think about it, doesn't really make sense. I'm not gay. I like tits. I may have had my fair share of one-night stands, but as my mother taught me, I always treat those women with respect. They know what they are getting themselves into before they fall in my bed anyway

I turned my truck in the direction of my best friend's autobody shop. Like me, Lance stayed put in this town. I've known him since we were in elementary school, and he's always been like a brother to me. He's had my back more times than I can count and in high school, he was practically my savior. If it wasn't for him calling me out on my bullshit, who knows where my anger would have taken me. Jail, probably, which is odd to think about since my father used to be our town's sheriff.

Lance's autobody shop was a large Morton building right outside of town. His doors were wide open and lights on, just as I had expected them to be. That shop was his entire world and has been since Old Greg gave him his first job there in high school.

When I pulled up, I noticed that Lance was wearing his navy jumpsuit and white beater, but he had the sleeves off and they fell around his waist. He was leaning on his work bench with what looked like a Miller Lite can in one hand and a cigarette in the other. His usual short blonde hair was getting long, almost falling into his eyes; it was the longest I've ever seen it. His face, which he always kept clean shaven, had light brown stubbles. I gave him a wave, and as I parked the truck, Lance started to walk towards me, his usual, goofy grin on his face.

"Hey, fucker," Lance called. "What the hell are you doing here? That POS doesn't need to be worked on, does it?" He grinned.

"Not today," I called. "I just thought I'd stop by for one of your shitty beers." Lance laughed and nodded to the mini fridge he kept in the corner of the building. I nodded my appreciation to him and walked across the shop, careful not to step on any tools he had laying around. He wasn't one to keep his workplace cleaned or even remotely organized. It used to drive me crazy, but after years, you get used to it.

I remembered the day Lance told me he was going to buy this place as if it was yesterday. Old Greg was getting too old to maintain it; his arthritis had been getting worse for some time, and he was ready to retire. Just as he promised Lance in high school, he called him up and gave him the first option to buy it. Lance pulled all his money together, but it still wasn't enough. He had to get approved for a startup loan, but he bought the building and ended up repaying the loan in full from profits after his first year. Old Greg did give him a decent deal for it; he wanted someone to love it as much as he did. That place was home to Lance.

"Last day?" Lance asked, puffing on his cigarette.

"Thankfully, yes," I said, popping open the can. "Need any help this summer, just let me know." I took a long drink of the amber liquid, letting the cool suds relax me.

Lance scoffed. "You say that now, but you probably already got every day lined up with something. You know, you need to slow down a little, and live some."

"You're one to talk," I mused. "When's the last time you've taken a day off?" Lance frowned and shrugged.

"Hell, if I know," he mumbled. "Wanna grab a drink tonight at the pub?" he asked.

"Nah, not tonight. Maybe tomorrow."

"What are you doing tonight?" he asked casually, looking off into the distance. I watched as he puffed on his cigarette a little more.

"Tonight, I'm going to relax. Order some food, drink a few beers, watch a little TV, and then pass the fuck out. I'll be doing baseball stuff all weekend."

Lance nodded and started to put his cigarette out in the nearby ashtray. "Thought about going back out with what's-her-name?"

That was Lance's nickname for any woman I'd been seeing at the time.

"Maggie," I added.

"Ah, yes, Maggie." Lance grinned a little. "She was hot."

He wasn't wrong there. She lived about thirty minutes away in the city. Lance I met her at a bar we went to sometimes after golfing. When we walked in, there was Maggie, sitting with a group of her friends, laughing and chatting—with her bright, fire red hair and soft, cream skin with a sprinkle of freckles on her face and shoulders. Normally I don't go for redheads, but the way she smiled at me intrigued me. She walked right up to me, sat down at the bar next to me and talked to me for hours. Her sunny personality is what brought me in; she was naturally a positive person and it rained off her. Lance ended up leaving me there after promises from Maggie that she'd get me home safely. And she did just that, but instead of dropping me off in the driveway, she ended up coming in. I had the pleasure of exploring her cream skin and freckles a little more that evening.

"She was pretty," I amended. He laughed out loud, shaking his head at me.

"Dude, when are you going to settle down? You're not even *trying* to find someone, and they *flock* to you. Here I am, honestly trying to meet someone and you have a line of women lining up at your door day in and out. Send them my way, would ya?"

"Maybe if you left this damn shop, you'd find someone," I challenged, taking a swig of my beer.

"Don't need to. I have Tinder."

I nearly choked on my beer. "No wonder you can't find anyone. Tinder is for fucking, not dating. Try other ways, brother."

Lance sighed and tilted his beer. "Maybe you're right."

"I am always right," I told Lance. "Whatcha working on now?" I gestured to the yellow Jeep in front of me.

Lance tossed his beer into the trash can. "Replacing brakes, changing oil. Got the time?"

I nodded and started to unbutton my dress shirt.

"Dude, I know I may be desperate, but I'm not desperate enough to change teams," Lance said in a mock tone. I rolled my eyes at him and flipped him off.

Underneath my dress shirt was my white beater that I could care less about if it got dirty. My dress pants and shoes though were a different story. As if already knowing where my thoughts were leading, Lance nodded at the faded blue jumpsuit hanging on the far corner on a single hook.

"Thanks," I said. I grabbed the jumpsuit, but to my surprise, on the breast pocket in red stitching, read *Sawyer*.

"Just got it for you," Lance grunted. "Just in case, you know."

"Thanks, Man," I mumbled, but even I couldn't hide the smile from my face.

"Don't turn into a woman." Lance rolled his eyes. "It's nothing." I could see what this meant to him though as I slid the jumpsuit on.

Chapter 2 - *Abby*

Remmy was a ball of excitement when I picked him up from school and required my undivided attention. His constant chatter was the perfect distraction from my failing marriage. As per usual, I pushed my feelings and thoughts aside and forced myself to appear happy in front of my boy.

We spent the rest of the afternoon as planned in the pool with his water toys and basketball hoop. His favorite swimming activity was to try to get the rings from the bottom of the pool, which was already a challenging task since he still wore floaties. After many attempts of trying and getting pissed, I would swim after them for him and loop the rings on the bottom of his little foot. He found this highly amusing and because his laughter was my favorite thing to hear, I did this for him over and over again.

After a lot of swimming, I grilled us a few chicken breasts on the grill, whipping up a side salad and my homemade macaroni and cheese. This was Remmy's favorite meal. Since this was Michael's *least* favorite, it only made me feel more inclined to make it tonight and I did so with a smile on my face. As usual, he never showed. I threw the leftovers in a Tupperware and placed it on the top shelf just in case, but like the other leftovers I stored for him, I knew it would end in the trash. *Just like my marriage,* I thought.

I wasn't too disappointed that Michael didn't come home for dinner tonight. I never called to check in with him as I might have done in the past. I was over it and honestly, starting to get over him. I didn't like to fight in front of Remmy, but if Michael would have come home this evening, who knows what would have flown out of my impulsive mouth. Remmy deserved better than to see my anger.

Remmy and I went through our normal evening routine: shower, teeth brushing, nighttime reading, and bed. Before leaving his bedroom, I turned around and glanced at my boy one more time. His eyes were already drooping from the long day of school and sunshine. He looked like his father so much; they had the same dirty blonde hair, eye shape, and nose, but his eyes—his pretty blues—matched mine and he had the same little dimples in his cheeks when he smiled.

I flipped on his night light and quietly shut his door. I glanced at the clock in the hallway; it was nine o'clock on the dot. I tiptoed through the house and peeked out of the windows. The sun was nearly set, with only the sun's glow on the horizon. It was a breathtaking scene, as it always was here in Florida, but I couldn't help but miss my hometown in Illinois. Ever since my mother's invitation from earlier, my mind was buzzing, and my heart longed to be there with her.

I leaned against the hallway and closed my eyes for a minute, trying to push positivity into my clouded mind. *What is one positive thing from today, Abby?* I thought to myself. *Remmy's last day of school was today and he had a great day.* That was the best that I could come up with. *Describe your perfect day, Abby.* I thought. *My perfect day...* The answer came to me, almost seconds later, but it brought me up short and I felt my lips purse into a hard line. My perfect day would be with Remmy of course, and we would be on the beach, enjoying the sunshine and having a picnic. We would make sandcastles and look for treasure. When we were done, we'd walk down together to the Concession Stand and get Remmy's favorite chocolate ice cream and talk together about whatever came to my son's brilliant mind.

My perfect day wouldn't have Michael included at all.

"I need a drink," I mumbled to myself.

I tiptoed to the kitchen and grabbed a bottle of my favorite white wine, the corkscrew, and a tall wine stem glass. I don't know why I had a collection of wine glasses because they were rarely used, except the one I held in my hand. It had light pink and purple watercolors splashed on the bottom of the cup, and it fit so delicately and perfectly in my right hand. I poured the wine halfway, and then with a heavy sigh, decided to pour to the top of the brim, knowing full well that today was one of those days. I took a drink of the white bubbly and let the sweetness cloud my tastebuds.

I hesitated in the kitchen, wondering what I should do next. I could go in the study and catch up on my reading, but I already knew that wasn't a good choice. My mind would not allow me to concentrate on the words today; it was far too muddy from the different emotions flowing through me. The best place for me right now was probably bed and to sleep this day away and start fresh tomorrow, but my mind was too powered to shut down.

I tiptoed back down the hallway and creaked Remmy's door open; his nightlight lit his room, flashing little dinosaur figures on the walls and ceiling. I closed the door softly shut and ventured a little further down the hallway to my oasis.

I punched in the code to unlock the backdoor. When Remmy started walking, I insisted on a code protected door and Michael agreed. Not only for stopping intruders, but for Remmy's sake. It scared me senseless knowing he could easily slip out the door and venture out into the backyard without me any wiser and fast asleep. I lost sleep over this nightmare numerous times. I loved our pool, but it frightened me with my little man being so young and so fearless. We had the door passcode protected, so only those with the code could open it. It may have cost us a pretty penny, but it made me sleep so much better.

As soon as I stepped out into the humid night air, I knew I made the right decision by escaping here. My backyard was my happy place, and I already felt my stiff shoulders relax. We had a nice sized backyard, enough room for our inground pool, patio, my outdoor kitchen, and Remmy's playhouse. We chose this home for the backyard itself, with full intent of having it be our 'happy' place.

Michael knew how much I loved to be outside, and at the time, he wanted to give me everything I desired. We had plans to host so many barbecues and swim parties, when in reality, we only hosted here a few times in the six years of living here.

The patio was my dream come true. The light gray patterned stone was in a large rectangle right outside the door. To the right was our lounge wear—an outdoor wicker sectional with beige cushions and matching chairs and end tables. There was an oversized rocker close that I sat on numerous times with Remmy. I used to rock him back and forth there as a baby when he was fussy, and it always worked; it was our special place.

To the left of the patio, was our large outdoor kitchen with an island and barstools; the countertops were a smooth surface gray, with white cabinets that barely had anything in them. The stainless-steel refrigerator outside held mostly water, juice boxes, and beer. Attached to the counter was Michael's gas-powered grill that I've only seen him use a few times. I was the one who generally grilled; if I would have known he wouldn't use it, I would have gone with charcoal.

I flipped on the twinkling hanging lights that dangled from the pergola and let out a sigh. I know I'm blessed to have all these things; the inground pool, the large playground for Remmy, and the beautiful home in a gated community. Onlookers looking in at my life would say I had it made; a husband who worked hard at his job to provide for his family, an amazing son that was sweet and caring, and the beautiful home with all the bells and whistles that you could ever ask for. It was the American dream.

And I hated it.

Another wave of sadness hit me as I plopped down in my favorite rocker, careful not to spill my wine. I swiveled around in the chair to take in my beautiful oasis; it looked enchanting out here at night with the twinkling lights and the soft glow from the pool. I took a large gulp from my wine glass, letting the cool liquid warm me from the inside out.

As much as I wanted to ponder further on my marital problems, I couldn't think coherently. Probably because I had no fucking clue what to do. Living in Florida was expensive enough; there's no way I would be able to financially support Remmy on my own. I was working reduced hours as it was. I could pick up a second job, but what would that cost me in the long run? It would take me away from my kid, and in the hands of a full-time nanny. That's not what I wanted, nor did Michael. In fact, he strongly encouraged me to walk away from work completely when I was on maternity leave. It was a blessing in disguise that I hadn't. Where would I be if I had?

I could look for other full-time opportunities; maybe even land a better paying job. At least I would be separated from Michael all together. I couldn't imagine going through a divorce with him and still needing to see him at work. It probably wouldn't even matter; they'd fire me as soon as the divorce was final if Michael asked them to.

Divorce. Even the word sounded nasty to me. Did I really want a divorce from my husband of six years? Was I at that point yet? I wasn't sure. All I knew, something had to change because I couldn't be this miserable old bitch anymore. I was tired of feeling tired. Feeling sad and lonely all the time was exhausting. Not only did I miss the old Michael, but I missed the old Abby.

My mind flitted back to Carol and what she suggested to me a few weeks ago; *counseling*. Maybe it was time to step up and go to a therapist. Hell, maybe we could even go to a marriage counselor together. Even I scoffed at the idea; there's no way Michael would go anywhere near a therapist's office, but the idea intrigued me, and I put it on the back burner to think about later. Even if he refused, it didn't mean that I couldn't go.

I was starting to feel desperate to get back to my old self.

I took another long drink from my wine glass, when I heard the backdoor lock *beep* and unclick. The sound made me freeze in my rocking chair, but I didn't turn around. My mind was already feeling a little cloudy from the sweet wine and if I rocked in the chair too much, I'd probably fall right out of it.

"Abby?" Michael's matter-of-fact tone called me.

"Yeah?" I called back. I frowned at my almost empty wine glass. I should have just brought the bottle.

Michael walked out onto the patio and around the chair. He was still wearing what he wore earlier today at the office. Dress slacks, and his white polo shirt. His hair, which was usually perfectly gelled and styled in a classy disarray, looked disheveled, which made me snort. Nothing about this situation was funny, but there's me, the drunk wine drinker, laughing about his messy hair. I could almost imagine Hallie's perfectly maintained fingers running through it.

"What's so funny?" he asked, his eyebrows raising.

"Oh, nothing," I replied with a smile.

"I'm surprised you're still awake. You weren't waiting for me, I hope?" His arms were relaxed at his sides.

I took a long hard look at Michael and wondered when the day was that he stopped loving me. I felt my lips fall into a frown and looked away from his gray eyes.

"No, not intentionally. How was your evening?" I couldn't mask the disappointment and hurt in my voice and knew from his changed posture that he caught on to it as well.

"Fine," he answered coolly. "Had some drinks with the realtors. You know, the usual."

I nodded and drained my wine glass. I swiveled my chair around and sat the glass down on the end table, not adding to the conversation. I couldn't find the appropriate words to say to him at the moment, especially with my hazy brain. I really wish I would have brought the bottle out with me.

"How was your evening?" he asked.

"Great. Remmy and I swam. I made dinner, yours is in the fridge."

He nodded. "Thanks, but I ate already."

"*I'm sure you did*," I huffed.

"What does that supposed to mean?" Michael challenged. "It's almost ten, of course I ate."

"Just that I'm sure you already ate."

I didn't look at him but stared out into our backyard oasis. I tried to calm my heart as the beats sped up sporadically. The last thing I wanted to do was fight with Michael as soon as he got home, but there was cause for the situation, and I knew deep in my heart, my suspicions were valid.

I watched Michael turn his back to me and walk to the outdoor refrigerator. He pulled out a bottle of Bud Light, opened the top, and threw it in the trash. He stood in the outdoor kitchen and took a long drink of the bottle and all I could do was just watch him. The man that I fell in love with was no longer standing in front of me, and just thinking about it shattered me. He no longer paid any kind of attention to me, to my happiness or sadness, or cared when I was upset. He used to dote on me and loved surprising me with flowers and gifts. He loved to plan romantic dinners, or surprise me by hiring a sitter so we could take a long walk on the beach. Gone were the days of his whispers of love while he passionately made love to me.

Gone was the Michael Carter that I knew and loved.

I felt a tear slip down my cheek and I tried to swipe it away before Michael noticed. The last thing I wanted him to see was any kind of weakness from me today. However, it was too late because he noticed the escaped tear.

"What is wrong with you?" he demanded. His voice was not caring or soft. He sounded irritated, almost disgusted, as I knew he would be if he noticed the tear slip.

"I'm fine," I answered softly.

"*Whatever*, Abigail." His voice had a bite to it as he drained his beer in a final gulp. He tossed the bottle into the trash can and said, "The last thing I want to do is argue with you tonight. I had a good day, and I'm not about letting you ruin it with your fucking attitude."

Don't say it, don't say it. I told myself. "You mean, you had a good day with Hallie?" I challenged. *Well, shit, Abby.*

Michael's intense look turned into an angry glare as his jaw clenched tightly together.

"Here we go," Michael scoffed. "Here we fucking go again, Abby. Let's just get this shit straight, once and for all. Hallie is a real estate agent, as you are fucking aware. I need her business, especially right now. The market is shit and our rates are not competitive right now. I need to be with these agents, making relationships, or all of this," I watched as he threw his hands up in the air, gesturing to the house and backyard. "Goes away! Your pretty, fucking life will disappear if I quit schmoozing these agents. Do you want me to lose this fucking house? Do you want us to have to sell and move?"

"I'd probably be happier." The words slipped from my mouth and even though they were true, probably wasn't the best thing to say when his anger was boiling over.

"Oh yeah?" he laughed. "*I doubt that*. You're extremely materialistic, Abigail. You're an expensive woman. I must work ten times as hard as the other Loan Officers, so you and Remmy can enjoy all of this!"

"Quit yelling," I chastised, "You'll wake the neighbors."

"I really don't care," he laughed, humorlessly. "I'm tired of having this same argument with you. You need to get this through your head. I'm. Not. Cheating."

It was probably the alcohol adding to my abnormal behavior right now, but I laughed. Hard, too. He stood there, fuming at me, which caused me to double over.

"This is not funny," he said.

"Yes, it is. It is funny, Michael, because here's the thing. You are cheating. I know you're having an affair with her. I don't know if you think I'm stupid, or what, but any woman knows when their husband is not faithful."

"Well, your radar is off," he spat, "Because you're *wrong*."

"You lie so smoothly. You're a great salesman," I nodded to him. I got up from the rocking chair and walked over to the refrigerator, really wanting that second glass of wine, but instead, opted for a beer. I popped the lid open as he had done and took a drink.

"What are you, an alcoholic now?" he chastised.

"Oh yeah, I just drink *so* much," I said sarcastically, gesturing my left hand in the air. "All the time."

"Looks like it to me."

"If you were around more, you'd know that this is the first time in weeks I even had a sip. Unlike you, at the bar every night."

"Again, *schmoozing* realtors. It's not my fault they like the nightlife. And don't you think I want to be around here more for you and Remmy? I would love to be here, enjoying my evenings with you both, but I can't do that. I must build these relationships. Right now, it's a sink or float scenario out there, Abigail and I will *not* let us sink."

"As in schmoozing, you mean with your dick?" I added, cocking my head to the side. My traitorous lips formed a cruel smile. Michael's eyes narrowed into slits and his face flushed a deep red.

"Just admit it Michael. I already know."

I took a long drink of my beer when Michael walked and grabbed another.

"What, your tenth drink tonight?" I flared.

"*Shut up,* Abigail. You have no idea what you're talking about," he spat.

I rolled my eyes, walked to the counter, and opened the drawer that contained a pack of Marlboro Lights, a lighter, and a clean ashtray. I know Michael hated my smoking, and I wasn't an everyday smoker. It was a bad habit I picked up from college and I only divulged in a smokey treat when I was extremely stressed.

I set the ashtray on the counter, took a cigarette out of the full pack, and lit it. I inhaled sharply, letting the smoke fill my lungs, and blew out.

"So attractive," he added. "Let's take more chances of getting cancer."

I responded by inhaling another long drag, and slowly, blew out the smoke. Michael rolled his eyes, his nose scrunched in distaste.

"Doesn't Hallie smoke?" I finally added. "Do you think it's attractive when she does it?"

"You're sounding childish now."

We stood there in silence as the anger and tension filled the backyard patio. I wanted to scream at him and tell him to quit fucking her and come back to our family. I wanted to beg and plead with him to quit having his affair, but all I could do was sit there in silence and let all the emotions wash over me. I didn't know which emotion to succumb to, since so many were filling me. Michael, with his disheveled, "just fucked" looking hair and literally lying right to my face about his relationship.

Finally, after finishing my cigarette, I put it out into the ashtray and whispered, "Just admit it, Michael. Please." I heard pleading in my voice and hated sounding weak. "I can't take anymore lies from you. *Just admit it.*"

I looked up at Michael and watched the different emotions flash across his face. His bottom lip was trembling slightly, as if he wanted to burst out and just say it, but I watched as he internally argued with himself.

Another tear slipped down my face and I whispered, "Please."

Michael sighed and ran his fingers through his hair, looking past me. He took a swig of his beer and then said, "I'm not having an affair."

An angry groan escaped my lips as I crouched down into a fetal position, pulling at my hair. A sob overcame me as an anguished cry escaped me. All the hurt was now spilling out in front of us and for once, I didn't care that he saw me this way. Michael didn't try to comfort me, which only validated my feelings. He stood there in front of me, looking helpless and a little defeated. I stood up quickly, turned from him and wrapped my arms around my chest to try to stop the pain.

"Just fucking admit it," I said through another sob. *"You. Are. Fucking. Her."* I wiped at my tears viciously from my cheeks and tried to collect myself together. The pain I felt in my chest flicked viciously, as if I was getting stabbed repeatedly in the same spot.

Michael's arms engulfed my own and I couldn't help but lean back into his embrace. It's been so long since Michael touched me that his hands felt foreign to me, as if it was a stranger trying to console me. I let out another sob and let my head fall.

"I'm sorry," Michael murmured. "I'm sorry for making you feel this way, Abby." His lips grazed my wet cheek.

"Just tell me," I replied through tears. "I need to know Michael. It's not the same with you anymore. You're never here. Remmy asks about you all the time and I don't know what to say except that you're working. You don't look at me the same anymore. You don't touch me. We barely talk. We are just going through the motions, and it hurts so fucking much, Michael. You're supposed to be my husband, but you've turned into a stranger."

"I'm working for you and Remmy. I told you. I have to be on my A-game to give you guys the best life possible." His voice was kinder this time, softer.

"That's bullshit Michael. We don't care about all this stuff. What we care about is spending time with *you*. Being with *you*. Being a family. That's what we care about. Do you really think

Remmy will care if we have to sell the house? *No.* All he will care about is his Mommy and Daddy. Why can't you see that? Why can't you make time for us?" I could even hear the pain from my voice.

I wiped at my face again as Michael's lips met my cheek again.

"I don't like to see you cry," he admitted. "It breaks my heart."

"Then why make me cry?" I challenged. "Why are you doing this to us?" I turned around to face him.

Michael remained silent, his lips pursed into a tight line, but I forced eye contact between us. I wasn't going to break it and knew we had to have this moment. Building the courage, I whispered, "Why don't you love me anymore, Michael? What did I do?" I choked out in a hoarse whisper.

Michael's face softened and I saw a flash of hurt cross his face.

"Abby," he sighed. "You didn't do anything."

"I had to have done something," I whispered. "You don't ever want to come home anymore."

"It's because of this," he said exasperated. "I don't want to argue with you, and that's all we ever do."

"Because you're never *home*. Be with us Michael, and I won't argue. I'll stop asking about Hallie. Just be with us," I begged. With my fist, I softly hit his chest.

"I do love you," Michael said. "Which is why I'm working so hard."

I rolled my eyes and stepped out of his tight embrace, immediately wishing I was back under his warm touch; I was so tired of feeling so freaking lonely.

"Let's go to bed," Michael whispered. "It's getting late. We can pick this up in the morning."

I stepped to the countertop, picked up the beer, and drained the bottle. "Yes, let's just stop this conversation we are having, sweep it under the rug, and act like this never happened."

"That's not what I'm saying," Michael said, with a tired sigh. "I'm saying, it's late. I'm exhausted, and we can discuss this further in the morning. I don't have any meetings until ten. I'll call Ralph in the morning and tell him we'll be late."

"I'm not going in tomorrow," I told him. "You'd know that, if you paid attention."

Michael frowned and sighed, ignoring my last jab at him. "You have to go in tomorrow, Abby. Ralph sent an email this evening. The sales team has a morning business update meeting, followed by the operation staff immediately after. Remmy can go to my mother's. She'll be home tomorrow, she already told me."

"What's the meeting about?" I asked him, my curiosity getting the better of me. I never go into the office on a Friday anymore, and everyone at work knows this.

"I don't know, they didn't give us any details," Michael said smoothly. His face hardened into a mask. *There he goes with the lies again.*

I nodded and accepted his lie. I knew Michael heard almost everything at the office, and I also knew Ralph confided with him. Ralph was our Branch Manager, but Michael was his right hand guy.

"Let's go to bed," Michael said again. "Let's get some sleep."

He held out his large, smooth hand. After a moment of hesitation, I slid my hand into his, wondering how numbered moments like these were with us.

Michael walked us up the patio, punched in the code to open the door, and we both slid into the house. We stopped at Remmy's door together to check on him; he was still fast asleep. He had his arm laid across his eyes and his mouth drooping open, which made Michael chuckle a little to himself. "He sleeps just like you," he joked. I couldn't help but return his smile.

We slipped into our bedroom and walked into our master bath. I started to wash my face as Michael discarded his clothing to step into the shower.

"Want me to join you?" I asked him playfully.

"Oh, that sounds nice, babe, but not tonight. I just want to take a quick shower and get into bed. I'm exhausted."

I didn't get too excited about the prospect because I knew he'd decline, as he has done so many times before.

I washed my face, added my moisturizer, brushed my teeth vigorously, and ran a comb through my tangled hair. Michael slipped out of the shower, steam rolling off him, and as he wrapped the towel around his waist, I couldn't help but stare at him through the bathroom mirror. He was extremely handsome. He still had his abs from his college days, and chiseled stomach and arms. I knew he took advantage of our basement workout gym. He worked hard to keep his body in perfect condition, whereas I, not so much. I couldn't muster the energy to join him in the morning.

Michael stepped up to the mirror and I watched as he ran a comb through his thick hair.

"What?" Michael asked suspiciously. I watched him grab his blue toothbrush and add the toothpaste. I shook my head and left him in the bathroom to do his brushing.

I slid my cell phone onto the charger, not even needing to check the phone for missed calls or texts, because really, no one calls or messages me anymore. I have little friends here, and I already talked to my mom earlier today. The only person who should get a hold of me regularly, is standing in the opposite room and his name rarely appears on my phone anymore.

Michael entered the room as I started to undress. This used to be Michael's favorite time. He used to pounce into bed, in a jokingly fashion and excitedly watched me undress with looks of eagerness in his eyes. As I slipped off my clothes to grab my nightgown, I looked up to find Michael's eyes on me, but quickly flitted away.

I added lotion to my legs and arms, turned off the lights, and slowly climbed into bed. Lately, Michael has been sleeping with his back to me, but tonight, he laid facing my direction and opened his arms to me. I knew I must have looked surprised because his face fell as I crawled my way into his embrace. He wrapped his arms lightly around me, kissed my cheek and whispered to me, "I do love you, Abigail."

"I love you, too," I replied weakly. Even to me, my words sounded robotic.

As I closed my eyes to succumb to the much needed sleep, I wondered when I became as good of a liar as Michael.

Sawyer

I woke up the next morning to my alarm clock blaring next to me. It was five thirty in the morning and it was my first day of summer break. I groaned out loud and aimlessly flung my arm in the direction of the obnoxious noise, angry at myself for not resetting the time.

I laid in bed for a few more minutes, trying to shut my brain back off to go back to sleep, but I knew the attempt was useless. When I was up, I was up; there was no getting me to fall back asleep.

I yawned and stumbled out of bed, wiping the sleep from my eyes. I staggered through my small hallway and into the kitchen and went right for my needed coffee. I grabbed the empty pot and groaned. I forgot to set the settings the night before, which happened more than I liked to admit. My mom bought this coffee pot for me last Christmas. She said she saw me too many times at Casey's Gas Station in the mornings getting coffee and that I needed to learn to save money. With an exhausted sigh, I went through the motions of starting the pot. I threw away the filter from the day before, soggy with yesterday's grounds and replaced it with a new one. I scooped a few scoops from the red Folgers container and then proceeded to fill the pot with water.

I hit the brew button and staggered to the refrigerator. My mouth was dry, probably from sleeping with it wide open, and grabbed a bottle of Dasani from the bottom shelf. My refrigerator was incredibly empty. I had a half gallon of milk, a few Gatorades, a half dozen water bottles and beer, and the usual eggs, butter, and dressings. I needed to make a trip to the store but knew I probably wouldn't. I ate out mostly, not really wanting to cook just for myself.

I chugged the bottle of water and closed the refrigerator door. The summer workout calendar I created and other summer reminders were stuck on the refrigerator with small circle magnets. So was Maggie's phone number that she'd slid into place before sneaking out that morning. I checked the schedule today, already knowing I didn't have anything planned today.

I collapsed into my small, oak dining room table. It was such a small table, with only two chairs. I stared at the other empty chair and waited for the loneliness to settle in, as it sometimes had before, but it didn't wash over me today. I liked my life for the most part, but sometimes being alone all the time stung. When that happened in the evening, I generally would find a companion to spend the night with, followed by instant regret in the morning. Like Maggie, for example.

I thought about Maggie and wondered what she was up to today but disregarded the thought immediately. I had a busy summer and the last thing I wanted to do was to start a relationship. However, the ache I was feeling of wanting to touch someone, to love someone, settled in. I tried to toss the impulsive thoughts from my head.

The pot made a last, soft gurgle sound, indicating that the coffee was ready. I slumped out of my chair, grabbed a mug from the nearby cupboard and poured myself a glass. I put the brim of the cup to my mouth, feeling the heat of the drink on my upper lip, and took a sip.

Maybe I should get a dog? I thought to myself. I've always wanted a German Shepherd, or even a lab would do. Chocolate labs were my favorite kind of lab, especially puppies. This thought occurred to me several times over the years. I loved all dogs, but knew in my heart, it wouldn't be fair to the dog with how much I'm gone all the time. A dog, like a woman, deserved constant love and attention, and that's not something I could promise anyone right now.

I stood in my kitchen and took sips of my coffee, letting the warmth soothe and bring life to my tired body. The sun was starting to poke through the dark sky and for a moment, I thought to go sit outside and watch it rise. I disregarded that, too, though, as that's something I didn't want to do alone either. Watching those beautiful moments all by myself, triggered the loneliness feeling I was trying to ignore.

My kitchen was very small. It had four, oak cupboards, matching oak counters, with a beige countertop. The refrigerator was here when I moved in, white and a little outdated, but I couldn't bring myself to replace it. As my dad once said to me, "Why replace it, if it isn't broken?" The stove and the microwave were also the same shade of white, and they, too, were here when I bought the house. Mom kept encouraging me to update my kitchen, but I always disregarded her suggestions. I did let her paint the kitchen when I moved in. It was a soft, yellow-ish color. I think she said it was called 'pear'. She chose the color because she said I should start my mornings with as much sunshine and happiness as possible.

She also got a little carried away and painted my living room and bedroom, which I hadn't agreed to. She freshened up the paint in the living room with a light beige color and my bedroom with a slate gray. When I came home one day to her painting the rooms, all I did was shake my head at her. There was no sense arguing with the woman, because she would, of course, win. I had to admit though when she was done, it did brighten the place up a little.

Maybe I could go over to Mom's and visit with her this morning, I pondered. She liked it when I dropped in to visit with her. I hated to think of my mom being in that big old house all by herself. I tried to talk her into selling and finding something smaller, but she always gave me the same response. "It's home." I couldn't disagree with her on that. It was her home, and any fixing she needed done, she had a son right at her disposal.

I drained the coffee cup, already feeling slightly better, and put the mug into the empty sink. I walked through the narrow hallway and into the bathroom. I brushed my teeth, gargled some mouthwash, and ran a comb through my brown hair. I needed a cut, it was getting much too long. I ran a hand over my scruffy beard and knew that I probably should also shave, but also knew that since it was now summer, I probably wouldn't. I always tried to be clean and professional for work, but during the summer, I turned into a caveman.

I walked to my bedroom and quickly changed my clothes into athletic shorts, white Nike socks and found my favorite, Nike black running shoes. I slid them on, laced up, and stood to start stretching. *Might as well get my run over with.*

I didn't bother to put a shirt on, as I knew the morning would be humid. The girls in the teacher's lounge yesterday were talking about how hot it was going to be right away this summer break. I knew about a half mile into my run, I would be drenched in sweat anyway. I grabbed my cell phone and AirPod case and slid the headphones into my ear. After turning on my music, I walked out of the house, did a few more stretches on the front sidewalk, and started jogging.

The neighborhood was starting to come to life right before my eyes. Mrs. Gibbons, my neighbor three doors down, was standing outside in her pink bathrobe, her gray hair in a tangled mess, as if she just woke up herself, and she was watering her plants already. She gave me a bright smile, as she usually did in the mornings and waved. I always returned the smile and wave. She was a sweet woman and sometimes, she made too much for dinner and would bring me her leftovers, knowing full well I was a bachelor at its finest. Sometimes, I thought she did that on purpose, but I always thanked her and invited her in for a cup of coffee, which she normally, always refused, stating she needed to get back to her cats.

My heart rate was starting to pick up as I made it around the corner, and I felt my speed pick up pace as my legs stretched and got used to the motions. I've always enjoyed and loved running. It was an outlet for my emotions, especially when I couldn't control them. I would go running for hours at a time in school, especially after what happened to my dad.

The music encouraged me to keep up pace and push me faster. I made it to the town square where the shops and businesses were lined up. The bakery already had its lights on and an open sign showing as some older folks were walking into the building. I stopped for just a minute outside of the building and decided to catch my breath. I waved at a few passersby walking into the bakery and I nodded at them in greeting. I looked into the large, square windows and saw a brunette woman greeting a group of four people. She was handing out menus to them with a big smile. I recognized her as Sammy's mom and made a mental note to myself to come back at a later time when she was working. I couldn't deliberately give them money, but I could always leave the waitress a generous tip.

I stretched my legs once more, and then continued back to my old jogging pace. I waved at several people as I jogged by them, not really having a direction in mind of where I was heading to, when I found myself at the familiar Victorian home of the Foster residence.

Mandy Foster was outside, sitting on her porch with her cup of coffee in hand and to my surprise, my mother was sitting right next to her. I glanced at my Apple watch on my wrist and noticed the time read six thirty AM. What in the world was my mother doing, up and about at this hour?

"Sawyer!" My mother beamed and waved at me brightly. "Sawyer, sweetheart, it's your first day off and you're up so early! I thought you'd sleep in for once." I took one AirPod out of my ear and smiled sheepishly at Mom and Miss Mandy. I tried to catch my breath as I walked up the sidewalk and to the front porch.

"Hi Mom," I said gruffly. "I forgot to turn off my alarm." I walked up the deck and kissed my mom on the cheek. She was already ready for the day. She was dressed in black capris and a white blouse. Her brown hair, that matched my own, was twisted into an elegant clip on the back of her head.

I looked over at Miss Mandy and nodded at her, as well. "Good morning, Miss Mandy. Hopefully my mother didn't wake you too early." I grinned at them both.

Miss Mandy laughed and waved the thought aside. "Oh, no, Sawyer, your mom and I have coffee this early every Friday."

"Every Friday?" I said, surprised. "Huh, you learn something every day."

They chuckled and Mom patted me on the hand.

"Would you like some coffee, Sawyer?" Miss Mandy asked politely. "Or some water?" She looked at the sweat beading on my forehead.

"Water would be great," I said with my best, winning smile. "You don't need to get up, Miss Mandy. Enjoy yourself with Mom here. Do you mind if I go get it?" I asked politely, nodding to her front door. Even though I haven't stepped in the house in years, I still knew it like the back of my hand.

"Oh, you're sweet, yes, you may. You know where it is."

I left the two women back to their gossiping when I walked into Miss Mandy's large white home. It's been the same after all these years. Immaculate wooden flooring that always looked polished and clean and her bright white walls that hung all different kinds of décor, from family photos to artistic paintings. I walked my way into her large, oversized kitchen when I was brought up short by Mr. Foster.

"Hello, sir," I told him with a nod.

Mr. Foster was sitting at the kitchen island with his reading glasses on, coffee in hand, and reading the newspaper. He looked just as surprised to see me standing in his kitchen at this hour as I was surprised to see him.

"Sawyer," his voice said, booming. "Good morning. What are you doing here?"

"I was out running when I saw my mom sitting outside with Miss Mandy. Miss Mandy invited me in to grab a bottle of water. Do you mind?" I gestured to his refrigerator.

He smiled kindly at me and nodded to it. "You know where it is," he said. I approached their stainless-steel refrigerator, but my attention was caught on a picture of a little boy hanging from a magnet. I stopped short and studied the little boy's reflection. He had dirty blonde hair, bright blue eyes, and an adorable smile that was missing his front tooth. In the photo, he was wearing a beach hat and was standing by the ocean.

Mr. Foster must have noticed my hesitation because he said, "That's our grandson, Remmy."

I nodded, assuming that this was Abby's boy; his bright blues reminded me so much of hers as I studied the photo further. I haven't seen Abby Foster in years. Frankly, I don't remember the last time Abby came home and visited. The Fosters never really spoke about her when I was around, and I never asked about how she was doing. I know she lives in Florida, she's married with a son, and that she's living in a beautiful large home, because that's all my mother told me. I was invited to her wedding, but I didn't go. Sometimes, I still kick myself in the ass for not going. It would have been nice to see her smile one more time.

"Cute kid," I added.

Mr. Foster nodded. "Yes, he is. We sure miss him. Wish we could see him more, but you know how life gets," Mr. Foster added with a slight frown.

"I do, sir," I agreed. "Hey, while I have you here, Mr. Foster, I wanted to ask you something, if you don't mind."

Mr. Foster set his paper down, so I continued. "Do you need any help around here? I know I volunteer to do these things for you, but I know a kid, my student, who's trying to earn some extra money. He told me yesterday that his mom is having a hard time paying the bills and he's trying to earn some extra cash to help her." I paused and watched as Mr. Foster took off his reading glasses, which gave me the impression I had his full attention. "I just thought I'd ask to see if you needed anything done that could help the kid out. He's starting to mow for people, but I was under the impression he'd be up for any outdoor work." I opened the water bottle and took a drink.

Mr. Foster nodded, pondering my words. "I probably have some stuff he can do. The fence out back needs mending, and I would be interested in hiring the boy to do the mowing for us."

I gave him my best, polite smile and said, "Great, thank you Mr. Foster. I'll get his information over to you or have him stop by and introduce himself. I appreciate it."

Mr. Foster smiled back at me and slid his reading glasses back on. "Always willing to help out those that want to work for it."

That is just one of the reasons why I've always admired Mr. Foster.

"Good day, sir," I nodded back to him and walked back to the two women on the porch. When I cracked the front door open, their hushed whispers fell silent.

"Are you two beautiful women behaving yourself?" I asked, giving them a smile. This caused them both to start laughing. I took another long drink of the water and slid the half empty bottle into my pocket.

"Of course we are." My mother said, "We always do. So, Sawyer, what's on your agenda for the day?"

I shrugged. "I am not sure. Probably finish my run and then shower. I was actually going to stop and see you but ran into you here."

Mom beamed. "Well, if you want, you can stop by at the house in about an hour or so and help me load up my things for the town bake sale. It starts this morning, and I could really use the help with the loading part. Maybe help me put my stand up as well?" she asked, hopefully, a twinkle in her eye.

I sighed, knowing full well of my mother's intentions. "Sure, Mom. I'll see you in an hour. I looked over at Miss Mandy and thanked her for the water. "I'll see you both later," I added. I slipped the AirPod back into my ear, and took off down the driveway once more, pushing harder than ever, to make it back home.

I knew I should have just waved at Mom and kept running. Now, it looks like I'll be helping at the damn town bake sale.

Chapter 3- *Abby*

The next morning, I woke up to Remmy peering over at me, with his small, black blanket in his left hand. When I opened my eyes, his face was in full view, and I jumped. Clearly, I wasn't expecting to see him up so bright and early. This was new.

"Morning, Mommy!" He grinned at me. His front tooth was missing, and he was proud of that missing front tooth.

"Well, good morning, Remmy," I said with a smile. "Are you ready to start your day?"

"Yes!" He giggled excitedly. "What are we going to do today, Mommy? Go to the beach?" he said, eagerly.

"Oh, that sounds so much fun, baby." I started to get up from the bed. I turned around and noticed Michael's side was empty and I frowned. "I do have a work meeting though, but maybe after, okay? I think I'm going to bring you to Nana's house for a little while this morning."

Remmy's smile immediately vanished from his face as he let out a loud groan. "Ugh...Mommy I don't want to go there," he pouted. I patted his head slowly as I grabbed my nightgown cover from the hook nearby.

"I know," I said, reassuringly. "It won't be long, just a little while. Would you like me to make you some... *pancakes*?" I tried to add as much enthusiasm to my dead voice as possible.

"Yeaaaaaaah," he sang, "With sausage."

I laughed. "Okay buddy, with sausage. Um, where's your dad?" I asked. The bathroom door was open, and the light was shut off. Generally, I'm a light sleeper, but this morning, I didn't hear or feel him leave the room as I generally did. It was probably the wine I drank last night; as soon as my mind stopped whirring, I slept like a rock.

"I don't know." He shrugged. He started skipping in his racecar jammies to the kitchen, his black blankie trailing after him. I followed him, listening for signs of Michael, but the house was quiet, except for Remmy's footsteps. I listened down in the basement for signs of the workout equipment being used, but none came.

I glanced at the clock in the corner, and it read seven AM. It was, indeed, time to start my day now that I had to go into the office for the abnormal morning meeting.

Remmy sat on the kitchen island, his two toy soldiers in hand. He played with them together, talking amongst himself as I started to prepare breakfast. I grabbed two separate pans, one for the sausage links, the other for the pancake and got to work in silence, listening to Remmy's pretend play.

It was unusual for Michael to escape so early in the morning. He did say that we would talk further this morning, but I knew that was a fluke as soon as the words left him. I peeked out of the kitchen window, expecting to see him running down the sidewalk to us any minute, but he didn't. Once I had Remmy's breakfast on a plate in front of him, I handed him a fork, napkin, and a glass of chocolate milk and kissed his forehead.

"Enjoy, Buddy," I told him, with a pat on his head.

"*Mmm....* thanks Mommy." He started to dig in instantly.

"Small bites," I reminded him. I walked to the garage door and quietly creaked it open. Michael's car was gone already. Typical Michael.

"So much for that talk," I said with a heavy sigh.

I grabbed a cup of coffee from the pot, added my usual cream and sugar, and took a drink. It was needed this morning. I couldn't fight off the peculiar feeling in my stomach. No, it wasn't about Michael and his affair, but it was a different, odd feeling that I couldn't explain. I went to my room and grabbed my cell phone, expecting to find a missed call or text from Michael. Again, nothing.

I sighed, and watched Remmy finish his breakfast. After he shoveled in the last bite, he waved and sang, "All done!"

I gave him a warm smile. "Great job, buddy. Now let's get you cleaned up for Nana's."

With a roll of his eyes, he obeyed, but only because he knew he didn't have a choice. I knew he didn't like to go over there. His "Nana" had an immaculate house, one that was larger than ours, and one that had to be kept in pristine condition. Therefore, Remmy couldn't behave or act like himself. If a mistake or mess would happen, he would be scolded immediately, and there were no toys there for him to play with. She wasn't a horrible grandmother, but she didn't have the same carefree grace as most grandmothers had, and only occasionally would offer to keep Remmy. Which was fine by me because I didn't like to send him over there anyway.

Today I had no choice since the meeting was so last minute. I couldn't call our usual sitter, Hannah, who loved watching him. She had a side babysitting business and was fresh out of high school, getting ready for college this fall. She was so busy watching other kids and her waitressing job, that I had to ask her at least a week in advance to watch Remmy.

Speaking of the devil, my phone rang a few times with Katherine Carter's name flashing on my screen. With a soft sigh, I answered the phone. I didn't like to talk to the woman that much either, to be honest.

"Hello, Katherine," I said politely.

"Why, hello Abigail. Good morning. How are you and my grandson?" she said brightly.

"We are good, I'm just getting Remmy ready."

"Oh yes, Michael said you needed me to watch him today. That's why I called, sweetheart. Something came up and I actually won't be able to anymore." I heard clatter in the background of the phone, and I swear I heard someone ask her if she wanted another mimosa.

I sighed. *Typical Katherine.* Just like her son, her social life came first. That's probably where Michael learned his behavior.

"Oh," was all I could say. "Okay. I'll think of something."

"Great, darling, take care. Give Remmy a hug from his favorite Nana. I'll see you Sunday for dinner."

"Sunday?" I asked, surprisingly. *What the hell was happening on Sunday?* I glanced at the calendar quickly on the refrigerator and nothing was noted for that day.

"Yes, dear, Sunday. Didn't Michael tell you? We are all having dinner at the club."

"I didn't know that Katherine, but I'll add to the calendar," I added. "Thank you. Have a good day."

"Bye, bye," she sang and hung up the phone. I stood there in the kitchen with the phone in hand and sighed. I guess I could call Hannah really quick to see if she *was* available. It didn't hurt and I would rather her watch him for a few hours anyway. I also didn't want to have to take Remmy to the office unless I absolutely had to. On the few occasions I had to do this, Michael always scolded me and told me that it was unprofessional. He wasn't wrong, but when you're in a bind, there's really nothing else you can do.

I could just blow off the meeting, too, but knew Ralph would have my ass for it. Or worse, my job. We were already on reduced hours as it is, and I enjoyed working in the office as much as I could. I grabbed my phone again and flipped through the contacts for Hannah's name. It rang once, twice, and then on the third ring, her chirpy voice picked up.

"Hi Abby," she sang. "How are you?" Hannah was always such a bright, cheery person. Her attitude was infectious, and it was no wonder Remmy adored her.

"Hi Hannah, I'm doing well, but I am in a small bind. I wasn't supposed to work today, but a mandatory meeting popped up that I can't miss. Michael arranged for his mom to watch Remmy, but she just called and canceled. Is there any way you're available?" I asked, crossing my fingers. "If not, I totally understand. It's so last minute."

Hannah laughed. "It just so happens that I am free this morning, until about three o'clock. Will you be back by then? I am working tonight's shift at the diner."

I sighed in relief and thanked my lucky stars. "I'll definitely be back by three. Thank you so much, Hannah. I appreciate it. When can you be here?"

"An hour fine? I just finished my run and will jump in the shower quick. Are you okay if we swim today? I'll bring my suit if so."

"Absolutely fine. Thank you again, Hannah. See you soon."

I hung up quickly with her and again, thanked God for something going right today. I ran up to Remmy and with an excited smile told him, "Well, good news, kid. Nana can't watch you, but Hannah will be here soon!"

"*Yayyyyyyy.*" Remmy started to run excited circles around his bedroom. "I'll get my swim trunks on instead!"

He always knew if Hannah was coming over, it was a swim day.

"Great buddy, I'm going to hurry up and shower and get ready. You play in here when you're done, okay?"

Remmy nodded and started undressing. I nearly ran down the hallway and into my own bathroom. I slipped off my clothes and like every morning, hurried through the motions of getting ready. I took the quickest shower of my life, when really, I wanted to enjoy the hot water and let it relax my tense muscles. Something about today just didn't feel right and I couldn't fight the feeling that today was going to be a hell of a day. I washed my hair and body as quickly as I could, quickly ran a razor over my prickly legs, and hopped out of the shower. I put a towel in my hair to help absorb the water and started drying off my body.

I quickly slipped into a black skirt and purple blouse and black flats. I washed my face quickly, moisturized, and while my face dried a little more, I took the blow dryer to my hair. My hair was naturally straight so once I finally dried all the way through my thick hair, I ran a brush through it once more and grabbed a black clip from my countertop. I pulled it up a bit, and in an elegant, librarian sort of way, clipped it in full in the back. I took a few strands of the front to form my face when I decided to add a little makeup. I had the irksome feeling I had to look a little fresher today. I added my foundation, beige eyeshadow, and a bit of mascara. Nothing over the top, just a little something.

Just as I was finished getting ready, Remmy came bounding out of his room singing, "The doorbell, the doorbell!" Sure enough, the doorbell was ringing throughout the house, and I saw Hannah's thin figure on the other end.

I greeted Hannah with the warmest smile I could muster, as exhausted as I already was from the morning.

"You are a lifesaver, thank you so much," I told her, as I let her in. Hannah was this adorable thing. Eighteen years old and beautiful as can be. Her skin was always sun kissed and she had the prettiest blonde hair that today was down and straight. Her eyes were a pretty green color, and she had the prettiest smile that could be seen for miles.

"Oh, it's no problem, Abby. I love watching the little man." She beamed at my son and said, "Hi Remmy! Are we going to do some swimming today?" I noticed she had her swimsuit on underneath her clothes already.

"Hannah!" Remmy ran up to her and gave her the biggest smile. "Mom bought me new floaties! They have sharks on them!"

Hannah grinned. "Awesome, Remster! Can't wait to see them. Let's get you sunscreened first, okay?"

Remmy made a sour look, which caused both Hannah and I to laugh. Hannah said, with her eyebrows raised. "We don't want you to turn into a red lobster." She made her fingers into little lobster claws, puckered her face into a funny expression, and started poking, or rather clawing, at Remmy, which made him fall into a fit of giggles.

"I'm going to get this breakfast mess cleaned up and I'll be out the door." I told her.

Hannah looked at the breakfast pans and plates sitting on the counter and waved her hand. "I'll clean it up for you, Abby. It's no problem. If you leave now, you can stop at Starbucks." She gave her kind smile. *God, I loved her.*

I touched her arm in a motherly fashion. "Thank you, Hannah," I said softly. "I really, *really* appreciate you."

I gave Remmy a hug and kiss goodbye and promised I would return as soon as I could. "Don't hurry too fast," he said. Which again caused Hannah and I to laugh. He loved hanging with Hannah, and I knew our time with her was going to be limited since she'll be going off to college soon.

I grabbed my purse from the nearby coffee table, snagged the keys out, waved and blew kisses at Remmy and was out the door in a flash. Quickly, I checked the time, knowing that Hannah was right. If I left now, I would have time to stop by Starbucks. A mocha iced coffee was calling my name.

The Starbucks line was *long.* Too long for my comfort, but I was committed to the idea of that iced coffee and waited with the little patience I had left. I checked the time, and I still had plenty of time to make it to the office. After all, the meeting started at ten, and it was only eight thirty. I didn't even plan to come into the office today at all, but I wanted to check my email before the meeting started. Might as well make sure all things were good in the mortgage world.

I started people watching around me. I glanced at the others in their cars, also waiting impatiently for their orders, when I noticed the Red Corvette parked in front of me. I don't know how I missed the flashy car in front of me, since nowadays, my eyes were drawn to each of them. I squinted, trying to see who the driver was, when I saw a thin, short hair blonde woman sitting in the driver's seat.

As if she knew I was watching her, Hallie's face looked up in the rearview mirror, and then ever so slowly, she took her black shades off and with an ominous, almost devious look, she smiled at me, and tantalizingly waved her four fingers at me.

My anger flared at once and I fought the urge to pump the gas pedal. This woman knew what she was doing to me. That evil smile right there told me all that I needed to know. My insides squirmed as I made myself look away from the flashy red before I really did accelerate right into her car. I took a slow, deep breath, trying to remain calm, but my hands were fidgeting against my steering wheel. She was still watching me in the rearview mirror when her drink order arrived. She turned her attention to the barista and accepted the coffee with her perfectly manicured nails.

I took that as the opportunity to flip her off as boldly as I dared. She wasn't paying attention anymore anyway.

"What a bitch." I said, as she drove off. I swear I saw her *laughing* at me. I crept my car up to the drive thru window and handed my card to the barista, trying to calm myself down from that wretched woman. The barista was a redheaded teenage girl, who had braces covering her front buck teeth. She beamed her toothy smile at me.

"Oh, the lady in front of you bought your drink. Did you want to pay for the person behind you?" she asked with an excited sort of smile.

"That *whore*," I breathed, my nostrils flaring.

The barista's eyes widened, and she took a step back from me. I closed my eyes, took another slow deep breath, and sighed.

"I'm sorry," I apologized, "It's just that, that *woman* is screwing my husband, you see, so the last thing I want is for the bitch to pay for my drink. But yes, I'll pay for the car in the back." I handed her my debit card matter of factly, and the girl's eyes widened even more. Reluctantly, she accepted my debit card, swiped, and handed it back to me.

"Erm, have a good day, ma'am," she spluttered; her toothy smile was completely wiped from her lips.

"I'll freakin' try," I told her back, and gave her the best smile that I could, and peeled out of the parking lot.

I was breathing fire the entire drive to the office, and I hoped like hell, that the wretched woman did not show up today. The last thing I needed was an office scandal but if I saw her today, I'd probably viciously go after her like a rabid dog. I was so pissed off from the entire situation. Yesterday, I was sad and felt sorry for myself, but today, I'm an angry bitch, and the world better watch out.

I slipped into the parking lot, parked in my usual spot, and hurriedly got out of the SUV. I walked, more like storming, into the office building before I remembered, I was at work. Time to flip gears to the office professional that I knew I could be. Before I opened the double doors, I took a deep breath and then whispered to myself to get my shit together, and then I opened the door.

As soon as I walked in, I could feel the tension in the air. The hairs on the back of my neck stood up. I glanced at the time, and it was nine AM on the dot. I looked over for Carol, but she had her head down in concentration, typing fiercely on her keyboard. I crept over to her desk area and whispered, "*Carol.*" I watched as she jumped in her chair, her glasses nearly tumbling from her face.

"Oh Abby, you scared me." She clutched her heart. "Good morning."

"Good morning," I told her, and then continued further in a hushed whisper. "What is up with this meeting? I didn't even know about it until Michael told me last night."

Carol's face grew serious, and she bent her head lower in her cubicle. Her words were so quiet that it was hard to hear her.

"I don't know, but I don't have a good feeling about it," Carol hushed.

"Me either," I admitted in the same quiet tone. "I guess time will tell. Is Michael here?"

Carol nodded. "Yeah, he got here before me, and I was here at seven thirty." She gave me a look and I sighed. "Anything to report...?" she asked inquisitively.

"Not yet, but maybe soon." I gave her a tight smile, patted her shoulder, and walked to my own cubicle, my eye on Michael's shut door. I opened my computer and powered it up as I dug through my purse for my phone. I expected to have at least a text from Michael by now, but again, nothing. I sighed. *What the flippin' hell is going on?*

I quickly typed my password into the encrypted screen and waited a few seconds for it to power on. The screen went black to blue and read *'Good Morning'* in a white font. "Good morning, to who?" I mumbled grumpily to myself. The screen finally came to life, and the first thing I did was open my work email.

I had a few emails from title companies with the documentation I requested and another few from various Homeowner's Insurance companies. I flagged them all to go back to them later, but then I caught Ralph's email with an urgent flag next to it. The subject line read *Mandatory Business Update Meeting, Conference Room 1, 10 AM.* I clicked it open, my heart rate picking up a beat or two as I quickly skimmed the email. It was vague, of course, telling us where to meet, and that it was a mandatory meeting for all employees who received the email. In the bottom of the email, it read in red, bold, italicized writing *'Please do not forward this email to other recipients.'*

I quickly checked my Outlook calendar and the meeting was added there automatically for me today, May 27th, 2022. A pit in my stomach started to form and I knew that this was not going to be good. *For fuck's sake.*

I had an hour to kill before the meeting, so I quickly entered our work database and uploaded the documents I received via email into them. I replied to other emails, sent various updates as needed, when my instant messenger popped up with Michael's name. *'Come to my office after the meeting'* was all it said.

I stared at his message, completely perplexed and again, getting even more pissed. No *"Good morning, Hun, Sorry for taking off so early. Chat soon."* Fuck *you*, dude.

I sent back the thumbs up emoji, exited out of his chat, and got back to my email. I put the emails I already took care of into their respective file folders in Outlook and then spent the remainder of the time trying like hell not to barge into Michael's office and demand answers. Instead, I perused my pipeline of loans, noticed that they were still all good and set and nothing new to report as of today. They were all closing the following month and were waiting on other third parties before we could do anything further.

The seconds ticked by slowly as I sipped on my Starbucks drink. I literally sat in my swivel chair and stared at my computer screen until the time finally read that it was ten til. *Well, it was now or never.* Might as well enter the room early and grab a good seat for the upcoming shit show.

I grabbed a notepad and a pen from my desk and walked over to Carol's cube. She was also gathering a notepad and pen and gave me a forced smile.

"Wanna walk with me?" I asked her. Carol nodded. I could tell she was also anxious, and her hand was shaking slightly. "You okay?" I asked her.

Carol nodded again. "Yes, I just hope this isn't what I think it is," Carol murmured next to me. I touched her hand and gave it a squeeze.

"Me too, Carol."

I didn't fail to notice that Michael's door had remained shut all morning.

Carol and I walked with our notepads and pens to Conference Room 1, which was just down the hall from the Processor's cubicles. We walked in and noticed there was quite a crowd already in the building. Most of the people who were here worked remotely and I haven't seen their faces in quite some time. There were underwriters, processors, and closers standing awkwardly around the room, all exchanging quiet chit chat. My favorite underwriter, Janelle, was standing in the corner and already had an angry, hardened expression on her face. Carol and I meandered over to her, and I gave her a quick hug.

"Hello Janelle," I told her. "How are you?"

Janelle gave me an impish smile and said, "Not good. I'm nervous as hell for this meeting. I wish they'd just get it over with." she admitted. "You know what this meeting is, right?" She stared at me pointedly.

"Well, I'm hoping it's not what I'm thinking," I added, trying to bring positivity to the situation.

"It is. *Brace yourself.*" She cocked an eyebrow at me with a forced nod.

I sighed and leaned against the wall next to her. All I could do was give Carol's hand another tight squeeze. This was going to be so hard on her.

A few minutes later, Ralph himself walked into the room, followed by a face I've never seen before. Ralph walked to the front of the conference room, head of the table with the unfamiliar female. She had her blonde hair piled on top of her head into a very tight ponytail. If she pulled it any tighter, it may tear off her head. She had a hardened expression, light makeup, and wore a black business suit and black heels that clattered on the floor as she walked. Ralph also, who normally wore khakis and a polo, opted for a business suit as well.

Ah hell.

You could hear a pin drop in the room. I saw everyone exchange nervous glances. There were probably thirty people piled into this small conference room. I noticed from the window, there was another large group gathering in Conference Room 2.

"Thank you all for being here today." Ralph looked up from his folder in front of him. His voice was full of confidence, but at the same time, sadness. "I appreciate you all making the trip here on such short notice. As you know, I'm Ralph, Branch Manager here. Alongside me is Patricia Waylon. She's from HR." He paused for a minute, sighed, and continued. "As you all know, you are here for an important business update. You all know the situation we are in. We have had a significant drop in volume in the last two quarters and unfortunately, we must make some tough decisions."

Carol's rough hand grasped mine and I squeezed hers back in support.

"First off, I just want you all to know that you are all exceptional employees. You are all hard working, and this was an incredibly difficult decision. This is also not a personal decision, but a corporate, business decision. You should also know; we did not get to choose the individuals. The corporate staff themselves made this decision for us."

This cannot be happening. This cannot be happening.

"Due to the business decline, rates increasing, it's been a tough few quarters and unfortunately, your roles for this business have been impacted and today will be your last day of employment with Home United."

I felt my knees start to wobble and my hands start to shake next to me as my stomach flipped. Carol's face scrunched up into what looked like an attempt not to cry. *God, my heart went out to her.* She was a widow who lived alone and finding this job was her salvation. She loved this job; she's told me numerous times.

"It will be okay," I whispered to her. I gave her a determined look as she silently wiped a tear from her cheek.

"I'm now going to let Miss Waylon explain the next steps."

He took a small bow and stepped away from the head of the table. Miss Waylon walked forward with a manila folder.

"Good day." She nodded to all of us. "As Ralph had mentioned, today is unfortunately your last day of employment with Home United. We ask kindly that after this meeting, you all return to your desk, type your notes on your current file statuses, and email them to Michael Carter. He will be taking the front position of re-assigning loans to other staff members."

Carol's and Janelle's eyes darted to me with accusatory glances. They both looked hurt, as if I knew this information all along. I shook my head at them, conveying silently that I didn't know. My entire body felt as if I was crushed by a million bricks. Michael knew I was getting canned today from a job that I loved and never even told me. What. The. *Fuck.*

The HR lady continued on, but her words seemed gibberish, as if she was speaking in a foreign language and my mind and body went still as I stared into the white wall.

I lost my fucking job today.

*****

I squeezed Carol's hand a final time, collected my folder, and abruptly left the Conference Room. Few people mingled to talk amongst themselves in hushed voices, but I needed to get the hell out of here, and fast. There's no way I was going to Michael's office. I knew my anger would reach high volumes and I didn't want to embarrass precious Michael. I stormed to my cubicle, Carol quick at my heels, and sat on my swivel chair.

"Do you want me to grab your box for you?" she asked. She touched my arm sympathetically.

"Sure, thank you, Carol." I returned in a clipped tone; I instantly regretted my tone. She was in the same predicament I was in.

She hesitated at my cubicle and quietly asked, "Did you really not know?"

I looked up at her quizzical gaze and watched as the tears started swimming. "I'm just as stunned as you are Carol. No, I did not know."

She sighed, patted my shoulder, and left me alone. I glanced at my pipeline that was ever so small. Six loans. No wonder I got fired today.

I opened a new email in Outlook and started to type my notes fiercely on each individual loan. There wasn't much to report to be honest. I added Michael's email to the *'To'* line and in the subject line wrote, *'File Notes'*. I left the email up, knowing full well that he would check my email first and the last thing I wanted was for him to come out of his office. At the end of the email, I wanted to tact on gracefully a big *fuck you,* but I refrained. These were monitored emails and I wanted that damn severance check.

Carol came back with a box for my things, and I started piling everything into it that was considered a personal possession. Pictures of Remmy pretty much, and a plant that was slowly dying. I considered leaving the damn plant, but hastily placed it in the box.

I watched Carol at her desk, piling her items into her box as well. She was sniffling and her eyes were brimmed with tears and my heart literally shattered for her. She of all people didn't deserve this. She knew the first thing of struggles and hardships and this job turned everything around for her. She gave everything to this company, like me, and helped and assisted with so many side projects she volunteered to participate in.

"It'll be okay, Carol. You will find something, I promise. You can add me as a reference, too, you know," I added. Carol offered me a tearful smile but remained silent. I wanted to wrap her into a big hug and knew I would do just that before I left.

Once I had my personal possessions all collected, which weren't much, I grabbed my purse and looked at my computer screen. I hit send on that email to Michael and powered down my computer. Quick in haste to avoid a scene with him, I went to Carol's desk, and wrapped her in a tight hug.

"I promise you will find something. Keep me updated. Call me anytime."

"Thanks sweetheart, I will. It was a pleasure working with you, you know. You always brought so much joy to the workplace."

I gave a weak laugh. "Is that sarcastic, or serious?"

She smiled, but it didn't meet her eyes. "Serious, my dear. You are certainly a spectacular person. I'll let you know where I land. Keep your head up as well. I know this will be tough on you as well." She was literally the most caring person on this planet. Here she was, hurting herself, and she was concerned for me.

I patted her hand again and said, "I will. This may be the change that I needed."

"Oh?" she asked, her eyes widening.

"Yeah," I told her, nodding, and then blew her a kiss as I generally did, and fled from the building, holding the small box the company graciously had for us.

As I opened the door to the employee parking lot, I heard Michael's voice boom from behind me.

"Abigail, I needed a word," he called after me. Without turning around to face him, I raised my right hand, high and proud in the air and flipped him off.

As soon as I reached my SUV, I threw the box in my backseat angrily; the box tumbled, and I watched as some of the contents spilled. I groaned, but instead of cleaning it up, I slid into the front, and let the angry tears finally escape.

"*Gahhhhhh*," I screamed into the car, hitting the steering wheel. "What the actual fuck is going on with my life!"

For one: I'm failing at my marriage. My husband is no longer attracted to me, and he's sleeping with other women. Two: I lost my job, and not only just a job, but a job that I loved. I thoroughly loved working at Home United, and I was damn good at it. The hurt and betrayal hit me so hard that I felt windswept. How many times have I, myself, volunteered to assist in extra projects during my stay? I helped launch the new Portal, trained countless other individuals, and volunteered to take point on the new process change. *With no extra pay.* I coached countless Junior Processors to help them achieve their goal of becoming a Senior and I did all of this, for what? To be shit canned in a large Conference Room with thirty other people?

"*Why does it have to be so hard?*" I screamed at my steering wheel. As the tears flowed, a loud tap from my window made me jump in my seat. I spun, clutching my chest as the anger boiled through me from my visitor. I wiped my angry tears away and rolled down my window, my lips pressed tightly together.

"You were supposed to come talk to me after the meeting," Michael said softly. For a moment, I saw a flicker of tenderness in his eyes as he scanned my face, but it was quickly masked by his usual cocky flare he had at work.

"I had nothing to say to you," I told him. I couldn't look at him anymore and looked through the front windshield deliberately.

"Well, I had some things to say to you," he said. "I'm sorry about all of this, Abby. I really am. I tried to pull for you and get your name off the list, but like Ralph said—"

"You and Ralph can go fuck yourselves," I interrupted.

"Abigail, this was out of both of our control. This was a *corporate* decision. The company had to let go of employees, we had too much staff and not enough loans."

"You also said that you had no idea what this meeting was about. To my surprise, Ralph said that you were taking charge of reassignment. You had to have known, Michael. I'm so fucking done with your bullshit lies. Everything that comes out of your mouth is a lie and I'm so *so* tired of it." I couldn't help but glare at him.

Michael rolled his eyes. "You are being dramatic, Abigail. Really, this is not a big deal for us. It's not like your money really pays much for our life anyway."

If looks could kill, this man would be dead. I glared at him and said, "That's not the fucking point, Michael. I *liked* my job. I enjoyed working here. This is *awful*. And not only for me, but for all those other people in there. They have *lives*, Michael and this is affecting them."

"The company understands, and which is why they are paying out severance."

"So, you admit you knew this was coming?"

Michael let out an exasperated sigh and had the good grace to look away. He ran his hand through his sandy hair, shaking his head slightly.

"Yeah," he admitted, "I knew. He told me at the end of the day yesterday. He also told me that I could not say a word about this to anyone and that if the news got out before the meeting, my own job would be at stake. He said the whole thing needed discretion and that I could not warn you about this. What was I supposed to do, Abby? Break protocol and tell you? The first thing you would have done was tell Carol, and God knows who she would have told."

"I'm your *wife*, Michael. And you knew I was getting fired today. You could have at least prepared me. Gave me a hint or something. That was awful in there." I wiped at my face angrily as more tears spilled from my eyes. "I lost my job."

"I'm not worried about it," Michael said. "You have your severance coming and you can stash that away for a rainy day if you want. You have all the money you need in our joint account. I pay for everything anyway. It will be fine."

"Again, Michael, that's not the point. I enjoyed making my *own* money. Do you really think I want to rely on *you* for cash?"

"You do anyway, so I don't understand the problem."

"I do not Michael! I pay for our groceries, and I pay for Remmy's and my things from my own account. I don't touch your paychecks unless it's for bills, but even I pay some of the bills from my account, too. I just can't believe you right now."

"We can discuss the money later. Just know, I'm not worried about it. If you want to find a job, then find another job. There are plenty of them out there right now."

"A job with the same flexibility will be hard to find and you know that," I snapped. "I need something flexible for Remmy."

"Or you don't have to work at all," he added again. "Lots of mothers forgo working to be stay at home, Abigail. It's normal. Practical, even, given Remmy's age."

I sighed, not wanting to continue this conversation with him anymore. There was no point arguing with him.

"Speaking of Remmy, I need to go back home. Your mother bailed and I have Hannah there right now."

"Of course, she did." He rolled his eyes. "She's so typical. She's the one who insisted on watching him."

"Yeah, well she's as dependable as her son," I snapped. I rolled my window up on my last statement and flipped him off again as I stared him straight in the eye. Michael rolled his eyes at me again and walked away.

When I got home, Hannah and Remmy were both still in the pool. I watched them through the window for a moment, before venturing out to the back patio, making sure my cheeks were dry from my earlier ugly cry session. Hannah picked Remmy up from the water and held him to the pool basketball hoop, when Remmy slammed the basketball into the net. He squealed with pleasure and was yelling, "Slam duuuuunk."

I smiled and let out a heavy sigh. If only I could be young again. Adulting straight up sucked.

I put the passcode in and walked out to the patio. Hannah and Remmy both turned to me, and Remmy yelled, "*Moommmmm, get in with us! It's fun!*"

I slipped off my shoes and found a dry spot on the pool edge. I sat down and let my feet dangle in the warm pool water. Hannah glanced at me for a moment, looked away, and then back at me, her brows puckering up as if she was trying to solve a puzzle.

"Are you okay, Abby?" Hannah asked with concern.

I put on a forced smile and gave her a slow nod. She nodded back at me and turned towards Remmy.

"Remmy, I have the best idea! How about we sit out and have a popsicle? Wouldn't that be so yummy right now?" Hannah added so much excitement to her voice and Remmy gobbled it up.

"Yeaaaah, I want the red one!"

"*I* want the red one!" Hannah said with a laugh. She placed her hands underneath Remmy's armpits and pulled him to the side of the pool. I watched them both step out and grab nearby beach towels. Hannah wrapped Remmy up in his blue *Power Ranger* towel and she grabbed the soft pink one and covered herself up.

Hannah moved around our backyard with ease, and I knew that I was going to miss her terribly. Help like her was hard to find and she was so unbelievably great to my Remmy. She cut the plastic off the top of three popsicles and handed Remmy the red one, where he instantly ran off to our favorite rocking chair. Hannah walked over to me and handed me my own, a blue one, with an impish smile.

"Popsicle for your thoughts?" Hannah asked. I accepted with a low chuckle. She sat down next to me on the pool edge with her own popsicle and we started chewing on the flavored ice. The sweetness lingered in my mouth for a moment and Hannah waited for me to start speaking.

"The meeting was a layoff meeting," I said with a sigh. "I was let go today."

Hannah's lips turned into a frown as she stared into the clear blue water.

"I'm so sorry, Abby. I know you liked working there."

I sighed. "It's okay. It's probably for the best. Working with your husband can be challenging." I smiled as best as I could.

"Oh, I'm sure," Hannah added. "Everything happens for a reason though. I'm sure you will find something different soon. Who knows, maybe you'll like it even more?" she said, brightly.

"Maybe," I said with a sigh. "I just don't know what to do right now. I have a lot going on and feeling just a little emotionally overwhelmed. Being an adult, you're supposed to have all the right answers, but right now, I don't, and it's honestly intimidating."

I sucked on the popsicle and glanced over my shoulder to check on Remmy. He was humming to himself and sucking on his own popsicle, perfectly content.

"Sometimes, you don't have the right answers," Hannah said. "But sometimes, finding the right answers can be fun, too. Challenging, difficult, yes, but I think that's the beauty of it. Life is a crazy kind of thing, but I believe that God gives us these challenges to show us how strong we are. Once you overcome a challenge, and find the reason, you will be blown away. Maybe this challenge right now is a sign for you. A nudge to point you in a different path of your life."

I looked over at this eighteen-year-old girl in amazement and wrapped my arm around her wet shoulder.

"You, my dear, are wise for your years." I gave her a tight squeeze and let my arm fall back down to my side. "Thank you, Hannah. For being so great to my family. I really appreciate everything you do for us."

Hannah beamed at me, and we sat in silence while we finished our popsicles. Sometimes, a sugar infused popsicle was the exact cure for a broken heart.

After we finished our popsicles, Hannah told me she still had time to stay with Remmy if I wanted to have a little alone time to think. She was seriously the sweetest girl I've ever met. I thanked her and told her that I would go take a quick bath. She nodded and her and Remmy decided they were going to play on the playset for a little while before getting back in the pool. As I walked up through the patio, I heard Remmy's giggles from behind me as Hannah chased him around the backyard.

I walked to my master bath and started filling the jacuzzi tub with hot bath water. I grabbed the bubbles from the nearby stand and poured in a few capfuls. I sat on the edge of the tub and watched as the tub filled, trailing my hand into the top of hot water. My mind was utterly blank, as if in shock, and I couldn't think about it anymore. I met my capacity for the time being. When the water reached half full, I slipped out of my clothes and left them discarded on the floor.

The water was hot to touch and stung my skin, but only for a second as I dipped my toes in. I slipped further into the tub and let the water relax my tense muscles. I thought about nothing except how great the water felt on my body and sunk deeper into the depths, letting my entire head submerge under the surface.

Under the water, my mind started sporadic thoughts.

I lost my job. My husband is screwing other women. I lost my job. I can stay with my husband and be a miserable hag or leave and be absolutely broke. Stay and have my comfort or leave and fight like hell to survive?

I came up from the depths of the water and grabbed a hand towel nearby and patted my face. The water was still running and almost overflowed the tub. I turned it off with my foot and sat up a little straighter in the tub.

Those really were my options. I am no longer employed, so there's no way I can save money on my own and leave Michael. I do have a severance coming, but that money won't last forever. I would have to find another job, but really, who is hiring Processors right now, especially considering how the economy is?

It's fine. I can make it work. I'll update my resume this evening and get it out there. First, I'll look for mortgage jobs. Second, for office admin. I can find an office admin position *somewhere* in Florida. It will all be okay. There are jobs everywhere right now and I can and will make this work. All I needed was a positive can-do attitude.

"You can do this," I said encouragingly. I laid my head back on the tub. *"You can do this."*

Even in my heart, I knew that staying with Michael was not an option. No, as I laid in his arms last night, I knew that staying in this relationship was not going to work. It wasn't healthy what we were doing, and I knew Michael was not about to change. I wasn't happy with our situation and Michael won't even admit to me that he's having an affair. You can't fix a problem if you won't admit to the problem. Hell, even Hallie knows that I know they are having an affair, but Michael can't be man enough to admit it. Even if he did admit it though, would it change my feelings? Probably not. I would still feel the same hurt and betrayal, probably even more. Michael would still not come home at night, be off fucking around, or "schmoozing" as he refers to it, and I would be at home, with Remmy, taking care of things as usual. All by myself.

I just couldn't do it anymore. I couldn't stay in a loveless relationship. It wasn't just picking at me anymore but swallowing me whole.

So, that's it. First, find a job and start the job. Second, save, save, save. Third, find my own place. Fourth, leave the cheating bastard.

I've got this.

I already felt exhausted from just thinking about it. I rubbed at my face with my wet hands and thought about what Hannah said earlier, about how everything happens for a reason, and mulled on it. What in the world was the reason for this? To get me away from Michael at work? To get me to slow down a little? I have been such a freakin' hot mess lately. Slowing down sounded nice, but I couldn't do it in this house, knowing Michael's out there running around on me. It hurt too much and really, it was just fucking embarrassing at this point.

Maybe you really should go visit your parents... I thought. It wasn't a horrible idea, to be honest. I missed home. I missed my parents desperately and my mother's needy, but wonderful hugs. Maybe this was a sign from God that I needed to slow down but go home and do it there. My mom did just mention me visiting the other day. Maybe this is the path He's pointing me down?

I mean, I could go for a little bit, clear my head, and really think about what I want to do with my life. I would probably have a clearer mind there anyway, and not surrounded by all my hurt emotions with Michael. I wouldn't be checking the clock all the time and wondering why he wasn't home yet. I wouldn't have to worry about what he was doing, because, who the hell cares?

Remmy also could bond with his grandparents more. He loved my mom and dad, but we seldom saw them. Remmy really could use the vacation, too. I mean, Illinois is no Florida, but it is home and right now, home sounded just where I wanted to be. *Just where I needed to be.*

I leaned out of the tub at that moment and grabbed my purse that I dropped nearby on the floor. Water splashed out of the tub, but I didn't care. I grabbed my leather purse and rummaged inside for my cell phone, tossing out old receipts as I did so. I found Mom's number in my favorites and hit the call button.

The phone rang several times and then it went to voicemail. Crickets, that's right, she had a bake sale today. She was probably too busy to talk. Generally, I didn't leave voicemails, but this time, I did, my heart hammering with each word.

"Mom, it's Abby. Listen, can you get that room ready? Remmy and I are for sure coming down to visit. I-I just really need you, Mom. I'm coming home, okay? Call me later."

I hung up and even though I was excited to see my parents soon, I started to break down and cry.

Sawyer

I loved my mother, but she drives me absolutely *insane*. I showed up at her house and as soon as I walked into the door, she turned into a warden. Her kitchen had baked goods *everywhere*; the counters full, table, and even a folding table in the living room as if she had her own damn bakery. She considered at one point in her life pursuing it as a career but decided to keep it as a hobby. Growing up, she'd call me into the kitchen all the time to taste test her creations and it was always so damn good. It took me seven trips to load everything into her car while she observed and each time, reminded me to be careful.

I was going to drive separately, but mom insisted that I drive her to the square. That should have been my first clue. She had every intention of holding me hostage today. I drove her to the bake sale, unloaded everything, while she gossiped and chatted with the others at the sale. Once we were set up, Mom directed on how she wanted the table to look. I added the tablecloths as instructed and then started arranging the baked goods, just so she could change it because she didn't like how I arranged it. "Presentation is everything, Sawyer."

She drove me absolutely crazy.

After she approved the table, Mom mingled a lot with the other bakers at the sale and gave me the 'cash box' duty. *For fucks sake*. I felt like I was five years old doing a lemonade stand all over again. Mom did well though and sold a lot of goods, while I continued to count down the seconds to when hell, I mean the sale, would be over.

Around three o'clock, when the sale was finally closed, Mom and I assessed her almost empty table. She still had a few cookies and cupcakes leftover. Everything else had sold to my mother's delight. "Sawyer, how did we do today?"

"You did great, Mom. I think the last time I counted the cash box you were up three hundred."

"Oh, that's so wonderful!" Mom smiled with delight. "*We* did great, Sawyer." She patted my arm. I didn't say anything, but just gave my mother a blank stare. It was time for me to get the fuck out of here. "Now, we can get this all packed up. Do you want to take the leftovers home?"

"Sure."

I started tearing down her stand carefully. Mom liked to reuse the signs, as the town had several bake sales throughout the year, and I carefully loaded everything back into her car. When I returned to my mother, Miss Mandy was standing next to Mom, and they were talking in hushed voices.

"What are you two whispering about?" I asked, cocking my brow. "What scandal happened today?"

Mom and Miss Mandy exchanged glances, and I noticed that Miss Mandy's eyes had tears, but it didn't match her smile; she was glowing.

"I just checked my voicemail and got a call from Abby. She's coming home to visit! She hasn't been here in such a long time. *Oh*, I'm so excited to see her and my grandson," she cooed.

I paused at her words, my head jerking to the side. *Abby was coming home?*

"Is that right?" I asked. I didn't fail to notice that my mother was eyeing me curiously with a hint of a smile.

"Yes! I have to hurry home and get their rooms ready. Oh, I'm just so excited! We should plan a dinner one night, all of us, just like old times."

I didn't say anything, but my mom answered for us. "We would be delighted to come. Let me know if you need any help with preparing their rooms," my mom offered. Miss Mandy pulled my mom into a tight hug and before she left, she patted my arm.

"Sawyer, did you give the earned money to Stephanie?" Stephanie was the treasurer of the bake sale.

"Yes, I did. Are you ready to go?"

Mom looked around the almost empty square and nodded. "Sure am, sweetheart. Let's go."

On the drive to her house, Mom was quiet and was staring out of her window most of the time. I didn't try to start a conversation because I didn't know where Mom's head was. Also, the silence was nice, after all the chatter from today. When I made it to her driveway and put the car in park, Mom placed her warm, papery hand on my arm.

"Sawyer, when are you going to start dating? Like *really* dating?" Mom asked. "Mandy just boasts about that grandchild of hers and I want one to boast about, too." Mom's eyes were filled with sadness.

I let out a grumbled laugh. I should have known this was where Mom's thoughts were. "*Mom*," was all that I said, just as I had done as a child.

"I'm serious, Sawyer. You are thirty-one years old, and you don't even have a girlfriend yet. Don't you want to settle down with someone and start a family?" she pleaded.

"I'm busy, Mom. Work keeps me busy."

Mom's face fell into a scowl. "I'm *never* going to meet my grandchildren, Sawyer, and I want grandchildren!" she demanded. Now she sounded like a child.

"And I want a million dollars, but we can't get everything we want all the time." I told her with a smile. She used that line countless times with me during my childhood. Mom's scowl increased.

"Mom," I told her. "I will date when *I'm* ready. I'm just... not there yet. I am *busy*. You know I give a lot of my time to this town. Hell, all weekend I'm going to be at the baseball fields for clean up. I will get to dating when I am ready to do so."

Mom rolled her eyes and opened her car door. I heard her mumble, "I won't even get to *meet* my grandchildren, I'll be *dead*."

I let out a groan and rolled my eyes. After I unloaded her car, I kissed my mother on the cheek.

"Do you want to stay for dinner?" Mom asked. "You can invite Lance. I'm sure he's *bacheloring* it up just as much as you are," she added with a scowl.

"Sure, Mom. I'll call Lance."

Mom glared at me as she stomped into her house. She was a stubborn woman, who normally got what she wanted, but in this case, she had to be patient. The right woman would come along eventually. When, I had no clue, but for now I was going to live my life the way she and Dad taught me; work hard and help others when you can.

The right one will come, I thought. I just haven't found her yet. I wasn't going to settle down with just *anyone*. The person had to really capture my attention and be the whole package. Fiery, but sweet. Kind, but someone who wasn't afraid to speak her mind. Beautiful, but not over the top. I preferred a woman's natural beauty, someone with a pretty smile and eyes. Someone that could make me fall to my knees with just a look.

Maybe someday.

Chapter 4- *Abby*

Our travel luggage was packed and sat adjacent to the front door. It would be the first thing Michael saw when he got home, but I didn't care. If he would have reached out to me at any point today, I would have told him that I was going home, but he never called or texted, so I really didn't give a damn either. He'd find out soon enough. Our plane tickets were purchased for the following morning at six AM sharp. It was going to be an early morning and getting Remmy up that early would probably be the death of me, but I kept reminding myself that it would all be worth it when we arrived in Illinois.

It took *forever* to get Remmy to bed that evening, but in the end, my excited little man succumbed to his droopy eyes and fell asleep. Exhaustion hit me like a ton of bricks in the last half hour, but I knew I had to force myself to stay awake and wait for Michael to bless me with his presence. I had an extremely emotional and taxing day and all I wanted to do was crawl into my own bed and sleep away this horrendous day.

While I waited for Michael, I finished the laundry, deep cleaned the kitchen and bathrooms, made sure I had mine and Remmy's outfits picked out for the next day, made sure the bills were scheduled to be paid by their due dates for the next two month, and even hired a maid to drop in next week to tidy up the place for Michael.

The plane tickets I purchased to Illinois were a one-way ticket. I was not going to purchase a return ticket until I was ready to come home. I needed the time away to think, process, and really dive into my emotions without being surrounded by my memories of Michael. It was hard to be in this house, *my dream house* at one point in my life, and think about giving it all up. Just being in here made my skin crawl and I felt like I was suffocating. If I was able, I would have just loaded up in the SUV and started driving this afternoon, but I was in no condition to start a nineteen-hour drive. Still, the idea was tempting.

I glanced at the clock and the time flashed ten-thirty PM. I sighed and decided that I couldn't wait for Michael anymore. My mind and body was over the day, and I needed to catch some z's for the following morning. I walked to the bathroom, got ready for bed, and climbed underneath my silk sheets. I glanced at the clock one more time, registering it was now close to eleven, and the thoughts of what Michael could be doing jumbled around my head, until finally, I fell into a restless sleep.

It didn't feel like I had my eyes closed for more than a few minutes when I jerked awake to a loud *thud*.

"WHAT THE FUCK, ABBY?" a male voice boomed. My eyes were droopy from sleep, and I vaguely registered that it was Michael standing, more like hovering, over my bed.

I pulled back at his deafening voice and tried to get my eyes to focus. Our bedroom door swung idly from the slam. I eyed the wall and noticed a small indent from the doorknob. I glanced up at Michael's face and recoiled from his cold, haughty stare.

"What?" I finally asked. I attempted to clear the sleep from my throat.

"Why do you have luggage by the front door?" he hollered.

I sighed, sat up a little straighter and rubbed at my eyes. "Will you please keep it down? You'll wake Remmy."

"I will not," he protested, but even so, his harsh voice lowered to an angry whisper. "What the fuck is going on?"

My eyes focused more on Michael in the darkened room. He smelled a mixture of beer and stale cigarette smoke, and his eyes had a reddish tint to them. He leaned slightly to the side.

He was drunk.

"I tried to wait for you, but you were out too late," I told him.

"Why is there luggage by the front door?" he bellowed again.

I flipped on the nightstand light to get a better look at my drunk, staggering husband and sighed again. "Why don't you get some sleep, and we can discuss tomorrow morning?" I told him, patting the bed.

"No, we'll talk about this *now*." He folded his arms across his chest, in a menacing way, but Michael Carter never has, nor never will, intimidate me. I felt my eyes roll.

"Remmy and I are going to visit my parents for a while."

"And you didn't care to tell me this? You're just letting me find out *this way?* That's kind of shitty of you, Abby."

"I was going to tell you when you got home, Michael," I replied quietly.

"Why didn't you call and tell me? Or text me?"

"Because I didn't."

"No, you're trying to get back at me about your fucking job," he sneered. "Real low of you, Abby."

"It has nothing to do with it."

"Whatever, it has everything to do with it," he scoffed and turned his head to the side, his hands clenched. "You're not going, *end of discussion.*"

For a minute there, I thought it was just my sleepy eyes playing tricks on me. My eyes did a double take and focused on the pinkish smear. My eyes dialed in, taking in the color, and slowly, I felt my body rise from the bed. I took a step closer to him. His chest was rising and falling rapidly, and he looked at me, his eyes still glaring, but now they were confused as I zeroed in on his neck.

On the side of his neck, was a light smear of red lipstick.

My stomach heaved as my insides boiled and I let out a nasty laugh and turned away from him. My eyes burned as the hot tears started to form.

"You have got to be fucking kidding me," I whispered, my back turned. I ran my hand through my tangled mess of hair. I spun around to face him, my hands shaking at my sides. Even though the tears started to flow, I let out another laugh.

"The reason I want to visit my parents is to get the fuck away from *you*, Michael." I snapped. "I need to get away. This…this is just insanity. *I can't believe you.*"

"Because of your job," he stated, nodding his head; his pupils were large as he took me in. "I HAD NOTHING TO DO WITH IT!" he bellowed.

"Nothing to do with my job, *Dumbass*. Look at your neck. THAT'S WHY I NEED TO GET AWAY FROM YOU, YOU CHEATING ASSHOLE."

Michael's glaring eyes turned bewildered as I pointed at his neck. He whirled around towards our full-length mirror and stared at the smear, his eyes going wide.

"I don't know what this is," Michael said coolly. He masked his expression well.

"Oh, here we go." Another angry laugh bubbled from my lips. "More excuses from Michael Carter. Can't wait to hear this. Actually, you know, I *can* wait to hear this. I can't even look at you anymore. You absolutely disgust me, Michael. You are a completely different person from the man that I married. Remmy and I are leaving tomorrow morning to go visit my mom and dad. During this time apart, I suggest you really think about what the fuck you are doing Michael because *trust me,* I'll be taking this time to think as well." My chest heaved.

Michael laughed and took a slow step towards me, his eyes narrowed.

"What are you going to do, baby?" he whispered haughtily. "Leave me? With no job? Sure, let's see how far you make it before you come crawling back. You can't do this without me. Sure, take the time that you need. Go visit your parents, but don't threaten me with that bullshit because you and I both know that you'll come back." He got close to me, his hot breath on my face, but I wouldn't back down from him. I stood taller, my eyes glaring right back into his.

"You say that I'm not the man you married? Look at you Abigail! You're one to talk! You used to be fun, *exciting*. We'd go out, have fun. You used to be fucking hot, now look at you. Up three, maybe four clothes sizes and letting yourself go. What man would want to come home to a wife like that? I don't ask you to go out with me, Abby, because I'm embarrassed to be seen with you.

"And yeah, you're right, I'm fucking Hallie. There! I said it. I'm fucking her, and have been for months, but what do you expect from me? I need to get it somewhere and I don't want it from you."

I jerked back from his malicious stare, my jaw dropping to the floor. His words stung my entire being in one fell swoop. Hot tears welled my eyes as the lump in my throat ached, but not as bad as my heart. He finally said it, admitted to the ongoing affair, and just as I expected, it didn't make me feel any better.

His drunken confession lingered around us; his chest rose and fell rapidly as his eyes glinted as if he was a warrior that just won a battle. I felt my entire body crumble to the floor. I didn't have words to say to his hurtful confession, because I knew what he said was real. He may not have raised his hand at me, but the words stung as if he had slapped me. He was honest with me for the first time in his life.

The man that used to be my best friend, my confidant, my love, was gone.

I bit down my lower lip to stop the trembling as the tears poured from my eyes. I looked away from his stare, slowly nodded, and wiped the tears from my face. I tried to regain my composure, but the tears made it difficult to speak as Michael waited for me to reply.

"Okay," I told him softly.

"That's all you have to say?" Michael sneered. I looked back up at him and gave him a sad smile.

"There's nothing left to say," I told him, giving him a half-hearted shrug. "Thank you."

"Thank you?" He cocked an eyebrow at me and started laughing again.

"Yes," I said, taking a step towards him. I forced myself to stand tall in front of him, even though it was becoming difficult to stand. "Thank you for making this decision easy for me."

"What the hell do you mean by that?" He smirked.

"You and me," I told him forcefully, looking right back into his cold stare. "It's over, Michael. I'm done. I am going to file for divorce."

Michael's lips pulled back into a sinister smile and he said, "Whatever you say, baby."

Sawyer

"Awesome job today, Sammy," I told him, clapping him on the back; his back was drenched with sweat as his shaggy hair clung to his skull. I wiped my hand on the back of my shorts and he gave me a wry smile. "Drink some water," I said, tossing him a bottle from the nearby cooler. He nodded his thanks and started drinking.

Today was the baseball diamond clean up. We had fifteen volunteers today, which was actually a great turn out. We were able to break up into small groups, and after six hours of raking, dragging fields, pulling weeds, repainting and restocking the concession stand, mending a few fences, staining the dugouts, and rechalking the fields, we were done. *Finally*. All that was left was the mowing, but Sammy volunteered to come back tomorrow. I was gracious for that; the last thing any of us wanted was to jump on a mower for another few hours.

"Text me after you're done mowing tomorrow, and I'll meet you here with your check." I didn't tell him that the check was coming from me directly. I didn't want him to have to wait for board approval, and after all, he worked the hardest today out of us all.

"Thank you, sir," Sammy told me with a nod. "Is there anything else that needs to be done?" All the other volunteers had left for the day.

"Nah, you're okay. I gotta head to the Commons though to start town ball registration. Got anywhere you need to be?" I asked him, eyeing the dirt on his forehead with a grin. He had smudges all over his face.

"No, sir. I can help," Sammy volunteered automatically.

I beamed at him and clapped him on the back. "That a boy," I murmured.

I threw the cooler in the back of my truck and slid into the driver's side. Sammy hesitated but slid into the passenger side as he eyed the truck with appreciation.

"Like trucks?" I asked him, as I pulled out of the diamonds.

"Yes, I have a 1977 Ford F-250 at home. It's a beauty." He grinned.

"That is a nice truck." I nodded with appreciation. "Do you know how to work on it?"

"Some. My dad was teaching me a little bit." His voice trailed off as he looked out of his window and my lips turned into a hard line as I pulled into the High School parking lot.

"My buddy Lance owns the auto shop in town. If you ever want to learn about cars or need help fixing anything on it, just stop by his shop. He'll lend you a hand."

I didn't have to ask Lance because I already knew how he'd respond. That's just the kind of person Lance was. He was always one to lend a hand to anyone that asked, especially a kid like Sammy. It had a lot to do with Lance's upbringing. He, too, grew up without a father, which is partly why he took my own father's passing hard. He grew attached to my old man growing up, because he was the only father figure he knew.

"That's awfully nice of you, Mr. Gibson," Sammy said softly.

"It's nothing," I amended quietly. *I wish I could do more for you, Kid.*

I parked up front and rummaged through my pocket for the keys to the high school. Sammy and I walked into the darkened Commons, the school eerily quiet as I flipped the lights on. Together, Sammy and I pulled out a few white folding tables from the closet and arranged the tables with registration slips and pens. Sammy grabbed us a few folding chairs and we sat back and waited.

After thirty minutes of no one showing up, I tossed my truck keys to Sammy and told him to run to my truck to grab a deck of cards. He did so happily, but when he came back, he said, "Isn't anyone coming? The parking lot is empty."

"A lot of people register and pay online. I wouldn't be surprised if no one comes." I said with a shrug. "I still do a few in person registrations for those that aren't tech savvy." Sammy nodded and tossed the cards into my direction.

"Ever play Texas Hold'em?" I asked him. Sammy shook his head. I explained the rules and just like in class, Sammy soaked in the information I tossed to him. The kid was sharp, you could practically see the wheels turning in his head as I explained the rules.

"Ready to start?" I asked.

"Sir, just to be clear, this is poker, right?" Sammy asked.

"Yeah. Erm…maybe don't mention to anyone that your teacher taught you to play poker, okay?" I said with a nervous laugh. Sammy grinned but agreed.

We played a few hands and Sammy caught on fairly quickly, as I knew he would. Just as I was about to deal the next round, the door opened, and a group of people started to file in. I looked over at Sammy with a knowing grin as he scurried the cards from sight.

Sammy was a great help; he helped collect money and provided thanks to each parent just as I did. A few parents stopped to chit chat and to my displeasure, a few mothers attempted to flirt. My face reddened more times than I could count at their presumptuous words. One mother even had the courage to ask me if I would coach their kid, simply so she could have eye candy at the games. It was bad timing when she said that; I took a drink of my water and nearly spit out its contents all over her. Sammy found all of it highly amusing and had to walk away numerous times from his silent laughter.

"Hush it, you," I told him finally. This was after a woman deliberately filled her form out right in front of me with her tits bobbing around; they practically slapped me in the face. Sammy's eyes widened as he choked back a laugh and I forcefully leaned back and stared at him the entire time. This right here was why I was over dating.

"I'm going to the bathroom," Sammy said, chuckling as he walked away from me.

"I can handle the next group," I told him, as the high school door swung open again.

"Oh, I'm sure you can, sir," Sammy said, still chortling. "Especially all of those *single* moms."

"Sammy, I'm still your teacher," I told him, tossing him a stern look. He slipped into the nearby restroom, and I could still hear his laughter echoing.

I turned my attention to the next group, a mother and son. My focus was more so on the little boy. He was practically skipping, his little hand in his mom's and he had a wide, infectious smile that popped out two little dimples in his cheeks. He was wearing athletic shorts, tennis shoes, and a white t-shirt with a baseball printed on it. He looked so familiar, too, but I couldn't pinpoint where I've seen him before. It was a small town, so maybe at a town function…

He had sandy, short hair and as he got closer to me, I noticed that his eyes were a mesmerizing, deep blue.

"Well, hello, little man," I said, flashing him a bright smile. "Let me guess…you're here to sign up for…*basketball*?"

His grin widened and he shook his head back and forth. "Baseball!" he chimed, giggling. Even his voice was adorable.

I laughed. "Oh…baseball. That's right. I should probably remember that," I teased again, making a face at him. I looked up to introduce myself to his mother, but I froze.

I nearly fell off my chair as I stared into her widened baby blues and quickly straightened in my chair.

"*Abby*."

Abby was…*different*. Way different than the last time I saw her, but that was, what? Thirteen years ago? *My times have changed*, I thought to myself. She definitely wasn't a kid anymore and I couldn't help but gawk at her. She blossomed into a beautiful woman and my heart jumped as I took her in. She was wearing black athletic shorts that showed off thick, tanned thighs and an oversized cotton white tee; the shirt hid her figure well, and I wondered what kind of curves she was hiding. Her hair was still the same light brown color I remembered her having, but it was hidden underneath a black baseball cap, her ponytail spilling from the back in wavy curls.

Her eyes, her pretty blues that I used to lose myself in as a teen, were still the same and I felt my heart kick into full gear as I gazed into them. She looked just as surprised to see me; her eyes also drifted over me, and I briefly hoped that I looked as good to her as she did me.

"Sawyer." Her voice was smooth and collected; she shifted her weight to the side and fidgeted with the strap of her black purse.

"Wow, it's so good to see you," I mumbled. Abby's eyes scanned my face, and slowly, she gave me a smile, popping out those dimples that I used to love.

"Sarcastic or serious?" Abby said, her delicate eyebrow in the air.

"Serious."

"Mmm…" Abby hummed, her eyes scrutinizing me. "So, you're on the town board?"

"Yeah. I guess you're here for registration?" I asked her, shaking my head slightly. I couldn't believe she was here.

"Well, I'm not here for school."

I narrowed my eyes. *Yes, this was definitely Abby.*

I grabbed a pen and a registration slip for her and slid it over to her. Abby grabbed it without a word and started to fill it out in front of me. I knew I shouldn't keep staring at her, but I couldn't help it. I went thirteen years without seeing this girl and now that she was right in front of me, I couldn't keep my eyes off her.

"You're staring," Abby said, and I felt my cheeks flush.

"Because I can't believe you're here," I said. "It's been a long time. How have you been?"

"Fine," she replied simply. I nodded and looked down at the registration slip. I watched as she filled out the paper with her elegant scrawl. My eyes glanced from the paper, to her left hand and widened; she had a fucking rock on her hand.

Obviously, I knew she was married. I was invited to her wedding, but I refused to go. My mother wasn't thrilled with my decision, but didn't push me on it, which I was thankful for. There was no way I could have told her that the reason I didn't want to go, *couldn't* go, was because I couldn't bear the thought of seeing her give herself to someone else.

Abby completed the form and slid it back over to me, digging through her purse.

"It's fifty," I told her.

Abby's eyebrows scrunched together as she looked back down at the form.

"It says sixty right there," she told me, her eyebrow raised. In a blink of an eye, I felt like we really were back in school, all over again. "Do you even know what you're collecting, Sawyer?"

I couldn't help but laugh as my heart came back to life.

"For your little man, fifty," I told her. I looked back up at her baby blues, but to my surprise, her face hardened into a mask.

"Why for us?" Her tone changed to accusatory, and I felt my eyes widen. "Did my parents tell you why we are here?" she demanded.

I put my hands up at once. She was getting fired up as her eyes glared into mine, and I stopped myself from laughing at her further; this was not a funny moment, but seeing Abby here, in the flesh, and having her argue with me, was just like the old days.

"Abby, I have no idea why you are here. I was just waiving the admin fee for you. I'm on the board and can do that for friends, but um, sixty, if you insist."

Abby's eyes probed mine for a second longer, before she decided that I was telling the truth.

"Sorry," she apologized, shaking her head. "Sure, okay." She continued digging in her wallet for the cash and slid three twenties over to me. I wasn't surprised. I fought my amused grin and looked over at Remmy, who was grinning at me, showing off his missing front tooth.

"Thank you both so much," I told her, forcing professionalism into my voice. I grabbed the money and slid the cash into the envelope and gave my usual spiel to the parents. "We are excited to start the baseball season. You'll hear from your coach probably late next week and practices will start the following week."

"Will you be there?" Remmy's tiny voice piped up.

"I'll be around," I told him with a smile. "Good luck, little buddy. Hope you have a great season."

I held out my knuckles to him and he was quick to respond by hitting his knuckles against mine. What took me by surprise though, was when he pulled his hand back, and with his tiny fingers next to mine, wiggled them back and forth and chanted, "*Woogie woogie*" with delight.

I couldn't help the belly laugh that followed as I took my right hand and ruffled his hair. "I like that addition; I'll remember that the next time I see you," I said.

Abby's smile instantly warmed me as I found myself staring back into her face. Her smile used to be my favorite. I used to act like a fucking idiot around her, just to see that smile, but more times than most, I would get a scowl and an eyeroll, but it was just as cute. She was always so annoyed by me, and it only encouraged me more. I gave Abby my best smile and watched as her eyes glazed over slightly; my insides started to burn as her eyes lingered down to my mouth. She took a slow breath and looked back down to her son and cleared her throat.

"Sawyer, thank you." She gave me a curt nod as she gestured to the slips in front of her. "Good to see you."

"Good to see you. I'm sure I'll see you around." Abby inhaled sharply as she fidgeted with her purse again.

"I hope not," she mumbled underneath her breath.

Fuck, have I missed her.

"What was that?" I asked, cocking a brow at her and letting out a silent laugh. "Did you just say what I thought you said?"

Abby tossed me a sarcastic smile, and said, "I said I hope to see you soon, Sawyer."

With a nod of her head, she grabbed Remmy's hand and ushered him to the front door. Remmy happily walked next to her, more like bounced, and I watched as he turned around to look at me one more time. With a bright smile he waved, and I hurried to return the gesture.

"Abby!" I called, as soon as her hand touched the exit door. I watched as she froze ever so slightly and then slowly turned around to face me, her eyebrow already cocked in the air.

"We should get coffee sometime. Catch up."

"Probably not." Abby scrunched her face. I let out a bark of laughter.

"And why not?" I challenged, eyes narrowing at her; I enjoyed this way too fucking much with her.

"Oh, because I don't want to," Abby said, nodding her head at me, but even as she turned away from me, I saw her lips pull into a smile. I chuckled, eyes narrowing more as I watched her walk away from me. She pushed open the doors, but before they shut behind her, she turned around to look back at me, her eyes dancing.

Chapter 5- *Abby*

Why the hell did Sawyer Gibson have to look *that* good? Why couldn't he have aged like the rest of us? At least go bald or have a beer belly or *something*. He was still gorgeous as ever; his blue eyes were still that deep color that nearly knocked me off my feet. His hair was still unfortunately firmly intact; a deep chestnut color that fell in a sexy as hell disarray. And his *arms*....

And that beard. My God, Sawyer with a beard was sexy.

Hands down, he looked like a fucking model, and I hated him for it; *why, why, why.*

When I walked into the Commons, I nearly sprinted in the other direction. I recognized that man right away and I was mortified. I looked awful. We just got off the plane a few hours ago and I haven't even had time to shower yet. Of course, the first person I run into in this damn town would be *Sawyer*.

That's just my luck.

"All registered?" Mom asked me. Remmy and I just got back to my parents. Mom was sitting on her porch swing, drinking her coffee and she was smiling at me. I wondered if she knew Sawyer Gibson was going to be there. Leave it up to her, to dangle him right in front of my face.

"Yes. Um, did you know Sawyer was on the board?" I felt my eyebrow raise inquisitively.

Mom's face looked way too innocent as her eyes widened dramatically.

"Oh, that's right. Yes, he is. Did you run into him?"

I narrowed my eyes on her. "As a matter of fact, we did."

"He's such a great man," Mom added, her eyes sparkling. "We just adore him. You know, he's the high school history teacher and he is so involved with the school and community. He's the football and baseball coach, too. We are lucky to have him here."

"Hmmm..." was all I said.

Mom didn't say anything else, but she didn't have to. She stood up swiftly and looked down at Remmy. "How does swimming sound?"

"I'm going to get my suit!" Remmy practically sang, with an excited fist pump in the air. He bounded through the front door, and I could hear his footsteps thud up the oak stairs. I turned to my mother, who in turn, was already staring at me.

"You know, Abby, you guys can stay here as long as you want," Mom offered.

"I know."

"Do you think you'll be here all summer?"

"Probably, I just need some time."

Mom patted my arm softly with her hand and whispered, "You take all the time you need here, my dear."

I watched Mom walk into the house, but I didn't follow. I took a seat on the swing and stared at the front lawn that I spent so much time playing on growing up. I closed my eyes and breathed in the Illinois air. It was a hot day, but not as humid here as the air was in Florida. A soft breeze picked up and I leaned my head back and slowly rocked the swing back and forth with my heels.

It was nice being back home. As soon as our plane landed in Illinois, I felt like I could breathe again. Away from Michael and his harsh truths, I finally felt at peace. My mom greeted us with her comforting hugs, and I instantly cried when her arms engulfed me. She patted my hair and told me that we would talk later; even she could tell something was wrong with me. My eyes were still puffy from crying myself to sleep the night before and they only started looking better a little while ago. Thank God, too, since I ran into Sawyer.

Sawyer Gibson, I thought to myself. I always expected him to go on to bigger and better things. He was our star athlete, the school's pride and joy in high school. Everyone doted on Sawyer Gibson; I was the only one who didn't. I saw right through that boy. He was obnoxious, annoying, and extremely flirtatious. He always found it humorous to hit on me and mess with me whenever he could; we argued more than anything.

But, even with his cocky flair and challenging ways, I would be a complete liar if I didn't admit that I felt attraction toward him. Whenever he gave me that grin of his and cocked his head to the side, I was a goner. Each smile and wink he gave me, he took a little bit more of my heart and I hated it. I hated how he made me feel and I hated that he was so damn talented at *everything*. The entire school expected him to play professionally; it wasn't a question of will he or not, but which one? He had a talent for baseball and football and had scouts on him for each. I think he surprised us all when he didn't show up at the scouting meeting. He just wasn't the same after his father left us.

Today though, he looked good. *Damn good.* He was smiling and he brought on all those old feelings I buried long ago. As soon as he said my name, the butterflies were in action, and I felt like I was fifteen all over again. It was ridiculous though to even think about. I was thirty and married, even if I didn't plan on being married much longer, and my being here was just a summer visit.

When he asked me for coffee though, my entire body sang, just like it did when he showed up on my doorstep for Prom. I wanted to shout, *yes, please,* but instead, I opened my mouth and smartass fell out. I couldn't help it; Sawyer just did that to me.

It was better that way though. There's no way I was ready to jump into anything else, especially when I was still legally tied to Michael.

And Sawyer Gibson…he was bad news. He probably did turn a new leaf, grew as a person and all that, but to me, he was my kryptonite and I had to stay far, far away.

But even so, damn did he look good.

Sawyer

"Dude, you really suck at darts," Lance told me, bringing his bottle to his lips. I scowled and flipped him the bird while I aimed at the dartboard across from me. I squinted one eye as I aimed, as if that would help my focus any. It didn't. The dart flew out of my hand and just like the last few times, it landed nowhere near my intended target.

I groaned.

"For someone who used to be so fierce on the field, you really can't aim worth shit." Lance said with a grin. "Maybe you should stick to Pool."

"Shut the fuck up," I told him with an eye roll. "I can kick your ass at anything else. I gotta let you have something that you're good at or I'll have to hear you whine like a little bitch."

"Whatever, I think it's you who whines like a bitch. Just listen to you now," he retorted.

"Let's get another beer, asshole," I told him with a huff.

Lance threw the remaining darts at the dartboard, each of them hitting the bullseye smoothly. I rolled my eyes at him as he turned to me with a smug smile. Younger kids stood huddled together by a nearby table, their attention clearly on our disastrous game. I heard Lance tell them we were done playing while I started to weave my way through the throng of patrons.

Many groups of people were standing in circles around the bar, their loud voices carrying over the DJ's music. Groups of older men and women mostly, but the younger generation was also out. Tonight, the bar was playing mixed music; a little bit of hip hop, but a whole lot of country music, just the way Lance and I liked. Country music was what Lance and I preferred to listen to anyway, but as the bar gets busier with the younger crowd around this time of night, the DJ accommodates their requests, too.

A group of younger women were standing adjacent to the bar area, singing off tune to Lady Gaga's latest hit. I thought it was Lady Gaga anyway, but I could be totally off. I never really cared to commit pop music titles to memory. This group of women all looked the same and how they dressed instantly shot red flags into the air. Their faces were each caked with an array of glowing colors that probably took way too much time to put on. Didn't they know that guys preferred to see their natural beauty? Their clothes looked as if they were painted on, with tight miniskirts and tops that revealed each of their stomachs and tits toppling over. In their hands, they each had a plastic cup filled with colors of the rainbow, some fruity ass drink probably.

As we stood next to the bar, I watched the group of girls toss hopeful glances in our direction. I watched as their eyes scanned us, wicked smiles playing on their lips. No fucking way was I going anywhere near them. I had no intention of falling as their prey. I nodded my head towards them respectfully, as they were obviously checking us out, but I quickly turned my attention to the flat screen television mounted on the wall above the cooler. The very last thing I wanted this evening was a group of barely aged women to be flocking to me. It didn't make a good impression since I was employed at the school, but even if I wasn't, there's still no way in hell I'd entertain the idea.

Lance, however, tossed the girls a grin, and then ended it with a wink. The girls fell into a hiss of giggles, which made me roll my eyes in turn.

"Too young," I grunted at him.

"They always are," Lance said with a small laugh. He turned his attention to the television as well, blocking the hopeful glances from view.

Mya was bartending tonight, as she usually did on the weekends. Today she was wearing tiny blue jean shorts that barely covered her small, yet tight ass. I've seen her wear these shorts numerous times, and one time, even had the liberty of slipping them off her waist with my teeth. Her black tank top snugged her tiny curves and revealed a silver belly button ring dangling below. Her tits were practically spilling from her shirt, and I noticed she had a few twenties tucked into her cleavage. Mya had barely any trace of makeup on tonight, which wasn't unusual because she didn't need any. She was a natural head turner and caught my eye on more than one occasion. Her thick long hair was piled on top of her head in a just fucked kind of way, but it worked for her. Her creamy skin was naturally glowing underneath the bar lights and you could just see the hint of freckles sprinkled on the top of her shoulders.

Before Lance and I could even ask for another, she slid two Coors Light bottles in our direction with a quick wink, as she put a finger up to another patron that was trying to demand her attention.

"One sec," she told the guy with a seductive smile. I glanced over at the poor bastard she was gesturing to and watched as his eyes started to glaze over, completely intoxicated by Mya's presence.

"Ready for those shots, boys?" Mya called loudly over the music. I turned my head from the poor guy and back to Mya with a bemused expression.

"You shouldn't do that, you know."

"Do what, exactly?" Her thin eyebrow arched perfectly, and she shared the same, seductive smile with me, except I couldn't help but notice that her smile seemed a little more genuine in my direction.

"Seduce the customers."

"Well, what can I say, Saw, drunk men are my specialty. Give them something nice to look at while they drink and then they become putty in my hands. Right Lance?" She wiggled her eyebrows at him.

I watched Lance's complexion turn a light shade of red as he took a long drink of his beer, shaking his head ever so slightly. A windchime laugh escaped Mya's lips as she put her hand in Lance's apologetically.

"Just teasing, you know I love you." She beamed at him. "So, again, are you both ready for those shots?" She slapped the top of the bar with her hands.

"Who said anything about shots?" Lance retorted, which caused Mya to roll her eyes at us, but I didn't know why.

"This is about the time you guys always order two shots of Jack. Do you want them, or not? I have a line waiting." Her eyebrows shot in the air as her charm quickly dissipated.

"Sure," I said. After all, she wasn't wrong. Mya's annoyance with us quickly disappeared as she nodded and got to work. In a quick fashion, she grabbed two empty glass shot glasses from nearby and with the other hand, she grabbed the bottle of Jack Daniels. My eyes were trained on her as she worked, but I wasn't staring at the shot glasses; my eyes couldn't move from her bouncing breasts in front of me.

"What are you doing after close tonight, Sawyer?" she asked, in a hushed tone that I knew all too well. My eyes darted up from her breasts to her coy smile. She obviously knew I was checking her out. Her dark eyes probed mine intensely and I forced my gaze away from her, my lips mashing into a hard line.

I told myself the last time I fell prey to her that it would be the last. I guess I said the same thing the time before that, too. She never took no for an answer though and I'm a very, *very* weak man. The dark memory flooded my thoughts as I remembered Mya cornering me in the men's bathroom that evening, after I declined her invitation. Before I could ask her what the hell she was doing, Mya had the door locked and she was on her knees in front of me, pulling at my jeans. It wasn't my proudest moment, but *fuck*, did it feel great. She won though; I followed her home that evening and as punishment for seducing me, she got her pretty little ass spanked while I pounded into her from behind.

Again, I'm a feeble, pathetic man.

I tossed a five-dollar bill over the bar for her tip, but she shook her head at me, her seductive stare never leaving mine.

"Not there, my friend," she said, her eyes now shining. "I'm only accepting the tips right here." With her black nails, she pointed at her breasts softly. I felt my eyes linger down for a moment, and slowly back into her stare.

"I don't think so."

"Then I can't accept the tip," she said firmly, eyebrows raised.

"Okay, then don't." I laughed at her. Her eyelids lowered and slowly, she leaned into me over the bar, her chest now inches away from mine.

"It's not like you haven't touched them before," she whispered.

Her breath tickled my ear and sent a shiver up my spine as I drew back from her. Her eyes flitted quickly down to my lips and then slowly back to my eyes. I squinted at her, my lips tugging into a smile, and I grabbed the five dollars from the bar and without breaking eye contact, I quickly set the five dollar bill into her bra, my fingertips lightly grazing the top of her cleavage.

"Only because you begged," I challenged. I leaned back instantly and took a drink of my beer, pleading with my dick internally to quit twitching in my jeans.

"You always take my women," Lance scowled next to me, shoulders now hunched. His words pulled me back into reality and I felt Mya's intense charm disappear as quickly as it had come. I forced out a laugh and lightly punched Lance's bare arm.

"You're way too fucking slow, buddy." Lance rolled his eyes, his attention back to the baseball game on the flat screen.

Mya snickered at us as she reluctantly turned away from us to go help the now pissed off guy down the bar. He was standing there glaring at me with a haughty expression, as if I was stealing his woman from him. My guess is that he probably thought *he* was taking Mya home tonight, but what he didn't know is that I prayed like hell that was the case. Maybe he could win over her heart, so she'd leave me the fuck alone. I knew that Mya didn't have any real feelings towards me, nor I her, but she liked other parts about me, and I sure as hell liked parts of her.

Lance and I fell into small talk then, talking about his shop mostly, and he admitted he overbooked himself yet again this week. I watched Lance as he talked. The way his eyes averted my gaze and how his lips pursed into a tight line, told me that he was stringing himself out. He needed the help, another full time set of hands, yet he refused to hire another full-time mechanic because he was a stubborn prick. However, I understood it, to a degree. That shop was his baby, and he did not want anyone to come in and screw up his reputation. In a small town like this, reputation was everything. It was still worth taking a chance on someone, if it meant he could lighten his workload and live a little.

I wish I could help him out during the summer, but Lance was right. I didn't have the time that he deserved. I did know one person that would be able to help him though. I immediately fell into conversation with him about Sammy and I watched as Lance's posture straightened as he listened. When I mentioned that Sammy's dad left and he was wanting work this summer to help his mom, Lance turned into stone, his eyes hardening into an icy stare.

"Send the kid over, I'll talk to him." He said automatically, without needing further explanation. I clapped Lance on the back in thanks.

Without needing to order another round, Mya firmly set two Coors Light bottles in front of us, and we nodded to her in thanks. From the corner of my eye, I watched Mya greet another customer, but I paid no attention to the person until I heard the voice.

"A Captain and Coke please, and two Gin and Tonics lined up."

The familiar pull that I fought for so many years tugged me into the direction of that sweet voice. My eyes jerked from their direction as I scanned the crowd for her, my skin rapidly tingling with an immediate ache, when finally, my eyes found her.

Abby.

Abby's eyes locked with mine and I felt my heart rapidly lurch underneath her gaze. I couldn't quite read her expression though; she was a mystery to me now that I intently desired to solve. For a second, I thought I was imagining her. I blinked a few times, expecting her to disappear into thin smoke before me, but she didn't. Her lips were painted a glossy pink and were pursed into a tight line. Abby's hair was no longer confined in a ponytail but tumbled down over her shoulders in soft wavy curls. She was wearing dark, faded blue jeans and a black tank top tucked into them, revealing unexpected, full curves. I longed for her to just turn around so I could really look at her, but her feet remained planted, and her questioning eyes never left mine.

"Is that *Abby?*" Lance thundered next to me. I felt his palm grab my shoulder, as if he had to brace himself.

"It sure is," I murmured.

Lance leapt from the barstool and bounded around the bar in a few, quick strides. I watched as he pulled a wide-eyed Abby tightly into his arms and crushed her against his chest. Abby stiffened, but instantly relaxed as she realized it was Lance.

"For fuck's sake, Abby. I didn't even know you were in town!" Lance bellowed. "Look at you. You're still hot as hell."

I watched as Lance pulled his arms away from her waist but left his rough hands on her forearms as he took a small step back to stare at her body openly. He wasn't even hiding the fact that he was checking her out. Abby's face flushed a crimson red and she glanced away from his stare shyly.

She was so fucking adorable.

"You're still a liar, I see," Abby softly said, a smile playing on the corners of her mouth. "It's great to see you." I watched as her delicate hand reached up and touched Lance's arm gently.

"Did you know she was back?" Lance turned to me, a goofy, eat shitting grin on his face.

"Yeah," I said roughly. I took a drink of my beer nonchalantly, averting my gaze from the happy reunion. For unknown reasons, watching the two of them embrace set my nerves on fire.

"What the fuck, dude? You didn't tell me that?" Lance accused, tossing me a dirty glare. "Sit and chat with us, Abs. What in the hell have you been up to?"

Lance quickly pulled out an empty barstool for her, right next to me. I secretly hoped that she would take it, but I didn't know how my body would react with her sitting so close. From the corner of my eye, I watched a look of uneasiness flash on pretty face. I noticed how she kept glancing over at the corner of the bar.

Is her husband here? Is that why she's acting so hesitant? I wanted to look for him, to see what kind of man Abby married, but told myself to quit being a nosy prick. Whomever she chose, he probably still wasn't good enough.

"I'd love to, but I'm actually here with...well, my mom." She chuckled a little exasperatedly. She gestured to the corner of the bar, where our attention followed.

Mandy Foster was sitting at a small black table in the corner of the bar. She was wearing blue jeans as well with a white blouse, her cream purse sitting in her lap. Her soft auburn hair was pulled back in an eloquent bun with strands of hair framing her face. With Abby here, it made me realize how much Abby resembled her mother. Mandy was just an older version of Abby; they shared the same distinct features. They had the same eye shape and bright blues, the same thin face, and matching deep dimples that only showed when they smiled. Mandy had her head bent and was chatting to another woman beside her. When I realized who she was chatting with, my jaw dropped. *My mother.* In all the time that Lance and I have been coming here, I've never seen my mother, nor Abby's, in this bar.

"What the hell is my mother doing here?" I asked Abby, bemused. "It's like, nine o'clock." I looked up at the time for validation.

"Well," Abby started with a bemused laugh, "They invited me for Karaoke Night." Abby's eyebrows rose. Apparently, she was just as surprised as I was.

"Oh, for fuck's sake…" I moaned and ran a hand through my scruffy beard. I looked back over at our mothers who were both now looking over at us, waving widely and whispering amongst themselves. I didn't even want to know what they were saying or cooking up this evening.

"Anyway," Abby said, tearing my attention from our moms and back to her, "I wouldn't want to interrupt your…um…" and then, in a typical, Abby fashion, her nose scrunched up in the cutest fucking way and her fingers gestured between Mya and me, whom was none the wiser pouring Abby's drinks. "Do you call that flirting?" She ended with a spirited whisper.

Abby snickered at her own joke, as she turned to Mya to accept the drinks that were on the bar for her. She quickly handed Mya money, told her to keep the change, and without glancing back up at me, she turned from us and said in a casual tone, "Great to see you haven't changed, Sawyer."

There she went, leaving me speechless yet again.

"Feels like the old days," Lance said with a low chuckle. I wanted to throat punch him in response.

I forced myself to look away from the wretched woman, but my eyes acted on their own accord, and I found myself memorizing her every move. Her hips were swaying side to side in a seductive, sensual way that caused my insides to warm. Dark thoughts interrupted my mind as I pondered about how wonderful it would be to put my hands around that waist and to really feel her. Just as I had expected, her ass looked round, but firm in her jeans. Her thighs grazed the other as she walked, and I was unbelievably speechless; the Abby I remembered was skin and bone growing up. I couldn't believe all the soft curves Abby had now, but I found myself reveling in them. She wasn't the teenage, bony girl that I knew from long ago, but now an exquisite beauty.

I noticed that I wasn't the only one staring at Abby either. Others recognized her natural beauty as well, and it took all my being not to get up and run over to her. I didn't like that they were all staring at her eagerly, but Abby's glow was hard not to notice. She simply shined without even trying.

"Let's do those shots," I told Lance in a now, hardened voice. I forcefully turned away from Abby, even though my insides were screaming at me to go to her, grab her hand, and claim her as mine. I forcefully grabbed the shot glass in front of me with a prick of irritation at my own thoughts. I was starting to sound like a possessive asshole over a girl that I haven't even seen in years.

I knew Lance was staring at me, but I refused to look at the bastard's face. I already knew what direction his thoughts were going and what he wanted to say to me, but I wasn't going to allow that to be open for discussion. I refused to give him any more satisfaction on the subject.

Abby and I were not good for each other. End of story.

Lance picked up his shot glass then, and we softly clinked the glasses together in unison, and then downed the shots in one, quick swig.

"Another," I called to Mya, who was walking back towards us. Her eyes widened slightly, but she grabbed the bottle of Jack and poured.

We cheered again, took the shot, and both of us let out a satisfactory sigh as we slammed the glasses, the whiskey burning all the way down.

"It's great to see Abby," Lance prodded. "She looks incredible."

I felt my eyes tug unwillingly again in Abby's direction. She was sitting next to her mom, their heads bent low together, whispering about something that evidently Abby found humorous because her head fell back in laughter. The dimples in her cheeks shined and I felt my own lips twitch into a smile. Her hair fell back over her shoulders, swaying as she laughed, and for a fleeting moment, I wondered how her hair would feel in my fingers.

"Yeah," I admitted earnestly, my eyes darting away from her. "She does."

Lance was eyeing me curiously again as he took a drink of his beer, but again, I ignored him. It felt like I was living in the twilight zone, by his pointed looks and telling glances. "There's something there," he always used to tell me. "I see it and I know you do, too, brother."

"Well, if you're not going to ask her out, I will." Lance finally said, slamming his empty beer down.

"What?" I snapped, my eyes narrowing at him. "What did you say?" Even I heard the anger in my voice. Never has Lance backed down from me though, no matter how pissed I was, and I knew he wasn't about to start now. His own eyebrows lifted at the challenge in my words, and I watched his lips turn into a cocky grin.

"I said, if you don't ask her out, then I will." He challenged back. I could tell he was trying to be serious, but I knew Lance better than he thought and I knew what game he was playing. I wasn't falling for it.

"She's *married*." I rolled my eyes and took a drink.

Lance cocked his eyebrow at me. "Married, but not wearing a ring?"

What the fuck, how did I miss that? I leaned back on the barstool and glanced back over at the chatty Abby in the corner of the bar. She held her plastic cup in her left hand, and I squinted to get a good look at it. The rock was no longer shining on her left finger. I looked back over at Lance, the questions evidently playing on my face.

"Well, there you go," I said in a forced manner. "Go for it."

"I think I will," Lance said, his eyes shining brightly. "Get me a beer, would ya?"

"Fuck you," I whispered back.

He tapped the bar a few times with his left hand and beelined straight for Abby. In the worst possible moment, the upbeat song changed into a slow one and to my dismay, many couples formed together in unison.

I couldn't keep my eyes away from them. He walked right up to her and held out his hand, waggling his eyebrows like a complete moron. I snorted, thinking there's no way Abby would fall for that, and I waited impatiently for reaction.

She fucking *beamed.* Her eyes widened with pleasure and lips broke into a full smile, showing off those cute as hell dimples again. Abby gave him a tiny laugh, but she placed her hand into his and let Lance drag her to the makeshift dance floor. I felt my jaw clench as Lance looked over at me, waggling his eyebrows again, as he pulled Abby into his arms once they reached their destination. I wanted to go over there and tell Lance that this wasn't a joke—*she* wasn't a fucking joke—but I knew my words would hurt Abby's feelings and I'd rather take a dagger to the heart rather than upset her in any way.

I felt a light touch on my right shoulder and turned to see Mya nudging a few more bottles in my direction.

"Thanks," I mumbled.

"What's got you?" Mya asked questionably. "You look…pissed."

"I'm fine." I snapped, causing Mya's eyebrows to shoot up.

"Is it because Lance is over there dancing with that beautiful woman and you're not?"

"No. I couldn't care less." I tried to sound cool, but even I could detect the jealousy in my tone. I scowled.

Mya's lips turned into a smile. "She is pretty," she mused. "Really pretty."

"Go away." I glared at her. She snickered.

I glanced back over at Lance and Abby and their heads were bent close to each other; Lance whispered into her ear, and Abby's face fell into an amusing grin. Abby's head fell back with a loud laugh, and I couldn't take my eyes off her; her smile was simply radiant, but it made me wonder what Lance had said that was so damn funny.

It irritated me that here I was, on the sidelines yet again with Abby while Lance gracefully strolled right back into her life. He always had a way with her; the two of them had such an easy-going relationship, while I struggled to even get a sentence in with her. If it was just her and Lance, they'd talk for hours, laugh, and had their own inside jokes. If I tried, Abby would practically spit fire at me. Even though I enjoyed it and maybe antagonized the situation, I was always jealous as hell when Lance didn't get the same reaction as me. She was always kinder to him; it made me think that maybe Abby had a thing for him, but they never started a relationship. Instead, Lance always pushed her into my direction, but I never understood why. Those two would be better off together. Hell, they'd still probably be better off with each other.

I wasn't going to let that happen.

I took a drink of my beer and set the full bottle down on the bar with a loud *thud*. I caught a few stares, but I ignored them. I pushed myself in between the dancing couples and didn't stop my feet until they were firmly planted right in front of Lance and Abby. Lance's eyes glanced towards me and the annoyance I expected to see didn't come. Instead, an impish smile sprang on his lips.

"My turn," I said.

Chapter 6- *Abby*

I have no idea what the hell is happening. All I know is that here I am, dancing with my old friend Lance, when I heard that husky voice say, "*My turn*." My entire body froze after my head whipped in his direction. I hated that after all these years, I was still so attuned to him—his voice, his intoxicating smell, and his overwhelming presence. My entire body hummed before he even said the words. Sawyer, with his featherlight touch, grabbed my wrist and slipped my arms over his neck and held me securely in place, like he already knew where my thoughts were leaning.

My eyes went wide as I looked over at Lance. He nodded in my direction, without a word, and my eyes flashed daggers on him. Lance's thin mouth slipped into a coy smile as he walked away from us. I wanted to shout after him to stay; I couldn't be alone with Sawyer, but Lance let out a small chuckle at my irritation. I'm so glad this was so amusing to him. Had this been his plan all along? It wouldn't surprise me if it was. Lance's mission in high school was to get me with Sawyer. So many long conversations were spent with Lance talking his buddy up, only for me to roll my eyes at him and tell him that it would never happen. I never understood why he kept pushing me towards him and frankly, after all these years, it was now just annoying.

I did not agree to this. I agreed to one dance with Lance, *not* Sawyer. There's a reason why I've always kept Sawyer at arm's length, and this was *not* arm's length. He'd always been too much of a player, even now. We were far too close for my liking. My head whipped to the side as I caught a whiff of his aroma as his arms tightened around me. Sawyer always had a certain odor, and it annoyingly always made my body come to life. He had a woodsy, yet fresh scent about him. The mixture of his strong fragrance started to light my nerves on fire and my head hazy. My eyes closed as I tried to commit the smell to memory; holy crickets, Mother of all that's Holy. No one should ever smell *that* good.

My head barely reached his neck; he was so damn tall, and I felt so tiny in his arms. Sawyer tightened his grip around my waist and my stomach curled with desire. I felt electrified as his large arms engulfed me tenderly. Being this close to Sawyer was dangerous and my entire body tensed as I tried to contemplate how to get out of this, without hurting Sawyer's feelings.

I decided I would count to ten. At ten, I would tell him I had to go to the bathroom. I could wait ten seconds.

One… two… damn, he smelled amazing…three….

"Is this okay?" His breath tickled my ear, causing another shudder to rip through me.

"Yeah," I said, a little too quickly. I leaned back to look up at Sawyer's face, but immediately wished I hadn't. His blue eyes engulfed me, searching my face, as if he was looking for an answer to a problem he didn't have. Finally, his full lips pulled into his cocky grin that I haven't seen in years; my heartstrings pulled, and I felt my own traitorous lips turn into a smile.

I allowed myself to really look at Sawyer's face. He's changed so much in the thirteen years since I'd last seen him, but then again, not at all. His jawline was still prominent, hard, nose perfectly straight, to die for eyes that now strongly reminded me of the Florida ocean. His face had a scruffy dark beard that only added to his perfection. Sawyer with facial hair was fucking hot; there's no denying it. It looked as if he had been running his hand through it this evening because the tiny hairs prickled in different directions.

A dark thought erupted through my head, and I instantly tried to push it away, but I couldn't help but wonder how that scruffy face would feel between my legs....

I practically shuddered when Sawyer cocked his eyebrow at me. "Are you okay?" he asked quietly.

"Just dying internally, that's all," I mumbled, but instantly regretted the confession. Here I go, with the word vomit. What was it about Sawyer that made me just say everything that popped into mind?

"Alrighty then," Sawyer let out his husky laugh that shot weird vibrations to my stomach. I've always loved Sawyer's laugh.

"This is just so surreal," I said.

"How?" I watched his eyebrow raise again and felt his arms tighten a little more around me.

"Um, I don't know, because I'm dancing with you. It's just...unreal," I added lamely.

"We've danced together before," Sawyer reminded me. I watched as his blue eyes danced underneath the dimmed bar lights. If I had the chance, I would dive right into them.

I snorted in response and then quickly tensed. My snort always sounded like an angry elephant. I couldn't believe I made such an unattractive noise right in front him. I felt the heat flush my cheeks as I looked back up at Sawyer, but to my surprise, Sawyer's head fell back into a fit of laughter, his eyes glistening. I felt my body relax, and smiled a little, too.

"You only danced with me out of pity," I said to him finally. This brought him up short. He stopped laughing and looked down at me with a questionable look, his eyebrow, yet again, cocked in the air. I wondered if it would just stay up there all evening.

"What are you talking about?" he asked me, exasperated.

"Oh, come on, you remember. Prom, you asking me to dance," I prodded.

"Yeah, I remember," Sawyer said immediately. "But I don't remember doing it out of pity." A frown pulled at the end of his lips.

"Well, yeah, but you did."

"No, I didn't," he protested.

The sensation of arguing with Sawyer after all these years brought me a strange sense of peace to me, as if everything was right in the world again. Saw and I used to argue about *everything*. Who was the fastest runner? Who could play first basemen best? Who could read the fastest? Who had the better grades? The arguments only changed and intensified as we grew older.

"Oh, come on. It was a pity dance," I said. I watched as Sawyer's stare intensified and it nearly made my heart combust. *My goodness, it shouldn't even be allowed to look at a person that way.*

"Abigail, I did not ask you to dance because I felt sorry for you. I asked you to dance because I *wanted* to. Just like now. I'm dancing with you, because I *want* to." As if he was proving a point, he squeezed my waist gently.

There he goes with my heart, all over again. I fought back a sigh, as my insides instantly turned into mush, but my mind went into overdrive. Was he telling me the truth? Was he just trying to use a pick-up line with me, like he used to? He was the famous Sawyer Gibson, after all, the town super star. How and why would that gorgeous man want to dance with me, out all people? Not even just in high school, but here, and now? There were plenty of other women here that were probably already lining up for a chance with him. I'm pretty sure after witnessing that little steamy exchange between him and the bartender, that she already has.

"You don't believe me," he stated, reading my mind. He was always good at telling my thoughts.

"Not at all," I said with an honest laugh.

"Well," Sawyer said, his full, tempting lips turning into a smile, "I guess I'll just have to prove it to you."

His eyes softened at his protest, and I felt my heart thud a little more loudly in my chest. Feeling Sawyer's arms so protectively, yet tenderly around me and seeing that fierce look in his eye, touched the darkened parts within me. I tried to remember when Michael danced with me this way, or even looked at me the way Sawyer was now. I couldn't think of one recent memory. I felt my thudding heart start to crack just a little bit more, as Michael's harsh truths flooded my memory.

I tried to push his words out of my mind, and be in this moment with Sawyer, but like a broken record, his words were fresh in my mind. Every time my thoughts went there, I felt more salt getting thrown into the deep wounds Michael left last night. If Michael, my own husband, had those thoughts towards me, what made me think that Sawyer wasn't thinking the same? I wasn't the thin Abby he once knew. I had put on more pounds and flab that I liked, and every time my body jiggled, I felt disgusted. I couldn't even look at myself in the mirror this morning. My thighs, that once had a perfect part, now brushed together when I walked. For the first time in my life, I felt disgusting in my own skin.

My head started to feel light, as the truths pounded into me; I wasn't the Abby I used to be, but now a mother, a jobless one at that, with no means of income and no clue on what she wanted to do with her life. My husband confessed his cheating, I was going to file for divorce, and here I was, dancing with my old high school crush.

My life was starting to turn out to be some kind of joke.

Thoughts of Remmy popped into my mind. I knew he was already fast asleep, but the worry that was already there, came to the front of my mind. My dad was home with Remmy, and he was well equipped to handle him, but the feeling of not being there if he woke up started to settle in. I shouldn't be in this stupid bar. I shouldn't have let Mom convince me to go out for Karaoke Night of all things. This wasn't my mother's usual scene, not at all, and it made the questions start to pop in. I couldn't help but wonder if she knew Sawyer would be here all along.

I forced my eyes to look away from Sawyer's and scanned the crowd quickly. Lance was nowhere in sight and my mother was animatedly chatting with Sawyer's mother. She was no longer paying attention to me anymore. Earlier I noticed she was eyeing us with a hopeful look in her eye. I don't know what she's so hopeful about, but I was going to put an end to all of this right now. The fact that she was cooking anything up right now, when I've been in Illinois for merely hours, was ridiculous. I literally just told my husband last night that I was done and was still trying to process everything.

And I couldn't process it here; especially with Sawyer's scent engulfing me in this perfect bubble.

The song ended right on time as I pulled my arms away from Sawyer's neck. I took a step back from him almost immediately, and his arms fell to his sides. He stared at me perplexedly, as if he was trying to read my mind again, but I refused to meet his stare.

"I think I should get going."

"Wait, what?" Sawyer tenderly grabbed my arm, but I recoiled from his touch.

Please don't get too close to me.

"It's getting late, and um, I shouldn't even be here." I let out a small, exasperated laugh as I covered my face with my hands. "I'm so freaking tired. I mean, I was just on a plane this morning and I got like, zero sleep last night, and you know, I have a kid, so… I have to do Mom things tomorrow. I, um, really should go home and rest."

Let's add 'rambling lunatic' to the resume, shall we?

"Abby, did I say something, or do something…?" Sawyer's voice lowered and heartbreakingly enough, sounded full of concern.

I finally looked back up at him. Right back into those pretty blues and my heart wavered at his, yet again, intense as hell stare. Seriously, what the fuck is he playing at? Does he really want to get into someone's pants that badly tonight? Pick another woman, dude because I'm getting the hell out of here.

"No," I let out, followed by a weird, nervous laugh. His eyebrows pulled together in confusion. "I just really have to go."

"Well, I can drive you home," he offered.

"No, Saw, seriously. You stay and have fun. I'll see if Mom's ready." *And if she's not, I'll wait in the car, because you're making my head spin and making me feel all these weird emotions about you all over again.* I started to dash away from him like a crazy person, but stopped abruptly, and turned to him. "Thank you for the dance."

Sawyer's eyebrows were scrunched together, clearly puzzled at what just happened here, but he quickly nodded. "No problem, I guess. But Abby, are you sure you are okay?"

"Of course, Saw. Don't worry about me." I waved it away nonchalantly and forced out a laugh, that came out a squeak more than anything else.

I was seriously losing it. Maybe I really did need a good night's rest and to wash away all of the idiocy that was pouring from me. All I knew was that I couldn't do this. Not right now anyway.

"Alrighty then… and goodbye," I said awkwardly. I quickly beelined for my mother, leaving a bewildered Sawyer behind.

Sawyer

"Come on, boys, you can do better than that!" I bellowed at my athletes, looking down at my stopwatch. "Again!" I blew my whistle.

A group of thirty teenage boys stood at the opposite end of the gym, gasping, and throwing me vengeful looks. I vaguely heard low grumbles come from them but couldn't make out what they were saying. It was probably a good thing, too, because if I heard any kind of negativity, I'd have to be the bad guy and that was the last thing I wanted to do. I didn't want to torture the poor kids, but I wanted them to see what they were made of.

The air around me smelled a mixture of rubber, rubbing alcohol, and sweat, but even I welcomed the blended odors. When I closed my eyes, I could vividly fall back into my old high school days of hammering a rubber dodgeball at Lance's awaiting face. I loved it here. There was always something about being in your old high school; even though I taught here, the building still felt like home. Even to this day, the vivid flashbacks of myself walking these halls would come back to me and sometimes they took me off guard.

I watched as the boys lined up on the white taped line, their chests rising and falling quickly as drips of sweat fell from their damp hair. A few of them shot daggers at me, but their faces ultimately showed the determination that I wanted to see. I blew my whistle again and watched as the boys took off towards the next painted black line; today was suicides and the kids despised me for it.

I watched the seconds tick by on the stopwatch, while also glancing up to watch the boys periodically with the whistle hanging from my lips. They were coming closer to the half point line, almost there. "You've got this, boys! Keep it up, almost there!" The whistle fell from my lips as I called out to them. I brought the plastic piece back to my lips, getting ready to blow the final whistle.

They each touched the half point line in unison, the boys groaning and panting as they each pushed themselves to run harder, and with a sense of pride washing over me, they each sprinted harder back to their starting line. When they each crossed, I blew the final whistle and looked at the time of the stopwatch with satisfaction.

"Awesome, you did it! Grab a drink of water, and let's hit the gym," I called out to them. A few of the boys groaned in response, which made me grin. "Would you rather do more suicides?" They quickly let out a howl of protests and I chuckled.

My black water bottle and matching hand towel laid on the gymnasium bench next to my clipboard. Our school mascot, a black panther, was printed on each. I grabbed the water bottle and took a long drink of the cool, icy liquid, wiping my own beaded sweat from my forehead with the hand towel. I didn't do the last few suicides with them, but I did the first two. I had to show them that we were all in this together. They weren't surprised when I started sprinting with them; this was something I always did, and it always seemed to push them harder to perform.

Sammy staggered up to me, his face a light red color, and he was drenched with sweat. His eyes looked murderous, and I tried like hell to fight my amusement.

"So glad you made it, Sammy. You did a hell of a job today."

"Whatever, I barely made it through," he said through deep breaths. "They are a lot faster than me."

"You'll get there," I told him earnestly, "Don't give up. Keep showing up and we'll get you where you wanna be."

He nodded and I watched his chest rise and fall in rapid breaths as he put his hands on hips. I clapped him on the back and said, "Drink some water, kid. We got more coming." His face fell into a miserable scowl. "Hey, at least you got a free water bottle and towel by joining us today."

"Not…worth it…" Sammy exclaimed, and I chuckled.

"Don't worry, kid. I'll be working out with you."

"You better…" he breathed.

The group of boys before me were not just my football players, but an assortment of our Carrington High aspiring athletes. Due to regulations, football practices could not officially start until July. To comply, the Sports Director at our school and I conversed to host a generic summer workout camp that didn't pertain to a specific sport, but fundamentals as a whole that would benefit all athletes; basically, it consisted of running and lifting weights.

"Alright boys, let's go!" I called.

In groups of twos, I watched the boys file out of the doors past me and to the hallway that led to our weight room. I started flicking off lights as I left the rooms and went down the wide hallway to our gym. The hallway smelled strongly of Pine Sol, and I felt my eyes glance around to make sure that the boys didn't track mud throughout the hall. Thankfully, the floors still shined as the janitor left it; the last thing I wanted was a pissed off janitor.

They flooded the weight room and fell into groups as they crowded the machines. I messed with the docking station, looking for amped music for them to listen to, when my eyes landed on an individual I hadn't expected to see. My lips turned into a smile as I watched Abby in the corner of the room. She was running on a treadmill, her brown hair piled on top of her head. She was wearing workout clothes, loose black running shorts, and a light pink cut off shirt that was tied in an elegant knot on her lower back. Her skin glowed a soft, natural bronze color, but it glistened with sweat. I watched her face intently; it was a soft red and her ears had little white earbuds placed into them. I wondered if she realized the weight room was crowded now; she seemed to be in her own personal bubble.

Her chest was rising and falling rapidly, and I noticed that her nose still scrunched up into that adorable fucking way she did when she was concentrating. My lips pulled into a smile as I watched her try to push herself harder. It was nice that some things about Abby never changed. I've seen that blazing look on her so many times in our past. She gritted her teeth and let out a soft groan as she punched the dial on the treadmill until the gears switched into a slower pace.

I hesitated on what to do next. It seemed rude not to go up to her, but I also didn't want to push her further away. Her behavior the other night puzzled me and left me thinking for hours that night. I came to the conclusion that she was a woman and I'd never understand. But now, I had a decision to make, and knew that whatever I chose, probably wouldn't give me a win. I sighed and decided to just get it over with. I would just say hello, that was all, and then leave her be.

"Hey," I told her, landing on the side of the treadmill.

Abby's flushed face turned towards me, and I watched as shocked recognition flashed across her face. Her eyes widened; lips parted into the perfect O shape as she tried to keep her steady pace.

"*Fuck*," she squeaked.

Without knowing how the hell she did it, she stumbled in her step with arms flailing around her like a sick bird. I instinctively held out my arms to catch her. Her upper body fell into my outstretched arms with her feet now dragging at the rolling treadmill. I had a good grip on her and wouldn't let her fall, but she was making it almost impossible to keep her steady with her arms thrashing around as if I was her kidnapper. I quickly shifted her weight into my right arm, while turning off the machine with my left. I turned my attention back to her, eyeing her ankles and legs to make sure nothing looked out of place.

"You okay?" I asked, hesitantly. My attempts to hide my smile failed as Abby's face flushed a deeper red. The immediate look of horror turned into her shooting daggers at me. I knew right when I saw those eyes, that coming over here wasn't the correct choice.

"Yes. Can you let me up now?" Her voice was full of annoyance which shouldn't surprise me at all since this is Abby. Without saying a word, I helped her to her feet and took a step back from her. Her sweet fragrance started to make my head swim and I refused to look like a swooning idiot. Not just to her, but to my kids. They would never let me live it down.

With the back of her hand, Abby wiped at the sweat on her forehead, and I watched as she examined her own body. I raised an eyebrow at her, wondering if she did hurt something in her fall. After her quick examination of herself, she took an earbud out of her ear and looked up at me.

"What are you doing here?" she finally asked me. My eyebrows shit up at her accusatory tone, and I stared at her with bewilderment. A witty comeback was playing on my lips, but I stopped myself. I didn't say anything as her eyes scanned the now crowded weight room. The kids no longer found her fall interesting and were back to concentrating on machines. "Oh, never mind. I should go."

"You don't have to," I told her. "We can share the equipment."

Abby turned her back to me as she collected her nearby belongings.

"No, really. I've embarrassed myself enough for one day."

"Abby, I promise you're fine. No one saw it anyway, except me. I apologize if I scared you on the machine. I was just coming over to say hi."

She didn't reply, but I watched as her lips pursed into a fine line. I wish I could read her mind to really crack the Abby puzzle, but I was not clairvoyant, and I knew better than to ask her.

"You didn't," she finally said. "I'm just..." she let her words trail.

"Just what?"

"I don't know, Sawyer," she snapped with a sigh. Her shoulders slumped and her arms fell to her sides in apparent defeat. She was starting to remind me of a lifeless shell, just going through the motions of life. Just by looking at her eyes the other night at the bar, told me everything that I needed to know. She was hurting.

"Do you want to talk about it?"

I knew I was going to pay for being kind to her; her eyes flashed anger, but I couldn't just leave her when she seemed so upset. My instincts screamed at me though to turn around and leave her be. Her face was scrunched up, as if fighting the urge to cry and my heart went out to her. I could never stand to see her looking so sad.

"Do I want to talk about how I can't run like I used to, or how fucking huge my ass has gotten? Or you know, we could talk about how my husband thinks I'm a disgusting cow. Yeah, let's talk about that, *Sawyer!*"

I felt my jaw drop to the floor and eyed the weight room quickly; a few athletes turned and stared at her in awe. I gently grabbed Abby's arm and ushered her towards the door. I had to get her out before her meltdown was heard by all my students. Abby has always been unpredictable and who knew what else would come out of that pretty mouth.

Once I had Abby outside, she jerked her arm away from me and turned around in an abrupt motion. She folded her arms around her chest and her face puckered into a deep scowl. Even though she looked as if she was about to rip my head off, I couldn't help but notice how utterly adorable she looked when she was so fired up.

"*What?*" she snapped at me again.

"Wow, okay. First off, I don't know why you're so mad at me. I'm just trying to help you." I lifted my hands in protest.

"Did I ever ask you for help Sawyer?" Her eyes narrowed.

"No, but—"

"Then maybe you should just mind your own business," she said flatly.

I spluttered. What the fuck is going on with this girl? Why is she so angry right now? Not even just at me, but at the whole fucking world? I hated that she was so upset but biting my head off like that...my God. I never responded well to pissed off Abby; she had a way with her words, and this wasn't the first time she lashed into me. I felt my eyes narrow in on her and tried like hell to fight the angry words that were bubbling at my lips. I never was one to coddle her. I'd leave that to Lance.

"*What the hell is wrong with you?*" I snapped. I was thankful that we were alone in the parking lot. My hand lifted and pointed at her. "I don't know what's going on with you, Abby, but don't act that way with me. I was just trying to help and be a friend. If you don't want to talk to me, then fine, but *clearly* you need to talk to someone. I don't know what shit you're dealing with, but keeping it bottled up the way you are, will make you *explode*."

"You would know," she snapped. "But I didn't ask you for advice."

"Okay, Abby." I rolled my eyes and shook my head at her. I didn't have time to deal with this. I had kids inside waiting for me and the last thing I wanted was to waste my time arguing with her. "I'm going back inside now. I hope you have a better day." I turned around from her and tried like hell to repress my last thought, but instead, let the words fly. "*I should have let you fall on your ass.*"

Chapter 7- *Abby*

I don't know why I behaved that way with Sawyer; it was insanely childish. I wish I could say that I felt better about myself, but the embarrassment of my actions was starting to eat away at me. The overwhelming urge to scream was starting to set in my veins, but like always, I tried to push away the anguish. My life was turning into utter catastrophe, but rather than bracing myself against it, I was now the creator.

Instead of driving home where I ought to be, to deal with these imploding emotions, I started to drive to the town square with no destination in mind. All I knew was that I didn't want to be alone, and my parents' house would be too quiet for my busy mind. They took Remmy to have a "Remmy Day", as they called it— bowling with a picnic lunch in the park. I was reluctant to let him go, but his bubble of excitement made me agree. It wasn't his responsibility to keep the pieces of me together, but his presence had a calming effect and made me feel complete. With him around, I had a purpose. When alone, I felt like an exploding hot mess.

I passed the familiar streets and houses, trying to keep my mind off my chaotic life, when finally I parked my father's truck into an empty parking space right off the town square. I looked around at the booming businesses and really soaked in the small-town atmosphere. Once upon a time, I craved to leave this town; dreamed of moving away to a bigger city where the sun always shines with sandy beaches and the ocean. Now here I was, thirty-one years old, and I had come running right back to it. The square was alive today, people bustling in and out of the businesses. There was a cute boutique newly added, a floral shop, and a bakery that I haven't seen before. When I was a teen, those businesses were entirely different—a bar, a video rental, and hardware store.

I started to take notice of a young, plain couple walking hand in hand down the sidewalk. At first glance, they looked ordinary to me, just two people walking down the street with each other, but as my eyes studied them further, I realized that there was nothing whatsoever dull about this couple. Her eyes were alive, yet soft, and her smile shined as bright as the sun as she gazed upon him. He gazed back at her with such fiery that my own cheeks started to flush. He stopped their pace and turned her towards him. My own heart started to quicken. Ever so lightly, he grazed her cheek with his outstretched fingers and after a slow moment, drew her in for a kiss. I watched as she closed her eyes and when their lips parted, she slowly opened them with such a glow. She no longer looked plain to me.

Love made all things beautiful.

Heat rose through my chest and sent a hollow burn through my veins as I watched the two of them embrace once more; his kisses were more insistent as she let out a fit of giggles and playfully swatted him away. Even though I didn't know this young couple, watching their pleasure from afar sent a piercing spasm through my chest.

What I wouldn't give to have someone look at me that way.

Michael's words sprang back into mind, as they have often been playing in my head today. Who would want someone like me; an oversized, bitter, jobless, angry, mother?

A throbbing pain hit my throat as I closed my eyes and willed it away. I took a slow, deep breath, but my eyes started to drop slow tears. I covered my face with my hands and shook my head frantically, forcing the pathetic thoughts out of my mind. Sitting here in pity and wallowing about how no one loves me, was not going to do me any favors. There's no reason to dwell on such shit feelings.

With a forceful nod, I got out of the truck and walked towards the town's Bakery and Restaurant. The door chimed as I opened it, and I watched as all the sitting customers turned their eyes towards me. Some of the people's faces puckered with confusion, others recognized me and waved. I nodded at them with a soft smile and scanned the busy room for an empty table.

The bakery was pleasant; it had that rustic feel, with wooden flooring and bright, white walls that made the room look larger than it was. Pictures hung from the walls with encouraging words and wisdom. I immediately felt that peace I desperately desired washed over me as I breathed in the sunny atmosphere. There were few tables available, but to my delight, there was one sitting in the far back, away from impending stares. Without meeting anyone else's eyes, I walked swiftly over to the table and fell into an oak chair quietly.

The special's board read *Salad Bar and Soup* in an elegant scrawl on the back of the wall. I didn't need to see the menu, the salad bar sounded just fine, especially after doing my run. The last thing I wanted to do was stuff my face full of crap after working out. That would be beside the point of the cardio that nearly killed me. A waitress quickly ushered over to me, young and bright eyed.

"Hey there, what can I get you?" she asked politely, her eyes scanning me. It may be the paranoia settling in, but I thought she was also trying to put a name to my face.

"I will just have a coffee, and the salad bar, thank you."

"Hot coffee, or would you like one of our cold options?" She gestured to the menu, and I paused.

"Oh, um, a caramel iced coffee, then?"

"You got it." She offered me a soft smile. "Feel free to go to the salad bar. Plates and silverware are up there. I'll have your drink back in a sec."

"Thank you," I mumbled. She offered me another kind smile before she left to check in on the table behind me.

Thankfully the Salad Bar was directly behind me, so I didn't need to walk back through all the stares. My stomach growled as I started to pile my plate with salad, Caesar dressing, croutons, tomatoes, and cheese. A silver container was next to the bar that was labeled Cheesy Potato in the same elegant writing as the board. As soon as I opened the lid to the soup, the steamy aroma filled my nostrils and my stomach lurched.

As soon as I sat back down at the table, the waitress returned with my coffee and left without a word. I felt the pang of loneliness wash over me as I realized that I have never in my life gone to a restaurant by myself. I wish I would have brought a book or something to divulge in while I ate. Like a modern cliché, I dug through my purse for my cell phone and perused the world of social media while I dug into my salad.

I flipped through my Facebook newsfeed, flicking over the many ads that have taken over the platform. In truth, I had more Facebook friends than real friends, and read and liked their posts as if we were the best of friends. I scrolled the feed with my forefinger, but abruptly stopped as I saw Michael's name tagged in a post update.

He was tagged in a post with Hallie.

I dropped my fork with a loud clatter on my plate as my other hand tensed around my phone. I felt the beats of my heart quicken as I devoured the words on the screen. Even though my eyes scanned the words many times, it was as if they were in a different language; they were not registering to mind. I read slower this time, taking in each word until they were charred to memory.

They read, *'What a great morning spent with those that I adore.'*

I pounded the screen of my cell phone so forcefully that it rattled to the ground, causing others to look back up at me again. I breathed slowly in and out through my nose as I picked the cell up with shaking hands. *What a great morning spent with those that I adore.* I knew I shouldn't look at the pictures that were included in the post, but like a traffic accident, I couldn't help but look.

Hallie, Michael, and another couple that I didn't know were sitting at a cloth linen table, their eyes and smiles bright. Displays of breakfast food were on their china plates of sausage, eggs, and bacon. They were holding champagne flutes in hand, which for a moment, took my attention from the fact that Hallie's other outstretched hand was grazing Michael's shoulder ever so slightly. I brought the screen to my face and that's the only thing my eyes zoned in on; her damn fingers touching my husband.

My throat made an almost gurgling sound as my stomach started to twist into knots. I flicked the photo away and to the next. I willed myself to put the phone away, to stop looking, but my eyes did not listen to my shouting thoughts. They were still with the same couple, but this time on the golf course. Michael wore khaki pants, his white shoes, and navy polo shirt that snugged his arms tightly while Hallie wore the cliché snug, short white dress, showing off those gorgeous legs of hers. She looked like a fucking Barbie.

There was another photo of just Michael, getting ready to tee off, his face in full concentration. I felt a lump start to harden in my throat as I flicked to the next; Michael driving the golf cart, a small smile toying on his thin lips; and to the next, Michael and Hallie smiling at the camera; Hallie's usual billboard flashing smile, her eyes shining, while Michael's smile remained mysterious. He was always a mystery to me.

I pushed my full plate to the side of the table, the salad losing its appeal from just a few minutes ago. I hated wasting food, but if I ate, it may all just well come back up. There were comments lingering on the post and my finger shakingly hit the comments to read. I bit my lip and eyed the words on the screen.

Sharon Conway: You two are just so adorable. Will we see you this evening?

Harrison Thomas: Hallie, bring him this weekend! We can't wait to meet him.

Jennifer O'Connor: Looks like fun! Call me later, I want to hear all about your day!

Madison Harper: Isn't he married?

Why yes, Madison he is married, I thought to myself. The anger bubbled underneath my skin as the images of Michael and Hallie together burned my retinas. The audacity of that woman…taking photos and blasting them over social media, when in fact, he was still married. She was dangling her relationship with him right in front of my face all the way from Florida. I set the phone down abruptly on the table and tried to gain my composure. I was in a restaurant full of people and the last thing I needed was to lose my shit. I could practically hear the rumors already circulate. *"Oh you know the Foster's daughter? She's unstable. Lost her shit in the town bakery…"*

Breathe, I told myself.

"Abby?"

I turned my head towards the direction of the familiar, sing-song voice and my eyes landed on a familiar face that I haven't seen in years, except for on social media.

My heart swelled when I saw my childhood best friend, Emma. Her light auburn hair was pulled into a messy, long braid that hung on her right side, with brown square sunglasses sitting on top of her head. She was wearing jean shorts and a fluorescent pink shirt with the words '*Kids' Haven*' in childlike writing. She still had the same cream skin, sprinkle of freckles over her nose and cheeks, and the exact same warm smile for me.

"Oh, Emma," I whispered. The tears were instantaneous as I got up from my table and wrapped my arms around her.

Then I lost it.

"*Oh,*" Emma responded. For a moment she hesitated, her arms outstretched as I cried on her shoulder, and then without a beat, Emma's arms engulfed me into a tight hug. "Oh, Abby," she whispered.

My eyes were a broken faucet, and I felt my breathing start to shudder. I wondered if Emma remembered how big of an ugly crier I was, because she quickly moved into action. The loud buzzing of the restaurant ceased, and I could feel the heat from the stares on my back. With one arm still around me, she leaned to my table, grabbed my purse and phone, and looked over at the waitress, who was also gawking at us. I heard Emma murmur she'd back in a minute to pay, and she quickly ushered us out of the bakery, her arm around my shoulder in a motherly way. She walked us across the street to the middle of the town square and sat us down gently on a wooden park bench.

"Oh, Abs…" she whispered. I let out a loud hiccup in response. I tried to talk, to apologize for doing this to her, but all that came out was garbled nonsense as my tears soaked Emma's sleeve.

I wasn't sure how long we sat underneath the oak tree; the branches were guarding us from the piercing sun and swayed noiselessly. The only sound was the nearby traffic, occasional honks, and my relentless tears. I tried to take a deep breath and to gain my composure, but every time I tried to get it together, the harder the tears came. I finally gave up trying.

Finally, the tears started to slow, and I sniffled, swiping at my eyes with my fingers. "I-I'm so sorry, Emma. I don't know what came over me. You caught me at a *very* bad time, if you couldn't tell," I blubbered, wiping at my eyes again. They were starting to ache, and it was getting harder to see. I felt drained.

"Or I caught you at a very good time," Emma said with a gentle squeeze. This was just one of the reasons why I loved Emma; she had such a kind soul, and my heart ached a little more as I realized how much I missed her.

"Oh my God, I'm snotting on you," I said through a mixed cry and laugh. "Emma, I'm so sorry."

"Eh, I get it all the time from my kids. Trust me, this is nothing." She waved it off with a low laugh.

"K-kids?" I dug through my purse for some tissues and started to dab at my eyes.

"Not mine, daycare kids. I run the daycare center here in town." She smiled gently at me. My heart swelled with a little pride as I stared at my old best friend. She always talked about one day opening the town's first exclusive daycare center.

"Wow, Emma, that's great. I could really use a distraction right now, tell me all about it," I said with a low chuckle.

Emma's eyes narrowed at me, and a smile sprang on her lips. She grabbed my hand gently, just like she did when we were kids, and said, "Next time. I think you're the one who needs a friend right now. Would you like to talk about what's bothering you?"

I opened my mouth to tell her no, that I didn't want to talk about it, but there was something about being in her presence. It could have been her soft, calming voice or the way she opened her arms to a now stranger, but I finally started talking. Emma listened without interruption as I spilled my story from start to finish. Her fingers squeezed my hand as I explained the fiasco of Michael coming home last week. I heard her draw in a breath when I told her he said he was screwing around because he no longer found me attractive. Just saying the words out loud felt like another punch to the gut.

"And then when I was eating, I saw these." I grabbed the cell phone from the top of my purse and shoved the photos in her face. She drew back from the phone and grabbed it from me. I watched as her eyes widened as she flicked through the photos, her lips pursing into a frown.

"Well," Emma said. "This just shows what kind of people they are. This has nothing to do with you." Emma handed me back the phone and I sniffled again. "I'm so sorry you are going through this right now and feeling this way. I wish I could take your pain away."

"I just don't know what to do," I told her with a heavy sigh. "I just don't know if I can go back there, you know? I don't know if I want to."

"Has he reached out to you?"

"Just to make sure we landed okay. He's also FaceTimed Remmy one time, but I wasn't in the room. I couldn't even look at him through the phone screen."

She patted my hand sympathetically and I watched as she bit her bottom lip in thought.

"You're thinking something, so just say it," I told her, remembering her facial expressions all too well. It was as if no time had passed between us. She smiled.

"Well, I think that if he hasn't reached out to you more since all of this happened, and he's publicly out with her while you're here, that kind of tells you right there what you need to do."

"But he's my husband and Remmy's Dad," I choked.

"Yes, he is. But do you really want to be with someone like that? Does he really make you happy? Also, don't you think Remmy would rather see you happy than sad like this?"

"Remmy doesn't know what's going on. Trust me, I act very well around him. This is the first time that I really cried about it all." I admitted. She nodded in understanding.

"Ahh, which explains the ugly crying," she gently teased.

"A whole lot of it." I dabbed at my eyes again with a low laugh. "I'm so sorry, Emma, you didn't deserve that. I probably embarrassed you in there. I know I embarrassed myself."

She waved the thought away. "You know me, I don't really care what this town says about me. I know what kind of person I am." She gave me a soft smile. "I do have to get back to the center though. And I need to go in there and grab my lunch."

"Oh God, Emma, I'm sorry. Let me buy your lunch at least." I stood up quickly, but Emma laughed and pulled me into her warm embrace. I felt my body relax in my old best friend's hug.

"Nonsense, my friend. I'm just so glad that I got to run into you today. I heard you were back in town, and seeing you made my day, even under the wet circumstances." She giggled. "Are you free the rest of the day? You should stop by my center and check it out." She gave me a soft smile.

"Yeah, okay, if I won't be in the way."

She shook her head. "Not at all, I'd love to show you around. I'm going to run inside quickly, follow me."

"I have to pay for my lunch," I told her, walking with her. She shook her head at me again.

"Honestly, I would just get in your car; you can buy mine next time."

I groaned.

"Everyone was staring, weren't they?" I couldn't wait to play the inevitable twenty questions from my mother later about why I was having a meltdown in the bakery.

She laughed in response. "Not everyone, buttttt...I would still maybe just wait outside."

*****

Emma's daycare was just a minute outside of town. It was far enough away from the bustling streets, but also, not too far away that made the location inconvenient. I vaguely remembered an old falling down barn that sat on this empty property years ago, but the barn was nowhere to be seen. Instead, a small, paved parking lot sat in the front of the property that led to the front doors.

The building was larger than I expected; two stories, in bright yellow brick. The front entrance had glass double doors with large and wide, inviting windows next to it. The front top of the building made a triangular shape with a huge red sign bolted into the brick. *Kids' Haven*, it read, in bolded, rainbow lettering. There was also a cartoon image of three children of different ethnicities holding hands and smiling.

From the sides of the building was a tall, wooden fence that was painted in alternating colors; blue, red, yellow, and green. From the outside of the fence, tiny handprints in assorted colors were painted on the fence as well as different murals—a painted sun, a tree, little stick figure people, and a lion. You can just see the tops of the bright playground equipment peeking from the top of the fence.

"Emma, this place is amazing! I am in awe of you," I told her, beaming. Emma's face broke into a smile.

"Thanks, friend. It took a long time to get it here, but I'm so happy with how it turned out. Come inside with me." She gracefully looped her arm into mine and together, we walked up the paved sidewalk. I noticed as we walked up the path that the sidewalk was also painted with random alphabet letters and numbers.

The front entry room was small, but the natural light pouring in made it look stunning. The walls were painted a bright, sunny yellow, with a large bulletin board that read 'Kids' Haven Summer Fun'. They had an assortment of kids' art crafts already pinned to the board and printed photos of children doing summer activities. To the right of the room was a waiting area, a purple leather sofa, a few purple chairs, and a coffee table. To the left, was a light blue large desk area that read *Check In* in black lettering.

"Wow, Emma..." I said to her. She beamed in response.

Behind the desk sat a young girl; her auburn hair was thrown up into a messy bun and her large black eyeglasses looked as if they were too large for her face. As she bounced in her chair, they were sliding down the bridge of her nose. She flashed us a bright smile, silver braces lining her teeth.

"Hi, Emma," the girl said, beaming. "I had the desk covered, just like you asked! I never left it either. Well, except when I had to pee, but I promise, I was quick. In and out, and right back here."

Emma chuckled and touched the top of the desk with her fingers.

"Thank you so much for covering the desk, Victoria. You can go to lunch if you want."

"Oh, I'm okay, I can manage the front desk longer if you need me to. I don't mind, at all. No messages when you were gone or phone calls."

Emma smiled kindly back to her. "Thank you, Victoria. I appreciate it. This is my friend, Abby. She's back in town for a visit, so I thought I would show her around. I'll see if one of the girls in the back can relieve you."

"Hi Abby! I'm Victoria!" she chirped and extended her hand to me. I shook it quickly and gave her a soft smile.

"Hello Victoria, it's nice to meet you."

"Well, we'll be around, Victoria. Thank you again. Page me over the intercom if you need me, okay?"

"Of course!" she said energetically. "Have fun!"

Emma led me through the second set of double doors and turned to me in a hushed whisper.

"She's our summer help. We get a lot of high schoolers in here to help during the summer."

"That's nice."

"Yes, it gives them some experience. A lot of the high schoolers that come here are going into early education, and it helps us tremendously since summer is our busy time with school being out. Let's start the tour." She flashed me a smile.

Emma showed me through her daycare building; the large playroom for toddlers, where there were so many different toys with a craft section and Ready to Learn area, the nursery room, where we only poked our heads in because there were two babies napping soundlessly in their cribs, the kitchen with large tables and chairs for the kiddos to have their lunch and snack, the nap room for toddlers, where a few of Emma's staff were getting five sleepy toddlers ready for their naps, and a large rec room area for older children.

"Emma, I'm so impressed by all of this. You did an amazing job. I'm so glad you brought this dream of yours to reality."

"Thank you," she told me. "It's a dream come true, that's for sure. I'm so blessed."

Emma brought me back into her office; she had a wide office, with glass doors and windows. The room was painted a light pink and she had pictures hanging on her walls of her and her staff; her Bachelor's Degree for Early Childhood Education was framed on the opposite wall; there was also a large canvas photo of her with a man that I didn't recognize. I studied the photo of the two of them, holding hands in a sunflower meadow, the two of them staring at the other with such adoration; the photographer caught the moment perfectly. I felt a heavy sigh escape me as I turned away from the photo. It was so nice to see Emma in love like that, but I couldn't help but think how I wasn't here to watch their romance blossom. It broke my heart in a way, that Emma accomplished all of this, and I wasn't around to watch her make it happen.

Emma sat down in her black swivel chair behind her desk and gestured to the two chairs in front of her desk. I sat down in one of the squishy chairs and smiled at my old friend. She laced her fingers together on top of the desk and gave me a calculated look. For a moment, I felt as if I was in a therapist's office.

"I love your daycare. It's really perfect, Emma," I told her again with a smile. "I'm just so sorry that I wasn't here to watch you make this all happen. I'm sorry we lost touch after all these years; it breaks my heart."

"I don't blame you," Emma said, her eyes growing wide. "It goes two ways Abby. I also lost touch with you. We both got so busy after high school; don't think I blame you for our friendship. Besides, you're here now."

"Well, me staying in Florida didn't help any."

"No, but I understood. You've always loved Florida. I knew a long time ago it was going to take a lot to get you away from those beaches."

I laughed. "Oh, I miss the beach so much...." I closed my eyes, imagining hearing the waves come in, the seagulls chirping above. I sighed. "Remmy and I practically lived there."

"I can't wait to meet Remmy. Gosh, I can't believe you have a Remmy! Tell me about him."

"He is a stubborn, strong-willed child that one day may break me, but he's also perfect, charming, and sweet and I just love him so much. He loves playing sports, going to the beach with me, and of course, swimming. We love to swim."

"Sounds like you," Emma said, her eyes twinkling.

"Whatever," I replied, but I also smiled. "Maybe a little." Emma laughed.

"So," Emma started, "how long do you think you are staying here?"

I shrugged and sighed again. "I have no return date in mind; all I know is that Remmy starts school in September. It's not like I have a job to go back to."

"Right," Emma said, nodding. "Well, question for you, Abby..." I raised my eyebrows at her and watched as she straightened her posture.

"I have an open position here if you want it. It's part-time and the schedule can be flexible. You can make your own hours, it doesn't matter to me when you work, but I just need extra help around here. I'm looking for an extra hand, basically, that can bounce between rooms to help with the kids. We are almost at capacity, and I know my full timers would appreciate it. I normally have more high schoolers that come, but only a few applied this summer. I also, if you would be interested, need some help in the office. Billing mostly, a little website cleanup, that kind of thing. I know you don't know how long you're really planning to stay, so if you decide you are going back to Florida, it won't hurt my feelings, but it will give you something extra to do while you're here if you want it."

"Oh, Emma...." My eyes started to sting. I reached over the desk and clasped her hand with mine. "Thank you. I appreciate it."

"There's a free t-shirt in it for you, too." She gestured to the shirt she was wearing, her hands and shoulders moving jubilantly. I laughed.

"You know, that might just be perfect. I would love to come and help you."

"You're the absolute best." Emma sighed in relief. "I'll get the paperwork printed. But, um, are you willing to get CPR certified?" She scrunched up her nose at me and I let out a low laugh.

"Of course. So tell me about your boyfriend," I asked, eyes flashing.

Emma's face blushed. "You mean, *fiancé*?" She extended her hand out to me and I grabbed it and gushed.

"That is beautiful! Engaged? Oh, my goodness, tell me *everything.*"

Sawyer

A line of coaches stood huddled before me by the storage shed at the baseball diamond. I got here early to start pulling out bags of helmets, all organized by age groups, as well as tees, baseballs, and softballs. I started to hand out the gear one by one to the Coaches, and slowly, the large group dissipated.

"Sawyer, how's it going?" I looked up from the bags of equipment to see Henry Parker, an old work out buddy from my younger days. Henry looked the same, but different since the last time I saw him. His jet-black hair was sprinkled with light gray, and his usual clean face was now scruffy.

"Hey, buddy, it's going good." I extended my hand to him and shook his firmly. "I saw your name on the roster for coaching." My eyes twinkled at him. "Good for you, bud. Thanks for volunteering."

"Ah, man I'm happy to do it. I've been waiting for this day forever. My little guy, Ash, is finally old enough for t-ball! We have our first practice tonight."

"That's awesome, I hope you guys have a great season. Well, here's the gear you need to start. Bucket of t-balls, a tee, extra helmets. If you need anything else, just holler."

He nodded, his eyes dancing. "Perfect, thanks Man. I better get over to the field, looks like parents are starting to show up." He smiled at me energetically, scooped up the equipment, and left with a quick wave.

I had a few more coaches to wait for, which already informed me they would be late to pick up, so while I waited, I leaned on the back of the storage shed and looked over at Henry's forming team. He had all the kids sitting in a circle around the pitching mound. As he talked to his team, his arms were swinging around jubilantly at his sides. Henry really looked like he was in his element. My eyes turned to the benches that were now full of waiting parents, when my eyes fell on a mother talking in hushed voices to her boy. My heart picked up a little as I recognized that beauty; it was of course, Abby.

Abby's lips were scrunched into a frown as she knelt down to Remmy's eye level. She had her hands on his elbows, drawing him into her. I glanced over at Remmy, his lips into a pout while he kicked at the grass with his foot.

I don't know why I was doing this; Abby has made it clear to me before that she did not want or need my help, but I started to walk over to her knowing that I was a damn fool for doing so. I stopped a little outside of their circle, not too close to invade their privacy, but close enough that I could hear Abby's words of encouragement to Remmy, her face lighting up.

"Can't we just go home?" Remmy groaned. "I don't want to play today."

"This is practice, Remmy. You need to practice to play in their games. Don't you want to go over there and make new friends? The coach will teach you all sorts of things today, like how to catch the ball and hit the ball."

"I already know how to catch, Mom." Remmy rolled his eyes. "And I can hit pretty far, you know, I did it at school all the time."

"Hey, Remmy, and Abby," I interrupted with a wave.

Abby's eyes darted over to me, and almost at once, her lips puckered into a tight line, and I watched as her posture tensed. I let out a small sigh. It didn't look like to me that Abby was ever going to like me being around. I should probably just taking the fucking hint and leave her alone; her actions were becoming very clear to me. Yet, like a damn fool, I stayed.

"Hi," Remmy said quietly, not meeting my eyes. I knelt on one knee, ignoring Abby's widened stare.

"Well, hey there, superstar. This is your team, huh?" I said, looking back at the team and Coach. Remmy just nodded.

"Wow, they look like a great group. You know, I know that coach over there. He is an awesome dude. You'll love being on his team." When Remmy didn't say anything, I continued. "So, you say you can hit the ball pretty far, huh?"

Remmy nodded again.

"Well, that's amazing. I can't wait to see you hit it." I paused. "But you can't show us what you can do, without going out there with your team. They need a great ball player like you, you know."

Remmy's eyes peeked up at me through his long lashes. I watched as his face flickered with different emotions, but finally, his stare widened, and face broke into a wide smile. He reminded me greatly of Abby. They had the same smile with the same little dimples.

"I can hit it all the way to the grass!" From the corner of my eye, I watched Abby's body relax as she let out a breath.

"I can't wait to see it, bud. Why don't you go with your team, and we'll see what you can do?"

Remmy nodded, grabbed his baseball glove from the grass, and took off running around the fence to the coach. Henry offered his fist to Remmy as he joined them, and Remmy energetically bumped his against it before he took a seat in the dirt with his team.

Abby and I stood up from our knelt positions, our gazes on the baseball field. I couldn't help but be fully aware of Abby standing next to me, her arms folded across her stomach, and her chest rising and falling rapidly. I knew I should say something to her, but I couldn't form a coherent thought for the life of me. Our last encounter wasn't the greatest, and the last thing I wanted was for Abby to go off the deep end on me again.

"Thank you," Abby murmured to me. I turned to her and drank in her expression. Her blue eyes were soft, and her lips were forming into a smile. I didn't realize how tense I was and slowly felt myself relax.

"For?"

"Getting him out there. I didn't think I was going to win that argument."

"I didn't mean to interrupt you both. I saw you guys, and before I knew it, I was walking over here." I shrugged. "I hope he enjoys the season." I offered a smile. I went to turn from her and head back to the shed. The last thing I wanted to do was push my luck with this woman, when Abby's hand outstretched to my arm, her fingers softly curling over my skin.

"Sawyer," she said, her lips forming a frown, "I'm glad I ran into you actually. I wanted to apologize for acting that way towards you earlier this week. I don't know why I acted that way. All I can say is that I wasn't having the best day, but that doesn't mean I should have acted that way to you. I'm sorry." Her smooth fingers fell from my arm, and it took all my willpower not to grab her hand and lace my fingers within hers.

"It's alright, Abby, we all have bad days."

Her lips pursed. "Yes, but it still doesn't excuse my behavior. You were just friendly, and I was acting like...well, a bitch." She laughed a little. "Thanks for not letting me fall on my ass."

I chuckled. "Sorry for saying that I should have let you fall on your ass." She joined in a little on the laughter, and we both turned our attention back to the field. Henry was getting the kids lined up in the dugout now and was handing out helmets. Remmy turned to us and gave us a thumbs up. Abby waved back enthusiastically, and I gave Remmy a thumbs up in return.

"This takes me back," I told Abby.

"How so?"

"Oh, back to our own t-ball days. You, of course, were trying like hell to beat me. I used to hate it when Coach made you first basemen instead of me."

Abby's eyes sparkled as she laughed. "It's not my fault I was better than you at catching."

"Oh, okay," I told her, chuckling, "It's just because you were cuter when you begged." Abby rolled her eyes, but I watched as her lips turned into a smile, exposing those cute as hell dimples on her face.

"No, it's just because I caught better than you at that age," she teased.

"If that was the case, then you would have caught the damn ball when I threw it to you. Instead, you let it hit you square in the face."

Abby laughed. "You gave me a black eye, Sawyer, and you threw it way too hard! I swear, you did it on purpose to make a point."

"I would never," I told her, clutching my heart with my hand. "Did you know when I got home later, I cried because I did that? Seeing you with a black eye the rest of the week broke my tiny heart."

Abby's soft eyes suddenly trained on mine and didn't leave my gaze. The air around us suddenly charged, making the hair on my arms start to prickle; it was like we were placed in our own little bubble for that sweet moment.

"I don't believe you," she finally said, turning her head away from me. I noticed her cheeks started to flush a delicate shade of pink.

"Oh Abby, come on now, you know I'm not a liar. I'm many things, but not a liar."

I swear, I heard her whisper to herself, "One of the many reasons why I like you, Saw."

We both turned our attention to the practice, letting silence fall between us. The coach was getting the kids moving now, interacting with them enthusiastically. I could tell Henry was going to be a great t-ball coach; he was engaging and getting down to their level. I hesitated in my step for a moment, not sure if I should leave Abby in peace, or if she'd be okay with me watching, but I didn't want to leave. I liked standing here with her, even if we weren't talking. It felt…comforting in a way, being so close to her. I also really enjoyed watching the kids participate in the sport I loved; they were also amusing as hell to watch. It looked like Henry was going to have his hands full, as he tried to get them to listen. Some of the kids were kicking dirt, others were making faces at their teammates. Coach Henry kept reminding them to listen up while he tried to teach them how to position their feet by the home plate. He didn't have to offer much guidance with Remmy though. Remmy walked right up to the plate, positioned his feet firmly where they needed to be, stuck out his tongue, and with one big swing, he smacked the ball hard as it soared into the air above the coach's head.

From the corner of my eye, I watched as Abby jumped into the air, clapping energetically for her boy. Her eyes were bright, and lips formed into the brightest smile I've ever seen her have. She laughed, whooped, and cheered for her son enthusiastically. I couldn't help but turn my attention to her, my heart swelling in my chest at the sight of her. *She was so fucking adorable.* I laughed.

"What?" Abby said, her eyes dancing. "Sorry, I got carried away. I didn't mean to embarrass you."

"You could never embarrass me."

She offered me a shy smile before turning her attention back to the practice. Remmy was on first base and pumped his fist into the air enthusiastically.

"Great hit, Remmy!" I shouted and I watched as he beamed with pleasure.

The rest of the practice went smoothly; Remmy got to hit a few more times, each time, soaring the ball high in the air. The Coach even got the kids to pay a little more attention, too, which says a lot for this young group. At the end of the practice, they each ran the bases together, the kids giggling and laughing, as the coach had them running to the bases in different ways: hopping like a bunny, running in zig zags, and bear crawling. Hearing their squeals and giggles had all the parents laughing.

At the end of practice, Remmy sprinted over to us, a huge smile plastered on his face. To my surprise, he didn't run to Abby though, but beelined straight for me. I watched as Abby's back straightened, her eyes wide again.

"Did you see me, mister? Did you see how hard I hit that ball?" I chuckled as he bounced up and down in front of us.

"Oh, I saw. You had *amazing* hits. You are going to be a great ball player, Little Man." I offered him a high five. Abby watched the two of us, with a mixed expression on her face that I couldn't read, but it told me that this was my time to leave. "I'm so glad I got to watch you practice today. You keep up the hard work and have fun this season."

Remmy nodded enthusiastically and turned his head to Abby. "Mom, we are getting ice cream, right? You said, we could get ice cream." Abby's surprised gaze turned into a kind smile.

"Of course. Ice cream seems appropriate after you did such a great job."

"Will you come have ice cream with us?" Remmy asked me excitedly.

I froze in my step and looked up at Abby's stunned expression. She quickly touched Remmy's arm. "Oh, he's probably busy, honey," she said quickly, but Remmy's eyes were trained on me, wide and hopeful with the most precious smile that tugged at my heart. I felt my body hesitate as I looked from him to his mother, who was now biting on her bottom lip.

"Um..." I was about to say maybe another time, but as I was about to speak, I watched Remmy's face fall, and I felt myself switching gears. Seeing his hopeful expression drop like that was like a knife to the gut. "I would love to come, as long as your mom is okay with it," I said.

Remmy's face brightened and looked up at his mom hopefully, his eyes pleading. "Please, Mom?"

I watched as Abby collected herself and put on a smile that didn't quite meet her eyes. "Yeah, of course." I also noticed how her eyes were looking at everything else, but me.

"Awesome, let me just lock up here quick." Abby quickly nodded in response as I flashed her a grin. "Abby, I don't have to go, if you don't want me to," I chuckled. "You're clearly having an episode or something."

Abby shook her head quickly and let out an exasperated laugh as she wiped her hands on her jean shorts.

"Don't be silly, Saw, you're invited." She gave me the tiniest smile.

Hearing her call me 'Saw' like she did back when we were in school sent a wave of heat through my body. A strange feeling that I haven't felt in such a long time entered me and I couldn't help but grin back at her.

"Okay," I told her. I couldn't stop smiling even if I wanted to.

"Okay," she repeated softly.

Grinning like a fool, I started to walk towards the storage shed to lock everything up, with a little more pip in my step than I usually had, when I felt a tiny hand reach mine. I glanced down to see Remmy's wide front-toothless grin beaming up at me with his tiny fingers pressed firmly into my palm. I automatically felt my hand clasp around his tiny hand, as if we did this every day. He swung his arm back and forth, skipping next to me and started chatting about baseball.

Even though I wanted to listen to what he was animatedly telling me, I couldn't because all I could do was think about how precious this little boy was, and how with just a simple gesture, he plopped right into the center of my heart.

Chapter 8- *Abby*

I have never in my life heard Remmy talk as much as he did now to Sawyer. He was a nonstop chatterbox. I barely even got two words in the whole time we're at the bakery. Remmy talked about sports, baseball and football, mainly, but also talked about dinosaurs, spacemen, aliens, and what kind of dog he wants for Christmas.

"I just really, *really* want a dog, but my mommy said that she doesn't know if Santa brings puppies for Christmas, but I just *really* want one. He brought my friend from school a puppy last year." Remmy sighed, exasperatedly.

"Oh, well, maybe in your letter to Santa you can ask for a dog?" Sawyer offered, taking a bite of his melting ice cream sundae. Remmy thought about it for a moment, but then made a face at Sawyer.

"I don't know how to read or write, mister, how old do you think I am?" Remmy rolled his eyes, which caused Sawyer to let out a booming laugh. Remmy giggled in response, soaking in all of Sawyer's attention. I, too, let out a small my eyes engrossing the two of them together.

For one thing, I loved that Remmy was interacting so well with Sawyer. It was nice to see him getting some male interaction; he didn't get too much of it these days, except for with my dad these last few weeks. What surprised me the most though was Sawyer. He was joking and laughing and making funny faces with Remmy over their ice cream. The entire time, the two of them ignored me, but that was okay with me. I was slowly melting into a puddle anyway.

"Well, maybe your mom can help you write the letter," Sawyer said finally.

"Can *you*?" Remmy asked, licking his dripping ice cream. The sides of it were starting to be a gloppy mess from us sitting here too long.

"Oh," Sawyer sat up for a moment, and he eyed me curiously. He quickly turned his attention back to Remmy though and said, "Sure, I can."

"Awesome, maybe he'll get me a new bike, too." Remmy's eyes danced mischievously.

"So, what are your plans tomorrow?" Remmy asked Sawyer speculatively.

This caused Sawyer to laugh again. He sounded like such a grown up when he asked.

"I don't know quite yet."

"Don't you have a job?" Remmy asked, his eyebrows raised. Sawyer's face looked like it may break from so much smiling.

"I do, but I'm off for the summer. I'm a teacher."

Remmy's eyes widened over his ice cream. "That's so cool. I don't want to be a teacher though."

"What do you want to be?" Sawyer asked.

"I'm going to be an office worker, like my dad." Remmy nodded conversationally. Sawyer's eyes flitted over to me, and I felt my body freeze. He's barely talked about his dad the last few weeks.

"Well, I *wanted* to be an office worker like Dad," Remmy corrected himself, making a face. His lips turned into a slight pout. "But he works a lot. And I mean a lot, *a lot*. I don't think I'd want to work that much, it sounds boring to me. I've been thinking about being a firefighter. I think that would be cool." He nodded.

Sawyer's eyes met mine for the smallest moment and I shrugged, offering him a weak smile. For a moment, I saw his lips turn into the tiniest frown, his eyes hardening. He glanced back over at Remmy.

"Oh, to be a firefighter would be pretty cool," Sawyer agreed. "You have to be really brave though."

Remmy nodded. "I am very brave, mister. Sometimes, I think it would be cool to be a cop, too, you know, catch the bad guys." Remmy thrusted his hand in the air, holding a make-believe badge and yelled, "*Freeze!*"

To anyone else, this little scene would probably make anyone laugh, but I knew what it would do to Sawyer, and my heart dropped instantly. *Oh, Remmy.* I glanced over at Sawyer quickly and saw his lips and eyes fall ever so slightly. My heart went out to him as I watched Sawyer try to regain his composure. I watched as brief pain flitted his eyes before Sawyer forced a smile on his face.

"Cops are pretty cool," Sawyer agreed, nodding. "My dad was a cop, you know."

Remmy's eyes widened and his little mouth fell open. He brought his face close to Sawyer's, grasping Sawyer's cheeks with his little hands.

"*No way,*" Remmy exclaimed. "That is so, *so* cool."

Sawyer's grin widened and he let out a low chuckle as Remmy let go of his face.

"Did he ever catch any bad guys?"

"Yes, he did. He was a true hero of this town," Sawyer said, nodding his head again. My heart nearly shattered into a million pieces listening to him. I had a sudden urge to reach across the table and grab his hand but refrained. Sawyer's eyes glanced over to me, and he gave me a sad, knowing smile.

"Did you get to ride in a cop car?" Remmy asked quickly.

"Oh yeah, all the time."

"Did you get to flash the lights?" Remmy asked again. Sawyer nodded, his lips twitching.

"Buddy, you really should eat your ice cream," I interjected. "It's getting so messy." Remmy turned his attention from Sawyer to the gloppy mess in front of him.

Raising his pointer finger in the air, he declared to us, "I will eat it like a lizard."

Sawyer's husky laugh filled the air around us and he shook his head at my crazy boy. We watched Remmy start to lick his ice cream cone like a lizard, when Sawyer brought his attention over to me.

"Your son is something else," Sawyer chuckled. "Very amusing kid."

"Oh, he's something alright," I murmured back, shaking my head at Remmy. He ended up getting chocolate ice cream on his forehead and giggled. "Remmy, wipe your face."

To my surprise, Sawyer took his chocolate covered spoon, and wiped the ice cream on his own forehead, announcing to the table that he, too, was also a lizard. I stifled a groan and placed my hand to my face; *what in the world.*

Remmy fell back in a fit of laughter, clutching his stomach as he did so. Sawyer also laughed and looked over at me, handing me his spoon.

"What do you think, Mom? Do you want to be a lizard, too?" Sawyer asked me, his eyes dancing.

"Don't you dare put that spoon on my forehead, Sawyer Gibson." I glared at him, but I couldn't keep the serious act going; seeing Sawyer with chocolate melting ice cream on his forehead was a sight to be seen. Sawyer's eyes narrowed at me, a smile toying on his lips that flashed bolts of lightning directly to my heart.

"Fine, Remmy and I will just be the cool lizards then," Sawyer declared. He looked over at Remmy and stuck out his tongue, which erupted another round of giggles from my boy.

I glanced at the time on my phone and couldn't believe how long we'd been sitting here. Sawyer must have caught on to my expression because he said, "Getting late, huh?"

I nodded. "Yes, Remmy has a bedtime soon." Remmy's lips puckered into a frown.

"*Mommmm*, can't we just like, hang out with mister a little while longer?" Remmy begged.

"His name is Sawyer, Remmy," I told him quietly.

Remmy said, "Can we stay with Soy-er, a little longer?" Sawyer's lips twitched into a grin.

"It is getting late, my lizard friend," Sawyer said, patting Remmy on his shoulder softly. "I bet you may even get to see me again soon." He raised his eyebrow at Remmy. Remmy's eyes widened.

"You promise?" Remmy asked, sitting up straight in his chair, abandoning his gloppy ice cream. He was right back into Sawyer's face, extending his pinky. Sawyer's face puckered into an amusing grin. Before they connected pinkies though, Remmy pointed at Sawyer, his nostrils flared, and lips pursed. "You know, you cannot break a pinky promise."

Sawyer forced a serious expression on his face and said, "Oh, I wouldn't dream of it. Pinky promises are life."

Remmy narrowed his eyes at Sawyer for a few seconds. He must have believed him because he quickly nodded and looped his tiny pinky around Sawyer's.

"Besides," Sawyer said, getting ready to stand up. "We have to write a letter to Santa Claus." He looked over at me with a sexy wink and irresistable grin on his face, and I swear my heart literally stopped.

Watching these two banter back and forth, Sawyer tossing me extremely sexy smiles all through our ice cream date, has turned my entire heart and body into complete mush. I didn't even know if I would be able to stand and walk out of here without someone carrying me. *Sawyer carrying me would be pretty nice....*

I tossed the dirty thought from my mind and focused back on my son, who was now giving Sawyer high fives over and over again.

"Remmy, let's pay for our ice cream and then let's get going," I said to him, fumbling with my purse.

"You are *not* paying," Sawyer said, raising a brow at me.

"No, I will pay for our ice cream. We invited you." Sawyer rolled his eyes.

"Actually, Remmy invited me, and he's not old enough to pay yet, so I will pay for him," Sawyer teased, making a face at me. Then, with a sudden change of emotion, he gave me a heated look and gently grabbed my hand and squeezed. "I insist," he whispered.

I've seen him give this look to many women; the flirty, *'I'm so fucking hot'* look that he does, but never in a million years, would I have thought I'd be on the receiving end. His intense stare was intimidating yet electrifying and it was like he was piercing my very soul with just his eyes. I drew in a breath, my gaze flitting down to his lips, that looked all too inviting.

Sawyer chuckled, and lightly brushed my forearm with his rough fingers as he walked away from me, leaving me slightly breathless and staggering.

Here he comes, I thought. *Right back into my heart.*

Sawyer

It was impossible to fall asleep last night. I laid awake in bed for hours, replaying the evening I'd spent with Abby and Remmy. I was in agreement with Remmy; I didn't want the night to end. Laughing and joking with that boy brought out a different side of me, and I didn't realize until last night how much I craved that lifestyle; a kid, an exquisite woman by my side... a family. It just felt *right*.

Abby was a wonderful mother, there was no denying it. She was so attentive and charming and just by the way Remmy acted and behaved all evening, spoke volumes to how amazing she was doing. He was a fantastic kid and funny, too. I haven't laughed that hard in such a long time; my cheeks even ached a little. He was such an easy-going kid. It was so hard not to be warmed by his instant charm.

I thought a lot about how Remmy said his dad worked a lot. When I looked over at Abby, I started to see the ghost of the girl I had seen spring back to life, her lips etched back into a sad frown. It made my heart ache to see her that way. She shrugged and forced a smile on her face, and the ghost woman quickly disappeared. It was like she was forcing that sadness away from her so Remmy wouldn't see it. It hurt to watch her have to try so hard.

No one should have to try that hard on something that's supposed to be so easy.

When I woke up this morning, I laid in bed for a long time, trying to remember the wonderful dream that I had. I woke up feeling so tranquil, but all I could remember was breathing in an intoxicating smell; it was like roses, or a familiar flowery smell. I had a brunette woman in my arms, but her face was turned from me. I wanted to take in her face and look at her, but she kept turning away from me. I woke up right at the moment as she was turning her head.

As soon as I got out of bed, I ran through my morning chore list that I was putting off for far too long. I swept, vacuumed, and scrubbed the bathroom clean. I was going through the chore list so robotically and was not at all focused. My thoughts were on Abby solely; her shy smiles she gave me last night, the way her eyes were so endearing towards her son, the way her eyes widened and softened when I grinned at her. The way her lips twitched into a smile when I joked with Remmy. I kept thinking about ways to get her to smile at me like that again. Seeing those dimples pop out at me was a sight for sure, and I craved to see that smile again.

I was hopeful that I would see her again today. To my knowledge, she has no idea that I arranged a visit this morning with Mr. Foster. Sammy asked me the other day if I would go with him to meet the Fosters and to help him with the fence. I quickly agreed, too, because I knew there may be a chance that I could see Abby. Running into her yesterday was just coincidence at the field; if she would have known I had plans to go there today, she would have mentioned it yesterday.

But now, it wasn't just Abby that I was anxious to see again, but Remmy, too. His laughter yesterday was contagious, and I was counting down the minutes until I could see both of them again.

Finally, busying myself with household tasks paid off because it was time to go. I leapt into my truck, a small smile playing on my lips the entire time. I started to whistle as I revved the truck to life and drove down the familiar streets to the Foster residence. When I pulled up into the paved parking lot, Sammy's truck was already sitting there, and he was leaning against the frame.

"Hey Coach," Sammy called to me. "Thanks for coming with me today."

"Not a problem, happy to help." I told him with a grin. Little did that boy know, he was helping me out today as well.

"This is a nice house," Sammy murmured next to me, looking at the Victorian home. I nodded back to him as we walked up the sidewalk together. I knocked on the door firmly and Sammy and I waited on the other end.

We heard footsteps on the other side of the wall. "I'm getting it!" I heard Abby's voice call to her parents; my skin tingled at the sound of her voice. The door swung open, and Abby's eyes instantly met mine as she froze into place.

"Oh shit," she said quickly. Abby had a coffee mug in hand, and I watched as the contents dripped onto the wooden floor.

I tried to stop the low laugh, but it escaped too quickly. Abby's eyes flashed back to me, and I watched as her delicate cheeks started to flush crimson red.

"Sawyer," she said quietly, "I didn't expect to see you first thing in the morning..." she trailed off.

I couldn't help but let my eyes linger on her. Her brunette hair was tousled on top of her head with a black clip; her face was framed with black, thick eyeglasses. My stomach curled as I took in her clothing. She was wearing short lavender boxers, fluffy pink slippers, and a baggy black tee that nearly engulfed her. I felt a burn settle into my chest and cleared my throat abruptly. I looked back up at her and felt my lips twitch into that grin I knew she loved.

"Obviously," I told her.

Her cheeks burned a little more as her eyes widened. "Well, what can I do for you and your..." she turned to Sammy, noticing his age, and added thoughtfully, "Friend?"

I licked my lips and gestured to Sammy. "This is Sammy. He and I have a meeting with your dad this morning."

The perplexed look never left her face, so I continued. "Your dad agreed to meet Sammy and to see about hiring him to do some projects around here."

"Oh. Alrighty then, sorry. Dad didn't mention anything to me. He's in the kitchen. Why don't you both come in?" She opened the door invitingly and I gestured to Sammy to go in first.

Sammy's eyes widened as he took in the beautiful interior of the home. I clasped my arm around his shoulder and gave him a reassuring nod to follow Abby in. Abby led us to the kitchen and the entire time we followed, I couldn't help but look down at her ass in those tiny shorts. Abby in her pajamas was a sight that I'd probably never forget, at least not any time soon. Sammy gave me a hard nudge to the ribs, and I looked up at him, eyes scowling. He eyed me knowingly and shook his head at me.

"Don't mention that to anyone," I whispered to him, causing him to chuckle.

"Dad, you didn't tell me Sawyer and his friend Sammy were coming by this morning," Abby accused, eyes daggers towards her father.

"I didn't think I needed to tell you who was coming in and out of *my* home," I heard Mr. Foster respond before we saw him. We entered the kitchen together, Sammy and I stopping right at the edge of the hallway. Mr. Foster was sitting at the kitchen island, his eyes on his newspaper and coffee mug in hand.

"Well, it would have been *kind* to let me know, so I could have not looked like this," Abby declared; she had a little bite to her voice, which in turn, made Mr. Foster give out a small chuckle. "They're here Dad."

"Oh," Mr. Foster said, lifting his eyes from the newspaper. He grinned over at us. "This must be Sammy then. Hello, Sammy, I'm Craig, Craig Foster."

Mr. Foster stood up and walked around the kitchen island to us. He extended his hand out to Sammy and Sammy shook it, a little nervously.

"Nice to meet you, Mr. Foster," Sammy said automatically. Mr. Foster offered him a kind smile and turned his direction to me.

"Sawyer, good to see you. Let's go out in the back and talk, boys. I'll show you what needs done and you can let me know if you can both do it." Mr. Foster led the way through the kitchen to the sliding glass door. Sammy hesitantly followed, but I hung back.

Abby was standing in the kitchen, a little awkwardly, her face still a light shade of crimson. She looked over at me and glared.

"What?" she snapped.

"Nothing," I replied with a grin. "I like your shorts. Your slippers are cute, too."

"Oh, fuck off Sawyer," she said, spinning around. I let out a small laugh and joined Mr. Foster and Sammy on the patio.

We talked briefly; I let Sammy do most of the talking, since it was his up-and-coming business after all. I just stood by for moral support, my eyes moving to the kitchen every so often, hoping to get a glimpse of Abby again in her cute as hell outfit. Mr. Foster clapped Sammy on the back, with a gracious smile, and told us to let him know if we needed anything.

Sammy and I looked at the fence together; noting the places that needed new boards, and what sections needed to be replaced all together. There were some parts of it that could be salvaged, so we got to work on those pieces first.

"Mr. Foster seems nice," Sammy told me, wiping his sodden forehead with the back of his arm.

"He is."

"His daughter seemed...." Sammy let his voice trail off, "nice, too."

I chuckled. "I went to school with her."

"Ah," Sammy said. "She didn't look that old."

"You saying that I am, kid?" Sammy laughed.

"No, you don't look old either, I'm just saying she looked...pretty," he added lamely.

"That's because she is," I told him in a matter-of-fact tone, ignoring Sammy's surprised grin.

Sammy and I worked in silence the rest of the time, only talking when we had to about the fence. My mind kept wandering back to Abby, her haughty expression playing over in my mind as she told me to fuck off. I chuckled at the thought of it, which made Sammy look up at me, but I shook my head at him. Abby was a firecracker, I've always known that about her, but watching that fire come back into her, made my whole body buzz. She was coming back to life right before my eyes.

"Soyyyy—errr," I lifted my head automatically to his call and grinned over at the little guy bounding over to me. Remmy was wearing a Batman cape and mask today. As he sprinted over to me, his little cape flapped behind him.

"Hey there, Remmy," I said to him. I dropped the tools that I had in hand and turned to him. Good thing, too, because he launched himself into my arms at once. I gave him a tight squeeze, my heart instantly warm from his sweet gesture.

"What are you doing?" he asked, grinning wide.

"My friend Sammy here is helping me fix your grandma and grandpa's fence." I told him, gesturing to missing boards.

"Can I help?"

"Well, yeah, of course; we can't do it without Batman, after all." I told him matter of factly. Sammy chuckled at my words, and Remmy's face brightened.

Sammy and I took turns with Remmy, showing him how to use a hammer properly, and what the other tools did. Sammy held the board up, while I crouched by Remmy, helping him hammer the nail into the board. His face scrunched up, his little tongue hanging out, while he hit the nail hard with the hammer. As soon as the nail was successfully in, I watched as his face lit and he let out a loud whoop.

"Wow, great job, little buddy," I told him. "On to the next."

Remmy stayed with us the rest of the time. My shirt was damp from the sun beaming down at us, so in the end, I took the shirt off and threw it to the side. Sammy did this, too, and used his shirt to mop the beads of sweat dripping from his forehead. Remmy took notice of us, working without our shirts on, that he decided, too, to take his off, but he kept his cape on, which made me smile.

"Only a few more," I told Remmy. "You are doing so great! Thank you so much for helping Sammy and me. We really needed Batman's help."

"I could tell you needed me." Remmy nodded, matter-of-factly, acting older than his years. "It's a good thing I came out."

Sammy and I chuckled together, and we continued to finish the remaining boards. I glanced up at the deck to find Abby there, leaning on the deck with a mug in hand, her eyes trained on us. She was no longer wearing her pajamas to my dismay, but now jean shorts with a white beater. Her hair was now down and hanging from her shoulders.

I sat up a little straighter and offered Abby a smile, but she didn't return it. Instead, her eyes went wide, and she looked away from me. I didn't know how long Abby was watching us, but I liked that she was. Abby's eyes glanced back towards me and even from all the way over here, I could see her eyes darkening as they snaked over my bare chest, her lips slightly parted. The Sawyer Gibson that I tried not to be around her, came into full force though, and I winked at her. Her face flushed red all over again, and she quickly turned around from me.

"Mommy, I helped them with the fence!" Remmy yelled, bounding back over to her. Abby offered her kind smile and gave Remmy a high five.

"I saw, you were a great helper to them."

"Yes, I was," Remmy said proudly. "Good thing I went out there to help, they *really* needed me."

"Oh, of course."

I tried to fight the grin, but I couldn't; Abby and Remmy just did that to me, and it surprised the hell out of me. Sammy and I cleaned up our messes, putting our tools back into place and in the back of my truck. Mr. Foster came out shortly after, with cash in hand. He handed it over to Sammy directly, and Sammy's eyes widened in response.

"Mr. Foster, we agreed on one hundred, this is a hundred and fifty," Sammy said, quickly scanning the money. "I can't take the fifty."

"Yes, you can, son, you both did a fine job today," Mr. Foster said. Sammy turned to me with the cash and tried to hand me some, but I shook my head at him quickly.

"It's yours, you earned it. Now that you know Mr. Foster, you can work with him directly; you also don't need my help, you did a great job today. I was very impressed. Why don't you talk to him about your mowing?"

Sammy beamed at me and tossed me a look of gratification as he turned to Mr. Foster and started to dive in on his mowing services. I stood close by, but my eyes were trained on Abby and Remmy. Abby had Remmy in her arms and was swinging him in circles around the yard. Remmy was giggling and yelling, "Faster, Mommy! Faster!" Abby obeyed, her own soft laughs filling the air. They both fell to the ground in another fit of laughter, and Abby said, "I can't do it anymore, I'm too dizzy."

"Me, too," Remmy said.

I sighed as I watched the two of them. They were a beautiful family, a beautiful mother and son duo. My chest warmed rapidly and I knew my face showed all my feelings for them. Mr. Foster's eyes trained on me, and averted back over to his daughter and grandson. He cleared his throat loudly, bringing me back to their conversation. I looked over at Mr. Foster and smiled sheepishly at his raised eyebrow.

Yes, Mr. Foster. Your daughter is slowly stealing my heart.

Chapter 9- *Abby*

I thought my heart was going to combust in my chest today, as I watched Remmy with Sawyer. Remmy was ecstatic to see Sawyer; I tried like hell to get him to stay inside while they worked, but Remmy was not having it. As soon as he saw Sawyer out in the backyard, he beelined straight for him. I couldn't help but hold my breath as Remmy darted for him; it was what I usually did. The last thing I wanted was for Remmy's little heart to get broken by another man. His dad never played with or really had any kind of time for him. I've watched Remmy's spirit get crushed again and again, after begging his dad to swim, or play basketball, or catch. It was always a no, and I always had a hurt Remmy afterwards. It's probably the reason why I give a hundred and ten percent to that little boy because if I didn't, who would?

When I watched Sawyer drop his tools, his grin so wide you could see it a mile away, I felt my chest relax and started breathing normally. Not only did Remmy run right at him, but jumped right into his arms, and Sawyer caught him, as if they've been doing that for years. It looked so natural as Sawyer ruffled his hair, commenting on how cool he looked in his Batman cape. Remmy's face glowed all day.

I found myself coming out to the deck every so often; I told my mom it was because I needed to check on Remmy, but I wasn't fooling her. Of course I had to check on Remmy though; I mean, Sawyer is a stranger to me now. I literally know nothing about him, except that he's a teacher and coach at the school, and he's also on the town baseball board. He also obviously takes a special interest in his students since he showed up today with one. As I watched Sawyer help Remmy with the hammer, his words of encouragement for my boy filling my heart, I found myself wanting to know more about him. What does he do in his free time, besides volunteer? Does he have a girlfriend? Why isn't he married yet? What made him choose teaching for a career when the possibilities for him were endless?

Remmy and I were spinning in circles; we've done this a million times. I don't know why he finds it so humorous, but he does. We spun faster and faster, Remmy giggling, and chanting, "Faster, Mommy! Faster!" I laughed, my head whirling and my legs and arms stinging from the constant movement. Finally, he and I collapsed into the grass, both of us falling into a fit of laughter.

"Mommy, do you think Soy-er will play catch with me?" I felt my body tense at the mention of Sawyer's name, but I shrugged.

"I don't know," I told him. "He may have to go. You can always ask though. If he says no, then I'll play with you." This was always my response to him when he'd ask his father to play.

Remmy nodded, popped up from the grass, and darted inside to his room. I laid on the grass though, reveling in the warmth and comfort the ground provided. I sighed, my eyes looking up at the brightened blue sky, trying to make shapes form in the puffy white clouds. My body was slowly relaxing as I breathed in the beautiful air.

"Soy-er," I heard my little man's voice say. "Will you play catch with me?"

I tensed again, straining my ears to hear his response, but Sawyer enthusiastically agreed and I relaxed. Remmy also asked Sammy if he wanted to play, but Sammy said he had to get going to his next job. I glanced up at Remmy and watched as he threw his tiny arms around Sammy's waist and smiled as Sammy gave him a tight hug in response. That little boy could charm just about anyone.

I watched as Sawyer slid on his shirt; I kind of wished he didn't. He looked so…chiseled. It made my stomach burn. Remmy and Sawyer walked further into the grass and Remmy threw the ball to Sawyer. Sawyer in turn, threw the ball lightly back at Remmy, but he missed and let out a groan.

"Oh, we don't have any of that," Sawyer said. "Sometimes, you just can't catch the ball, and that's okay. You just practice and before you know it, you'll catch them all."

Remmy nodded, his eyes focused on Sawyer. I leaned up from the grass area on my elbows and continued to watch the two of them together, my heart swelling into a balloon all over again. Remmy threw the ball back to Sawyer and he gracefully caught it in his outstretched hand. I watched as Sawyer threw it back to Remmy carefully, and Remmy lifted his little glove, his tongue sticking out with concentration and this time, he caught it. I let out a sigh.

"Wooooooooo," Sawyer chanted, raising his fist into the air. "That's what I'm talking about, bud!" Remmy beamed back and jumped into the air.

They continued that way, and Remmy started to catch more and more; each time, Sawyer let out a hoot of encouragement, and each time, Remmy's face danced with excitement.

I heard the sliding glass door open and my mother's voice calling to me.

"Abby, you have a phone call." My mom's voice was calculated, which caught my attention. I glanced up at her and her usually sunny demeanor was replaced by a slight frown.

Sawyer and Remmy paid no attention to me, but Mom walked out with her cell phone in hand. As she got closer, she mouthed, "*Michael.*" I felt my body stiffen at his name. I sighed, got up from my seated position in the grass, and grabbed the phone from Mom.

"Hello," I said into the phone.

"Abigail." He already sounded annoyed, and I sighed.

"Hello, Michael." I told him. I turned from Remmy and Sawyer and walked to the deck, my mother's eyes trained on my face, a look of worry starting to etch into her features.

"I've been trying to call you on your cell all day. Why haven't you answered?"

"I haven't been around my phone."

Michael paused. "What if it was an emergency?" he asked.

"Is it an emergency?"

"No."

"Well then, okay. What can I do for you?"

"I would like to know when you're coming home," he said; I could tell from the sound of his voice, he was gritting his teeth.

"I'm not sure."

"What do you mean, you're not sure?"

"Just what it means; I don't have a date in mind."

"You haven't bought a ticket home yet?"

"No," I responded simply. I started messing with the strands of my hair. My eyes flitted back to Sawyer and Remmy and I noticed that Sawyer's eyes kept glancing back to me between throws.

"Abigail."

"What, Michael?" I heard him sigh on the other end.

"I'm glad you are spending time with your family. I'm glad Remmy's having fun, but I think it's time for you to come home now. I mean, you have responsibilities here. The house is a fucking mess, the gardener didn't show up like he was supposed to, and Charlene from the HOA stopped by this morning and said that we could get fined if we don't get our bushes trimmed soon, and—"

"Then you handle it, Michael," I interrupted.

"*What?*"

"Handle it. I don't know what to tell you. The home computer has everything you need to know. If you can't get the gardener to show up, then grab the trimmers and start trimming. It's not hard."

"It's not my job, Abigail, it's yours," Michael snapped.

"Well, considering I'm not there, no, it's not."

"When are you coming home?" he snapped.

"I. Don't. Know." My tone was matching Michael's now.

"I haven't seen my kid in weeks, Abby. You can't just take off like you did."

"Would it have been any different if we were home?"

"Oh, here we go." Michael let out an angry sigh. "Here we fucking go with that bullshit again."

"Okay Michael, I have to go. I'm not going to be arguing with you. Would you like to talk to Remmy?"

Michael paused. "Yes."

I held the phone out from my ear and yelled for Remmy. He looked irritated with me for interrupting his time with Sawyer, so I added, "Remmy, it's your dad, bud. He wants to talk to you."

Remmy's face brightened as he tossed the ball back to Sawyer and bounded over to me, his little cape flapping behind him.

"Hiya, Dad!" Remmy called. I couldn't hear what Michael was saying on the other line, but Remmy continued to smile. "Oh yeah, I'm having so much fun here. Mom signed me up for t-ball, and I have my first game here soon! I'm so excited!" Remmy paused. "Yes, I'm practicing *a lot*. I'm playing catch right now with Soy-er, and he said I have a really good arm! You should have seen me hit the ball at practice, it went all the way to the grass!" Remmy paused again. "I miss you too, Dad! But I have to go back and play catch now, byyyye!" Remmy threw the phone back to me and raced back over to Sawyer. My eyes went to Sawyer's face and my chest fell as I watched Sawyer's lips pull into a frown.

I put the phone back to my ear. "Hey," I said.

"Who the fuck is Sawyer?" Michael fumed. I sighed and rolled my eyes.

"A family friend, Michael. He was here fixing the fence and Remmy has really taken a liking to him."

"Huh," Michael said. "Well, I'm going to start FaceTiming Remmy daily, so make sure you have your phone on you. I shouldn't have to call your mother to get in touch with you and my son."

"Okay, Michael." He sighed.

"I really wish you would come home, you know. I really miss you."

"Oh, you do not." A dark laugh escaped me.

"Yes, I do, Abby."

"I highly doubt that, but it was a good attempt."

"We really should talk, you know." Michael's voice lowered.

"I have no interest in talking with you."

"Abby, the last night you were here, I was..." his voice trailed off. " I vaguely remember saying things that I shouldn't have."

"Like I said, Michael, I have no interest in talking with you about this. You were very vocal and honest that night. I've been doing a lot of thinking about it lately."

"I didn't mean what I said."

"Oh, you did too. It's fine, Michael. Honestly, I'm glad you finally fessed up. But, like I said, I don't want to talk about it right now, or any time soon. Remmy and I are really enjoying our time here, and I think it's really good for us to be here. If I were you, I would get to trimming, Charlene doesn't mess around."

Michael sighed.

"I will call you tomorrow," Michael said. "Answer, please."

"I will answer. Bye Michael."

"Bye."

I hit the end call button and didn't realize that my mom was still standing there. I handed her phone to her, ignoring her frown and her cautious eyes. I wasn't ready to talk to her about it either. I didn't need my mom to know what a colossus mess my life has become.

"Everything okay?" she asked, brightening.

"Yep."

"Remmy really likes Sawyer," Mom said, staring at the two of them. They were now chasing each other around the yard playing tag. I sighed.

"Yes, he does."

"I really like Sawyer, too. He has a gentle heart." Mom hesitated. I turned to her, my eyebrow pulling up.

"What does that mean, Mother?"

"Nothing, just that he's a gentle one. He hasn't let too many people in, you know."

"I don't know why," I told her. Mom sighed.

"Me either. He'd be the perfect Dad."

Sawyer caught Remmy with one of his arms and twirled him around in the air. My mom brightened again and started walking over to them.

"Anyone want to swim?" Mom asked. She was gobbling all of this up.

Sawyer set Remmy down in the grass, his giggles able to be heard all the way through town. Remmy turned to Sawyer, his face beaming again. I haven't seen Remmy look like this in such a long time.

"Sawyer, will you swim with us? Puh-lease." Remmy pouted his lips and put his hands together in prayer motion. Sawyer chuckled and turned his gaze over to me. I offered him a kind smile in return, as if saying yes.

"Sure, buddy, I don't have my trunks though. I'll have to run home quick."

"You will come back, right?" Remmy said, his face slowly falling. My heart panged in my chest all over again; he's been let down so many times, it hurt to watch him doubt Sawyer's intentions.

Sawyer ruffled his hair, knelt to one knee and extended his pinky to Remmy, his eyes dancing. Remmy's face lifted as he wrapped his little pinky around Sawyer's. "I pinky promise."

*****

Sawyer was back within minutes; Remmy and I barely had time to get our own swimsuits on. I hesitated in my room, trying to pick which suit to wear. Remmy was growing impatient with me from the hallway. I decided to pick my one-piece black suit. I knew I would never have the courage to actually wear the two piece in front of Sawyer, and I wanted to be comfortable out there with them. There's no way I was about to show off my stomach to Sawyer; the once, smooth hardened skin, was now rippled with tiger marks, and too soft for my liking.

"Come on, Mom! He's already back!" Remmy sighed.

"There's no rush, Remmy. He'll still be there," my mom said to him. I opened my bedroom door and found the two of them standing outside the door. She was also wearing her swimsuit, a light green one piece. I've always admired my mother; even after all these years, she still looked great. Her legs were starting to sag a little, but still kept its firmness for her age.

I pulled my hair up in a quick ponytail and grabbed my sunglasses and the pool towels on the countertop.

When we walked back out on the deck, Sawyer was already swimming in the pool, doing circular laps. I watched as his arms pushed him forward, his muscles tensing and flexing. My heart started to pick up as I gawked at his flawless body in the water. My mother nudged me gently in the side, her eyebrows pulling up at me. She was clearly amused and calling me out. I shook my head, my cheeks slightly burning, and Mom stifled her laugh.

"Sawyer!" Remmy waved at him excitedly. "I'm coming in!"

Sawyer stood up, the water dripping from his brown hair, and I watched as his eyes set on me. I bit my lip, my stomach instantly doing flips from his intense stare. I felt my insecurities get the best of me and went to grab for a towel to wrap around my too exposed body, but my mom gently nudged me forward, as if she knew where my thoughts were leading.

"Hang on, little guy," I told a jumping Remmy. I grabbed his arm gently and pulled him to the patio table. "Sunscreen and floaties." Remmy stuck out his tongue in response.

I quickly lathered sunscreen on Remmy's body, all the while getting urgent protests to hurry up. Sawyer chuckled in the water, waiting patiently for him by the stairs. I slipped on his arm floaties and watched as he darted to the pool's edge.

"Sawyer, I'm going to do a cannonball!" Remmy chimed. Sawyer flashed him a bright smile.

"Oh I can't wait to see this!" Sawyer fell back into the middle of the pool. Remmy leaned back on the deck, his eyes focused, and then he leapt forward into the water, holding his legs as the water splashed around him. My mom giggled next to me.

As soon as Remmy's head was above water, Sawyer called out, "I give that a ten! *Wow*, that was huge!"

Remmy giggled and started to swim after Sawyer. My lips pulled into a frown as I watched the two of them together. It was difficult for me to process why an almost stranger could give him this much attention, when his own father shunned him away. My heart was full of mixed emotions for the two of them; sadness, for Remmy missing out on these times with his own father, yet a twinge of happiness as I watched him get to know Sawyer.

"Are you getting in?" Mom nudged me again, a smile toying on her lips.

"I think so."

"Good, I think I'll join you guys." I felt her hand clasp around mine with a squeeze.

Mom and I got into the pool, not doing cannonballs as Remmy insisted, but we used the ladder instead. Mom got on top of her floatie and sunbathed, while I lurked in the corner of the pool, watching Remmy and Sawyer engage. Sawyer had Remmy in his arms most of the time, either throwing him around in the pool, or putting Remmy on his neck.

"Let's play Marco Polo!" Remmy insisted. "Mom, you play, too."

"Of course," I replied. Together, the three of us started the game. Remmy was a cheater, peeking through his fingers to try to find Sawyer and I. Sawyer let Remmy grab him, and then he went to the middle of the pool for his turn.

He spun underneath the water while Remmy and I quickly swam around to get away from him. Sawyer got up, eyes closed, and called out, "Marco."

Remmy squealed, "Polo!" but I kept quiet.

"Now, now, miss Abigail, you know the rules," Sawyer chided playfully.

"Polo," I called out quietly, a giggle escaping me.

"Marco," Sawyer called out again, his smile radiant with droplets of water slipping off his face.

"Polo," Remmy and I chanted together, both of us giggling.

Instead of swimming after Remmy, Sawyer's head cocked in my direction. His lips pulled into a mischievous grin and he prowled closer to me. My heart started to quicken, eyes wide as I tried to quietly pass him. I should have known the fucker would seek me out first.

"Marco."

"Polo,," we chanted again. Sawyer was getting closer to me now with his cocky grin and I couldn't help but laugh. I tried to get away, but I was making too much noise and Sawyer's face darted to me.

"Marco," Sawyer said, laughing.

"Polo," we chanted again. Now Sawyer was really close, his fingers very close to mine. I felt my breath catch in my throat as Sawyer's arm extended to me, his wet fingers grazing my upper arm. He pulled me closer to him by a few inches, his eyes opening and face hardening.

"I caught you," Sawyer whispered, drawing me in. His eyes snaked over me, his pupils dilated. His eyes lingered down to my mouth and back to my eyes and I watched as they slowly darkened.

"Are you going to let me go?" I asked, my breathing unsteady.

His eyelids lowered, his lips turning upward into a half grin "Not likely," he whispered. My eyes widened in response. He grabbed my waist firmly, my insides flashing red hot pleasure, and he picked me up and slammed me into the depths of the water.

I erupted from the water fiercely, the chlorine water stinging my nostrils, and glared at Sawyer. Sawyer let out a howl of laughter and turned to Remmy, who had an eager smile on his face as he swam determinedly towards us, wanting to be in on the fun. I took the hair tie out of my hair, shook my head, and let the damp hair fall around on my face.

"Asshole," I whispered. Sawyer heard, and he grinned back at me, tossing me another one of his winks that seared my heart.

We played in the pool for hours; the sunshine felt wonderful on my face and skin. Being outside was my happy place, no matter where I was. The smell of my mother's flowers, the trees, even the chlorine, brought an overwhelming sense of peace to my soul. I was relaxed in the water with Remmy and Sawyer. My mom ended up getting out to dry off, announcing to us all that she was going to start dinner and invited Sawyer to stay. Sawyer agreed all too quickly, and I felt a pang of pleasure course through my chest at his response. Just like Remmy, I didn't want him to leave us so soon, even though he's been here with us all day. I told my mom I'd get out and help her, but she waved her hands at me dismissively and told me to stay and have fun with the boys.

Whenever Sawyer tried to talk to me, or splash me with the water, Remmy called his attention right back to him, but Sawyer didn't mind. Every time Remmy called Sawyer to him, Sawyer turned to him with a bright smile and got back to what he was doing. It was odd for me to see another man be so taken with my boy, and it caused me to feel so many mixed emotions. On one hand, I loved that Remmy was so taken with Sawyer, but on the other, it frightened me. The last thing I wanted was Remmy's heart to be broken.

I laid on the float, reveling in the sun's warmth, when I heard Remmy and Sawyer whispering. They were tossing a squishy ball back and forth in the water when I decided to hop onto the float. I glanced over at them in the corner of my eye, and started giggling; they were clearly plotting something, as Remmy kept pointing at me and snickering. I closed my eyes again, pretending to be asleep, and strained my ears to hear the two of them. Their quiet splashes rippled the water around me, but I still pretended to be asleep, joining in on their game.

Remmy and Sawyer sprang from the water on my left, yelling, "*Rawr!*" I pretended to jump and clutched at my heart, which made Remmy fall into a fit of giggles. They started splashing me, the water drenching my face.

"Ahh," I let out. "You scared me!" I poked at his cheeks.

"Let's do a cannonball contest," Remmy insisted. He looked at Sawyer to gauge his reaction, but Sawyer agreed. The two of them got out of the water and one by one, jumped into the water, creating large waves in the pool.

"My turn," I called out to them. Remmy's eyes brightened again with excitement as I slid off the floatie and swam to the stairs. I felt Sawyer's gaze on me, and I turned to him grinning. Sawyer dipped half of his face into the water, but it didn't hide that desirable smile on his face.

"Mommy has the best cannon balls," Remmy told Sawyer seriously. "We do this all the time at home."

Sawyer grabbed Remmy and put him on his shoulders to judge my cannonball. They gave me plenty of room to jump in. I ran straight into the water, and curled my body into a tight position, and plunged into the water, instant waves erupting all around me. When I stood up from the water, blinking and wiping the water from my face, both boys were clapping and announced that I received a ten. Sawyer's face transformed into a look that I haven't seen before and

I wondered what he was thinking, as his lips turned into a coy smile.

My mother came out of the sliding glass door and said, "You guys, I'm afraid I'm making too much food. Should we invite others to join? Sawyer, how about your mom? Anyone else you both want to invite that would have hungry appetites?"

Sawyer suggested Lance and I suggested Emma. Mom beamed at the both of us, clearly excited for the impromptu gathering and told us to invite them over. I slipped out of the pool with Sawyer on my heels. I glanced around for my towel but noticed that Sawyer had it in his hands.

"Pink towel for you?" I asked him, cocking my eyebrow. He gave me his half smile and took a step towards me, his eyes full of heat. I swallowed hard, as Sawyer gently placed the towel around me, his eyes taking over my body. I expected to feel the insecurities to start flowing in, but they didn't come. Instead, I flashed Sawyer a knowing smile and let him drape the towel around me.

Mom brought my phone out to me, and I texted Emma the invite and Sawyer texted Lance. Our phones instantly pinged, both of them accepting our invitations.

Remmy was not quite ready for the fun to end, but my fingers and toes were starting to wrinkle, and the chlorine was starting to sting my nose. I hesitated when asking Remmy to get out, but Sawyer said he would continue to swim with him. I pulled over a patio chair and watched the two of them, as the others joined us on the patio.

Emma beamed when she saw me and wrapped her arms around my almost dry shoulders. I noticed she had a swimsuit underneath her tank top and jean shorts. I told her to go right in and swim if she wanted, but she opted to sit next to me instead. Lance on the other hand, instantly took off his white tee, trunks already on, and dove right into the pool.

Remmy was attached to Sawyer's hip the entire time; he clung to him like he was his lifeline and my heart swelled more than once at the two of them. Soon enough, he started to relax around Lance, too. Lance bellowed out laughter at Remmy many times, and soon enough, he captured Lance's heart, too. Remmy and the two guys were playing pool basketball now, shooting hoops together and picking Remmy up in turns to allow him slam dunks.

"Remmy really likes Sawyer," Emma whispered next to me, eyeing the boys. Remmy had his arms tightly around Sawyer's neck as they swam around the pool together.

"Yes, he's really taken to him," I agreed. I watched Emma's eyes glance over at me, a smile playing on her lips.

"And you?" she asked, her eyes dancing.

"What about me?" I asked.

"Are *you* really taking to him?" she whispered, her eyes glinting. I pointedly ignored her, my eyes back on the boys in the pool, which only increased Emma's enthusiasm. She gave a little shriek and I tossed her a look of death.

"You know, Sawyer is a really good guy. He's really matured since high school," she whispered.

"I can tell."

"He's not so hot headed anymore."

"He's still Sawyer though, I'm sure it's still there somewhere," I said, eyebrows raised. Emma laughed.

"He's not dating anyone," Emma added. "I know that for a fact because the women are always gossiping about him around town. They all want to land him. I see why, too, he's quite a catch."

I rolled my eyes at her. "Don't," I told her.

"Don't, what?" Emma said, eyebrows raising, fighting back her smile.

"You know, what." I pointed a finger at her as she looked back over at the boys.

"He's extremely attractive," Emma added. I rolled my eyes, but heard the words pile out of my mouth before I could stop them.

"He's always been attractive."

Emma grinned in response.

My parents came out of the house with Mrs. Gibson. She beamed when she saw me and instantly engulfed me into a tight hug. She still looked the same to me, except for the gray strands now playing in her hair.

"Oh, Abby, I'm so glad you're still here! It's been wonderful seeing you around town." She kissed my cheek, and I patted her hand with mine.

"We are loving our stay. It'll be hard to leave." I told her honestly. Mrs. Gibson's eyes flashed to the boys, her expression softening as Sawyer held Remmy tightly to his chest.

"Oh, isn't that a sight," Mrs. Gibson whispered with a warm smile. "*Ugh*, he would be such a good dad." I looked back at the boys and sighed, too.

"He really would," I whispered honestly. Mrs. Gibson's eyes sparkled in response.

Sawyer lifted Remmy in the air and announced that he thought it may be time to get out of the pool. Remmy protested, but Sawyer told him that if he stayed in any longer, he would turn into a wrinkled old man. Remmy looked down at his hands, wide-eyed, and quickly agreed. I handed Remmy a towel, drying him off lightly, when Sawyer collapsed into a nearby patio chair, water dripping from his chest and legs. I forced my eyes to look away from his wet body; just by looking at him, waves of heat shot through me. Remmy pulled out of my grasp with his towel and climbed on top of Sawyer's lap, snuggling himself instantly into his bare chest.

My heart lifted as Sawyer re-positioned Remmy, engulfing the little man in his large arms. You could barely see Remmy underneath his biceps. I felt a heavy sigh escape me, my heart feeling so heavy and full. Lance ruffled Remmy's hair as he walked by towards my dad, who was now working on firing up the grill. The smell of the charcoal made me close my eyes and my stomach lurch in response; anything on the charcoal made by my father was going to be delicious.

The bright sky started to slowly darken as the time flew by. We all fell into conversation, conversing about everything and anything that came to mind. Lance, Sawyer, Emma, and I reminisced about some of our high school days, recollecting old memories that made us all laugh. Mom, Dad, and Mrs. Gibson joined in, giving us their point of view of the memories, there's a little more humorous than ours. The sides of my stomach started to ache from the constant laughter.

My mom and Mrs. Gibson prepared a lovely meal; we had hamburgers and brats, potato salad, pasta salad, chips and dip, and Mrs. Gibson brought over Scotcharoos for dessert; my stomach was going to burst if I ate anything else. Emma and I helped Mom and Mrs. Gibson clean up, while the boys fell into discussion about the housing market. I felt my body tense at the change of the subject, and kept my mouth tightly shut.

"Rates are so high," Lance said with a sigh. "I thought about refinancing, but my loan officer suggested waiting for now."

"Abby said they were going up," Dad sighed. "I haven't paid much attention to it though. It'll get worse before it gets better; let's hope it gets better for Abby's sake." I tensed again, looking up at my father. Dad took a drink of beer and I felt Emma's eyes glance towards me.

"What do you do?" Lance asked interestedly. I paused, cleared my throat, and set the plates I was gathering back down on the table.

"Well, I was a Loan Processor," I replied.

"Was?" Lance caught. Sawyer's eyes were trained on me, and I felt my face flush from the attention.

"Yeah, I, um, I got laid off right before I came home."

"I'm sorry to hear that," Sawyer said automatically, his lips turning into a frown.

"Yeah, that sucks," Lance agreed. "If you need a job, you can clean my shop," he added playfully.

"Now, now, don't take away my help, Lance," Emma said with a laugh. "Abby's been helping me at my daycare."

Sawyer looked back over at me, questions toying on his face. I gave him a small smile, a shrug, and went back to helping my mom clean up the dishes; I was thankful that the conversation was turned from me.

The sky started to darken; the nightlife erupting around us with the crickets starting to sing their songs; soft chirps from the birds above us started in. My mother got up and turned on her patio lights, which made the air around us feel more like home, raying comfort all around. I fell back in my patio chair and sighed, closing my eyes. I could feel Sawyer's gaze on me; it sent prickles of pleasure up my arms.

Emma and Lance announced that they had to get going but thanked us all for the evening. I got up and gave Emma and Lance a hug in turn and Lance squeezed me a little harder. "Glad your back, Abs," Lance whispered in my ear and kissed my cheek.

I glanced over at Remmy, who was back in Sawyer's arms, his eyes drooping on his chest. The warm smile on Sawyer's face told me that he was enjoying the moment with Remmy. There was no better feeling than snuggling with that boy. I walked over to them, touched Sawyer's arms lightly and whispered, "I'll take him. He needs to get up for bed."

Sawyer nodded, and tried to hand him over, but Remmy clung to Sawyer. "No," Remmy yawned. "I want to stay."

Sawyer hesitated, looking back up at me. "Remmy, it's time for bed, buddy. You can barely keep your eyes open."

Sawyer started to stand up, cradling Remmy in his arms gently. "Show me the way," Sawyer said.

I walked through the house with Sawyer right behind me, as we walked up the stairs into Remmy's room. Mom transformed her guest room into an exclusive room just for him, with dinosaurs and astronauts decorating the walls. His bedding was tiny astronauts and moons. Sawyer gracefully laid a yawning Remmy into bed, and I started to dig through his dresser for pajamas.

"I'll give you a minute," Sawyer whispered, stepping outside of the room. I tugged the clothes off my sleepy child and slipped his pajamas on. Remmy's eyes were already drifting, and I knew that there was no way I was going to get the little guy to brush tonight. I sighed and started to tuck him in. As soon as his head hit his pillow, he was out. I kissed him on the forehead, whispered the words I say to him every night, *"Love you forever, like you for always,"* and quietly tiptoed out of the bedroom.

Sawyer was waiting for me in the hallway, his eyes gazing intently of the old family photos of us when I was younger. I gently touched his arm, and he looked over at me, with a soft smile. "You've changed a lot," Sawyer said, gesturing to the teenager in the picture.

"I know," I said, "I was a lot thinner then." I sighed, looking down at my enlarged body. Sawyer's eyes and lips puckered into a frown.

"Abby," he started to say, but he paused abruptly. "You clearly don't see yourself the way others see you." I rolled my eyes.

"I don't know what you mean by that, but I think I see myself just fine. I'm aware enough to admit it."

Sawyer shook his at me, a sad smile on his lips. "You're wrong, Abby. I don't know why you think of yourself that way, but just know, you're wrong." I felt my cheeks burn a little. Sawyer sighed and ran a hand through his tousled hair.

"I guess I should get going," Sawyer said, eyeing me. "Little man is out, mission complete." He laughed softly.

"Sawyer," I said, as he turned away from me. He looked back up at me, waiting for me to continue. "You can stay…if you want. Have a beer with me?"

Sawyer's eyes quickly scanned my face and nodded in agreement.

"Okay," he said.

"Okay," I said, my spirits lifting. "I'll be down in a minute; I just need to change quickly." Sawyer's face fell into a mocking expression.

"Back into your slippers?" he asked. I lightly punched his arm.

"You'll never forget that, will you?"

"Oh, Abby, it'll be seared into my memory forever." He laid his hand over his heart. "I'll be outside waiting for you." He turned around and started walking down the stairs. Instead of turning to my room, I watched him walk away from me, his back to me as my heart rate started to pick up again. When he reached the bottom step, he also turned to face me, flashing me his brilliant smile, before walking through the house.

Sawyer Gibson really had a way of playing with my heart strings.

Sawyer

My mother looked surprised when I told her that I was staying at the Foster's house a little longer. Her eyes widened in response, excitement evident on her face, but I shook my head at her.

"Mom," I started to say, but she didn't say anything more. She just gave me a hug, a pat on the cheek, and told Mr. and Mrs. Foster good night. Mr. and Mrs. Foster stood awkwardly in the kitchen, their eyes trained on me. I fidgeted in the kitchen a little, not knowing what to say.

"Are you both okay if I stay? Abby invited me, but I don't want to put any of you out," I offered.

"Oh, of course you can." Mrs. Foster forced a smile on her lips. "Just, I have to say something." She let out. Mr. Foster tossed a furtive look at Mrs. Foster then, his eyes appraising her.

"Mandy," Mr. Foster said.

"Oh, don't Mandy me. Go to bed." Mrs. Foster rolled her eyes at her husband. He sighed, kissed his wife on the cheek and left us alone in the kitchen.

"You can say anything to me," I told Mrs. Foster politely. I was honestly curious about what she wanted to tell me. If it was anything to help me figure out Abby, I was all ears.

"You know I love you, Sawyer. You've always had a special place in my heart..." Mrs. Foster started.

She was looking everywhere but at me. *Fuck*, this must be bad. Is she telling me to stay away? I would, if she really wanted me to, I had the utmost respect for the Fosters, but after spending such a great day with them, it would be hard to keep my distance. Their laughter had become music to my ears. When they laughed, I couldn't help but laugh. When they smiled, I smiled. I wiped my sweaty palms on my jean shorts, waiting for Mrs. Foster to continue. She sighed, finally making eye contact with me. I never realized until today how much her eyes resembled Abby's.

"I guess I don't know what I'm trying to say. I'm just...concerned a little, about Abby. You know, she hasn't really talked to us about what is going on with her. I know it's not good, but she hasn't opened up to me yet, and I am not pushing her. Honestly, we just love seeing her back home with us. I guess what I'm trying to say is to be careful." She shrugged halfheartedly.

"You're asking me to be careful?" I clarified, eyebrow pulling together. *Shouldn't it be the other way around?*

Mrs. Foster sighed again, her fingers now toying with loose strands of her hair.

"Yes, and no, *I don't know*. I probably shouldn't say anything. I need to butt out, it's not my business, but Sawyer, I saw the way you were looking at her today." A warm smile played on her lips. "It was the same look you used to give her all the way through school," she added, eyebrows raising. I didn't deny it, but I couldn't continue to look into her eyes; I chose to stare at my feet instead.

"I adore you, Sawyer. Like I said, you have always been in my heart, thoughts, and prayers. So, I guess what I'm trying to say is, the last thing I want to happen is for you to get so attached to her and Remmy, just for her to go back to Florida. That's her home, Sawyer. It's not here anymore, no matter how much we want it to be. It needs to be her choice to come back here, not ours."

I thought on her words, nodded, and walked over to Mrs. Foster and engulfed her in my arms. Her eyebrows raised in response, but she wrapped her soft arms around me and pulled me in and hugged me as if I was her own child. That's why I've always loved Mrs. Foster; she had a kind soul.

"You don't need to worry about me, Mrs. Foster, but I really appreciate it nonetheless." She patted my cheek in response, just like my own mother does and sighed.

"I just want to see you happy, Sawyer. Just like my Abby. I want to see her happy, too. It has been killing me for years to see her so unhappy with Michael, but her marriage with him is not my place to interfere." Her lips turned into a sad smile. "You'd be good for her, if you want my opinion, but I also don't want to see you get hurt."

I didn't know what to say back to that, so I didn't. Mrs. Foster sighed again, patted my cheek once more, and said, "I'm going to turn in before I say anymore. I won't bring this up again. Good night, Sawyer."

"Good night, Mrs. Foster," I told her softly.

"My goodness, Saw, we've known each other for years, you can call me Mandy."

I chuckled, waved good night, and decided to go outside and wait for Abby like I said I would. As I opened the sliding glass door, insects fluttered above my head around the patio light. I quickly shut the door and stepped into the cool air.

I walked over to the deck's railing, leaning against it, as I stared into the darkness that now swallowed the yard. The crickets were still chirping as I quietly listened to the night coming to life. It was a beautiful evening; a perfect evening, but it wasn't because of how peaceful the night air was.

Mrs. Foster's warning started to swim in my mind. I didn't know what to make of it. I knew her intentions were well, but her words kept spinning around.

I let out a low breath, knowing that Mrs. Foster's warning was real, but on the same point, I knew she was getting a little carried away with it all. There was nothing going on with Abby and me. Sure, a few shared glances and smiles today, and maybe, just maybe, we had a moment in the pool, but there was nothing to worry about. I know Abby's home is Florida and that she will be going back home eventually, but why should I miss the opportunity of spending time with her and getting to know her son?

There was nothing going on with us, I thought. Just friends, catching up, enjoying each other's company.

I nodded to myself, getting my head firmly back in place, as I turned towards the cooler that was filled earlier with Bud Light. I grabbed a bottle, opened the tab, and took a drink.

The sliding glass door slowly opened, and my head jerked towards it. Abby was walking out, in short, flannel shorts with a gray, plain crew neck sweatshirt. I felt my breath catch in my throat, as she offered me a kind smile.

"Yes, I'm back in my pajamas, go ahead and laugh," Abby said quietly. I just smiled in response.

Abby walked over to where I was standing and looked out into the darkness with me. "I forgot how pretty it can be here," she said with a smile. "It's so peaceful at night."

"Yes, it is."

"Do you want to sit on the patio?" She gestured to the seats. I quickly nodded. I didn't know why my voice was suddenly feeling dry, but I took a drink of my beer as I followed Abby over to the patio chairs, licking my lips nervously. I quickly stepped in front of her and pulled out her chair for her, watching her face glow and blush.

I sat down next to her and started fiddling with my beer bottle. I glanced up at Abby underneath my eyelashes, but her attention was up to the sky, her eyes gazing at the twinkling stars.

"No stars in Florida," she told me. "They are hard to see where I live. This is what I miss most about home."

"Do you miss Florida?" I asked her, picking at the label on the bottle. Her lips pursed in response as she thought how to respond.

"Yes, and no," she said honestly. I took a drink of my beer again. "I think I need one of those," she gestured to the beer.

"I'll get you one. I need another anyway," I replied. I quickly got up and grabbed two cold bottles from the cooler, popping her tab open and handing it over to her. She offered me a kind smile.

"Thank you, Sawyer."

"You're welcome." I loved hearing her say my name on her lips; it brought on a weird sensation through me; all I knew was that I wanted to keep hearing her say it.

We sat in silence for a moment, both of us drinking our beers, looking around her mother's patio. I glanced over at Abby, really taking in her expression, and wondered if I brought up her homelife situation, if she would run the other direction, or confide in me. I started to pick at the label on the bottle again.

"What I miss most about Florida," Abby started to say, but she paused. I looked up at her, waiting for her to continue, "Is the beach. Remmy and I spent so much time on the beach. I love hearing the ocean waves, having the sand between my toes, and underneath the sunshine all the time. Remmy would be there all day if I let him." She chuckled. "We'd have picnics on the beach, look for seashells, and have ice cream dates."

"The beach sounds nice. Do you live close to it?"

She nodded. "About fifteen minutes away. It's gorgeous there." She sighed. "I also miss my backyard." She laughed a little. "I know that may sound silly, but my backyard was my happy place. Remmy and I spend most of our time back there during the day and when he's asleep, that's where I escape most evenings to unwind."

"Tell me about it," I asked. I listened to her explain her backyard in detail; the pool, the swing set, her kitchen and grill area, the rocking chair.

"My favorite thing about it though are the lights that I have. I have those twinkle lights strewn from the pergola and around the patio, and it just looks beautiful out there at night. It brings a sense of calm to me that I can't explain."

"It sounds wonderful," I told her honestly. Her smile turned into a frown.

"It can be. We did the backyard that way because I love to host parties, but we've only hosted a time or two."

"Why is that?" I asked.

"Well, you need friends in order to have parties." She laughed a little. "I don't have many friends in Florida, to be honest." That surprised me; Abby was one of the kindest people that I've ever met. Correction, she was kind to others, to me, she would always be the spitfire Abby.

"What?" I asked. "That can't be true."

"It is," she said with a dry laugh. "I'm just so busy with Remmy that my social life kind of took a dive. The college friends that I had moved away, so it's just me and Remmy."

"And your husband," I heard myself add. I watched as her body tensed and she sat up a little straighter in her chair.

"And Michael," she added earnestly.

Silence fell between us for a moment as I watched Abby's gaze turn back towards the yard. I wanted to reach over and grab her hand, but I didn't. I felt the impulse to tell her that she could confide in me, tell me what's going on in that pretty mind of hers, but I was hesitant to continue the conversation.

"Michael and I..." Abby started to say. My head snapped over to her, my hands still on the bottle before me, "Well, we aren't doing all that great, I guess you could say."

"I figured," I said. "Do you want to talk about it?"

"Honestly, no. I hate talking about it. I hate even thinking about it, but it's been eating me alive keeping it inside." She sighed.

"I hope you know, you can always tell me anything," I told her. Her eyes looked up at me.

"I know that, thank you, Saw," she replied quietly.

I waited for her to continue; to see if she would continue on her own. I took a drink of my beer and set the bottle back down. I tried to think of a back up conversation, anything to see her smile. I didn't want her to be sad, and I could already tell this conversation was bringing back the ghost of the girl I saw the first day.

"Michael is having an affair," she whispered, her eyes trained on her hands in her lap. I felt that familiar burn that I used to try so hard to repress run through my veins and my hands stilled around the bottle.

"Are you sure he is, Abby?" I asked. How in the world, a man could cheat on a beautiful thing like Abby was beyond me.

"Yes." She told me matter of factly.

"Ah. Well, I'm sorry to hear that," I told her honestly, my lips pulling into a tight grimace.

"I knew he had been for awhile now, but he finally admitted it the night before I came home. It's not like he really had a choice though," she let out a small laugh, but it didn't sound like hers. "He came home with lipstick on his neck." She rolled her eyes.

"He, *what?*" I felt the red hot flashes start to spring within me. Abby could tell, too, because she gave me her look; the one she used to give me in school when I needed to calm down.

"Yeah, he came home late, drunk, and pissed off that I had suitcases by the door. He woke me up, to ask me what was going on, when I saw the lipstick on his neck. That was the day that I got let go from work, too. It was a hell of a day." She sighed and took a sip of her beer.

"Damn, Abby."

"Yeah, it wasn't the best. The next morning, Remmy and I got on a plane and came here." She gave me a shrug. "I know I have a lot of decisions to make, things to figure out, but I just can't." She sighed again.

"What are you going to do?" I asked her.

"Hell if I know," she whispered, taking another sip. "But, it looks to me that I'll be needing a divorce lawyer and a job."

"Are you sure that you want to do that? I mean, the divorce. That's a big step. I'd hate for you to go through all of that and realize that it was a mistake." I was being honest with her, saying what a friend would say, but my insides secretly screamed at me to shut the hell up.

"I really think that I do. He's just not the same person anymore. I mean, you heard Remmy. He works *all* the time. During the week, he's never home by nine. Remmy's always asleep before he comes home. On the weekends, he's out golfing or out with his co-workers. He doesn't make any kind of time for us anymore. It's always just Remmy and me."

"What is he doing?" I asked, bewildered. Hearing Abby saying this to me, made my heart hurt not only for her, but for Remmy, too.

"He's out with his friends or co-workers most of the time. He's a Loan Officer, so it is important for him to establish relationships with our Real Estate Agents. He has many real estate friends and they do give him a lot of business, which is great. But that's all he does. Also, the person he's having an affair with, is our top Real Estate Agent in our area, so there's that." She sighed.

"He's cheating on you with a co-worker then?"

"Client Partner," she said with a shrug. "Worst of all, they were doing it right in front of me, basically. I worked at the same company as Michael. He was the LO, I was the Processor. I couldn't work with Michael exclusively on loans since we are married, conflict of interest basically, but I had a desk diagonal to Michael's office, and she would come in all the time. They'd be in there for hours with the door shut and locked. I'm not stupid."

"What the fuck, Abby?"

Abby shrugged half-heartedly and took a drink of her beer. "Then, the day that I ran into you at the gym, right after that anyway, I went to lunch and saw a Facebook post of pictures of her and him. They are no longer hiding it anymore, so there's that. Basically, Saw, my marriage is over."

I looked over at Abby, my heart breaking for her. She offered me a sad smile as she took another drink of her beer. I didn't know what to say or think; how could any kind of man do that to their wife, but most of all, how could anyone do that to Abby?

"And you want your marriage to be over?"

"Well, it's hard to be with a man that tells you that he's no longer attracted to you because you've gone up three or four clothes sizes."

"He said, *what*?" I nearly shouted. My hands clenched tightly around the beer bottle and all I could see was red. The blood pounded in my ears as my eyes trained on Abby's look of defeat. She gave me another small shrug.

"Yeah, pretty much he said that I used to be fun and exciting and that I used to be fucking hot and now here I am, up three or four clothes sizes and letting myself go. He said that he has been screwing her for months and that he needs to get it from somewhere because he doesn't want it from me."

I watched as her nose scrunched up on her last words and she looked away from my stare, wiping at her eyes. I slid out of my chair and walked over to her instantly, crouching down to her eye level. She wouldn't look at me, so I gently moved her chin with my pointer finger to force her eyes towards me.

"Abby," I whispered. Her eyes started to brim with tears, and it nearly broke me into two to see her hurting. "That guy sounds like a fucking douchebag. You are literally the most exquisite woman that I've ever met in my entire life; you're funny, smart, and you are *beautiful*."

"Sawyer, you don't have to say that." Abby's lips were now slowly trembling, and she swiped at her eyes again.

"I'm not saying it to make you feel better, Abby. It's the truth. When I first saw you back here, I thought to myself, wow, she is as stunning as ever."

Abby rolled her eyes at me and tried to pull away from me, but I didn't let her out of my grasp. "I'm serious. Do *not* believe what that asshole said to you. You are letting him take the fire right out of you. Don't let him. That fire that you have, is the most stunning thing about you."

I let go of her chin gently and slid back to the patio chair, hoping like hell I didn't cross a line with her. She looked away from me again, and I could tell she was trying to gain her composure as the silent tears continued to slip down her face. Abby was never one that liked to show her emotions to others; especially to me.

I also needed to cool off; the intense feeling of needing to punch something was hitting me square in the chest, but I didn't want to lose my shit in front of her. The red, hot anger was puddling into my veins, and I felt absolutely ridiculous for feeling this way. There was no reason for feeling so angry towards someone I didn't know, but the words he shared with Abby, felt like a punch to my own gut. I stood up from the patio and started to pace back and forth on the deck. Abby looked up at me, suddenly bewildered. "What's wrong, are you okay?" she asked.

"I just need a minute," I told her gruffly. I placed my hands on the top of my head, walking back and forth.

"*Why?*" she asked, confused.

"Because it just really pisses me off that he said those things to you," I admitted.

"*What?*"

"You deserve better than that, Abby. He's a real jackass for doing that. And not only saying those awful things but *cheating* on you. I don't understand how a man could do that to his wife, or his son. Remmy is an awesome kid; he's so lucky to have a kid like that in his life, and to have you as his wife. He's just....*ugh*," I groaned. "He's just a very lucky man, and the way he's treating you…you don't deserve it, that's all."

Abby stared at me wide eyed as I continued to pace back and forth. Finally, I stopped and turned to her. "You must think I'm crazy."

"Well, yes," Abby admitted, "But I also know that you just have a really big heart."

I rolled my eyes and plopped back down on the patio chair next to her. "Remmy is an awesome kid, you know. You did a great job with him." I told her, kindly. She smiled at me.

"Thank you, Sawyer."

"You're welcome, Abby." I sighed.

"You are kind of scary when you get mad like that, you know. You go into Hulk mode or something." She smiled sheepishly. "Even in high school, you would scare me."

"I'm not scary," I told her.

"No, but you can be, like I said."

"Abby, I'm really sorry you're going through all of this," I told her. "Just know, you're not in this alone. You have great people here who want to support you."

"I know," Abby sighed, "But that's the thing, Saw. We live in Florida, not here." She gave me a sad smile.

Her mother's words from earlier sprang into mind. *She has to be the one to decide to stay, not us.*

"Yes. I know."

"Just another thing to think about." She sighed. "But right now, I'm just going to make the most of the time that I have here with Remmy."

"I think that's a good plan."

We fell into another long silence, listening to the crickets and the other nightlife. Abby leaned her head back into her chair and closed her eyes again. I couldn't help but stare at her as she did so; such an amazing human being, being treated as though she were dirt. Watching her today with Remmy made my entire day; I couldn't get enough of the two of them. Watching them laugh together and play, made my entire body sore. And when Remmy climbed up on my lap and cuddled against my chest, it made me feel like I was on top of the world. How could a man have a woman and son like that, and just ignore them?

It didn't make sense.

Abby swatted her leg quickly, and my eyebrow raised in response.

"I'm getting bit," she admitted with a low laugh. "The mosquitos are attacking me."

"Me, too." I admitted. I've been feeling the tiny insects assault my legs all evening, but I was too engrossed in Abby to pay attention to the tiny stings.

"Shall we call it a night?"

"I suppose so, it is getting late," I told her, even though I really wasn't ready to leave. I stood up from the patio and threw away our empty beer bottles into the outside trash can. Abby stood up, too, but hesitated in her steps.

"Thank you so much for spending your day with us. I know Remmy enjoyed it." Abby smiled.

"I did, too. Thanks for putting up with me all day."

"It's the least we could do," Abby said. "I mean, you did fix the fence."

Slowly, Abby's footsteps came towards me, and I felt my body tense as she approached. I wanted to wrap her in my arms and hug her tightly, but I didn't know how she would react, or how I would react once I had her so close to me. The last thing I wanted to do was scare her away.

"Well, let me know any time that fence needs fixed," I told her. "Happy to come over, anytime."

"We will do that," she said with a soft smile.

"Well," I said, glancing at the sliding glass door, "I suppose I should hit the road. Thanks again, Abby. I had a great time."

"You're welcome," she murmured. I glanced down at her mouth; she was biting her bottom lip again and I felt my insides squirm. I'd give anything right now to bite that lip myself.

"Bye, Abby," I told her.

"Bye, Sawyer," she whispered, her eyes trained on mine.

I awkwardly waved at her; I didn't fucking know why, but I turned to the sliding glass door, when I felt Abby's soft hand, close around my wrist. I turned to her, breath catching in my throat, and looked into her pretty blue eyes. They were sparkling in the darkness, the porch lights illuminating her face.

"Sawyer," she said quietly, "Um, tomorrow. If you're not doing anything, Mom, Remmy, and I are going to the park tomorrow evening. They are having a movie night in the park, I guess." I watched as her shoulders turned into a shrug, a soft smile playing on her lips. I looked down at her lips for a moment too long, and turned my eyes back to hers, noticing that soft crimson started to flush her cheeks.

"Sounds fun, I'll be there."

"Only if you're not busy or if you want to. But if you don't want to, you don't have—"

I interrupted her ramblings by placing two of my fingers to her lips gently; her lips felt soft underneath my fingers and I had the intense urge to find out how they would taste; probably as good as they felt. Her eyes widened and then slowly darkened, as if she knew where my thoughts were leading. I felt the corner of my lip turn upwards as her chest started to rise and fall rapidly.

"I'll be there," I murmured.

Abby dropped her hand from my wrist, and I felt the skin tingle where her hand was. I moved my fingers from her lips slowly, my thumb lingering on her chin a second later.

"Okay," she said, softly.

"Okay," I told her. I turned my body from her, forcing my legs to leave this damn patio before I did something I would regret later. I opened the sliding glass door, but before I escaped into the dimmed kitchen, I turned around to look at her one more time.

She was touching her parted lips where my fingers laid moments before, her eyes bright, and eyebrows raised as she watched me leave. I felt my entire being hesitate; I didn't want to leave her. I could spend all evening on that porch with her getting stung by those damn mosquitos. It would be worth it. I felt my breath catch in my throat again and let out a small sigh.

We're just friends, I told myself.

It would make matters so much easier if my heart would just believe those words, too.

Chapter 10- *Abby*

"Mom, I don't see Soy-er," Remmy said to me with a heavy sigh. "Did you make him pinky promise?"

"He'll be here, Remmy," I replied soothingly. I ran my fingers through his hair, but he quickly moved away from me and glared.

"Mom, you needed to pinky promise with Soy-er!" He rolled his eyes at me and started kicking at the grass next to me, clearly irritated with me.

I let out a sigh and glanced around the park, scanning the large crowds of townsfolk for Sawyer. I knew he would come, but Remmy's anxiety was starting to loom over me. The park was busy with people; all talking in large groups, carrying their chairs and blankets for the upcoming show. Children were running all around the park, giggling with their friends. The playground was the exact same as it was when I was a child; merry-go-round with chipped and faded paint, yellow faded slides and blue equipment. Surrounding the park area were your classic black swings and benches that looked like if you sat on them, they would give you a splinter right on your ass.

"Well, maybe we should get the popcorn and find a seat," I told him, gesturing to the made-up concession stand underneath the pavilion. People I did not recognize were running the stand, handing out popcorn, drinks from a cooler, and a variety of candies. I noticed that my mother was standing by the concession stand, talking to a group of her friends. The flier said the movie night would start at dusk and the sky was slowly darkening into light and dark blue.

"Okay. Soy-er will want some popcorn," Remmy said matter-of-factly. "Maybe some M&M's, too."

"Do you mean *you* want popcorn and M&M's?" I laughed, poking his stomach with my pointer finger. Remmy giggled, his eyes still searching the crowd for Sawyer. His posture suddenly straightened; eyes lighted.

"There he is!" Remmy squealed.

Remmy started sprinting towards the parking lot and I felt my momma fear kick in as my stomach dropped.

"*Remmy!*" I yelled.

I dropped the blankets in my hand and started to take off after him, my flip flops making it near impossible to catch him. The gravel parking lot was dimmed by the nearby timber's lingering shadow and was lined with vehicles. My mind started to race through unthinkable scenarios that only a mother could think of. Sawyer's face suddenly came into view as I sprinted towards them when my flip flop caught on the side of the sidewalk and before I could control myself, my foot slipped and I fell. *Right on my fucking ass.*

I didn't move from my position, but I heard the gasps of the people around me and strangers calling out to me to see if I was okay. I grumbled and nodded to them, waving my hand at them in a carefree way as I laid down in the grass. I wanted to die right here in this park.

"Jesus, Abby, are you okay?" Sawyer's voice was above me and I opened my eyes to him. Sawyer had Remmy securely in his arms, but his eyes were trained on me, with a look of concern and amusement toying on his features.

"Oh you know, just a bruised tailbone and ego," I said with a sigh.

Sawyer extended a hand to me, and I reluctantly accepted it. I looked down at my legs and ankles. All was well, but my face was still heated from all the attention. The group around us disappeared and Sawyer's lips twitched into a smile as he helped me brush off the grass from my back.

"When did you turn so clumsy?" he murmured to me. I laughed.

"When I had Remmy." He grinned at me, when finally I let my eyes devour him. He was wearing gray cotton shorts with a black tee shirt that snugged his biceps. Seriously, every shirt I've seen him wear snugged him so deliciously and I wondered if he had a problem purchasing clothes that were too tight. His head was covered by a plain baseball cap, and he looked casual, relaxed even, as he twirled Remmy in his arms. The grin on his face could have been seen a mile away.

"Remmy, did you run away from your mom?" Sawyer asked, turning his attention to him. Sawyer re-positioned Remmy and held him on his side, as I used to do with him when he was a small toddler. Remmy molded right into him and clung to Sawyer's neck, giggling in response. "Next time, just wait until I get closer, okay? We don't want to give your pretty mom over there a heart attack." Sawyer looked over at me with an impish grin. "Or a broken ankle." He added. I scowled.

"Should we try this again?" Sawyer murmured to me, his eyes scanning me. "Hi."

"Hi."

"How was your day?" he asked casually, lifting his chin to me. *How was your day?* When was the last time a man asked me that? His simple question caused my heart to beat in overdrive all over again. It didn't help that he was close enough that I could smell his rich aroma; his sweet scent filled my body and caused my stomach to turn.

"Great, thanks for asking," I told him. "How was yours?"

"Long. I've been looking forward to this all day." His eyes twinkled.

I turned my face from Sawyer so he wouldn't see the blush and the child-like smile that erupted on my face. The last thing I wanted to do was show him what he was doing to me, but as if he did this all the time, he gently placed his finger on my chin and turned my face back towards him.

"I've been looking forward to seeing that smile all day. Don't hide, now." He flirted. I nearly fell on my ass all over again as the blush on my face intensified.

"How about popcorn?" Sawyer said, turning his attention to Remmy. Remmy nodded fervently.

"And M&M's!" Remmy chanted.

"M&M's it is," Sawyer agreed with a smile.

Together we walked and collected the blankets I dropped, and then we headed to the concession stand. I watched as Sawyer dug through his pockets for his wallet, but I put my hand over his. My fingers tingled as I touched his rough hand.

"It's my treat," I told him, dropping my hand from his. Sawyer rolled his eyes and raised a brow.

"Yeah, that's not happening. I got this, Abs. I want to." He told me. He meandered through his wallet and grabbed out a twenty. "We will do three popcorns, a box of M&M's please, and…" Sawyer scanned the drink menu, glancing over at me. "What would you like to drink?"

My heart was sputtering all over again as I looked at Sawyer. I didn't realize how much I craved simple moments like this until now, and here I was, experiencing this with a man that I never intended to.

"Water would be great," I quietly said. Sawyer must have caught something in my expression because he stared at me for a second longer, his gaze penetrating my very being. His lips turned upward ever so slightly, and without turning away from me, he said, "Three waters, please."

*****

For how busy the park was tonight, we scored decent seats. I laid out large flannel blankets for each of us on the grass and all three of us sprawled out with Remmy in the middle. I laid out a blanket for my mother, but she was nowhere to be seen; eventually I quit looking for her. She'd come around soon enough. The light blues of the sky was changing into a darker color, casting a stunning scene before us; it was soothing to look up at God's beautiful work at hand.

While we waited for the movie to start, Sawyer entertained Remmy and I by throwing pieces of popcorn into the air and catching it with his mouth. Remmy clapped for Sawyer each time, and after a while, tried to intercept the pieces of popcorn with his tiny hands. His fits of mischievous giggles erupted in the air.

"Oh, interception!" Sawyer called out when Remmy batted the piece out of his way. He grabbed Remmy playfully with his arm and gently placed him on the ground, ruffling his hair.

Remmy swatted his leg then, his lips pulling into a slight frown as he stared at his leg. Sawyer got up in a swift motion, pulling a small green bottle out of his other pocket.

"It's buggy out here," Sawyer said. "Let's get some bug spray on you. Is that okay, Mom?" He cocked his head in my direction, waiting for my response. I nodded quickly, unable to speak. *Be still my heart*, I thought to myself. This man was going to have me melt into a puddle by the end of the evening.

I watched as Sawyer sprayed Remmy down, my little boy closing his mouth and eyes tightly shut with his little nose scrunched up in displeasure.

"It smells weird," Remmy said.

"It does," Sawyer agreed, "But with this on, the pesky mosquitos won't feast on you." Remmy's eyes widened and Sawyer chuckled and turned the bottle to me. "Abby?" I nodded, but just as I went to grab the bottle from him, Sawyer's lips pulled back into his carefree smile, and he started spraying me. I closed my eyes and mouth as Remmy had done, and let Sawyer spray the misty liquid over me, goosebumps prickling over me.

"All done," Sawyer whispered. In turn, he started to spray himself, when I noticed a woman hovering over us.

She had short, bouncing blonde curls, and her skin looked unnaturally tanned. Her eyes had a dark eyeshadow and lips painted a bright red. She wasn't smiling though, but rather pursing her lips and she reminded me profoundly of an ostrich, ready to peck the living shit out of us. I tensed in position, ready to pull Remmy to me if I needed to. She looked scary.

Sawyer turned, and I watched as he jumped in place, his mouth dropping in an *"oh shit"* kind of reaction. In his jump, the green bottle tumbled out of his large hand and smacked me right on the forehead.

"Oh, shit, Abby, I'm so sorry," he mumbled quickly, touching my forehead with his hand. I rubbed the spot and glared at him, almost throwing the bottle right back at him.

"Fuck, I mean, *hello*, Miss Edeen," Sawyer said, his face smoothing collectively. He tossed me an apologetic look from beaming me in the face. "How is your summer going?"

"Hi Sawyer," she said, in a clipped, sing-song tone. Her voice to me was like nails on a chalkboard; it hurt my ears. I glanced over at Remmy and watched as his nose scrunched up as well, as if he was chewing on something sour. He leaned backwards and hid behind Sawyer's leg, his eyes never leaving the woman. O*h, for the love of God, please do not say anything, Remmy.* The woman put her hands on her hips and looked down at us.

"Summer is fine. It looks like you're having a cozy little gathering." She eyed me and Remmy speculatively, her fingers waving at the three of us.

"Oh, yes. We are looking forward to the movie," Sawyer politely said. "Miss Edeen, this is my good friend, Abby and her son, Remmy. They are visiting from Florida for the summer." He gestured to us.

"Ah," Miss Edeen said, her eyes studying me. I quickly sat up; her stare wasn't intimidating by any means, but it was…scary. "Nice to meet you."

"It's nice to meet you, too." I told her, forcing a smile on my lips. Remmy thankfully remained silent behind Sawyer. I watched Sawyer's hand come down and rested on Remmy's back. The small gesture sent my heart rapid again.

"This is my co-worker, Miss Edeen. She's the librarian at the school," Sawyer explained. "I hope you enjoy the movie, Miss Edeen. Are you here with your family?"

"My nephews," Miss Edeen said, in the same clipped tone, her eyes now glaring at Sawyer. I have no idea why she was glaring at him, but I had a good guess. I swear if Sawyer slept with that woman, I would probably become violently ill. His bar could not have been that high. "I have to say, Sawyer, it's surprising to see you here. I didn't think you were into this...sort of thing."

Sawyer's eyebrows raised, but he regained his cool expression quickly. I could tell from his posture that he was ready for this conversation to be over. He rubbed Remmy's back soothingly and I eagerly waited for Sawyer's reply.

"What can I say, when a lovely woman asks me to watch movies in the park with her son, I can't say no." Sawyer smiled down at the two of us and I felt my cheeks heat again. Would I ever get used to that smile of his? I looked away from him and Miss Edeen and out into the sky. "And, the movie is *Toy Story*. Who can say no to *Toy Story*?"

Sawyer scooped Remmy up in his arms then, which caused Remmy to erupt in a fit of giggles all over again. Sawyer set Remmy on his shoulder and held on to him tightly, his muscles tensing with the motion. He raised his other arm straight in the air and chanted loudly, *"To infinity, and beyond!"*

I let out a soft laugh, but Miss Edeen did not find it humorous whatsoever. Her beady eyes narrowed more, and she started to cluck her tongue impatiently. *What's with this freakin' woman? I can't believe she works with kids.* Sawyer laughed too, and set Remmy down next to me. I opened my arms to him, and he cradled his tiny body into my embrace. I kissed the top of his head and leaned my chin into his ruffled hair.

"Are you two dating?" Miss Edeen asked, gesturing to the two of us. A loud cough escaped me. I tried to clear my throat to no avail and Sawyer's eyebrows shot up.

"That's kind of a personal question, there Miss Edeen." Sawyer replied, his eyebrows pulling together now. "But if you must know, Abby has been a lifelong friend of mine, and I'm greatly enjoying her company as of late, along with her son's." He paused for a moment before continuing. "It was great to see you, Miss

Edeen. I hope you and your nephews enjoy the movie," he said dismissively. Miss Edeen's eyes widened, narrowed again, and she let out a small huff. *Good, gracious, woman. When did he turn you down?*

"Have a great evening," she said, and she finally walked away from us.

Sawyer let out a soft sigh and sat down next to us, and in a whisper, said, "That woman scares the living hell out of me."

"She is kind of scary," I agreed.

"Terrifying," he mouthed and I couldn't help but smile.

Remmy and Sawyer fell into an amusing game of rock, paper, scissors while we continued to wait for the movie. My heart swelled watching the two of them; Sawyer was making faces at him during each round and Remmy ate it all up.

"Soy," Remmy said, getting up from the ground, "You know I have my first t-ball game soon? Mommy said two more sleeps and it'll be here."

"A little birdie told me that the schedule was up," Sawyer said. "You're going to do awesome, little man."

"Will you come?"

Sawyer hesitated for a moment and glanced at me from the corner of his eye. I remained silent, but secretly hoped in my heart he would agree. Not for me, but for Remmy. He would love a crowd to come and watch.

"I'll be there, buddy," Sawyer agreed. "I'll have to get the schedule from your mom."

"I have a copy in my car," I told him quietly. No need to explain that I made an extra copy, just in case.

Remmy stood up and extended his pinky out to Sawyer, which caused Sawyer to let out his husky laugh; I closed my eyes, soaking it in and memorizing the sound. Sawyer looped his large pinky with Remmy's instantly.

"Pinky promise," he told Remmy sincerely. I wondered how many pinky promises Remmy was going to make him endure until he realized that Sawyer always kept his word.

The projector screen sputtered to life and the crowd around us erupted in cheer. Sawyer clapped among them as Remmy scampered into the middle of us, his eyes alight with excitement. The glow from the screen casted around us as I leaned onto the back of my elbows, kicking off my flip flops into the grass nearby. A soft breeze picked up, and I lifted my head into it and sighed slowly. I noticed from the corner of my eye that Sawyer wasn't watching the screen, but me instead. He was propped on one arm with his front facing us, and he was smiling.

"The screen is over there, Sawyer," I whispered to him, pointing to the movie. The credits just started rolling with Toy Story's theme song, singing, *"You've Got a Friend in Me."* Remmy's eyes fixated on the screen while he shoveled in a large handful of popcorn into his mouth. "Careful, Remmy," I whispered, but he wasn't listening to me.

"I'd rather look at you," Sawyer whispered back, his gaze intently on me. The corners of his lips were turning into that smile again. It was a good thing I was already lying down; if Sawyer kept looking at me like that, I'd probably fall all over again. I tried to cover my impending blush by rolling my eyes at him, but I knew my false attempt probably looked hopeless; the smile on my lips told Sawyer all he needed to know.

"You know, you sure are cute when you blush," Sawyer whispered. Before I could respond, Remmy threw up his hands at us in annoyance.

J. Glassburn

"SHHHHHHH!" Remmy hushed us. *"Woody is coming on!"*

Sawyer and I fell into a fit of chuckles, which made Remmy roll his eyes at us. With his two tiny fingers, Remmy pointed at his eyes, and then back at the screen, which only intensified our laughter. I covered my mouth with my arm to muffle the sound, my eyes the entire time on Sawyer's dancing expression.

Not wanting to piss off the little guy anymore, we fell into silence and watched the movie. Every so often, Remmy would break the silence with his giggles, which always caused Sawyer and I both to look down at him, and then back up at each other. It took everything that I had to look away from Sawyer, but I forced myself to focus on the screen before me. In turn, I could feel Sawyer's gaze on me on numerous occasions and it made my stomach pool with desire. I glanced back at him, gnawing on my lower lip, and found his blue eyes back on me with that cocky grin shining.

I really hated how attractive he was.

I was surprised when I realized we were already halfway through the movie; I could barely pay attention to the screen. Feeling Sawyer's eyes on me and feeling that pull, had all of my attention. I glanced down at Remmy and noticed he was starting to rub at his heavy eyes. I laid out my arms for him, expecting him to cuddle right into me, but instead, Remmy leaned into Sawyer's chest, his head nuzzled right into the crook of Sawyer's neck. I looked at Sawyer's face, to try to gauge any kind of reaction from him, but it didn't seem to faze him. Instead, his face relaxed and he looked perfectly content.

My mind started to work in overdrive as I tried to analyze the situation before me, but I kept telling my busy mind to knock it off. There was nothing to analyze. I was overreacting, like I generally do. Sawyer was just a family friend that Remmy was really starting to like. It was great that he was forming a relationship with a male figure, and Sawyer was one with a kind heart; he was a good one. Sweet. Kind. Charming. Handsome.

Perfect.

I glanced back over at the two of them. Remmy's eyes were closed, fast asleep now on Sawyer's chest. Sawyer's face was tender, and my heart was puddling at my feet yet again. From how Sawyer has been interacting with Remmy the last few days, I knew deep in my heart that he would make a fantastic dad someday. It was a shame he didn't have a family of his own already; he was a natural. He would make any woman proud to be hers.

It nearly crushed me right there to think about how that woman couldn't be me.

Sawyer

"Saw, I swear if you keep whistling like that, I'm going to kick your happy ass right on out of here," Lance said to me, underneath the hood of a beautiful Ford Ranger.

I volunteered to help Lance today at his shop; he has never been one to ask for help, but when he mentioned in passing that he had a lot of work lined up, I told him I'd be there. After delegating some of my summer work out activities to the other coaches in the district, I cleared my schedule for my best friend...and maybe for some other people, but I haven't had the courage to call them yet. I was currently working on a Chevy Equinox and hadn't even realized that I was making any kind of sound.

"Don't be so damn grouchy," I mumbled, but I made a conscious effort to stop. He really would throw me out of here.

"I never knew happy Sawyer was so damn annoying," Lance mumbled.

"I'm always happy."

"No, you're normally brooding."

"That would be you," I retorted lamely. I slid out from underneath the vehicle and looked over at him. He had his back to me, messing with a part on his stool.

"Are you going to see Abby again or something?"

"Remmy wants me to watch his t-ball game, so I'll be seeing them tonight at the field."

Lance nodded, concentrating on the part in hand. He turned his stool over to me and eyed me speculatively.

"You like her, don't you?" Lance scanned my face. I shrugged in response, and he rolled his eyes. "Will you just fucking admit it? This isn't high school dude."

I threw the dirty rag in my hand at him in response. I went back to the Equinox to work on replacing the filter. I could tell Lance was eyeing me, but I ignored him. I wasn't about to start spilling my feelings about Abby, especially to him; mainly because I honestly didn't know how I felt. I've always been comfortable with Abby. She has always been someone that I could talk freely to, someone who's always been a friend, even if we spent most of our childhood fighting.

She was Abby. *My Abby.*

That thought made me pause a little and I shook it away quickly. She couldn't be *my* Abby anymore because she was married. To a douchebag nonetheless, but the last thing I wanted to do was cause Abby more confusion. I didn't want to disrupt her household or be *'the other guy'*, even if her husband was a cheating asshole. I didn't want to put her into a position like that of having to choose. Part of me wondered though, if the real reason was that I was scared that she wouldn't choose me.

I was surprised how great of a time I had with them at the movie night the other day. Remmy was a ball of excitement; he enjoyed it so much, until he fell asleep on top of me. I can't even describe that feeling, I just felt *whole*, like finally I mattered to someone. It also broke me a little knowing that his own dad was missing these moments with him. If I had a kid, especially one like Remmy, there's no way I would miss a beat out of his life.

"It's okay to like her, you know," Lance told me, bringing me out of my own mind.

"Really, though?" I mumbled in response.

"You've always liked her."

"You mean, you *think* I've always liked her," I amended.

"No, you have. Don't forget, I was there, buddy. I got to watch it all."

"Watch what?"

"You falling in love with Abby," Lance said. As he said it, he looked up at me, a somber expression on his face. "When she moved away, and didn't come back, I saw what it did to you."

I clucked my tongue in response and looked away from his sudden intense stare. "I've always liked Abby as a friend."

"That's a lie, and you know it, brother." He went back to messing with the part in hand. "Remember in high school when you punched Luke James in the mouth because he cheated on her? I bet Abby doesn't even know that."

I rolled my eyes, but the memory came back to me vividly. All I remember was seeing red, but it didn't take much back then to set me off. I was angry all the time and I used my fists as my outlet. I'm not proud about it now, especially as a teacher, but back then, if you even looked at me the wrong way, I was ready to go. I scared the hell out of Lance, but he was always by my side, until one day, he told me he was done with my shit and wouldn't back me anymore. That was after I had punched Luke in the jaw.

"He deserved it," I mumbled with a frown.

"He was a douche; I'll give you that," Lance said with a sigh. "But still, there's a reason why you did it."

"Because he was taunting me."

"Maybe," Lance offered, "but I think it had more to do with Abby."

"He was telling everyone at that party, Lance, that he was done getting a piece from Abby and that she was up for grabs." Even thinking about it now sent my blood boiling. "He was a fucking jerk."

"Yes, I remember. I didn't like it either, but I didn't punch him for it."

"That's because I handled it." I said, clenching my teeth. Lance rolled his eyes at me.

"That is beside the point," Lance started. "What I'm trying to get through that thick skull of yours is that Abby is here now. Don't let this opportunity pass you by."

I didn't have a response to that.

*****

"Soy-er!" I was walking up to the baseball diamond, water bottle in hand, when I heard his voice calling to me. I loved the way he said my name and knew right away that it was Remmy. He was standing on the field and waving at me sporadically. I chuckled and waved back to him and gave him a thumbs up. I scanned the fence line, looking for Abby, when my eyes fell on her. She was sitting in a lawn chair next to her mother, her gaze shifting from Remmy to me.

My heart stilled when our eyes locked and she smiled; *God, I loved the way she smiled.* I breathed in and out slowly and approached her.

"Hello, ladies," I said to them both. Her mother beamed at me.

"Sawyer, so good to see you." Mrs. Foster said. "I didn't know you were coming."

"Oh, I wouldn't miss this for the world," I replied. Mrs. Foster smiled at me and turned her attention back to the field. "Hi," I said, crouching down to Abby's level. Abby's eyes were practically sparkling at my words.

"Hi," she said softly.

"How was your day?" Watching her face lift from my simple question made me feel like all was well in the world.

"Great, how was yours?"

"Good, I was at Lance's shop most of the day."

"Oh, I didn't know you worked there," Abby said, scanning my face.

"I just help out when he needs it."

"That's kind of you."

"It's nothing," I said back. I nudged her shoulder with mine and looked back at the field. "How's Remmy today? Excited?"

Abby turned her attention back to the field. Remmy was listening to his coach intently, but I noticed his attention kept averting back over to us.

"Yes, very excited. But I think he was more excited to see you tonight, to be honest." My heart swelled at her words. "Thank you for coming. I appreciate it."

"Oh, I am just as excited to see him. Thank you for inviting me to come." Abby's eyes studied my face for a moment before she quickly turned her attention away.

"Do you want a chair?" Abby asked. "I have an extra in the car. Dad was supposed to come, but he got held up at work."

"I'm okay," I told her, "If I change my mind, I'll let you know."

She nodded and looked straight ahead. I noticed from the corner of my eye that she was fidgeting in her seat. Oddly, the thought that I was making her uncomfortable excited me. I glanced back over at her at the same time she glanced at me, and I smiled sheepishly at her.

"What did you do today?" I asked, fully interested. She could tell me she watched paint dry today and I would be fascinated.

"I worked at Emma's daycare most of the day."

"Oh, how is that going?"

"Good, she runs a great daycare. Good kids, too. I got to hold a few babies today, it was precious," she beamed. "I miss that age."

"Do you plan on having more kids one day?" I blurted. *What the fuck, Sawyer.* Abby's eyes widened a little but I watched as she thought how to respond.

"Maybe," she hesitated. "If I met the right guy, then I would be open to discuss it."

"You will," I told her sincerely.

My stomach started to do an insane amount of flipping as Abby's eyes studied me.   A shy smile appeared on Abby's face and the blush that I loved spread on her cheeks as we looked at each other. Mrs. Foster brought us out of our trance.

"Okay, you two," Mrs. Foster said. "The game is starting." I could hear the humor behind her words and broke eye contact with Abby.

The game started with our team up to bat. The coach was running around in circles; it was clear that he needed the help, but no one had volunteered. He was running back and forth from the dugout, to the batter, helping the kids as much as he could. His face puckered up with apparent stress. I glanced around the parents again, hoping someone stepped up to help, but all the dads remained seated.

Ah, hell.

I glanced over at Abby; she was frowning, too, noticing the same thing as I was. I leaned in over to her and whispered, "Would it be totally weird if I volunteered to help him out? He looks like he's struggling."

Her eyes widened. "No, but Sawyer, you don't need to do that." She placed her hand on my arm, and I felt my body start to burn from her soft touch.

"I don't mind. I just wanted to clear it with you," I said to her. I leaned out of my crouch and looked down at her again. Her eyebrows puddled together. "Are you okay with it?" I asked again; I was having a hard time reading her expression.

"Yes," she said, but her eyes still studied me.

"Then why the look?" I asked her, grinning.

"I'm just trying to figure you out, that's all," Abby said with a sigh.

"Good luck with that," I replied, eyes shining. Abby's lips turned into a smile. As I walked behind her, I couldn't stop my hand from reaching out to her and lightly brush her shoulder as I walked by.

Before I talked to the coach, I had to look back at her. If she was looking back at me, that was a good sign. If she wasn't…well, I'd just have to try a little harder with her. I reached the dugout and cocked my head to see her. She was watching me, her face shining, and I felt a low sigh escape me.

My kryptonite, I mused to myself.

"Hey, man," I said to Henry. "Want some help?"

"Oh, dude, thank you so much. I didn't think it would be this hard to do on my own," he said slowly. "Yes, thank you." I watched Henry's shoulders sag in relief.

I chuckled at him and walked around the fence area to the dug-out entry. Remmy was jumping up and down in his place and barreled right into my legs as soon as I entered the dugout. I gave him a quick side arm hug and ruffled his hair. "Hey, buddy, ready to play some ball? Grab your helmet, let's get lined up."

The game started to transition smoother. The coach stayed with the kids at home plate, helping them plant their feet by the tee while I managed the dugout and first base. The kids all acted as if their parents shot them up with sugar before the game, *holy shit.* I never realized how hyper five-year-olds could be. Remmy was quiet though; he sat on the bench when instructed, cheered his team on when I reminded them to, and when it was his turn up to bat, he gave me a high five, and walked to the plate with his little tongue sticking out in concentration. Before he got his feet lined up by the plate, he turned his head over to his mom and gave her a big wave. I laughed; it was so Remmy.

He cranked that ball all the way to the outfield. My heart leapt as Remmy sat his bat down and sprinted towards me, his face scrunched up with delight. I yelled encouraging words as he sprinted towards me, until his feet hit the base. The other kids didn't even have the ball in their hands yet when he flew by me. The boy had wheels.

"You did it!" I told him, ruffling his hair. I put my fist out and he bumped his against mine. He was grinning ear to ear.

"Yes!" Remmy's little voice said. "That was a great hit, huh?"

"Yes, it was buddy! Now, when the next kid hits the ball, you run to second base, okay?"

"Okay, Soy-er," Remmy said, nodding. I jogged to the dugout and called the next kid up.

Being out in the outfield with the kids was a nightmare, but I tried to keep the kids as enthusiastic as I possibly could. Henry was trying to pump them up, too, but honestly, the kids really could have cared less. They were either kicking at the dirt, picking their nose, or looking up at the sky. A few girls were chatting, holding hands in the field. I looked over at Henry at the same time as he looked at me, and we both started laughing. Five-year-olds were rough.

I showed the kids how to scoop up the ball correctly and how to throw to first base. A few paid attention, but no one paid attention as much as Remmy did. He was soaking in all the information Henry and I gave. When the other team hit the ball close to Remmy, he shagged it up pretty well, and threw it to first base. First basemen didn't catch it, but that's okay. It was the attempt that mattered. I gave Remmy and the first basemen both a fist bump. Remmy positively beamed at me.

"Alright team, that's game!" Henry called. "Great job, everyone! You all did great today! Don't forget to grab your treat at the concession stand before leaving."

The kids ran off to the concession stand like a pack of wild turkeys. Remmy hesitated at the dugout and looked up at me, uncertain.

"You can go with them," I told Remmy. He nodded, gave me a thumbs up, and darted to the concession stand.

"Wow, man, I really appreciate your help today," Henry told me, shaking my hand.

"It was fun," I told him with a chuckle. "And you definitely needed the help."

Henry quickly glanced around, as if he was looking to see if anyone could hear us, when his voice lowered to a whisper. "Is Remmy your boy?"

I shook my head. "He's Abby's. His mom is over there." I pointed over to Abby.

He still looked puzzled as he looked from Abby to me. Abby wasn't paying attention to us; she was packing her chair and talking to her mom.

"Are you dating her?"

My lips pressed into a hard line, but I shook my head no. "We go way back, old friends. She's home visiting for the summer," I told him.

"Ah," Henry said, "I was going to say, way to go Sawyer. He's a great kid, he's the only one who really listened, including my own." Henry made a face, patted my arm, and walked out of the dugout. "Thanks again for your help!" he called to me.

I nodded in response. I grabbed Remmy's baseball stuff and started putting it all into his baseball bag for him. I looked up and saw Abby eyeing me now, her face still looking like she was still trying to figure me out. I wished she would, for the both of us. I gave her a half smile, slung his bag over my shoulder, and walked over to them. As soon as I was in arms reach, Mrs. Foster quickly wrapped me in her arms.

"That was so nice of you, Sawyer. Thanks for helping," she gushed.

"Oh, it was my pleasure. It was hard to sit there and watch Henry struggle like that, yeesh." I chuckled and turned back to Abby, who was still staring at me with a puzzled expression. "How did I do, Abby?"

Abby's eyebrow raised. "Okay, I guess; I mean, you didn't give anyone a black eye, so that's a positive."

I groaned and rolled my eyes. "It was an *accident*, Abby. Will you ever get over that?"

Mrs. Foster started giggling next to us. She touched my arm gently and turned to Abby. "I'll be in the car," she said and I swear, Mrs. Foster winked at her before she left us. I glanced back over at Abby, and she was staring back at me, a small smile on her lips.

"That was nice of you," Abby said.

"It's what I do," I told her. "I love to coach." I shrugged. Abby smiled again as she swayed her hips back and forth, her eyes looking back over at the concession stand for Remmy. He was standing in line quietly, while the other kids erupted in chaos next to him.

"You really do have a great kid," I told her. "He's so well behaved, compared to others. You did a great job."

"Thank you, Sawyer."

"You're welcome."

My eyes zeroed in on the chair slung over her shoulder. "Here, let me grab that from you." I took a step closer to her and lightly grabbed the strap from her shoulder. I noticed a small shudder escape her as my fingertips lightly brushed her collarbone. My eyes zoned in on her pretty blues again and I breathed in a little with my mouth shut.

"Abby," I said to her, taking another small step closer to her. My fingers were messing with the strap on her shoulder.

"Yes?" she asked; it didn't pass my notice that she was now sounding a little breathless. I smiled more widely.

"Would you like to go to dinner with me tomorrow night?" The words tumbled out of my mouth before I could stop them. I had no intention of asking her out, but seeing her standing there before me, wearing damn yoga pants that made her ass look magnificent, a tank top that showed off her smooth shoulders, and the way she smelled like a fucking goddess had me acting like a fool.

One thing was certain though; if I kept repressing my feelings for this girl, I was going to combust. As I watched her from the sidelines today, cheering for her son, jumping in the air when he hit the ball, made me realize that she was a girl that was worth all of the unknowns and uncertainties. I had to get to know her more and break that wall she so carefully surrounded herself with.

Abby's eyes widened, and her lips mashed into a tight line. She tried to take a step back from me but staggered in her steps. I caught her arm, my eyebrow raising speculatively.

"Oh," Abby said quietly. She looked away from me to Remmy, who was still standing in line, and then back at me. "Sawyer, I don't know," she whispered to me. Her eyes looked around the crowd of parents who were waiting for their own children. None of them were paying attention to us and even if they heard me, I didn't care. I'd shout from the rooftops and ask her out if that's what it would take.

I've cared for this girl since we were kids, and I was finally going to chase her.

"You don't know because you don't want to go with me?" I grabbed the chair from her and slung it over my own arm.

"No, it's not that...."

"Then, your hesitation is because of...?"

Abby tried to look everywhere but at me, but I moved my head into her eye direction, a smile playing on my lips. Abby sighed and looked right at me, biting on her bottom lip. Her nose scrunched up in the cutest way.

"I just don't know if it's a good idea," Abby finally said.

"Ah," I told her. I tried to hide my own disappointment with a smile, but I knew it probably looked weak. "I get it Abby. It's no problem." I took a step away from her, but before I left her alone, I turned back and leaned into her, my lips close to her ear. I grinned as I watched a shudder rip through her. "I'm going to keep my schedule free tomorrow night regardless. If you change your mind, call me."

"I don't have your number," Abby said weakly, turning her pretty blues to me.

"Your parents do," I told her, walking away from her before I said anything else fucking stupid. "I'll put this in your car for you."

It hurt like a bitch to walk away from her, but I knew I had to let her process what had just happened. If there's one thing I remembered about Abby is that she didn't like change; she didn't like to feel cornered or pressured into anything. She needed time, and I understood that. Even as the words tumbled out of my mouth, I knew I was probably asking way too soon, but it was those eyes and that damn smile.

Even as I approached her mother's car, I knew I'd wait forever for that girl.

Chapter 11- *Abby*

"You told him no?" Emma asked, appalled. We were sitting in her office on lunch break; I was eating a sub sandwich and she was picking at a salad. I had just taken a big bite of my sub so I couldn't speak, but nodded, covering my mouth.

"Why on earth would you say no, Abigail?" Emma asked, her face suddenly stern.

I rolled my eyes and grabbed my napkin, trying to swallow quickly so I could answer.

"Emma, are you forgetting that I'm *married*?" I told her. I grabbed my soda and took a long drink of it. Emma's face turned to disbelief.

"For how long, Abby? Aren't you looking for divorce attorneys?"

"That's not the point," I told her. "I'm still married." I took another bite of my sandwich as Emma shook her head at me.

"It is the point, Abby. Do you not realize how big of a catch Sawyer Gibson is? He's a fucking god! He's gorgeous, he's kind, and smart, and he likes you!" Emma said. She dropped her fork and fell back into her chair dramatically. I rolled my eyes at her again; always the dramatics with that one.

"He is kind, and sweet, and yes, he's kind of sort of perfect, but he has no idea what he's getting himself into," I told her, avoiding eye contact with her.

"I think he does," Emma said. She raised her fingers in the air. "For one, he swims all day with you and spends time with you and Remmy. Two, he goes to the movie night with you and Remmy, and you all have a blast. Three, he goes to Remmy's baseball game and ends up not only watching but coaching. Four, he adores Remmy, and Remmy likes him too. He knows what he's getting himself into, Abby. He knows you have a child, so it's not like it's a surprise at this point."

"It's not all fun and games sometimes. It can get messy, too. Sawyer was never one to deal with that kind of stuff. I just don't want to get Remmy's hopes up, ya know?"

"Get Remmy's hopes up, or *your* hopes up?" she amended, her eyebrows raising.

"Remmy's."

Emma pursed her lips and shook her head at me. *"Bullshit,"* she said, picking her fork back up again. "And is it really fair to say that Sawyer can't handle messy? You don't know him anymore, Abby, and you can't compare him to his high school self. Plus, he was going through a lot back then. He's older, more mature, and we can't forget that he's sexy as hell. Please go out with him. I need *details.*"

We both started laughing and I clutched at my sides. "Stop making me laugh, I have to pee," I told her. Emma grinned and shook her head at me again.

"I'm not joking though; can you imagine how great he is in bed? Wowza." She stabbed her salad with her fork. "Talk about yummy."

"You're too much," I told Emma, picking at my sandwich. "It's not all about sex, either."

"Mmm..." Emma said, nodding her head at me. She swallowed the bite she had and continued. "No, it's not, but it's a great compensating factor, and just by looking at his abs at your swim party the other day, he would be fabulous."

I giggled. "Maybe he's really bad." I told her, shrugging. "You don't know that he's good. The abs could be his way of overcompensating."

She swayed her head back and forth, contemplating my thought, but shook her head quickly. "No, I bet Sawyer is very good in bed. The only way to know for sure, is to take the plunge and find out. How long has it been for you anyway?"

I pursed my lips, trying to think of the last time that Michael and I did have sex, but came up blank. I shrugged. "I can't even remember."

"Ugh, I hate that for you."

"How often do you and Dustin have sex?" Emma grinned mischievously.

"Whenever we possibly can." She sighed. "Dustin is extremely good in bed. Well equipped, if you know what I mean." Emma waggled her eyebrows at me. I let out a playful groan but snickered.

"Oh, stop, I don't want to hear that."

"It's the truth," Emma said with a smile. "The first time I saw it, I was nearly speechless. I almost fainted, swear Abby."

I giggled again and shook my head at her. I reached over the table and lightly grabbed her hand into mine.

"I've missed you," I told her genuinely, giving her a sad smile. "I'm so glad we have reconnected."

Emma beamed back at me and patted my hand with hers. "Oh, my Abby, I missed you, too. You've always been the sunshine in my life."

"I'm not very sunny lately," I mumbled, taking my hand from hers. Emma's lip turned into a frown, and she looked at me, her eyes suddenly intense.

"You are. You just need to look for that ray within yourself. It's there, you just don't see it right now."

I sighed and set my sandwich down and took another drink of my soda. Emma went back to picking at her salad, when she whispered, "Soo...you gonna call Sawyer and go out with him tonight or what?"

"Emma..." I groaned.

"I think you're looking far too into this situation. You go out tonight, just as friends, catch up without Remmy there. Get to know Sawyer again, the *real* Sawyer," she encouraged.

I groaned again in response.

"You know you want to. You can't deny that," Emma said, pursing her lips into a know-it-all look that I knew so well. I let out a sigh.

"I don't have anything nice to wear," I mumbled.

"My closet is at your disposal. Looks like we are close to the same size," Emma said, waggling her eyebrows again. "I can even do your hair, if you'd like."

"I don't have his number."

"Oh, that's too bad. But I do!" she added brightly. She snatched up her cell phone and pulled up Sawyer's number in her contacts. I cocked an eyebrow at her.

"Why do you have Sawyer's number?" Emma shrugged nonchalantly in response.

"He helped me out here quite a bit in the beginning phase."

"*Of course, he did,*" I mumbled. Emma put the phone by my sandwich and grinned at me. I slowly shook my head.

"Emma..." I said again.

"Again, it doesn't have to be anything more than two friends catching up, Abby. Go out and have fun." She cocked an eyebrow at me, waiting patiently for me to decide. I mashed my lips together, sighed, and then grabbed my cell phone from her desk. I glanced down at Sawyer's number which was displayed on Emma's phone and started dialing. I had to stop, clear, and re-dial again from missing the correct buttons.

Emma squealed and clapped her hands together as I brought the phone to my ear. The dial tone came on the other end and my heart started racing. *Don't pick up, don't pick up.*

"Hello," Sawyer said, breathlessly on the other end.

"Hello," I responded. I turned my back to Emma because she was grinning like a fool and I couldn't look at her anymore, afraid I would start busting up like a crazy teenager. For a split second, I felt like we were back in high school; Emma and I had this moment too many times to count.

"Abby?" Sawyer asked. He sounded surprised.

"Yes, this is Abby," I said quietly. There was a pause on the other end.

"It's great to hear from you," Sawyer finally said.

"Yeah, well, Emma gave me your number. I'm at her daycare center right now."

"Ah," Sawyer said. "How's your day so far?"

Why is it, when Sawyer asks a simple question like that, my heart and stomach both flutter? I closed my eyes and slowly drew in a breath.

"It's pretty good so far. I'm just having lunch. How is your day?"

"Pretty good, I'm helping Lance again today. I would be having lunch, but Lance is a damn drill sergeant." I heard a muffled sound on the other end and snickering. I held the phone out a little, a smile playing on my lips. God only knows what those two are up to. Sawyer started laughing. "Lance says hello."

"Hi Lance," I said brightly.

"So…what can I do for you, Abby?"

I hesitated, drew in a breath, and tried to get my heart to simmer down. "Um. Well. I was thinking about… well… I am free for dinner later," I added lamely. I rolled my eyes and cursed myself for sounding like an idiot. Emma giggled in the background, and I threw her a stern look. She muffled her giggles with her hands. Yep, this was just like our high school days.

Sawyer didn't say anything, and my heart sank. "Unless you don't want to go anymore, that's completely fine. I totally understand since—"

"Abby," Sawyer said, chuckling. "Of course I still want to go. I was hoping you'd call today."

"Okay," I said. *Okay? What?* Sawyer chuckled again.

"Okay," he replied softly. "I'll swing by and pick you up. How about six? Too early? Too late?"

"Six is fine."

"Awesome, well I will see you then."

"Okay," I said again.

"Okay," Sawyer replied.

"Bye, Sawyer," I told him.

"Goodbye, Abby." His voice sounded lifted on the other end, and I heard Lance whistling in the background, and Sawyer telling him to fuck off. I laughed a little and hit the end button.

I looked up at Emma, and she was staring at me, her eyes bright with excitement.

"Time to hit my closet," she said, nodding.

What the hell have I gotten myself into?

Sawyer

I have no idea what's gotten into me. All I know, is that I've been acting like a fucking chick for the last forty minutes and it's starting to piss me off. My bedroom was torn apart; I had several discarded shirts lying on the bed and the floor and I still had no idea what to wear tonight. It would help if I knew what Abby was going to wear, but that's not something a man asks. I didn't want to dress up too much if she didn't and make her uncomfortable, but I also didn't want to dress too down and give her the impression that I didn't give a fuck.

"Quit acting like a fucking girl," I mumbled underneath my breath.

I stared at my closet again and with a heavy sigh, said, "*Fuck it.*" I grabbed my navy-blue dress jeans and my white collared button up shirt. The shirt had a soft gray intricate pattern. I quickly pulled on the clothes and stared at my reflection in my bedroom mirror. I rolled up my sleeves to my elbow and started to button up the shirt. I opted for my light brown belt and matching shoes and took another long look at myself in the mirror. It would have to do.

I had plans to take her to *Brenna's* this evening; it was a nice restaurant in a nearby town, but now I was second guessing my decision. I already had the reservations made, but now wondered if it would be *too* much. Maybe Abby thought this was just a casual dinner? *Brenna's* could be a casual dinner, I guess, but the ambiance is what *makes* the restaurant. Their menu was a tad pricey, too, but not that I was worried about that. I *wanted* to take Abby somewhere nice with a quieter setting, so we could talk freely, but I also didn't want to scare her off.

I walked to the bathroom and started to gel the ends of my hair, noting to myself that I probably should have gotten a haircut today. It was too late now, though. My beard was also becoming entirely too scruffy; I quickly unbuttoned my shirt and threw it over the top of the bathroom door and started trimming.

I glanced down at the clock, and it was five forty-five; *time to go*. I slid my shirt back on, buttoned it back into place and looked around my house for my keys and cell phone.

"Keys, keys..." I mumbled to myself. "*Fuck*, where are they?" I looked all around the house, the kitchen a few times, only to discover they were right where I left them earlier; in a small bowl I kept on the kitchen counter, *for my keys*. "Jesus, Sawyer," I mumbled.

My hands started to get sweaty, and I decided to wash them again in the kitchen sink. I spent a little too much time scrubbing at my hands, letting the hot water sting my skin, my mind racing a million miles per minute; I took a deep breath and rinsed the suds off my hands.

My heart rate was increasing with every step I took to my truck, and I felt like my stomach was doing rapid somersaults, my insides slightly squeamish. I don't know why I was acting this way. This was just dinner with a friend; that's what I kept telling myself anyway. I started the truck and let the engine come to life before I backed out of my drive.

I was at the Foster's residence all too quickly; my hands were starting to feel clammy again. I cursed at myself silently, took a deep breath, and forced my legs to move out of the truck. My heartbeat matched every step that I took to the front door. I wiped my palms on the back of my pants, took a deep breath, and knocked on the familiar, red door.

Mr. Foster opened the door; he was in blue jeans and a white polo, reading glasses still on; his glasses didn't hide the apprehension clouding his eyes; he scanned me up and down, lips pursed into a fine line.

"Sawyer," Mr. Foster said in a clipped tone. *Jesus, why did I feel like I was suddenly back in high school?*

"Mr. Foster," I said, forcing a smile on my almost trembling lips. I extended a hand to him. Mr. Foster didn't hesitate to shake it, but he eyed me with a penetrating glare the entire time. "How are you this evening?" I asked.

"Confused."

"Ah," I said. I wanted to take a step back from his intimidating stare, but knew it was best to stand my ground with him. I never found Mr. Foster to be an intimidating man; he and I shared many conversations together, and all in all, I thought he respected me, but at this very moment, I was second guessing every thought I had towards him.

"Oh, knock it off," I heard Mrs. Foster say from the hallway. She walked behind Mr. Foster and looped her arm casually into Mr. Foster's. "Come in, Sawyer," she told me. I couldn't help but notice that the smile on her face didn't match what her eyes were telling me.

"Thank you," I said, forcing confidence into my voice.

I took a step into the entryway and glanced around the living room looking for Abby, but she wasn't in the room. I suddenly felt very warm. I almost told them that I would wait outside for her but refrained. I wasn't a kid anymore, I was an adult, and I knew I should be more equipped to handle situations like this.

"You look very handsome," Mrs. Foster said kindly. I nodded my appreciation towards her with a smile.

"Thank you."

"Where are you taking her?" Mr. Foster piped in. I cleared my throat before responding.

"I have reservations at *Brenna's*," I offered. Mrs. Foster's eyes widened a bit.

"That's a nice place. I haven't been there in ages," she said with a warm smile. "I'm sure Abby will love it."

"I hope so."

"She's just finishing up upstairs," Mrs. Foster said with a nod.

"Great," I replied weakly and cursed at myself internally. I was not acting like the confident person that I knew I was.

I felt as if the tension in the air would swallow me whole. I didn't know what to do with my hands, so instead of letting them dangle like a fool next to my sides, I shoved them into my pocket hoping it would calm my fidgeting hands. I kept glancing up the oak stairs for her and strained myself to listen for her footsteps but all I could hear was the silent ticking of the Foster's nearby grandfather clock.

"No funny business," Mr. Foster said, breaking the silence. Mrs. Foster threw him a scathing look that greatly reminded me of Abby's.

"Not at all, sir," I replied.

Yep, I was back in fucking high school.

"She is married, you know," Mr. Foster told me.

And now I wanted to crawl in a hole and die.

"I'm aware of that, sir. I promise, it's just dinner." I nodded at him, mashing my lips into a tight line. He eyed me shrewdly and Mrs. Foster nudged him.

"Craig, why don't you go into the kitchen and order that pizza for us?" Mrs. Foster said. He grunted in agreement and threw me a cold stare before he disappeared into the kitchen. Mrs. Foster watched him go, and then turned to me, offering me a kind, but somewhat forced smile.

"Don't mind him, he's just…processing," Mrs. Foster said. I nodded, not knowing what to say.

"It was kind of you to ask her to go out," Mrs. Foster said. "She's been kind of down, with all this divorce business. I know she's looking forward to your dinner."

I offered her the best smile that I could, but the lump in my throat was getting larger. I hadn't even known that Abby was expressively talking about divorce, let alone with her parents. I wondered how much they knew about her situation with him and if she told them what she shared with me about Michael.

I heard the quick footsteps on the wooden floor before I saw him. Remmy came bounding down the stairs, with his usual goofy smile. I opened my arms to him and felt my body instantly relaxed as he lunged towards me. As he threw his tiny body into my outstretched arms, I felt the strings of my heart tug a little.

"Hi, Soy-er." Remmy sang. "You are very dressed up." He eyed me up and down, his little eyebrows scrunched together. My heart panged a little in my chest at his words. Did that mean his mother wasn't? Was I overdressed? *For fuck's sake...*

"Hi, Remmy. Yes, I am." I looked down at my outfit and chuckled a little.

"Mommy looks *real* pretty," Remmy said, beaming. "She's wearing a dress. Mommy *never* wears dresses."

I let out a low sigh in relief and crouched down to his level.

"I can't wait to see her." Remmy grinned his front toothless smile at me.

"Mommy said I can go to dinner next time," Remmy said, nodding. "I'm going to have pizza with Grandma and Grandpa tonight and we are going to watch *Spider-Man*!" Remmy flailed his arms around, acting like he was spinning webs with his hands. I chuckled at him and ruffled his hair.

"Absolutely you can go next time. Pizza and *Spider-Man* sounds cooler though. I think you have the better end of the deal tonight," I said. Remmy beamed.

"Do you like *Spider-Man*?"

"Uh, *yeah*. Who doesn't like *Spider-Man*?" I made a face at him and poked his side with my finger; he giggled.

Just then, I glanced up at the wooden staircase and felt my breath catch in my throat all over again.

"Wow," I said out loud. "You weren't wrong, kid." I mumbled to Remmy. He beamed in response and looped his tiny hand into mine, looking up at his mom. I stood up from my crouch slowly, my heart taking off as if I just ran a marathon and drunk her in. She was wearing a light blue sundress that magnified her eyes, intensifying her pretty blues. The top of her dress swooped loosely into a V, and the bottom was hanging loosely around her, the front shorter than the back, but still exposed those perfect legs of hers with her feet strapped into clear heels. Around her waist, she had a brown belt hanging loosely around her.

Abby was slowly walking down the staircase towards me; her eyes were drinking me in as I was her. From the way her mouth slowly popped open, I think she liked what she saw, too. I felt a satisfied sigh escape me as I beamed at her. I couldn't help but be in complete awe of her.

I was a lucky son of a bitch.

"Hi," I forced out.

"Hi," Abby said, flashing me a wide smile. Her cheeks pulled together, exposing those adorable as fuck dimples again.

"You look beautiful," I told her; I knew I was grinning like a fool. Mrs. Foster was suddenly biting her thumb nail, looking back and forth between the two of us.

"Thank you," she whispered. I watched that beautiful crimson color that I was growing to love flush her cheeks.

Abby looked down to Remmy, who was still holding my hand and opened her arms to him. He leaned into her embrace, and she kissed the top of his head.

"Mommy, you smell good," Remmy said. Abby giggled and patted her son's cheeks.

"Thank you, baby," Abby said. I felt my heart constrict at her words, wishing for just a second that she was directing those words to me. "You be good for Grandma and Grandpa tonight, okay? When they say it's bedtime, *it's bedtime.* No fighting." She raised her eyebrows at him and pointed a finger at him. Remmy rolled his eyes and made a face. "I'm serious, Remmy." She leaned back down and kissed his cheek.

Seeing Abby as a mother was so damn attractive; I don't know what it was, but it was fucking adorable, and I couldn't get enough of seeing her this way.

"Okay, Mommy."

"I love you."

"I love you too, Mommy." He leaned back in and gave her a hug. "I'll miss you." Remmy's lips started to pout, and I felt my stomach flip again. *Fuck.* I didn't even think about what this would do to him. Abby's lips fell into a frown, too, but she gave him a reassuring pat on the arm.

"You will have so much fun with them, I promise." A look of concern washed over Abby's face, and it made me look from Abby back to Remmy several times.

"I bet you that Grandma will even read you a story tonight if you ask her really, really nicely," Abby said. Remmy looked up at Mrs. Foster, who nodded quickly.

"Anything you want," Mrs. Foster said to him.

She held out her hand for Remmy. He looked back up at me with sad eyes; I felt my heart nearly crumple in my chest at his faltered gaze. I held out a fist to him and he bumped his with mine, but the smile I was growing accustomed to seeing, didn't quite meet his eyes.

"You will be fine," Abby told him with a low laugh. "I promise."

Remmy's face went into a pout, and I prayed to the Lord above that he didn't start crying. If he started crying, there would be no way I would be able to steal Abby away from him tonight; it would crush me. Remmy didn't cry though and instead took his grandma's hand. Mrs. Foster offered us a reassuring nod.

"Have fun, you two," she said.

"Not too much fun," we heard Mr. Foster boom from the kitchen. I let out a low chuckle, and Abby rolled her eyes.

"Goodbye, everyone. I love you," Abby said, waving. Her eyes met mine and it was like they were holding me in place; I was frozen and in complete admiration of how beautiful her eyes were. Blue was a wonderful color on her, and it was starting to become my favorite.

"Ready?" she asked.

I nodded quickly, clearing my throat and opened the door for her. I waved goodbye to Remmy and Mrs. Foster. Mr. Foster was now leaning on the kitchen doorway with his arms folded across his chest with a sour expression. I nodded in his direction politely, but before I left the house, I took a few strides over to Remmy and held out my fist to him again.

Remmy's pouty look sprang into that goofy smile of his as he crushed his fist against mine again. "Have a great night, buddy." I ruffled his hair quickly and took off after Abby.

Abby waited for me on the sidewalk, clutching her tiny purse tightly. Her body was rigid as she waited for me patiently. I shut the door and quickly sprang to her side.

"You ready, Miss Abby?" I asked her, holding my arm out to her. She nodded solemnly, her gaze going back to the house, and I followed her line of vision. Standing in the living room window was Remmy. The curtain tangled around his head as he waved sadly at us, his little lip pouting out.

"Oh, man, that's enough to break my heart," I said, clutching my chest. I waved back at the little guy, my own lip pouting now, and Abby chuckled at me. She blew Remmy a kiss and a wave, and we watched as Mrs. Foster ushered him out of view. I turned back to Abby; my lip still puckered out.

"*Do we stay?*" I asked her incredulously. Abby let out her loud, sweet laugh and took a step toward me. She looped her arm in with mine and pulled me in the direction of my truck. The parts of my arm that she was touching started to prickle; I loved the way her arm felt intertwined with mine.

"We don't stay," she said, still laughing. "He'll be okay. He's just not used to being without me, that's all."

I sighed dramatically.

"There's no way I'd be able to handle that little lip; he'd get his way every time with me. You have grace, Abby Lou," I said to her, using my old nickname for her. She stopped short and looked up at me, her eyes and lips pulling into a smile.

"No one's called me Abby Lou in such a long time," Abby said with a small laugh.

"Well, now you can't say that." I walked Abby to the passenger side of the truck and opened the door for her. Her eyes opened in surprise, and she gave me a teasing look.

"Well, well, well, Sawyer, good looking *and* chivalrous?"

My heart rate took off like a bat outta hell. I narrowed my eyes at her and took a slow step toward her. I almost laughed out loud as her eyes and mouth popped open.

"You think I'm good looking, Abby?" I asked her softly, leaning closer to her. Instead of backing up, I noticed she was drawing nearer, her eyes narrowing and her lips pulling upwards.

"Caught that, did you?"

I nodded in response and looked into her eyes again. A strand of her hair moved with the breeze, and I reached for it with my fingertips. Her hair felt soft in my fingers, and I fought the desire of putting my hand further into her hair. I wanted to feel everything about this woman; how her hair felt in my hands, how her lips would feel against mine, how her bare chest would feel against my own…

This woman absolutely terrified me.

I put the strand back in place and held out my hand to her, to help her hop into my truck, but she was staring at me still, trancelike. I chuckled softly and closed my eyes before I gave in to the desire of pushing her against my truck.

"Up now, Abby," I said. Abby shook herself out of the reverie and nodded quickly.

"*Right*," she mumbled. She grabbed my hand, and I helped her into my truck. I closed her door for her. I opted to walk behind the truck to my door; as soon as I was behind the cab, I quickly adjusted the growing bulge in my pants.

If this was how it was already starting, this was going to be a difficult night.

Chapter 12 - *Abby*

As soon as I laid eyes on Sawyer this evening, I felt the immediate fluttering in my stomach, and the feeling still hasn't gone away. He was too handsome for his own good; his cocky smile, the way his eyes lit up when he laughed. He also smelled unbelievably good; *too good*. When he leaned into me by his truck, I couldn't help but inhale his husky scent. I probably would have let him take me right there and then if he tried.

Thank God he didn't.

I was nervous when he got into the truck; my heart rate wouldn't slow down, and my legs were starting to tremble. Being in his truck though eerily sent a wave of comfort through me. After all, I've been in this same truck before. I found myself looking around, taking it all in. It was meticulously clean; typical Sawyer, and his husky, sweet scent lingered in the air around me. I was inhaling sweet smell, trying to stick it to memory. It was a mixture of cologne with a woodsy smell. I forgot how intoxicating his aroma was to me. When he slid into the truck next to me, he looked over at me with the same cocky smile. He leaned back in his truck before he started it, and said, "Never thought you'd be back in this truck, Abs."

"Me neither," I told him with a laugh. "I'm pretty sure the last time I was in here, I told you that you were the most despicable person that I've ever met in my life."

Sawyer let out a booming laugh as he turned the truck on. I listened to the engine roar; it was the exact same sound that I memorized once, long ago. In my teen years, I used to listen for that sound, hoping I would hear it, just to get a glimpse of the Sawyer Gibson.

"You did," Sawyer agreed. "And I'm pretty sure you flipped me off all the way to your front door." He chuckled again and pulled out the driveway.

"Sorry," I said, "I was very dramatic back then. I sort of still am," I admitted, thinking of how I flipped Michael off back in Florida.

"I wouldn't expect anything else," Sawyer said with a smile. "Honestly, I kind of liked it when you got mad at me."

I pulled my eyebrows together and looked over at him questionably. He the glanced from the road to me and snickered.

"You were so cute when you were mad," he admitted with a shrug. "I used to love to get a rise out of you."

I rolled my eyes at him.

The entire drive was easy conversation. We talked about his summer plans, and how football camp would be gearing up in the next few weeks. He asked about Emma's wedding, and how she was doing with the planning. I didn't really know how to answer that because Emma never really talked about her wedding that was slowly approaching, which I thought was odd. I made a mental note to ask her about it the next time I saw her.

When we reached the restaurant, I couldn't help but smile over at Sawyer.

"Brenna's?" I asked. He nodded sheepishly.

"Is that okay? Is it too fancy? If it is, we can go anywhere else. It doesn't matter to me." Sawyer shrugged nonchalantly. To shut up his ramblings, I put my hand lightly on his arm.

"It's perfect, seriously. I haven't had this since...well..." I tried to think. "Probably homecoming?"

"Nope," Sawyer said, disagreeing with me. He waited for me to guess, but I honestly had no idea what he was referring to. "Prom," he prompted.

My eyes widened and I put my hand to my lips.

"Oh, that's right."

The memory flashed back to me as I looked at Sawyer, my heart fluttering again. He was referring to the time that he swept in and saved the day; more than he knew, too. He had pointedly refused to go to his Senior Prom. He wanted nothing to do with it, even though Lance had a date and was going. He told anyone and everyone that would listen that Prom was fucking stupid. He was asked to go by so many girls, too, but he turned all of them down. Not nicely either, might I add, which was so unlike Sawyer. I knew why he was acting that way; he was going through a very dark time and used his anger as his shield. He used to scare me sometimes when he went off the deep end. There were times that I didn't even want to approach him.

"You saved the day," I told him earnestly. He shrugged, his face suddenly reddening. "Sawyer Gibson, are you blushing?" I teased.

"Let's eat, shall we?" Sawyer said, ignoring me with a chuckle. I laughed, too. I went to open my door, but Sawyer pulled my arm back quickly. I raised my eyebrows at him. "I will get your door," he said.

"Oh, knock it off, I can open my damn door." I brushed him off and pushed it open. Sawyer was at my side in a flash though, pretending to glare at me. I made a face at him in return, which caused his face to light up.

Sawyer extended his arm to me, and I looped mine in between his. I was surprised by how easy and comforting I felt with him; it felt like we'd been doing this for years, when in reality I only had the opportunity to do this a few times with him. Touching his bicep sent a trickle of shivers through my spine; I was enjoying this all too much with him, more than I should.

"Hope you're hungry," Sawyer said, eyes dancing, while he opened the door for me. As soon as I was out of Sawyer's reach, I craved to be nestled right where I was.

I followed Sawyer to the hostess station; a teenage girl stood there; she had her black hair pulled up in an unkept ponytail, her eyes gazing off into nothing it seemed, as she said in a monotone voice. "Welcome. Name?"

Sawyer cleared his throat before exchanging glances with me. "Sawyer Gibson, reservation for 2."

I nudged Sawyer's shoulder with mine. "Reservation?" I mouthed, eyeing him. He grinned at me but turned his attention back to the hostess.

"Yes, follow me," she said with a heavy sigh. I looked back over at Sawyer, scrunching my nose, and making a face at him. He looked away quickly, stifling a laugh.

We followed the hostess throughout the restaurant; I blinked my eyes a few times, as if that would help me adjust to the dimly lit room. The restaurant looked the same to me as it did over ten years ago. Some of the walls were brick, while the others were painted a dark maroon red. Pictures of wine glasses and bottles and other abstract paintings hung on the walls. I looked around the restaurant seating and noticed that there wasn't an available table in sight; each dark cherry wooden table had occupants. The smells of fish, chicken, and potatoes and intense seasonings wafted in the air; it made my stomach gurgle.

The waitress brought us to the corner of the restaurant and dropped two menus on a smaller booth. It was perfect for two people. The table had a lit candle and cloth napkins.

"Your waitress will be with you momentarily," the hostess mumbled. Sawyer and I both thanked her and slid into the smooth black booths.

As soon as I sat across from Sawyer, I felt my heart start to sputter again. In the truck, it was so easy conversing with him, but now, sitting across from him directly, his piercing eyes on me, made me almost want to throw up. Sawyer looked at me briefly, and then started to fidget with the black menu in front of him, and I wondered if he was nervous, too.

"I don't even remember what's good here," I told Sawyer, picking up my own menu.

"Hmm…" Sawyer mused, glancing at his menu. "If I remember correctly, they have really good fried chicken."

"That sounds good," I offered.

Sawyer nodded, looking down at his menu. I started to peruse my own menu, seeing if anything stuck out to me. All that really sounded good was a glass of white wine to calm my shaky nerves.

The waitress popped in quickly with her notepad. She was a pretty girl; maybe early twenties, and she had slick blonde hair that was pulled up into a bun. She wore little makeup, but that's because she probably didn't need it. She was naturally pretty. She wore black dress pants, a white button up shirt, and had a black apron overtop. She beamed at us, but maybe a little too much at Sawyer. I couldn't blame her though; the dim lights just added to Sawyer's glory.

"Hi," she said, looking right at Sawyer. To my surprise, Sawyer paid no attention.

"Hello," he said, still looking down at his menu.

"I'm Hallie and I'll be your server today," she chimed.

I felt an intense groan escape my throat at her singsong voice and her *name*.

Sawyer and the waitress Hallie both shot me puzzled looks, Sawyer's eyes widening with a bemused smile.

"Something wrong?" the waitress Hallie asked haughtily. Her delicate blonde eyebrow shot in the air.

"Oh, I'm *so* sorry, I didn't mean to do that out loud. Hello Hallie," I said quickly and apologetically. She didn't look any happier though, but rather sourer. "Sincerely, I'm so sorry."

I felt my cheeks slowly burn as Sawyer started to laugh out loud, and not just a chuckle, but a gut-wrenching laugh. "Maybe I should give you both a moment," the waitress said, in a rather clipped tone.

"No, I'm so sorry. Um, I'll have a glass of white wine," I offered.

"What kind?" she asked, not making eye contact with me; she was rather snippy, not that I can blame her. "Um, Moscato will be fine, thank you." She turned to Sawyer then, who asked for a bottle of Bud Light. She nodded, threw me a distasteful look that I rightfully deserved, and then shot towards the bar.

I groaned again once she was out of earshot and put my face in my hands; my cheeks were still burning. Sawyer leaned over the table at me, snickering and tried to pull my fingers away from my face.

"What the hell was *that*, Abby?" he asked, trying to contain himself.

"I don't know," I admitted. I closed my eyes again, as if I was physically in pain.

He fell into another fit of laughter and clutched at his sides. I finally pulled my hands away from my face and glared at him, which only increased his hilarity. He started to collect himself and wiped at his eyes with the cloth napkin. "Oh, Abby Lou, you made me cry," he said again. "God, you really pissed her off." He started to shake from laughing.

"It wasn't that funny," I told him shrewdly.

"Oh, it was," Sawyer said, with a heavy sigh. "Care to explain why you made such a noise because of her?"

I shook my head at him because the waitress was walking back towards us, her face expressionless. She set the drinks down and asked us if we were ready to order. I nodded, trying to be as polite as I could. I quickly glanced down at the menu, ordered the chicken marsala, and Sawyer ordered a steak with shrimp. She nodded again and walked away, without a word to us.

"She's definitely going to spit in our food," Sawyer hissed over the table.

"She will not," I said, but secretly, I agreed with him.

"Will you explain *now*?" he asked, his eyes bright with amusement. I sighed.

"Her name is *Hallie*," I told him. He shrugged.

"So? Do you hate that name or something?" he asked, searching my face. My eyes narrowed a little and sighed. I must not have mentioned those details to him the other night.

"I guess I do." I shrugged. "The woman that Michael is having an affair with, her name is Hallie. *And* of course, she's a gorgeous blonde, too."

I watched as Sawyer's face quickly transformed. The laughter from his eyes dissipated almost instantly. He straightened his posture and leaned over the table and grasped my hand. He gave my hand a little squeeze, his lips pulling into a frown.

"Well, that's not funny at all," Sawyer murmured. "I'm sorry for laughing."

"It was kind of funny," I told him, the corner of my lips twitching into a smile. Sawyer scrunched up his nose.

"I mean, yeah, it was," Sawyer said with a nod. "But I shouldn't have laughed like that. I'm so sorry. Forgive me?"

His eyes probed mine, the humor starting to light his features again. I smiled back at him and nodded.

"So, in the truck, you changed the subject pretty quick about our last time here," I told Sawyer, raising my eyebrows at him. I took a sip of my wine and waited for him to respond. Sawyer's half cocky smile appeared again, my insides fluttering again.

"Ah," he replied. He took a drink of his beer.

"Don't feel like going back down memory lane?" I asked. He set his beer down and leaned over the table at me. For a moment, I felt like he and I were in our own little world.

"I don't mind it, but I think you just remember it differently than I do," he replied simply, shrugging.

"Sawyer, you didn't want to go to prom. If my memory serves me correctly, you *refused* to go. Then out of the blue, you showed up at my house, in a suit, to take me to my prom. You literally saved the day."

Sawyer looked down at his hands for a moment, as if he was thinking how to respond, when finally, his eyes pierced mine.

"I was at home," Sawyer said. "Just listening to CDs, not doing too much. I didn't have any plans to go to prom, you were right. I was a brooding, angry kid then and couldn't care less about shit like that. Until," he paused, his lips twitching into a smile, "my mother got a call from *your* mom. Apparently, you were upset. Your douche of a boyfriend bailed on you, hours before prom, and you didn't want to go alone since all your friends had dates."

I nodded. "Yeah, that Luke was a real tool," I said, shuddering. "I cannot believe I dated him for so long. *Ugh*."

Sawyer nodded in agreement. "Which is why I punched him in the face."

My eyes popped out of my head. "You did *what*?"

Sawyer grinned and shrugged. "I punched him; right in the jaw." Sawyer mocked punched himself. "Lance stopped me before I could get another one in, the bastard."

"*Sawyer Gibson*," I told him. "I cannot believe you did that." Sawyer shrugged again, his lips twitching, and he took another drink of his beer.

"I can. I was always pissed, and it felt good at the time."

I shook my head in disbelief. I cannot believe I never knew Sawyer did that. Living in a small town, news travels fast, but apparently, not all the time.

"So, you heard that I didn't have a date, and came to my rescue…" I told him kindly. "I'm guessing your mom strong armed you into doing it?"

Sawyer shook his head, and I felt my eyes widen again. I always assumed that Mrs. Gibson guilted him into doing it.

"No, Mom just told me what happened. She didn't even approach the subject of me going, she knew how I felt about it. She told me that Luke bailed on you, and you were home upset, and I got up, found my suit that I was going to wear to the scout meeting and put it on. At least I got use out of it." He rolled his eyes. "Then, the next thing that I knew, I was pulling up into your driveway."

My heart raced again as I watched Sawyer, and I shook my head slowly at him. "I always thought your mom made you come, which is why I was kind of a bitch to you at first," I admitted. "I'm so sorry, Saw."

Sawyer grinned. "Don't be sorry. Remember, I *liked* getting you mad. It made my night. It was worth going anyway. You looked beautiful."

His confession melted my heart and made my cheeks burn all at the same time. This time, I didn't look away from his stare, but embraced it, savoring it to memory. The way he looked at me made me feel…*whole*. And *wanted*. Like an entire new Abby.

"You looked very nice, too," I told him sheepishly. Sawyer's lips pursed into an adorable as heck way as looked around the restaurant. He still didn't like the compliments I see.

"Would you like another?" Sawyer asked me, gesturing to my empty glass.

I hesitated, clenching my teeth. "It's okay if you want one, you know," he added, with a grin.

"I normally just stick to my one glass rule," I admitted. Sawyer's eyebrow raised questionably. "I get kind of messy if I have more than two. I don't like it."

Sawyer chuckled and shook his head at me. "I highly doubt you get messy."

"No, I do," I told him. "I get kind of obnoxious. It's embarrassing."

"Well, whatever you decide is fine. I promise, messy or not, Abby, I won't take advantage of you." He was clearly joking with me, being lighthearted, but I felt my eyes burn into his.

Before I could stop the word vomit, I said, "What if I *wanted* you to take advantage of me?"

Shit Abby.

Sawyer's eyes widened slightly, but then turned dark, the sudden intensity of his stare captivating. I swear, if he kept looking at me like that tonight, he would have my panties off in a heartbeat. Sawyer opened his mouth to speak, but no words came out. He closed his mouth, biting on his own bottom lip.

"You shouldn't talk like that with me, Abby," Sawyer said, eyes narrowing. "Because I might do just that."

I felt a shudder course through my body and then suddenly I was leaning towards him, my eyes scanning his face. For the first time in a very long time, I let my mind wander there. I wondered how Sawyer's body would feel against mine; how his abs would feel underneath my fingertips, his lips mashed with mine, and how that scruffy beard would feel between my legs. I felt my insides charge and legs slightly twinge.

I couldn't deny it anymore. I *wanted* Sawyer.

He must have noticed the change in my expression because he shook his head at me, laughing.

"Abby, we are *so* not going there tonight," Sawyer told me. He firmly looked up at the ceiling, not wanting to make eye contact with me. I pulled my face into a slight pouty expression; not too pathetic, but cute enough, when finally, he looked back down at me. "*Oh, no*," he said, shaking his head again. "Do *not* give me the lip. Come on, now, that's not fair. I'm trying to help *you*, Abby, so don't make *me* the villain."

"How are you trying to help me?" I asked incredulously. Sawyer gaped at me.

"I don't want to take advantage of you, Abby!" he said in a hissed whisper. "Will you please, let me *honor* you?"

"I'd rather you *dishonor* me," I heard myself say. His mouth gaped open, and he shook his head at me.

"Jesus Christ, Abigail. *Stop it.*"

I couldn't help but laugh at him. He looked so confused, but turned on at the same time, it was quite hilarious. I didn't miss the fact that he placed his hands underneath the table to tug at his pants.

"And can you please stop biting your fucking lip?" Sawyer hissed. I looked up at him, my lips twitching into a smile. I didn't even realize I was biting my lip.

"Sorry," I told him. "I will let you *honor* me. But honestly, it really would be helping me out by *not*. I mean, it's been forever and a day for me."

Sawyer shook his head again and firmly planted his fingers in his ears. "I can't with you anymore," he said, fighting back his smile.

"Can't what?" I asked innocently.

"Converse. Talk with you. This is *not* how I thought the evening would go."

"Sorry," I said again. "If it makes you feel better, I didn't think so either. But I forgot how easy it is to talk with you."

"Talking is fine, Abby, but doing anything more, is *not*." He glared at me. Just then, our food appeared from our still haughty looking waitress. She still didn't say anything more to us but placed our food silently in front of us. I was honestly nervous to take a bite, thinking that maybe she *did* spit in it.

"Um, can we get another round?" Sawyer asked her before she could walk away. "Abby, did you want something different?" He gestured to my glass.

I shook my head. "No, I would love another glass, thank you," I told the waitress politely. Sawyer raised a brow at me but smiled. I was clearly breaking my one glass rule tonight.

When the waitress was out of ear shot, Sawyer said, "Abby, I have to say, this is one of the most entertaining dates I've ever been on."

I smelled the chicken marsala and sighed, my stomach gurgling. It smelled amazing.

"It's been fun," I told Sawyer, grabbing the knife and fork. "I'm so glad you invited me."

Sawyer beamed at me, his eyes sparkling underneath the dimly lit lamp. He grabbed his own silverware and dug into his steak. We chewed in silence for a minute, and I moaned a little as I tasted everything on my plate. Sawyer's eyes looked up at me, and I heard him chuckle.

"What are you doing?" he asked.

"It's *so* good," I told him. The waitress came back with our drinks. I gave her a polite thank you, but she only responded with a glare in my direction. I grabbed the wine and took a drink. "Do you want to try?" I asked, gesturing to my plate. He looked over at it, and a smile slipped on his face.

"Switch plates for five seconds, and then switch back?" Sawyer asked, his eyes light.

I let out a small laugh, reminiscing of our prom dinner; we switched plates then too, and knowing that Sawyer remembered that from so long ago tugged at my heart.

J. Glassburn

Sawyer

I lost count of how many times I laughed tonight with Abby. Her laugh and her smile were becoming one of my favorite things to see and hear. The way her head fell back and her body shook with silent laughter was one of the most sensual things I've ever seen. Even when she did the simplest things, like scrunching her nose or playing with the ends of her hair made my heart and soul freeze. She was mesmerizing and I knew in my heart and soul that this memory would sear my mind forever to come.

We finished our meals swiftly; we ended up putting our plates in the middle and both ate a little off each one. I must admit, I enjoyed my plate more than hers, but seeing that look in her eyes as we shared was well worth it. I was already planning our next dinner in the back of my mind, and that was new to me. On my previous dates, I was always contemplating my escape route and what I would say to not give them hope of another. I knew from the bottom of my heart that I had to have another chance at this with Abby.

When we left the restaurant together and headed back towards my truck, my mind and heart were both racing; I didn't want this night to end with her. I was having such a great time with her but didn't have the slightest clue of what to do next. Bars were out of the question; nothing good came out of ending the evening with drinks. I also didn't want to have to share her tonight; I wanted her attention all to myself. I opened Abby's door for her and helped her slide into the truck, her eyes flashing the same burning look she gave me at dinner.

Abby was one to always surprise me, but her casual jokes at dinner about me dishonoring her, took me by surprise. I never had the slightest thought or hope to end this evening with her in my bed. Not that I didn't want her there, but she was too special, too important. I didn't want to give her the impression that that's what I was looking for this evening because it was far from my mind. It made me question though if that's what she was wanting from me tonight. Was she just looking for a hookup, and that's why she agreed? I didn't know how I felt about that.

I hoped it wasn't.

I slid into the driver's seat and let the engine kick in. I looked over at Abby, who was staring outside of her window silently. I wanted to take her hand in mine but couldn't pucker up the courage to do it. Instead, I put the truck into gear and started driving.

The sun was now setting, giving the country sky a soft glow with its rays of oranges and yellows. I rolled down my window to let the country air in and watched as Abby did the same. She put her head back and let the wind hit her face. I was trying like hell to focus on the road but kept glancing over in her direction; she had her eyes closed and was smiling.

"What are you thinking?" I asked her softly. I couldn't stand it anymore; I had to know what was going through her mind.

"How much I missed Illinois," she answered simply. "In Florida, it's always so humid. This is nice."

"I'm glad you're back."

"Me, too. It's been way too long." She let out a heavy sigh.

A sudden thought hit me, and I knew where we were going next.

I pulled the truck into a different direction, going from paved roads to dirt roads. I watched as the dust kicked up behind us in my rearview mirror. Abby's face scrunched up as she glanced at me, and back to our surroundings, but to my pleasure, she never asked where we were going.

I pulled the truck up an old beaten up path and into a grassy field. Abby's face scrunched together and she looked over at me.

"Should I be worried?" She asked. I chuckled.

"No," I replied simply.

"You're not taking me here to kill me and bury me in the middle of nowhere?" I chuckled again and pulled the truck into park.

"That's *way* too much work." I rolled my eyes playfully. "Are you up for a little walk?" Abby looked down at her shoes and frowned.

"I'm not really wearing shoes for walking," she admitted.

"Then take them off," I offered. Her eyebrow cocked, but she shrugged.

"Okay...."

I hopped out of the truck and left the keys in the ignition. Abby opened her door as I was walking around the truck. She knelt to slip off her shoes, but I reached out for her instead. Slowly, I placed my hand on the back of her heel and slid her shoes off, one by one. I felt her freeze underneath my touch and couldn't help but smile. I looked up at her and saw that hunger filter beneath her eyes and felt my own heart start to beat a little faster. She was going to be the death of me tonight, I swear.

I held out my hand for Abby and watched her body hesitate for a moment. She placed her hand in mine as I helped her out of the truck, straightening out her dress as she stood on the tall grass. This time, I didn't let go of her hand and she didn't pull it away.

"It's not a far walk, I promise," I told her. "Just down the hill." She nodded, her eyes scanning the area around us. I could practically hear her brain whirling inside of her head.

I led her up the hill, my eyes on our steps as we walked to make sure she wouldn't step in anything that would hurt her bare feet. I heard her staggered breathing from behind me and wondered briefly if this was a good idea. Too late now though. Before we reached the top of the hill, I turned around to her, not able to contain my excitement anymore.

"Okay, are you ready?" She nodded, a bemused expression on her face. "Okay." I gave her hand a squeeze and together we walked a few more steps up the hill.

Down at the bottom of the hill were an abundance of tall viny greens with large yellow and orange sunflowers blooming; the field was larger than the last time I visited, it multiplied, making my own breath catch. The sunsetting against the timber around the field casted a soft glow against the sunflowers which only intensified the beauty of it. I bit my bottom lip, my breath caught in my throat and looked over at Abby. Her eyes simply sparkled as her mouth dropped open slightly. She placed her free hand over her heart.

"Sawyer," Abby whispered. "This is *beautiful*. I never knew this was here."

I felt a sigh of relief escape me as I watched her take in the country's beauty. She started laughing and in a quick, childlike motion, let go of my hand and started running down the field. I watched her run for a moment down the hill, my heart beating against my ribcage, before I ran after her. Abby instantly touched the sunflowers as lightly as one would a feather and buried her face into the flowers. Without hesitating, she stepped into the flower garden.

"You might want to be careful," I told her. "You don't have shoes on."

She didn't give it a second thought though; she buried herself into the rows of rows of sunflowers and out of sight; the vines were taller than her head as she ran from me.

"This is amazing!" I heard her call. "I can't believe I never knew this was here."

I put my hands in my pockets and listened to the chimes of her laughter. Occasionally, I saw her head pop up between the rows; her eyes were bright with excitement and smile wide; you could see those dimples of hers a mile away.

The sun was setting quickly, and I knew we wouldn't have long until darkness succumbed us, but I had no intention of rushing her out of here. Watching her underneath the beams of the sun was a sight I'd never forget. This moment with her was already stitching a permanent place in my heart. I watched as she popped up, sniffed the sunflowers, and touched the rows with her fingertips as she walked by them. She did a little twirl in the field, and I couldn't help but laugh with her. Seeing her this way, guard down, and full of excitement, filled my body with so much contentment. I could stay here forever with this girl.

"Are you going to come in here or what?" she asked me, a slow smile slipping on her lips.

"I'm enjoying watching you way too much to join in."

She rolled her eyes at me playfully and went back to enjoying God's work. She lifted her face into the country air, eyes closed, and arms above her head. The sun rays beat down on her face, as if they were purposely giving her her own show. I secretly wished I had a camera or my phone to take a picture of her like this; I wanted to burn this carefree Abby into memory forever.

Slowly the sun started to settle beneath the timber, darkening the field around us.

"Abby," I called to her. "We should head back." I tried to look for her, but she was deep into the field and out of my vision. I was starting to grow uneasy with her out of my eyesight, but knew I was being foolish. All I heard back was her soft laughter. "Are you hiding from me?" I asked, cocking an eyebrow to no one but a sunflower that was staring me straight in the face. She giggled again, sounding farther away from me than I liked.

I sighed and started to make my way into the field, knowing this was probably what she wanted me to do.

"Marco," I called out. She let out a loud laugh that echoed throughout the air.

"Polo!" she sang. I narrowed my eyes, trying to concentrate on the direction of her voice.

"Marco...."

"Polo." She giggled.

Her giggles were coming from the right; I sidestepped and kept walking, my heart racing. I heard her footsteps through the vines before I saw her. She let out a shriek of laughter and started running from me as fast as she could. To my surprise, I was laughing, too. I chased after her, the vines hitting my shoulders and chest as I went after her. It wasn't hard to reach her; it only took a few long strides. I wrapped my arm around her waist and drew her into my chest, her face only inches from mine. Her eyes widened with pleasure, sparkling even underneath the dimmed sky. Her lips turned upward in a sexy, longing way and I tried to fight the temptation of leaning in closer, but the intensity of her stare was overwhelming.

And I went for it.

I secured her waist in my right arm and pulled her closer to me until her chest was brushing mine; I could feel her rapid heartbeats underneath me and I smiled. Her breath caught, eyes scanning my face, when I slowly leaned in and crushed my lips on hers.

Her lips were soft, just as I had expected them to feel against my own. My insides twisted as our lips moved in slow synchronized motions. I yearned for more of her but forced myself to keep my steady pace; it wasn't too hard, she felt heavenly wrapped in my arms with my mouth pressed on hers. I wanted to savor every second of this feeling; the way her mouth moved so effortlessly with mine, her chest pressed hard upon me. I set her down on her feet slowly, my mouth never leaving hers, as I brought both of my hands and cradled her delicate face.

When our lips parted, she let out a heavy sigh as I leaned my forehead against hers, my fingertips caressing her soft face. I wanted to kiss her again. And again. And again.

And I did. I pulled her face back to mine and lightly pressed my lips to her, her breath hot against my face. I breathed in slowly, inhaling her sweet smell.

She was textbook perfect. No, she was better than that.

"I can't believe I waited this long in life to do that," I whispered. She let out a heavy sigh, wrapping her arms around my neck.

"To kiss a woman, or just me?" she teased.

I rolled my eyes at her and leaned in again. I knew I was testing my luck, but I had to feel her lips just one more time. They were soft and full against my own and I knew right then that I could do this forever with her. I felt her lips part underneath my own and gently collided my tongue with hers; a soft hum ruptured from her throat, and it made my insides pull with intense desire.

"I should get you back," I told her breathlessly, pulling away from her lips. Her eyes slowly fluttered open, and I saw the want and need reflected; a half smile slipped on my face and I fought the urge to whoop into the country air. I wanted to scream and shout and let the world know that I kissed Abby Foster. Well, Abby *Carter*. She nodded slowly and let her arms fall from my neck. She started to walk in front of me, but almost tripped over a vine. I let out a low chuckle and wrapped my arm securely around her waist to guide her. With my arm around her waist, I leaned into her neck and planted a light kiss, her hair falling into my face. I sighed.

It didn't take us long to get out of the sunflower field; we were at the corner's edge in just a few minutes. Abby kept walking, stumbling a little in her steps and I couldn't help but smile at her; I liked to think that I was having that effect on her, though I knew the glasses of wine may be the real culprit. I turned around and plucked a sunflower from the vine. When Abby turned around, I was holding it out to her. Her perfect, kissable lips turned upwards, popping out those damn cute dimples again.

"To remember me by," I told her, my eyes on hers.

"It's not likely I'll ever forget you, Sawyer Gibson," Abby whispered, taking the flower from me. Her face was glowing, even under the dimmed sky.

I grabbed her freehand and brought it to my lips softly, my eyes never leaving her blues. For the briefest moment, or maybe it was a trick of the light, I'm not sure, but I swear, I saw a pool of tears start to form in Abby's eyes. Why she was about to cry, I wasn't sure, but there's one thing I was very sure of.

I'm falling hard for this woman.

J. Glassburn

Chapter 13- *Abby*

I've been smiling like a fool all day. I tried desperately to keep my body and mind busy with mundane household tasks, but my thoughts kept going back to Sawyer. I kept replaying the moments we shared last night over and over in my head, but what kept my heart flying wasn't how perfect his lips felt against mine, it was his *eyes*. They pierced me so many times last night and every single time I looked into them, I felt as if I was puddling at his feet. Sawyer's eyes have always been captivating, but they were different last night; it was like they were burning into my very being.

No one has ever made me feel that desirable, that *wanted* before in my entire life. Just planning the dinner would have left me thinking it was a great evening, but Sawyer Gibson took it to the next level when he brought me to the sunflower field. It was the most perfect, beautiful moment I've ever experienced. I couldn't even imagine experiencing it with anyone else but him.

And that kiss. When he grabbed my waist, it was the most agonizing seconds of my life. I was screaming on the inside for him to kiss me; I burned to feel his lips on my own and when he delivered, I thought for a second that I was daydreaming. Surely nothing that perfect happens in real life…?

But it did. I wasn't dreaming. His lips were on mine, and I molded perfectly into his embrace. His hands were perfection as they tugged me closer to him and featherlight when he caressed my face.

And it was such a damn good feeling.

"You know," Mom said, breaking me out of my Sawyer reverie, "you've been scrubbing that same plate for a good five minutes. I think it's clean, my dear."

I jumped, startled from my mother's sudden intrusion to my thoughts. I dropped the wet plate into the sudsy water, causing the water and suds to spill over the counter. My cheeks started to slowly burn as my mother's eyebrow rose in my direction.

"Sorry," I mumbled. I grabbed a dish cloth and started drying the wet counter. I grabbed the plate and quickly rinsed it underneath the hot water and set it into the strainer.

"Nothing to be sorry about," my mother said. She sat on the kitchen island close to me, her elbow propped on the counter with her face in her hand. She eyed me shrewdly. "You've been very quiet this morning."

Please for the love of God do not be observant with me today.

"Oh?" I asked, grabbing another dirty plate. She nodded and grabbed the newspaper in front of her.

"Mhmm…and I believe I heard humming while you were doing the dishes."

"I do that often."

"I've never heard you before," Mom mentioned. "Care to tell me why you're so…distracted?"

"Mom, I'm not distracted."

"Mhmm…." Mom answered. From the corner of my eye, I noticed that she was folding Dad's paper into triangle pieces.

"Where's Remmy?" I asked her, scanning the kitchen. "I thought you both were out watering the flowers."

"Your father took him for ice cream." I rolled my eyes and shook my head at her.

"Didn't think to maybe, I don't know, ask me?" I asked; I knew I had a little bite to my tone.

"I didn't think you'd mind. Plus, I wanted to hear about your evening." I looked over at Mom, and she had a bemused smile on her face. "Care to share?"

I rolled my eyes at her and went back to doing the dishes. "We had a great evening."

"Is that all I get, Abigail?" I didn't even have to look at her to know that her eyebrow was in the air again.

"What do you want me to tell you?"

"I don't know, maybe what you did that has you smiling so damn much. Did you have sex with him, Abby?"

I jumped and spun into her direction; my eyes wide at how casually she was throwing the word *sex* around. Good Lord, this was not a conversation that I wanted to have with my *mother*. The plate I was holding nearly slipped from my grasp, but I caught it this time and set it back into the dishwater carefully.

"*Mom!*" I said to her, throwing her a furtive look. "That's *not* something a mother asks a daughter."

"So, you did have sex with Sawyer." Mom sighed and put her face into her hands. "Abby, you're going to get yourself into a sticky mess. I know he's good looking and man does he keep himself in wonderful shape, but you shouldn't be having—"

"*Mom, I didn't have sex with Sawyer!*" I nearly shrieked. I threw the sponge into the water. "Even if I did, I wouldn't tell you." Mom waved her hand at me.

"Don't be so dramatic, Abby. You're an adult and there's nothing wrong with being a sexual woman or having sex. I'm just saying that maybe this isn't the best time to be, you know, having sex with another man."

I felt like my eyes and ears were burning and fought the urge to clap my hands over my ears to tune her out. This was *seriously* not happening.

"Mother, I cannot talk about this with you."

"Oh, stop it Abigail." Mom rolled her eyes at me again. "Your father is going to be back soon, and I want to talk about this before he returns."

"There's nothing to talk about, we didn't have sex. It was just a date. A first date even. Do you really think I'm that kind of woman?"

Mom sighed and shook her head. "I do not think you are, Abby, but you and Sawyer have known each other for *years*. If you would have, I wouldn't have thought badly of you. You and Sawyer were a long time coming. I used to say it all the time when you were younger that you two would end up together and here we are."

"Mom, it was just a date."

"Yes, and you haven't stopped smiling or humming or singing all morning. So spill. I want to know what happened."

"So you can call Mrs. Gibson and tell her?" I offered, giving her an eye roll. Mom's lips pursed into a guilty smile.

"I won't call her if you don't want me to. She's dying to know how it went though...."

"So, if we had sex, would you have called her and told her that we had sex?"

"*Of course not*, Abby." Mom brushed me off. "But you didn't, right? Or did you?"

"I didn't, Mother."

"Did you have a good time at least?"

"The best," I told her. Mom smiled at me, urging me to go on. I rolled my eyes. "We went to dinner and had a great time. After dinner, he surprised me by taking me to this amazing sunflower field. It was beautiful there. We stayed there until the sun set and then he brought me home."

"He took you to the sunflower field?" Mom said, her face melting into a smile. She clapped her hand over her heart. "Oh, that's adorable." I felt my cheeks blush. "That explains the sunflower in the vase." Mom said, eyeing my beautiful sunflower sitting on the counter. I nodded, trying to fight back the smile that was exploding my cheeks.

"That's so sweet, Abby. No wonder you are all smiles. Very romantic." She sighed.

"It was perfect. The sun was just setting and it casted a pretty glow over the field."

"Oh, Abby," Mom said, clapping her hands together, her eyes misty. "I'm so glad you had a great time. Did he kiss you at least? You are quite full of smiles for just seeing some sunflowers." I felt my cheeks flush at her words and couldn't meet her eyes. "He did, didn't he? Oh, where did he kiss you? Here, when he dropped you off, at the restaurant, at the field?" Mom sat up straighter, clutching the counter.

"Mom, I'm not telling you anymore. We had a great evening, and that is all. Besides, I shouldn't kiss and tell," I told her with a wink. She beamed.

"I love seeing you so happy, Abby. It makes my heart happy."

"It's not even just Sawyer, Mom. I mean, he's great. Don't get me wrong, but it's just being back home. I feel like my old self again and just... free." I sighed, looking at my mom directly in the eye. "I don't think I can go back to Florida. I don't want to."

Mom's shoulders slumped a little and her smile turned halfhearted. She got up from the kitchen island and walked her way over to me and pulled me into her arms. I laid my head on her shoulder and fell into my mother's warm embrace; her hugs were always comforting to me.

"I know, baby girl. You have a lot to think about."

"Even thinking about returning just makes my stomach hurt. Michael's not pushing on it right now, but he will eventually."

Mom sighed and said, "You'll figure it out." Her hand went to my hair, and she started smoothing my hair in slow motions.

"I need to find a divorce lawyer." I sighed. "The whole thing just gives me a headache."

"You'll find one."

"I never thought I would need to be looking for one."

"I know, baby. But you deserve happiness, Abby. If you're not happy, and you know it can't be fixed, it's time to walk away."

"I don't want to fix it," I admitted. I pulled from my mother's embrace and looked into her face. "Mom, there's a lot I didn't tell you. He's just...not the person I expected him to be."

"He doesn't hit you, does he?" Mom said. She stiffened, her nostrils flared, and her eyes were misty again. I shook my head.

"No, he's not an abuser by any means, he's just…not faithful, Mom." I felt the sad smile fall on my lips. "He also admitted to me that he's not faithful, and that he's not attracted to me anymore, so there's that."

Mom's eyebrows scrunched together as she scanned my face. Her hand went to my arm as she slowly rubbed it back and forth.

"I'm sorry, Abby," Mom said. "That's awful. I can't imagine how you feel." I shrugged in response.

"I was upset, at first, but now, I'm just kind of over it, you know? It's been hell living in that house, knowing what he was out doing, while I was home or out with Remmy. It's just time. Remmy and I need a clean start." I shrugged and clapped my hands together. "I'm already feeling better about my decision, and I'm ready for what's to come."

Mom's eyebrows rose and a soft smile appeared on her face. "You're a lot stronger than me, Abby." She patted my arm again.

"You would be, too, if you were in this situation. You were very lucky to find Dad." I smiled at her. Mom laughed but agreed.

"You know I love you," Mom said. "I'll support whatever decision you make in the end."

I nodded, smiling at my mom and pulled her back into a quick hug. "I love you too, Mom."

Mom squeezed and pulled my face away from hers. Her lips were pursed though, eyebrows scrunched together as she scanned my face.

"What do you want to say, Mom? You're holding something back, I can tell." I rose my brow. "Just say it." I sighed. I knew this look well. I watched as Mom hesitated, her hands fidgeting with my shirt sleeve. She sighed and looked up at me; her face was trying to compete with different emotions.

"Just be careful with Sawyer," Mom said. "Don't hurt him, Abby."

My eyebrows lifted and my mouth opened to say something snarky, like, *"What the hell,* I'm *your daughter,"* but I mashed my lips shut as my mother's eyes turned misty again, her nose scrunched up, as if she was in pain saying those words to me. I let my head fall to the side and shook my head slowly at her. She's always had a soft spot for Sawyer. It used to piss me off so much growing up.

"I have no intention of hurting, Sawyer," I told her. Mom patted my arm again, her eyes averting my gaze.

"He's got a gentle heart, that one. I love you, Abby, very much. You're my daughter; the last thing I want is for *you* to get hurt, but Sawyer is…well, he's just Sawyer. He acts so tough, but he wears his heart on his sleeve. I can tell he's really taking to you and Remmy." Mom sighed and looked me straight in the eye. "If you're second guessing your divorce with Michael, don't pursue this with Sawyer."

I bit my bottom lip but held my head high as I looked directly into my mother's gaze.

"I'm not second guessing it." Mom searched my face, as if she was trying to validate my words, when she slowly nodded. She patted my cheek softly.

"I love you, Abby."

"I love you, too, Mom."

Mom sighed, shook her head slowly and clapped her hands together again. "So, what's on the agenda today?"

I looked up at Mom with a wide smile.

"Well…" I told her. "Fresh start comes with fresh beginnings."

Mom leaned on the island. "Oh?"

"I want a new look," I admitted. "You know, new Abby, new beginnings. Do you think Dad would keep Remmy for us for the rest of today?"

Mom's lips flashed into a brilliant smile. "Yes, he would; sounds like a brilliant idea. *Let's go.*"

Sawyer

I'm bordering on creepy stalker status right now, but the last few days without seeing Abby has literally been eating me alive. Every time I close my eyes I see her face, and when I'm walking through town or out running errands, I find myself scanning the area around me, hoping to just get a glimpse of her. My skin has felt like it's been crawling all day and I'm starting to become a fucking mess. Or a douche. Who fucking knows at this point.

Kissing Abby was like heaven, and I was counting down the minutes until I could feel her against me again, but we never set up a follow-up date. There are rules, I know the damn rules, on when you can reach out for a second date but fuck those rules. I want to see her. And I want to see her now.

I am turning into a psycho.

Abby and I have texted here and there since our date. The last few mornings I've texted her good morning and, in the afternoons, I've texted asking how her day was going. Her replies were always short and to the point which has me scratching my head. Didn't she have a good time? Why isn't she texting me back more? And why the hell, am I acting like a fucking chick again? I know I'm probably reading way too much into it, but it still made me wonder if she enjoyed herself as much as I did.

Which is why I'm driving to the Foster's residence right now. Just showing up, probably wasn't the best idea. They were probably busy, or she was at the daycare center, I didn't know, but I was about to find out. I loaded up my fishing gear in the back of the truck before I headed out, and decided if they wanted to go with me, then great. If they didn't, that's okay, too. I'd still go fishing; it was something I wanted to do this summer anyhow.

I pulled up to the Foster's driveway faster than I had expected; my heart was starting to thud viciously in my chest, but I ignored it. I was about to see Abby again and I already felt lighter. I hopped out of the truck, and noticed the front door swing open instantly. It wasn't the beautiful lady I wanted to see, but her *dad*.

Oh, fuck.

"Hello, Mr. Foster," I called to him, shutting the truck door. He nodded in my direction, his eyes piercing me as I jogged up the driveway.

"Sawyer," he said curtly. "What can we do for you?"

Are we still doing the cold shoulder, kind of thing? I planted my feet confidently in front of Mr. Foster and gave him the best smile that I could muster under his stare.

"Well, I was hoping Abby was home," I admitted with a shrug of my shoulders. Mr. Foster clucked his tongue, but slowly nodded.

"Yeah, she's inside. I'll send her out." He turned from me abruptly, and I noticed how he didn't invite me in. *Shit*; getting closer to Abby was pulling me out of Mr. Foster's good grace, but that's okay. Hopefully he'll warm up to me again eventually. I tried to put myself in Mr. Foster's shoes, but couldn't. I didn't have a daughter, so I couldn't relate to what he could be feeling right now. I mashed my lips together and turned around to face the town, while I leaned on the deck railing. The air was light today, a soft breeze, and wasn't humid; that's a plus, as it was the end of June. The sky was blue as it could be with white puffballs littering the sky.

It was a perfect day for fishing. Now I just hoped for the perfect company.

The front door clicked open, and I spun around quickly, my fingers fidgeting; *finally.*

I leaned back as I stared at the woman coming out of the front door; it was Abby, but it *wasn't* Abby. The long brunette hair woman that I just saw a few days ago, now had cropped hair, just brushing her shoulders. The back of her hair was a bit shorter than the front, and now her hair wasn't all that brunette, but had light blonde color in it; it made her skin look darker than I remembered it being. She was also not wearing her usual athletic clothes that I was accustomed to seeing on spur of the moment occasions, but wearing black, snug capris and a white blouse that framed her waist and breasts well. *Very well.*

"Sawyer," she said, smiling at me.

I clutched my hand over my heart and gazed at her.

"Abby. Wow. You look…" I didn't know what to say; all I knew was that if I continued gawking at this beautiful creature, I would probably fall right to my knees. "Beautiful."

I watched her eyes light up and her face flush. In a few quick strides, I reached her and stood before her; those adorable as fuck dimples popped out again. I glanced behind her, to make sure the little man wasn't trailing behind her, and before I could stop myself, I leaned into her and brushed my lips against hers.

"Hi," I told her, smiling, my lips inches from her. I opened my eyes to see that hers were still closed and I felt that piercing stab to my heart.

"Hi," she said, giggling. I took a step back from her, forcing myself not to steal another kiss. "What are you doing here?"

"Well," I said, giving her my best, apologetic smile, "I just wanted to say hello."

She eyed me, her lips pulling into a halfway grin, and I felt as if my heart was soaring into the sky above. God, she was breathtaking. I resisted the urge to pull her into me; knowing full well, if her dad saw, he may come out and pummel my ass to the ground. I also didn't want Remmy to see me kissing his mom.

"Well, hello," she said, with another small laugh. "Did you want to come in?"

I shook my head no.

"Okay…" Abby said with a shaky laugh. She was starting to fidget with the bottom of her blouse.

"What do you have planned today?" I asked her, cocking my head to the side.

Abby's eyes widened and she glanced back at the house and back to me. "Nothing much." She shrugged. "We were just kind of relaxing today."

"How about you and Remmy come with me?" I offered. Her eyes widened again, but slowly, there was that smile that I loved to see.

"What did you have in mind?"

I glanced at the window and the closed door quickly before I reached for her hand. Her fingers felt smooth and so small against mine as I intertwined my fingers with hers. I pulled her closer to me, my other hand resting on her hip. Her eyes were bright and glossy, and I noticed as her face was approaching mine, that Abby was wearing makeup. She did the other day too, but I assumed it was because of the date. The black mascara magnified her eyes, and I felt a heavy sigh escape me.

"I am going fishing," I told her. "Would you and Remmy like to join me?"

"Fishing?" she asked, giggling. I nodded.

"When's the last time you've been fishing?"

She shrugged in response, trying to think "Probably with you guys," she admitted.

"Well, then, let's go."

Abby laughed, shaking her head at me. "I have to stop and get my fishing license. I don't have one anymore."

"That's okay."

"I don't have a pole and neither does Remmy," she countered.

"That's okay, I have an extra for you, and I bought Remmy one already." I nodded to my truck. "It's got Spider-Man on it."

"You are full of surprises, Sawyer." She let go of my hand and I immediately wished she hadn't. She shook her head at me, that sensual smile playing on her lips. I fought the urge to kiss her again.

"So, is that a yes?" I put my hands into my pocket, rocking on the back of my heels. I started to bite the inside of my cheek, hoping she'd agree.

"That's a yes," she said with a sigh. "I have to change though. Remmy and I will have to drive separately; you don't have room for his car seat in that truck of yours."

"Perfectly fine," I offered with a smile.

"Do you want to wait inside?"

"I'll wait here," I said, gesturing to the deck with my head. "Your dad is turning out to be scarier than shit."

She let out another musical laugh as I watched her turn away from me and head right back inside. I sat on the porch steps and said a silent prayer to the man above, thanking him for another beautiful day.

*****

"Okay, little man, have you ever been fishing before?" I asked. I already assumed the answer but wanted to ask anyway. Remmy was standing before me, bouncing

up and down. He shook his head no with his goofy grin. Abby was sitting in a lawn chair next to us, her face up into the air, letting the sun rays beat on her face.

"Okay," I told him. "So, this is your pole. Here's the hook. This is what will catch the fish, okay? You have to be very careful with the hook because you don't want to accidentally hook yourself." I showed him the hook, and he nodded firmly. "Alright buddy, so what we'll do first is have you practice casting into the grass before we get it into the water. Before you cast out, the most important thing is to look behind you. You don't want to cast out when there's someone behind you because you can hook them accidentally. We don't want anyone to get hurt."

Remmy nodded again and together we walked into the center of the grass area. My truck was parked behind us with the tailgate open, our fishing supplies littering the tailgate. I demonstrated how to cast out a few times for him and reeled it back in; he soaked in my movements. I handed the pole over to him and asked him to try. The first time, he hit the button too quickly, the second time, he had a nice, long cast. I beamed.

"Awesome!" I told him. "You are a pro. Try again, maybe a few more times."

Remmy nodded and tried again, another perfect cast. And again.

"Perfect," I told him. "Now, we'll get the bait on." I turned back towards the tailgate, looking for the wax worm canister.

"What's bait?" Remmy asked, hopping next to me towards the truck.

"It's what attracts the fish. You have to put something on your hook that will catch the fish's eye. Now choosing your bait is very important; it depends what kind of fishing you want to do and what you want to catch. Today, we are just going to use wax worms. Next time, I'll let *you* choose the bait." I opened the clear canister and sifted through the shavings. A squeamish yellow worm popped up and I grabbed it with my fingers and put it in my hand for Remmy to see. His nose scrunched.

"Can I touch it?"

"Sure you can." I handed it to him. With his little fingers he grasped the worm and brought it to his face; it was squirming and he gave it a weird look. "I'll put it on your hook."

I showed him the best way to hook the worm through the hook and his eyes and mouth popped open.

"Soy-yer, you're hurting the worm!"

"That's the point, little guy. Fish eat the worms."

"That's kind of disgusting," Remmy admitted, his nose scrunched again. I laughed.

"That's part of fishing, little guy. Are you sure you want to do this?"

"Yeah, I want to catch a BIG fish." He held out his hands demonstrating the length of the fish he wanted. I nodded, grinning.

"Awesome, okay, so now we'll cast out into the water, but first, I think it would be smart to put a life jacket on you," I told him.

I grabbed the life jacket I purchased at the store when I did his pole. It was blue and white, and Remmy eyed it, uncertain.

"*Why?*"

"In case you fall in the river accidentally. You probably won't, but it's just to be safe."

Remmy nodded and we slid the life jacket on and buckled it into place. He and I walked together with his little Spider-Man pole to the water's edge, and I handed the pole to him. I stepped away from him and waited for him to remember the steps on his own. He scrunched his nose, looked quickly behind him, and stuck his tongue out. In a swift motion, he casted the pole out and we watched the line soar into the river.

"I did it!" he whooped. I laughed.

"Great job, little buddy. *Beautiful* cast."

"Now what do I do?" Remmy asked, holding the pole with one hand.

"Now, you wait for a fish to grab your worm. You'll know when you have one because the pole will start tugging. You see that red and white bobber out there?" I pointed out to the river. Remmy nodded. "When it bobs up and down into the river, that's when you know you have a fish playing with the worm. When the bobber goes all the way under the water, that's when we'll pull it back together and reel it in real fast to catch that fish."

"Okay, Soy-er."

"Alright, little guy. I'm going to grab your chair, okay? You watch that bobber while I get Mommy's pole ready."

I hurried to get everything else ready to go. I gave Remmy his chair and got Abby's pole ready for her. I went to bait the hook, but she already had the worm in hand, and gestured for her pole. I shouldn't have expected anything less from her. I watched as she baited her own hook and walked towards Remmy, a satisfied glint in her eye.

"Do you want me to help you cast out?" I asked her.

Abby turned to me and rolled her eyes. "Have I *ever* needed your help, Saw?"

I shook my head at her stubbornness and waited for her to cast out; I'm not gonna lie, I was kind of hoping she *did* need my help. I wanted a reason to touch her hand and show her the proper way to cast, but of course, she did it gracefully and the bobber landed beautifully into the water. She turned around and gave me a smug smile, the same one she used to toss in my direction when we were kids. I rolled my eyes at her and went back to getting my own pole ready.

Sitting out with Abby and Remmy on a beautiful day like this and doing something that I loved, was the epitome of a perfect day. I expected Remmy to get a little annoyed and bored after a few minutes, but he didn't. He watched the little bobber intently and I prayed like hell he would catch a fish. I wanted to make his first time memorable and there's nothing better than catching a bunch of fish on your outing. I ended up turning some music on with my radio, and the three of us enjoyed the breeze and the river.

"Soy, Soy, Soy..." Remmy stammered. I turned quickly to him and noticed that he was on his feet, bouncing from foot to foot. His eyes were wide and shining. "It's *doing* something!"

I dropped my own pole to the ground, which Abby hastily scooped up for me and I sprinted to Remmy's side. His bobber disappeared into the river and Remmy was holding and eyeing the pole as if it was a foreign object. I went behind him and placed his hands where they needed to go.

"Alright, buddy, jerk up." I jerked the pole up with Remmy and told him to start reeling fast. I watched his little hand spin faster and faster and I took a step back, my hands in my hair, as I watched the water's edge. My heart rate was starting to pick up as I prayed like hell there would be a fish on the other end. Remmy stuck out his tongue as Abby and I shouted words of encouragement.

After what seemed like an eternity, flapping on the water's edge, was a fish. I let out a sigh of relief and a small whoop. Remmy bounced up and down eagerly, showing off his front toothless smile.

"*Mommy*! Look!" Remmy pointed with his free hand.

"Awesome job, baby!" Abby called to him. I helped Remmy reel it in all the way until the fish was flapping in the grass. It wasn't large by any means, but it was perfect for Remmy's first catch. Remmy spun in a circle with his hands flailing in the air.

"It's a bluegill," I told him. I picked up the fish that was dangling on the hook and watched as Remmy's eyes widened. "Do you want to hold it?"

Remmy nodded quickly, a large smile plastered on his tiny face; I've never seen him smile so widely before. I watched as his body tensed as I handed it over to him and quickly wiped my hand on the back of my shorts. Remmy's nose wrinkled and he held it gingerly in his hand.

"It's so slimy! And kind of stinky," Remmy protested, but he tightened his grip on the fish as it flapped its fins. Remmy let out a shriek.

"Before you throw it back, we need a picture," Abby declared.

"*Throw it back*?" Remmy protested. "But I just caught it!"

I laughed and ruffled his hair. "Today, Remmy, we are only catching for fun. Another day we'll catch them to eat."

"*To eat?*" Remmy exclaimed, his mouth dropping open into a perfect O. I chuckled again.

"Yes, to eat. When you're older, I'll explain hunting to you."

I looked up at Abby then and caught her gaze; her expression was soft, and I felt my heart jump and stomach twist at her burning gaze. I forced my attention back to Remmy before I got too caught up into Abby's stare. Abby put her phone up for a picture, and I took a step back, but Abby shook her head at me.

"Sawyer, you should be in the picture with him," Abby said. "You helped him catch it, after all."

I hesitated, looking at Abby, but she nodded encouragingly. I took a step toward Remmy and crouched down to his level, the bluegill flapping in his tiny hands. Remmy's mouth widened and I felt my heart tighten as I watched his delight.

Nothing could bring me down from this high I was experiencing; Remmy's triumph lifted my climbing spirits and there was absolutely nothing better in this world, than to see him smile like that.

Not only was his mother catching my once cold heart, but this little boy right here was, too.

And I prized every minute of it.

Abby

We fished for hours today; to my surprise, Remmy never got tired of it. He was having way too much fun with Sawyer, catching fish and taking pictures. Every time he caught one, he and Sawyer would both let out a loud whoop that caused others to stare, but we didn't care. Sawyer ended up catching a lot, too, and he let Remmy help him throw each one of them back into the water. I caught a few, but not nearly as much as the two of them.

Close to the river was a playground that Remmy was currently playing on. He begged us to let him play for a little bit after we were done fishing. Sawyer agreed first and told him to go have fun before I could even respond; I didn't know how I felt about that, but after Remmy took off, he turned to me, and asked me if that was okay. All I could do was nod; he had no idea what he was doing to me.

Sawyer was running around with him, playing tag and trying out the monkey bars. Now he was plopped down next to me, running his fingers through his hair; it was getting long, almost passing his ears. I had to stop myself from taking my own fingers and running it through his hair just because. Instead, I had my hand laying on the bench next to me.

Sawyer quit fiddling with his hair and laid his hand close to mine on the bench, our fingers barely an inch away from each other. His proximity sent my fingers blazing and I wanted nothing more than to be able to hold his hand freely. Sawyer's gaze was on Remmy though, a wide smile on his face. I wished he wasn't wearing sunglasses today; I wanted to see his eyes. I've always felt I could read Sawyer like a book, if only I could see his eyes.

Sawyer's fingers lightly grazed my fingertips, and I felt my body shutter from his gentle touch. He slowly moved his fingers back and forth over my fingertips. I looked over at Sawyer and hadn't realized he turned his attention to me, but instead of his usual cocky grin, his smile was soft, almost endearing.

"Thanks for coming today," he murmured. "It was fun."

"Thanks for inviting us," I answered.

Sawyer glanced at Remmy, and then back to me. "If I asked you two over for pizza tonight, what would you say?"

I pursed my lips and placed a finger to my lips. "Hmm... depends what kind of pizza."

Sawyer chuckled. "Whatever it takes to get you both over." He stopped moving his fingers back and forth over my fingertips but didn't move his hand. His touch made my hands start to prickle.

"If it's pepperoni, we are both there." Sawyer grinned his cocky grin and looked back over at Remmy, who was now trying the monkey bars.

"It's a date." He squeezed my hand and looked over at me. "Remmy, how does pizza sound?" Sawyer called to him. Remmy whooped in response which made Sawyer chuckle.

He sprang from the park bench and sprinted over to Remmy. Remmy's giggles could have been heard a mile away. Sawyer quickly snatched him from the monkey bars and tossed him into the air in a fluid motion; I felt my breath catch in my throat as Remmy soared upward, and felt my body relax as he fell back into Sawyer's arms. He lifted Remmy on top of his shoulders and boomed out, "*Pizza time!*"

Seeing Sawyer like this, so carefree, sweet, and kind was completely new to me. This wasn't the Sawyer I used to know. I liked that Sawyer, but I liked this Sawyer more. I liked this Sawyer a lot.

And it absolutely terrified me.

*****

Remmy and I ran home before heading to Sawyer's. He and I both quickly showered to get the fish smell off and changed our clothes. Remmy threw on a pair of athletic shorts and a white t-shirt; I opted for jean shorts and a black tee. My mother tried to hide her surprise when I told her we were going to Sawyer's for dinner; she acted excited and encouraging, but she didn't hide the hesitation well from her eyes.

Sawyer texted me his address earlier and I plugged it into my maps app. We zoomed through town, Remmy chatting excitedly behind me, and we were at his house within minutes. It was perfect timing, too, because Sawyer was walking inside, juggling a pizza box, bag of chips, and juice boxes in his hands. He waved his head at me, his cocky grin plastered on his face. Remmy zoomed out of the car in a flash and left me behind.

I took a deep breath before I exited the car; my fingers were trembling far too much for a casual pizza dinner. I licked my lips and opened the car door. As I walked up his gravel drive, my eyes scanned the house before me. It was a one story, smaller home, with white siding and navy shutters. He had a small porch, with a few rocking chairs out front. He didn't have any flowers planted outside, but there were a few green shaggy bushes. I noticed Sawyer had the door propped open with the back of his leg, waiting for me, so I hurried my casual stroll towards him, my heart rate matching each step I took.

Remmy ran into the house, but before I stepped onto the porch, I hesitated. I don't know why I was acting this; after all, I spent most of the day with Sawyer. It was like Sawyer was reading through me though because he narrowed his eyes at me and nodded his head toward the door. I took a deep breath and stepped onto the porch, taking the juice boxes and chips out of his full hands, my eyes averting his. I glanced up at him quickly and almost took a step back; his eyes were smoldering, and it made my insides churn.

"Ready to eat?" he murmured. The frog in my throat prevented me from speaking, so I quickly nodded.

When I stepped inside, I took a step to the left to let Sawyer pass freely, my eyes absorbing Sawyer's living room. The house was quaint, and it was the typical bachelor pad you would expect Sawyer to have. As I glanced around, I noticed the decor was probably planted by his mother, a few pictures I hadn't expected to see in Sawyer's house. The living room had your basic items: navy sofa and a large black recliner, a TV stand with a large flat screen TV. He had a large wooden stand in the living room with what looked like framed family photos. Remmy flopped instantly on the sofa. "Take your shoes off," I instructed. He knew better. He let out a sigh and rolled his eyes at me but slipped his shoes off onto the wooden floor.

I walked to the framed photos on the stand; there were a few of him and his mom, but the one that caught my eye was a larger frame of Sawyer and his dad. My breath caught as I looked at Sawyer's dad. He was an exact replica of Sawyer. I forgot how much Sawyer resembled his father, the same built body, strong jawline, short brown hair speckled with gray, and a fiery stare. In the photo he was wearing his policeman uniform with teenage Sawyer by his side. He had his arm wrapped around Sawyer's shoulder and the two of them were beaming at the camera. Sawyer had shaggy hair then and he wore jeans and a collared white polo. This was exactly how I remembered the two of them; proud, energetic, and always smiling. The two of them were together often, whether it was running or working out, or playing ball outside; he was Sawyer's best friend, besides Lance, that is, but Lance was with them a lot, too. I gently touched the picture with my freehand, wishing like hell I could turn back time to see his face once more. Sawyer walked slowly over to me and stood next to me as I looked at Sawyer's dad's face.

"I haven't seen a photo of your dad in a long time," I told him with a small voice. Sawyer nodded slowly. "I miss him," I admitted.

"Me, too..." he whispered. He shuffled his feet next to me and let out a soft sigh. I knew this was a delicate subject with Sawyer; it was back then, too, so I quickly switched my focus. "Your house is cute," I offered, glancing around the living room. Sawyer's posture straightened.

"Thanks; bachelor pad at its finest. Would you like a quick tour?" he asked. I nodded.

"Well, this is it." Sawyer said with a chuckle. "Living room, of course, kitchen back there, and down this hall is your bathroom on the left and my bedroom. The second bedroom is there, too. I use it as an office." He shrugged. "It's small, but it works just fine for me."

"I like it." Sawyer rolled his eyes.

"I'm sure this is *nothing* compared to your casa back home." I shrugged nonchalantly in response; in truth, Sawyer's whole house could probably fit into my living room, but I wasn't going to tell him that.

"*Soy*, I'm hungry." Remmy called to us with a dramatic sigh. Sawyer's eyes brightened as he walked over to Remmy and scooped him up with his freehand. Remmy let out a shriek of giggles as Sawyer carried him to the kitchen and I followed, shaking my head at the two of them. I sat the items down on the gray countertop and

Sawyer set the pizza box down on the small circular oak table. I noticed there were only two chairs to go with it and I felt my lips pull into a frown. How incredibly lonely it must be to live alone. I couldn't even imagine it.

I watched as Sawyer moved around in his kitchen, grabbing paper plates for each of us. Sawyer gestured to the refrigerator with his head and told me to help myself to whatever I wanted. I thanked him and opened his refrigerator door, but looked back over at Sawyer, my eyebrow cocked at him.

"Your fridge is so empty..." I said with a small laugh. "Do you even eat?"

"I eat," he said with a shrug. "I just don't do a lot of grocery shopping. Here, put these juice boxes in there for Remmy." He tossed me the box and I set them on the almost bare shelf; this was crazy to me. Back home, there was barely any room in the fridge, or the freezer. I pulled a water out for me and a juice box for Remmy. Sawyer was already getting to work on divvying out pizza slices to the plates.

"Thanks, Soy," Remmy said, taking a big bite of his pizza. Sawyer ruffled his hair and handed me my plate. He gestured to the empty oak chair with his elbow.

"Sit," he told me.

"You can sit down," I argued. "I can stand."

"*Sit down,* Abby." Sawyer rolled his eyes and propped himself against the counter. I shook my head at Sawyer but listened.

Remmy entertained us throughout dinner; he was sharing stories about his adventures back home, from the pool to school, all the way to our beach adventures. Sawyer listened intently the entire time, never taking his eyes off Remmy while he shared details of his room, and his night light.

"Maybe sometime you can see it," Remmy said brightly. "It would be so fun for you to swim with me there. And maybe we could go to the beach."

Sawyer's gaze faltered for a moment, but he forced a smile on his face anyway. "That sounds like so much fun." His eyes glanced at me, but quickly flitted away. I couldn't help the gnawing feeling at my stomach, wondering what was going through Sawyer's mind at that moment.

After we were done with our pizza, I helped Sawyer clean up what I could. Sawyer showed Remmy how to use the television remote, and Remmy started clicking away, his blankie in hand.

"Soy, you got Disney Plus?" Remmy called.

"Do I have Disney Plus? *Of course,* I have Disney Plus." Sawyer grabbed the remote and went to the app for him.

"Why do you have Disney Plus?" I asked, raising a brow at him. Sawyer laughed.

"All of the Marvel movies are on there."

"Of course," I sighed. Sawyer snickered and handed the remote back to Remmy as he propped his head on the couch cushion, tugging his blankie into place as he flipped through the choices on the app.

"Want me to show you the outside?" Sawyer asked, nodding to the backyard. I glanced over at Remmy, who landed on a *Spider-Man* movie. He was already becoming engrossed in it.

I followed Sawyer throughout the kitchen and to the back door and was surprised at how large it was back there. He had a fenced in yard, but not much else out there. He had a small patio with a few lawn chairs propped open, cooler in the middle, and your basic charcoal grill.

"You could do a lot with this back here, you know," I told him, eyeing around.

"I know, I'm just never home." Sawyer shrugged. "Someday, maybe, but it's enough for now."

I nodded. "You have a lovely home, Sawyer. Thank you for inviting us over."

"Well, it was clean for once, so might as well," he joked. I grinned and shook my head.

Before I knew what he was doing, Sawyer pulled on my arm and tugged me towards him, that crooked grin on his face as his eyes devoured me. My heart sputtered in my chest, and I couldn't help but glance at the back door.

"He's fine, I promise," Sawyer whispered. He wrapped his arm around my waist and pulled me in until our faces were just inches apart. I held my breath. "I've been wanting to do this all day." I felt my eyes widen as Sawyer leaned in and pressed his lips lightly to mine.

The kiss was slow at first, sensual, and perfect, but as soon as my fingers weaved into his hair, his kiss strengthened, scorching my lips. I pressed my chest tighter into his embrace and he held me firmly with his arm. I felt my insides pool as my heart thumped against my ribcage rapidly. Sawyer quickly picked me up with his arm and moved me to the back of the house, out of the back door's line of vision and gently placed my back on the siding.

Sawyer's lips moved from mine, and he started trailing kisses down my jawline and to my neck, causing a shiver to shoot up my spine. I felt my leg wrap around his hungrily and pulled him closer to me; he pressed tighter against me, but it wasn't tight enough for my liking. Sawyer's teeth grazed my earlobe and I let out a gasp. He trailed kisses further down my neck and close to my chest, making my lower body tremble; I felt my nipples tighten as I ached for him to continue to kiss me.

His trail of kisses burned me and I felt his free hand touch my stomach. I almost recoiled from his touch, but his featherlight graze felt way too perfect to back away. His face was now inches away from my breasts and I felt my mind start to cloud.

God I wanted this man. But this wasn't the time or the place.

"Saw," I breathed out heavily, my head held back. "I-I can't." Sawyer pulled his face from my chest, his eyes dark. He let go of me instantly as he took a step back, his breathing rapid.

"Sorry, Abby," Sawyer said, his voice huskier than usual. "I got carried away, I'm so sorry. That was…." He was trying to think of the correct word as he ran a hand through his hair.

"Amazing?" I offered, trying to lighten the mood. His eyes averted back to me, his stare still intensely dark.

"Well, of course, but I was going to say, inappropriate."

"You were fine. I just knew I couldn't let you continue," I told him kindly.

Sawyer sighed and turned away from me. "You do things to me, Abby." He turned back to me and smiled. "I'm sorry."

"There's nothing to be sorry about but maybe we should go back inside." Sawyer nodded and placed both of his hands on top of his head.

"I'll be there in a sec," Sawyer said. "I just need a minute." I gave him a look, and listened to him laugh.

"Like I said, you do things to me Abby." I couldn't help but glance down and noticed the slight bulge in shorts. I grinned, a little triumphant.

"You do things to me, too, Sawyer, if that makes you feel better," I said.

"A little," Sawyer admitted. "I'll see you inside."

I nodded. Before I stepped inside though, I turned around and faced Sawyer. His eyes were sparkling as he watched me walk away. "Maybe we can pick that up another time though?" I offered.

Sawyer's eyes narrowed as he scanned my face, a hungry smile spread on his face. "That day can't come soon enough, Abs, but for you, I'll wait an eternity if I have to."

Chapter 14- *Sawyer*

The summer weeks flew by, too fast for my liking. I purposely took my calendar off the hook in the kitchen because it started to make my insides ache. I couldn't bear to see the upcoming month being August because I knew what it would bring. Every available minute that I had, I shared with Abby and Remmy. I've been with them almost every day, even if it was only a few hours here and there. If our time is short, I take them out to lunch, dinner, or ice cream, whatever works for their schedule. We've gone to the park many times, fished on several occasions, took Remmy to the Children's Museum, and to a movie. A few times a week, Remmy has his tee ball games and I haven't missed a single one. I'm always out on the field helping his coach out wherever I'm needed, and I love every second of it.

I loved every moment with them, even when Remmy cried at the movies because he wanted candy and popcorn, but Abby told him no. That was the first time I saw Remmy have a fit. I didn't know what to do, but Abby handled it gracefully and I watched her in absolute awe. He quickly gathered himself, chose the popcorn, and we went on with our evening.

My mother had been insistent that I bring Abby and Remmy over to her house for lunch. To my surprise, Abby quickly agreed. I took the two of them over there yesterday, and I had no idea why I was so nervous. It wasn't like Abby was new to my mother; she watched her grow up after all. Regardless, I was a bundle of nerves in the beginning. My mother greeted the two of them with welcomed arms though and my mom was instantly puddy in Remmy's hands; she adored him, and he fawned over her, asking so many questions, like he usually does, but my mom gobbled it up.

The two of them made chocolate chip cookies together in the afternoon while Abby and I watched, a satisfied, content smile on Abby's face the entire time.

Abby and I haven't had the chance to have any alone time though, or a second *official* date; Remmy is always with us, but it hasn't even crossed my mind to not include him. Whenever I'm with the two of them, my heart feels like it's on a cloud. Whenever I'm away from them, I'm counting down the minutes until I can see them again, which is thankfully the very next day nine times out of ten.

The only times I wish we were alone is when I catch Abby's blazing look; it almost knocks me to my knees, and it takes all my strength not to scoop her up and kiss her. That's all I want to do, is just hold her, kiss her, and keep her close, but we haven't shown any kind of affection in front of Remmy. It's better that way, but I have been able to steal a few kisses here and there to get me by.

When Abby is busy with work or plans with her family, I've been working away on a special project—"The Abby Project" as I've been referring to it. About a week ago, when we were watching Remmy swim, Abby talked about how much she was starting to miss Florida; she missed her house, her backyard, her own space. She said she loved staying and visiting with her parents, but she was starting to miss her own rhythm. I understood that; it would be difficult to live with my mother again—even if it was just visiting for the summer. Abby gushed about her backyard to me though, all the flowers and her twinkling lights; she said when she had a bad day, that's where she would be with a bottle of wine. As much as it killed me that she was missing her Florida home though, it lit a fire within me.

The Abby Project was finally complete after weeks of work, and I think it's about time that I got that second date.

I was standing in my kitchen, leaning on the counter with sweat dripping off of me; I just worked my ass off underneath the sun, but I wanted to call Abby before I showered. She answered on the second ring, like she had been, but unlike the other times, her voice sounded off.

"Abby, everything okay?" I asked her instantly. I straightened my posture, alert. Abby hesitated on the other line and let out a sigh.

"Not really," Abby confessed; she sounded as if she'd been crying.

"What's wrong?" I asked her. The seconds ticked by, and I was still waiting for a response from Abby. It was starting to eat away at me. "Abby?"

I heard a sniffle on the other end, and I clutched at the cell phone tightly; wondering what the hell could have happened today. I talked to her a few hours ago and everything was fine; she was bubbly and all.

"It's nothing really, Sawyer…I just had a hard phone call," she whispered.

"With?" I asked, but I already knew the answer. My stomach started twisting aggressively; I took a deep breath, trying to slow my now racing heart. It wouldn't do Abby any favors if I went off the deep end; I already knew my temper was short when it involved Abby.

"Michael," she said.

Fucker.

"Ah," I said. "Do you want to talk about it?" Not that I really wanted to talk about Michael, but if she was upset, I was all ears for her. Whenever Michael's name was brought up, by her or Remmy, it made my skin crawl and stomach clench. He was a constant reminder to me that everything that I wanted could be easily taken away from me.

"Honestly, no. Not really," she said with a sigh. I closed my eyes. If she doesn't want to talk about it with me, then I can't push. I started pacing in circles around the kitchen, wondering when the hell this girl would start opening up with me.

"Okay," I said softly.

"But I guess I should tell you," she said. I let out the breath that I was holding.

"Michael was served the divorce papers today, so he's a little…. irate." My body stilled in the kitchen, and I almost dropped the cell phone from my hand.

Hell yes.

I sent a silent prayer to the man above and almost did a fist pump into the air, but said, "Abby, I'm so sorry. I guess I didn't realize how far you were into the process."

"Yeah, I've been working on it the last few weeks. I found a divorce lawyer in Florida, and she and I have had a bunch of Zoom meetings. She emailed me the paperwork earlier this week and I signed and overnighted them back. Apparently, he got them today."

"Wow."

"Yeah, Michael's pretty pissed, to say the least. He's saying that I blind sighted him, which I really don't know how I could have. He's said some pretty nasty things, but it's just typical Michael."

"Nasty things…like?" I stilled again in the kitchen, my jaw clenched. I already felt the blood start to boil.

"Like how he'll take Remmy from me, and I'll never see him again." *There it is.*

My legs started to shake as I heard her sniffle again. I closed my eyes and took a deep slow breath before I could respond.

"That will never happen, Abby. No judge would *ever* allow that. You are a great mom." She sighed in response.

"I know, but he'll still try to make it hell for me. It won't be an easy process. I honestly don't know why he's so upset; I thought this was what he wanted." Her trembling voice shot a pain so far deep inside of me. I hated that she was going through this. It wasn't fair. It wasn't right.

"Is this what you wanted?" I mumbled into the phone; I waited with cautious breaths for her response, but she didn't; my heart prickled in my chest. "Abby, if I'm complicating things for you, I'll step away. I hope you know that. I would never try to go in between you and your husband." I cursed at myself internally for saying those words; they were true though, I would bow out for the sake of Abby's and Remmy's happiness. But would they actually be happy if she stayed with him? It would hurt like hell stepping away, knowing that she wouldn't be.

And I wanted her. I wanted her in my life so fucking much that it about killed me.

"Oh, Sawyer," she said in a wavering tone. I hated that I wasn't there to console her right now, but I knew my presence would only complicate things more. I had to brace myself that maybe this thing with Abby wasn't going to work out like I hoped. If Michael was already playing dirty, then he could get what he wanted: scaring Abby into staying.

"I know that, Saw. You are not complicating anything. Even without you, this is what I would do. I can't be married to someone who doesn't love me. Honestly, I can't be married to someone that *I* no longer love." She let out a heavy sigh, and I listened to her heavy breathing, my lips mashed into a tight line and eyes closed.

"Tell me what I can do for you," I murmured into the phone. She let out a little chuckle, that sounded more like a hiccup.

"Thank you so much, Sawyer, but I'll be okay."

"Do you want me to kick his ass?" I asked, trying to lighten the mood. She hiccupped laughed again in the cutest fucking way. I felt my lips pull into a half smile.

"No, we don't need to go down *that* road again." I grinned, recalling the last time I went to her aid.

"I miss you," I murmured into the phone; I hadn't wanted to say those words to her, but they slipped out.

"I miss you too." Her voice was barely above a whisper, and it sent a dagger to the heart for the fact that she had to whisper those words and not speak them freely.

"Listen. I'm going to let you be tonight. You should relax tonight, spend the time with Remmy alone, and just think about everything, okay?"

Abby hesitated. "Sawyer—"

"No, I'm serious, Abby. This is a big ordeal you're going through. I'm not saying I won't be there on the other side of it all, but I just want you to go through this with a clear mind. I don't want to get in your way or confuse things for you. I know you say I'm not, but I feel like I am. Take the time tonight, think about everything, and I'll let you decide tomorrow if you want to see me."

My heart hammered in my chest, and I prayed to God that she would call me tomorrow. If she didn't, I didn't know what I would do.

"Okay," Abby said softly.

"Okay," I replied, smiling at our banter.

"I'll call you tomorrow," Abby told me. I let out a small sigh.

"Looking forward to it. Bye Abs."

"Bye."

Abby

I worked at Emma's daycare for a few hours today. I couldn't bear to get through an entire shift. My mind was buzzing all day and it was getting harder and harder to concentrate as the minutes ticked by. I felt like hell when Emma suggested that I go home; she could tell that my mind just wasn't in it today.

"I don't blame you, Abby," Emma told me kindly. She wrapped an arm around my shoulders and gave me a tug. "After having a conversation like that with Michael *and* Sawyer last night, there's no wonder you're all over the place. Go home, take a bath, relax, and I'll see you next week."

My mind was still going a million miles per minute as I drove home. I knew my mom had Remmy at the park right now, so the house would be empty; what a better time to go home and really think about my feelings. *Not.* Going home to an empty house was the exact opposite of what I wanted to do, but still, I drove home.

What I really wanted to do was go see Sawyer and let him take my mind off it all, but that's exactly what he didn't want to do. He was right; I did need to take a minute and just think everything over. Before Michael's phone call, I was certain that divorce was the right answer for us. He was a lying, cheating bastard that didn't have time for Remmy and me; I knew that, and I knew he wasn't going to change.

So what has me so hung up on it all now?

My conversation with Michael started playing in my head as I pulled the car into the driveway.

"What the *fuck*, Abby?" Michael yelled into the phone. My ear started ringing and I took the phone away from my ear. I glanced around at my parents and Remmy, who were sitting nearby, and I excused myself to the patio.

"How are you?" I asked him, nonchalantly.

"Oh, I don't know, Abby. I guess you can say I'm just a little bit confused over here. I'm sitting at my office today when someone walks in and serves me with papers. *At the office, Abby!*" I didn't say anything; I knew there wouldn't be a point. "Do you know how fucking embarrassing that is?"

"Do you know how embarrassing it is, to be the topic of gossip at that office? Because I've been there, done that."

"Oh, shut up," he snapped. I rolled my eyes and took a deep breath. I needed to calm myself down.

"Then, I open the papers, to find out that I'm being served by my *wife* for a *divorce*. What the *hell* is wrong with you, Abby?"

"And, this is a surprise to you because…?"

"Well, since you haven't *told* me that you wanted a divorce, yes, it is."

"Michael, we don't talk. When you call once a week, I hand the phone to Remmy. You're posting photos on social media with Hallie almost every day; you're clearly open about your affair with her to the world. I'm happy for you, *really*. Now, since you're moving on, I'm ready to as well." I was proud of myself for acting so calmly on the outside to him; underneath my skin, I was shaking.

Michael paused for a moment; I could hear his heavy breathing on the other end. I started pacing the outside deck, my hand on my hip, and kept telling myself to hold my ground and stand tall. I wasn't going to let him walk all over me anymore.

"Abby, we are not getting a divorce," Michael said, he, too, was trying to calm himself down.

"Michael, I no longer want to be a part of this marriage."

"We are not divorcing Abigail."

"Yeah, we are." I said, choking out a laugh. He can't be real right now?

"We made vows to each other, and we are sticking to them." I felt my jaw drop.

"Our vows were kind of shot the moment you started screwing Hallie…" I said, my eyebrows pulled together; this man infuriated me to no end.

"You're being immature," he said flatly. "Husbands sometimes screw around, it's just a fact of life." My jaw dropped more.

"Um, no Michael, that is *not* normal, nor will I be with someone who thinks that's okay. You said yourself when I was in Florida that you are no longer attracted to me because, what was that? I went up a few clothes sizes. Here you go, here's your out. *I'm done.*" Even though Michael couldn't see me, my hands were flailing all around my face; I was always one for the dramatics. Whenever I was angry, I couldn't contain them by my side.

God, I wanted a cigarette.

"I'm not letting you leave me."

"*Why?*" I said incredulously. "Michael, you don't *want* to be with me. Go be with Hallie, I don't give a shit anymore, just let me out of this marriage."

"Because I love you," Michael said simply; his tone was kinder than normal, but I still felt my insides raging.

"No, you *don't*," I nearly shouted into the phone.

"Abby, I don't know how to do all these things without you. This summer has been hell without you here."

"Because I'm not there to spend it with you, or there to take care of your responsibilities?" He hesitated. "That's what I thought. You will be fine, Michael, trust me. Find someone to help you with those things and you'll be golden. I'm sure your mother has a few suggestions. As for the divorce, I don't know if you read the papers, but I'm not asking for much at all. I just want *out*. Get with your attorney Frank, read them over, and we'll go from there. There's a section in there about Remmy."

"I read it," Michael seethed. "You want me to pay *you* child support?"

"It's a standard calculation, Michael."

"And you want full custody?"

"Well, since I'm with Remmy all the time, yes. I can barely get a hold of you; let alone get you to spend time with him."

"You've been in Illinois all fucking summer. How can I spend time with him?"

"*Get real*, Michael. Even if we were in Florida, you wouldn't be around and you know it." I felt my teeth clash together.

"You're not getting full custody; he's my boy and I want him raised right. Hell, you'll be lucky to even get *joint*. I know the judges around here, Abby, much better than you think. You want to go down this road? Fine. But don't be upset when tables are turned and he's all mine, and not yours."

My lower lip started to tremble, and my hands started to shake around the cell phone. *I can't lose my boy.*

"Michael," I said, trying to control my voice, "don't threaten me."

"Have it your way, Abigail. You want this, I'm all for it, baby. Can't wait to not be married to your bitchy ass, but just remember what you asked for in a few months' time." Michael lowered his voice. "If I were you, I'd get your ass back to Florida."

Then he hung up on me. Even recalling the conversations with him, made the tears start to flow. I've replayed this conversation with Michael repeatedly in my head today, contemplating if his threats were real. I couldn't imagine that he would want full or joint custody of Remmy. He was never home, always working or out socializing. Not that he would give any of that up, he'd probably hire a nanny and continue what he was doing. But still, he could just go through with it to make a point to me. His parents were very involved in the community and knew all the right people; Michael always boasted about that to me. That should have been my first red flag with him.

There was no way in hell I was losing my son to that fucking asshole.

Instead of falling apart in the car, I got up and walked up the sidewalk to the front porch. The last thing I needed was someone in this small town to see me crying in my car; rumors would spread like wildfire, and I knew it was best to go inside and fall apart there. I was digging in my purse for my parents' house key, finally locating the key as I stepped up on the porch. Something caught my eye though and I glanced over and stood up straighter as I focused on the object before me.

Lying ever so still on my mother's rocker was a single sunflower.

I quickly ushered over to the rocker and stared at it, eyes wide. There was a small note tied to it with string. I picked up the stem gingerly with my fingers and inhaled the beautiful yellow pedals. The note, in a messy, but familiar scrawl, read, *"A reminder for you that you are stronger than you think. Love, Sawyer."*

My lower lip started to tremble as I fought back more tears that were trying to escape. My eyes kept scanning the simple, yet perfect words from Sawyer and I clutched the single flower to my rapid heart. I glanced around outside, hoping that Sawyer was still here, but I already knew he wasn't. I knew he meant his words last night, that he wanted me to have time to think about everything, and I knew he was right; yet, this kind, sweet gesture from him, was my reminder of what I wanted.

I wanted to be with Sawyer.

I quickly unlocked the front door and stepped inside, letting my purse crash to the floor next to me. The house was still, as I had expected it to be. I walked over to the kitchen and placed the beautiful sunflower into the vase with the dying one. The two of them clashed together in the vase as I stared at them, my mind racing all over again.

I felt chills course up my spine as I thought about my decision. Sawyer was sweet, kind, maybe cocky at times but that just added to my attraction for him, and he was good to my son. He always made time for Remmy, and he never complained that he was always with us these last few weeks. He cared about Remmy, it was evident all over his face. I knew Remmy was loving Sawyer. Being with Sawyer this summer was as easy as breathing. He made me feel beautiful, never contradicted my thoughts or told me that I was stupid for thinking a certain way; he validated my feelings and listened to me when I talked. He was the whole package, and he was right here in front of me with open arms.

I grabbed my cell phone and noticed I had a text from Michael. I wanted to ignore it, but instead I clicked on it. *Have a flight home yet?*

Fuck you, dude, I thought. I ignored him, went to my contacts, and dialed Sawyer's number. He answered on the third ring.

"Hey, is this a bad time?" I asked.

"No, not at all," Sawyer said, heavily. "I'm just at the gym. You're good."

"Oh, well, I'll keep this short," I told him. Sawyer waited for me to continue; I could hear loud clanking of the gym equipment in the background and Sawyer's staggering breaths. "I'm getting the divorce; there's no question about that, okay? Also, I want to spend my time with you as much as I can this summer. I have really enjoyed your company, Sawyer, and if you want to see where this goes, then I'm in."

"Abby, are you sure?"

"Positive."

"Okay," Sawyer said.

"Okay," I said, smiling. "I loved the sunflower, by the way. I just got home."

"I'm glad," Sawyer said. "So, is it too early to ask you out tonight? I mean, we haven't had a second date yet."

"Not at all," I told him. "What do you have in mind?"

"Oh, something lowkey, if you're okay with it."

"No sunflowers?" I asked.

"Not the field this time, but there may be some flowers involved, yes." He chuckled. "How about you meet me at my place tonight and I will cook you dinner?"

"Okay," I replied instantly. But I was instantly full of nerves; my stomach clenched as I thought about his invitation. I wasn't sure if I was ready for that kind of alone time with Sawyer yet.

"Okay," Sawyer said. I could practically see his grin through the phone. "I'll see you later, Abby."

"Bye," I said, hanging up. As soon as I hit the end button I jumped into the air like a deranged person and let out an excited shriek. Who the hell was I?

Dinner at Sawyer's tonight, just the two of us?

This could be very, very bad, or very fun.

I was about to find out.

*****

It was seven o'clock and I was finally pulling into Sawyer's driveway. He texted me earlier to show up around seven if I could, and I quickly agreed. It gave me time to help Mom make Remmy's dinner and for me to give him his bath. Remmy surprised me tonight; I thought he would fall to the floor when he found out he wasn't coming with, but he was okay with it. He gave me a tight hug that warmed my heart and said, "Go have fun, Mommy." He was the sweetest boy I could ever ask for.

I couldn't seem to get my legs moving out of the car. My hands were trembling like mad, and I couldn't calm the fluttering of my heart and stomach. I was looking forward to my evening with Sawyer, but the thought of spending alone time with him terrified me to no end. One touch from that man would have me spinning like a top. Hell, one *look* would probably even do the trick. I also didn't know what Sawyer expected from this evening. Just dinner, or did he expect more? I wasn't sure, but I also knew he wouldn't pressure me if I wasn't ready. That's what I was trying to figure out, too. Was I ready for that next step in our relationship?

My body screamed yes, *absolutely*. I wanted him, craved him. Just the thought of him on top of me sent my insides writhing. But was my heart ready for that? Could I let Sawyer see that vulnerable side of me? Hell, would I be able to let Sawyer see me *naked*? The thought of it terrified me; what if he didn't like what he saw? What if he didn't like the softness of my belly, or the stripes that now bore on my stomach?

I was a fucking mess.

I looked at the front of Sawyer's house, trying to get the courage to go inside. I could see the lights shining inside from the curtains and I knew he was probably impatiently waiting for me; he had never been a patient person. I swear I even saw his face emerge into the curtains for a second. I licked my lips, closed my eyes, and counted to ten out loud. One…two…three….

I heard his front door open and opened my eyes. Sawyer stood there, his eyebrow cocked in my direction and that oh so fine smirk on his lips. He leaned on the side of the door frame, arms folded across his chest and my goodness, did he look amazing. How the hell he could make a simple outfit, jean shorts and a black snug tee, look like he was a runway model, I had no idea. He had a white hand towel draped over his right shoulder that caused me to smile. My stomach fluttered again.

"You comin' in or what?" he called to me.

I nodded, turned to my passenger seat, and scooped up my purse and the cake. I opened the front door and on shaky legs, walked up to him, my eyes on my steps as I walked. I heard a low chuckle from Sawyer, but I ignored him; one look up at him, I'd probably run like hell in the other direction.

"Hi," he said to me, as I stepped in front of him. I forced my eyes to look at him. He had his crooked grin on and soft eyes.

"Hi," I replied.

"What do you have there?" he asked, nodding to the cake.

"Oh, um. We made you a cake today," I said with a low laugh. "Chocolate, nothing fancy." Sawyer's eyes sparkled as he took the cake from my hands.

"You made me a dessert?" I nodded, not being able to find my voice. Did he think that was stupid, or what? Why the hell was he looking at me that way?

"Abs, thank you so much. You didn't have to do that."

"We wanted to. Mom and Remmy helped." Sawyer stood up from the doorway and ushered me in.

"Can't wait to try it," he said, his eyes shining. He took a step inside and nodded to the house. I kept my feet planted on his patio, clutching my purse tightly. He cocked an eyebrow at me. "Are you coming in, Abby?" He let out a soft laugh, eyes dancing.

"I-I think so," I told him; I felt my breathing start to pick up. I heard Sawyer let out another small chuckle as he took a step toward me, his eyes narrowing in my direction.

"Just dinner, Abby," Sawyer whispered; his husky voice sent my heart racing even more.

"I *know...*" I told him, biting my lip.

"You know, the dinner, that's going to get cold if you don't get your cute ass inside." He nodded to the door. I took a deep breath, smiled as best as I could, and stepped inside.

The aroma from the kitchen filled me as soon as I stepped inside; garlic, oregano, and something else. I lifted my head to the smell, my stomach gurgling in response. Sawyer heard and grinned.

"Glad you're hungry, I made a lot." I went to slip out of my shoes, but Sawyer shook his head. "Leave them on, I thought we'd eat outside." I nodded and set my purse down next to the front door. I took a step towards the kitchen, but Sawyer stopped me abruptly. He leaned in and planted a soft kiss on my cheek. "Glad you're here," he whispered. His husky voice sent chills up my spine.

"Me, too," I whispered, trying to relax.

Sawyer led me to the kitchen and I followed slowly behind him, the smells from the kitchen making my stomach lurch. It really smelled *amazing*. He set the cake on the counter and grabbed gray oven mitts nearby, motioning to the stove. "I made you chicken parmesan," he said triumphantly, his eyes beaming. He was clearly proud of himself.

"I hope you like pasta," he laughed, opening the stove.

"I love it," I replied softly. What I didn't tell him was that he could have made Ramen Noodles and I probably would have been just as elated; no one has ever prepared anything for me before, let alone cooked chicken parmesan for me. I watched as he worked away in the kitchen, taking a large pan from the stove.

"I didn't think you cooked though," I teased. He chuckled.

"I don't, but I *can* cook, there's a difference." He shrugged and turned to me, bowing. "For you, sweetheart, I'd do anything."

My lanta....

"Can I help at all?" I asked, looking around the kitchen. He already had most of the dishes washed and it didn't look like there was anything left, but I felt useless standing nearby.

"Oh, no, this is all for you," he said, looking around. "Okay, plates…" He went to a nearby cabinet and pulled out a few white square plates.

"Saw, I can help," I said. "Let me help you." Sawyer sighed and rolled his eyes.

"Okay, you can get the wine out of the fridge. You like wine, right?" I nodded and turned to grab the wine. "There's white and red, you pick. I like both."

I found the wine bottles and scanned them each, before deciding on trying the white.

"Winking Owl, I've never heard of it," I told him, taking the bottle to the counter. It fittingly had a picture of an owl on the label.

"It's from Aldi," he told me, which caused my eyebrow to lift. He was scooping chicken parmesan to each of our plates but let out a chuckle. "Don't knock it until you try it. I've heard so many good things about it, I had to pick up a few bottles. We'll try it together."

"Glasses?" I asked, looking around the cabinets. He nodded in the direction of the cabinet right in front of me. I pulled out two wine glasses, impressed that he even had tall, stemmed glasses. They were beautiful, and they reminded me of the ones I had back home. Sawyer opened the silverware drawer, taking out forks for each of us, and handed the corkscrew to me. I got to work popping the wine bottle open and started to pour each of us a glass. The bottle was already half empty by the time I was finished. I internally reminded myself of my drink rule, determined not to get messy tonight. I wanted to savor every second of this evening with Sawyer and did not want to have a cloudy head with him. I gingerly placed the corkscrew back on, and went to put it inside the fridge again, but Sawyer shook his head at me again.

"We'll bring the bottle out."

I held the two glasses out in front of me and was about ready to walk out to the back, when Sawyer quickly stopped me, his eyes light.

"What?" I asked. "I thought we were eating outside."

A wide grin spread across Sawyer's face. I felt my eyebrow lift and tilted my head to the side.

"Yes, but first, I want to show you something," Sawyer said. He took the glasses from me quickly and set them nearby; he was practically skipping in front of me. "Do you trust me?" His eyes searched mine, wide and excitement spilling from his pores. I let out a laugh.

"I don't know, depends, I guess so...."

Sawyer bit his bottom lip and walked behind me, putting his hands over my eyes. I recoiled and went to grab his hands off me. He lifted his head close to my ear and whispered, "I have a surprise for you." I froze and felt a shiver shoot up my spine.

"And I can't see where I'm going...?" I asked, hesitant.

"Nope, part of the surprise. Just walk straight ahead, I'll get the door."

I groaned, my curiosity peaked. "Sawyer..."

"Don't ruin my fun, Abs. Please," he begged.

"Okay..."

"Cover your eyes for me." He moved his hands, and I replaced it with my right hand. I felt Sawyer's hand reach my free hand as he led me to the back door. "Okay, no peeking." I heard the creak of the screen door as he led me closer, my steps slow so I wouldn't trip. "Okay, you have a step here, careful now." Sawyer murmured. His grip was firm around my hand as I gingerly took a step out, my shoes hitting the pavement.

The summer air blasted all around me, but that wasn't what caught my attention first; there was a radio nearby playing soft music, old country songs that I hadn't heard in ages. I couldn't hide the smile from my face, curious to see what he could have done back here that he was so damn excited about.

"Okay, okay," Sawyer said. "*Open.*"

I removed my hand from my eyes quickly and took in the area before me. I caught my breath as I scanned the transformed backyard. I felt the tears wielding in my eyes as I looked from the beaming Sawyer back to his creation. My fingers lifted to my lips, and then fell to my skipping heart.

If I didn't know any better, I would never guess I was standing in Sawyer's backyard. My eyes flitted back and forth wide in amazement of what he had done. I didn't know what to look at first, there was so much to see that caught my attention. On each corner of the patio were large wooden barrels that had beautiful red and white petunias planted around large wooden posts. Each post had a string of beautiful twinkling lights that dangled from post to post with intricate matching hooks that held beautiful hanging plants, of what kind of flowers, I wasn't sure, but they were wonderful additions; reds, blues, and greens hanging from each pot. On the patio—where the folding chairs and cooler once were—a large, black, square dining table with matching black chairs and beige cushions sat; it could fit six people comfortably. On top of the table, was a large clear vase with an arrangement of sunflowers, daisies, and baby's breath. The table had three white single candles already lit.

I had no words. I was beyond touched and looked back over at him, shaking my head ever so slightly.

"Sawyer..." I whispered.

"Do you like it?" he asked, scanning my face. His nose was scrunched, and his lower lip pulled in by his teeth.

"I can't believe you did this," I said, looking around. "It's beautiful. *When* did you do this?"

Sawyer sprang to my side, taking his hand within mine in seconds.

"I've been working on it all week. I had a little help. Lance helped some, and my mom," he added sheepishly, grinning a little. I looked back around the patio and turned to see a wooden bar painted black sitting there, with more candles lit on top of the bar, a silver ice bucket next to the radio.

"This must have cost you a lot..." I murmured. He shrugged.

"I wanted to do this for you," he mumbled quietly. "You said you missed your oasis back home, so I thought I'd make you one here." He shrugged again, as if this was no big deal when, this was the most spectacular gesture anyone could have done for me. I turned my head toward him and caught his sheepish grin. My insides were turning into mush in front of him. I was surprised that I wasn't melting into a puddle at his feet. I brought my hand to my heart again, touched from head to toe by Sawyer Gibson.

"That," I said softly, "is probably the sweetest thing anyone has ever done for me." I told him sincerely; my throat started to tighten as tears clouded my vision. *Do not break down like an emotional fool, Abby.*

I turned to him and watched his eyes practically dance before me. I couldn't help myself anymore. I leaned in, inhaling his scent; I could never pinpoint Sawyer's smell. I was determined to savor this very moment for years to come. My eyes looked down at his parted lips, and then back to his now smoldering stare. I leaned in closer, my hands lightly gripping each bicep, and gently placed my lips against his; the softness and fullness of his mouth on mine sent my mind into a hazy fog. His soft kisses sent shivers up my spine as I melted into him, my body molded against his perfectly. He moved his hands to my face, cradling me so gently as his kisses intensified, crushing harder into my own.

He buried his hands into the back of my hair, cradling my head carefully with delicate hands as if I would break; when what I wanted him to do was hold me tighter. He parted my lips with his softly, his tongue lingering against mine for the slightest moment. A soft moan escaped the back of my throat, when Sawyer finally lifted his lips. He placed his forehead on mine, trying to control his staggered breaths. His eyes were closed, showing off those long lashes of his, when finally, he met my gaze.

"I think we should stop," Sawyer said, a low chuckle escaping him.

"Probably," I agreed, smiling. "Thank you so much for doing this for me, Sawyer. You have no idea how much this means to me."

He grinned, kissed me lightly once more, and then said, "This is all yours, Abby. You can come over here whenever you want and enjoy your oasis." I stole another kiss from him; this one lingered when Sawyer chuckled and pulled me away from him.

"We should eat before the food gets cold," Sawyer said, his eyes mischievous.

My stomach grumbled in response as he took my hand in his and led me back into his kitchen. Together we brought everything that needed to be taken out to the table. I put the wine bottle into the ice bucket and turned my attention back to the table. Sawyer was staring at it, his eyebrows scrunched together, when he turned to me, a frown on his face.

"*Fuck* Abby, I forgot to throw in the garlic bread." He scowled. I giggled and grabbed his hand.

"It's *fine*, Sawyer, we don't need garlic bread. This looks amazing." I told him, gesturing to the table. He smashed his lips together still though.

"I bought one of those stupid bread bowls for the garlic bread and everything," he said with a growl. "Can I please make it, just real quick?" he asked. I shook my head at him.

"We'll use that stupid bread bowl a different time." I brushed his arm. "Just sit and relax and let's enjoy this wonderful meal you made us." He grumbled and walked over to my chair, pulling it out for me. My heart lifted again as I sat down, and he slowly pushed me in. His hand lightly brushed my bare shoulder, and before he sat down next to me, he leaned down and kissed it, and then my cheek. I felt my head lean into him and closed my eyes.

He's so fucking perfect.

Sawyer plopped down next to me and together we grabbed our forks. At first bite, I chewed carefully, savoring the taste. I let out a satisfied hum and turned to him. He was watching me intently, his teeth clenched, and nose scrunched.

"You like it?" he asked. I nodded, covering my mouth with my hand.

"Sawyer, I'm so impressed; this is *delicious*." He let out a satisfied sigh and dug into his own plate.

We talked very little while we ate our food; in truth, I was starving. I hadn't had much of an appetite lately and proudly dug into my plate. The sky was starting to darken around us, and the twinkling lights and candles started to give his patio a soft comforting glow. I cleaned my plate, probably a little too quickly for a lady, but I didn't care. Sawyer didn't seem to care either. He was thrilled that I enjoyed the dinner so much, and he cleaned his, too. We both sat back in our chairs, looking up at the darkening sky; the clouds were barely visible, soft gray swirls up in the sky now. Soon the stars would shine above us.

I cocked my head toward the song that was playing on the radio; it was Keith Urban singing *"Making Memories of Us"*. I felt my heart constrict while I listened to his soft melody.

"Abby Lou, will you dance with me?" Sawyer asked, hesitantly. I opened my eyes at once; Sawyer was already standing, I didn't even hear him shuffle to his feet, and he extended a hand to me. My lips turned into a soft smile as I gently placed my hand in his. He pulled me in the direction of the radio and then drew me into his warm embrace. He squeezed my hand in his and wrapped his other arm around my back. I laid my head on his chest as he gently swayed us back and forth.

"Abby?" Sawyer whispered. I could hear the vibrations through his chest and his quickening heartbeat.

"Mmm?"

"I'm so glad you came home."

"Me, too, Saw." I whispered; I wrapped my arm tighter around him as he squeezed me.

"I would do anything for you, you know that, right?" he murmured, his lips brushed the top of my head.

"Yes," I whispered back.

"You mean the world to me; you always have." My eyes popped open; I didn't know what to say back to him. "Even then," he whispered, "I knew you were it for me."

I pulled my head from his chest to meet his gaze. His softened expression nearly tore at my heart. I searched his eyes, trying to find what, I didn't know, but I felt my lower lip start to tremble again. He gave me a kind smile, as his cheeks started to flush. Sawyer Gibson was embarrassed. I thought his bravado wouldn't allow such an emotion.

"You couldn't have known that," I told him, eyes narrowing a little playfully. I was trying to make light of how serious he was making this out to be.

"Oh, but I did." His face fell a little, eyes looking around us, as if searching for the right words to say. "When you showed up to my dad's funeral..." he started to say, but he hesitated. My heart instantly crushed in my chest as I saw the tears start to pool in his baby blues. His voice lowered, choking a little, "And when you took my hand in yours, I knew it right then. Everything my dad said to me about you, I knew it was true. You stayed with me, Abby. You hugged me, you consoled me, and you never left my side—not once that day. I can't tell you how much that meant to me." I watched as a tear trickled down his face and he casually brushed it away with his shoulder.

"Saw," I murmured, holding him tighter. I rubbed his back softly, "I wouldn't have had it any other way. It destroyed me to see you in so much pain."

"I was in such a dark place, Abby. There were times that I thought I'd never be happy again. But then I would see you, walking the halls at school, or running around town." He looked back at me, his eyes fierce. "I saw you, and you were the light for me. Everything about you glowed and I knew even then that I wanted to be with you. But I was always so angry, and I knew you deserved better. When you told me to fuck off that one day in my truck, it was like a switch for me. I knew I had to work on myself and get better before I could start anything with you. Plus, you hated me." He chuckled a little. "Which didn't help."

"I didn't hate you, Sawyer. I liked you, probably more than you think I did. Seeing you like that, so mad, it terrified me. I was scared for you. I didn't know how to help you, but you pushed me away. You acted like you didn't want my help. I talked to Lance, and he told me to just give you some time, so I did. I never hated you though. I could never hate you, Sawyer, no matter how much I tried."

Sawyer sighed and hugged me closer to him. "I wish it didn't take me so long to get my shit together. You and I could already be together." I laid my head back on his chest, my heart ramping from his words. "Then maybe you wouldn't have married that asshole," he mumbled.

"He may be an asshole, but that asshole gave me my son. I wouldn't change a thing. Besides, Saw, I'm here with you now. We didn't lose that much time," I told him softly. Sawyer sighed.

"I know, and I love that kid. I really do, Abby." My heart lifted at his words and a contented smile spread on my lips.

We were still swaying to the music. I wasn't aware that the song changed, but it was another soft country song, still appropriate for us to be dancing to. I listened to Sawyer's heart race in his chest as I wrapped my arms around him securely; I never wanted to let go of this man.

"Do you remember what I said to you at graduation?" Sawyer murmured to me. I cocked my head up, looking at his eyes, my brows lifted.

"You mean, when you walked up to me, looked at me straight in the eye and said, *'Abigail Foster, one day, I'm going to marry you.'*" Sawyer lips turned upwards into an impish grin.

"And you said, *'You fucking wish, Sawyer Gibson'*," he said with a low chuckle. "Such a potty mouth, Abby. Tsk, tsk." He narrowed his eyes on me. I laughed.

"What made you even say that?" I asked him. "I've always wondered."

Sawyer grinned. "Well, first off, you beat me at Valedictorian. I remember sitting with our classmates, listening to you give a speech that should have been mine." He narrowed his eyes at me, "And I just kind of watched you. You were exquisite up there, so poised and I remember thinking how perfect and beautiful you looked. Everyone threw their caps up in the air shortly after, but I didn't. Instead, I looked over at you." He gave a noncommittal shrug. "You were laughing, looking up, and I thought, 'Sweet Jesus, I would be so lucky to have her as mine'."

"Oh you did *not* think that, Sawyer." I rolled my eyes at him. His stare widened purposely.

"No, I did. When we walked back out, instead of standing in the line, I walked right up to you, and told you that I was going to marry you. I just wanted you to know."

"I couldn't believe you said that," I said. "But, I have to say, on my wedding day, your words did pop back into my head. I actually thought to myself, well, Sawyer was wrong."

Sawyer's eyes narrowed a little. "I got drunk on the day of your wedding, if that tells you anything."

"What?" I asked, eyebrows pulling together. "*Why?*"

"Because I couldn't bear the thought of you marrying some douche look alike."

"You never met him before," I chided.

"I didn't have to; he looked like a douche on the Save the Date card." Sawyer rolled his eyes. "Sorry, Abby, I shouldn't say that, but it's the truth, really. My mom went to your wedding and begged me to go with her, but I just couldn't go."

"I wish you would have," I told him.

"No, I knew I couldn't, because I'd probably embarrass the fuck out of you in some way, shape, or form." I rolled my eyes at him, shaking my head. "Sorry I didn't go though. My mom said you were pretty. I wish I could have seen you; I probably would have tried to steal his spot as groom though…so…" he joked.

I laughed and shook my head again at him. "It did break my heart, just a little, that you didn't come, but I understood why."

What I didn't tell him, was that at the reception, I was secretly scanning the crowd just for him. I just wanted a glimpse of the famous Sawyer Gibson to see how he turned out. Was he still moody and sullen, or was he back to his charismatic self?

I leaned back into Sawyer's embrace, my head back on his firm chest. I warmed into his arms, feeling his strong muscles wrapped tightly around me; he made me feel more secure than I've ever felt before. Sawyer kissed my head again, his fingers lightly tracing shapes on the back of my arms, leaving a trail of goosebumps behind them. I knew that I could probably stand in this position with Sawyer forever; I nearly pinched myself to make sure I wasn't dreaming of this picture perfect memory with him.

When the song ended, I looked up at Sawyer and met his gaze. He grinned down at me and lightly kissed the top of my nose. I laughed. "Should we clean up?" I asked gesturing to the table with our dirty plates. He nodded and reluctantly broke free from me. I helped him scoop up our dirty plates and silverware and together we made our way back into the kitchen. He started rinsing in the sink as I looked around for his dishwasher.

"Saw, where's your dishwasher?" I asked. Sawyer cocked an eyebrow at me, and chuckled.

"Right here, Abby Lou," he said, wriggling his fingers. My eyes popped open.

"You don't have a dishwasher?"

"No, Abby, I don't have one. It's just me here. I don't need one. Plus, I never really understood dishwashers. Don't you have to rinse them pretty well, practically wash it, before putting them in the dishwasher to be cleaned anyway? Why not just clean them yourself and save that extra step. Also, they use a lot of water, so I hear."

I shook my head at him and patted his shoulder. "I guess you're right, but it just kind of saves time."

"I'll just take the extra few minutes and wash them," Sawyer said with a mischievous glint in his eye. I approached him.

"Like, right *now*?" I asked, my eyebrow raised. I was slowly meandering close to him when Sawyer whipped his head around. His eyebrows rose into the air as I wrapped my arms tightly around his waist again, my eyes never leaving his.

"Abby…" he said cautiously, but I felt his hands touch my waist and my back.

"Hmmm…?" I asked, stepping on my tiptoes to plant a kiss on him. He chuckled underneath my lips and shook his head at me.

"Don't you want to go back outside?" he asked between kisses.

"If you want to," I told him politely, but now my lips were on his cheek and trailing down to his neck.

I heard a low growl come from the back of Sawyer's throat as he quickly plucked me up and set me on top of the counter, as if I weighed nothing. I wrapped my legs around his waist automatically, drawing him in close; still, he felt too far away. His eyes blazed mine, a look of hunger and need dilating his pupils. I felt my breath catch in my throat from his burning stare, but it didn't stop me from touching him. I wrapped my arms around his broad shoulders, my hands touching shoulders, his back, and then his chest. I wanted to feel him without the shirt and watched as his eyes narrowed as my hands snuck underneath to feel his soft skin. I nearly moaned from just grazing his pecs, feeling the chiseled lines. His eyes slowly closed, his head lowering as he let me touch him. I brought my hands up to his shoulders, touching and grazing them with my fingertips. I watched as a shutter escaped Sawyer and I knew right then I was all in; I was all fucking in for this moment with him.

I gripped the bottom of his shirt and slowly tugged it upward, Sawyer's eyes instantly finding mine again with that same scorching look on his face.

"Abby," he said, clearing his throat. He placed his large hand on top of mine. "If we start this...." He was lost for words, just like I was, but his eyes were pleading with me to understand.

"Just shut up and kiss me," I told him. Sawyer's eyes turned dark as he mashed his lips against mine, giving in to my needs. I was all hands; I tugged at his shirt again, only removing my lips from his to pull the shirt off completely. Before going back to our kissing, I examined his chest and felt a gasp erupt me as I laid my hands on his pecs, giving in to the urges that I'd been controlling every time I'd seen him in the pool. Underneath the soft glow from the kitchen light, he looked like a freakin' god, and all I wanted in this very moment was to be destroyed by him.

Sawyer leaned in and pressed his lips to mine again hungrily; his urgency stung me, but it wasn't nearly hard enough. I wanted more. I clung to his upper body, my chest pressed against his, when Sawyer's kisses went from my lips to my neck. I lifted my head and closed my eyes, letting out a soft sigh. I wrapped my arms around his neck, drawing him closer to me as he sucked and left trailing kisses from my throat down to my chest. In a fluid motion, Sawyer went to tug at my own shirt, but I quickly froze in place. I clutched his hands tightly, my eyes alarmed.

"Are you okay?" he asked breathlessly, the burn in his eyes switched to concern as if he flipped a switch. I nodded and cleared my throat.

"Y-yes," I stammered. "I just...." I looked down at his hands on my shirt when it clicked with Sawyer. Every time we were in the pool together, I always had a one piece on, never two.

Sawyer lifted my chin until my eyes met his; his eyebrows were lifted, jaw clenched. "Abby, you are beautiful. Nothing will change my mind about you."

I sucked in a breath and bit my lower lip, trying to calm my blazing nerves. I was having an internal debate with myself to just freakin' cool it and told myself that my insecurities were ruining the mood when Sawyer lifted my hand and kissed the top of it with his mouth.

"Let's just take this slow," he told me, his eyes soft. Slowly, he placed his hand on my stomach and slipped his large hand underneath my shirt. I felt my skin sizzle where he touched, and the desire pooled over me all over again; my insecurities be damned.

"I do *not* want slow," I told him breathlessly.

Making a quick decision, I slipped the shirt off me and tossed it on the floor next to his. Sawyer's eyes widened ever so slightly, the burn evident all over his face. He gave me his cocky grin and it sent my knees trembling. Without looking down to my stomach, he came back in for an urgent kiss, whispering, "You are so fucking beautiful," in between kisses. I felt my body melt into him, clutching him as hard as I dared.

Sawyer quickly lifted me from the counter, my legs still wrapped around him tightly, and carried me out of the kitchen, his arm cradling me to his chest. My hands were now in his hair as his lips hungrily ravaged mine; he stopped walking, pushing my back into his hallway wall, his free hand trying to turn the doorknob. I felt a soft moan escape me again as his tongue flitted into my mouth and tasted him; his sweet kisses burned my lips, and I couldn't wait for this part to be over with. I didn't need any more foreplay. I was all in, and I wanted him so fucking badly.

He staggered into his bedroom, still cradling me tightly and flopped me on the bed, his body instantly on top of me. His mouth left mine and he started trailing kisses down my neck, to my chest, and then to my stomach. He softly touched my stomach as he kissed my lines.

"Is this what you're so worried about?" he murmured, his lips still on my stomach. I felt my back arch as his fingers gently slid up and down my stomach.

"Y-yes," I stammered.

"I'll just have to show you how beautiful you truly are," he whispered, his lips trailing soft kisses over my stomach. I pushed more into him, a soft hum erupting from me.

Sawyer, Sawyer, Sawyer....

Sawyer's lips trailed up ever so deliciously. I felt my fingers dig into his bedding, wanting, and craving so much more. His kisses tingled my skin as his fingers trailed up my stomach, to my waist, and much too slow. I felt his fingertips trail up my sides, shivers shooting head to toe. I felt my body shake from his gentle touch. Slowly, his fingertips cascaded upward to my chest, and I drew in a breath as he freed my breasts. A low appreciative hum erupted from Sawyer's throat. He cupped my breasts into his large hands gingerly, his mouth back to mine as he slipped his tongue into my mouth. I arched my back once more, pressing my lower half harder into him. I wanted this man more than I ever wanted anyone and felt a heavy sigh escape me as I felt his hardened bulge pressed into me.

Sawyer's eyes met mine. I bit my lip at his hardened stare as his hand flitted to my back, unhooking my bra, and helping me escape the tangled lacy wire. He threw it to the side of the bed, his eyes never leaving mine; my heart thumped wildly underneath his penetrating stare.

His mouth went back to mine, but much to my liking, trailed down to my breasts, my nipple hardening underneath his mouth. My nipples tingled deliciously as my body started to shake underneath him. His other hand cupped my other breast and I let my head fall back into his pillow. I was going to lose all control with Sawyer on top of me, but it no longer frightened me. I welcomed it, and needed it. I needed him.

Sawyer's hands left my chest and slowly drew to my legs, his fingertips featherlight on my skin, burning me the entire way. I shuddered. His eyes shot back to mine, determination blazing his features. I watched him slowly lift my flowing skirt up, up, up... my heart thudding fiercely as his fingers trailed my thighs. Another small moan escaped me as his fingers touched my satin panties; I watched as Sawyer's eyes glazed over and he shook his head at me.

"Abby, you are *so* damn beautiful," he whispered earnestly. I bit my bottom lip as his lips met my panty line; I whimpered, my fingers digging back into his soft comforter.

Sawyer glanced back up at me, his mouth on my panty line as he slowly moved his hand underneath. I felt my mouth drop as his finger slowly entered me. I closed my eyes, but Sawyer stopped.

"I want to see your eyes," he murmured. "Don't close them." I sucked in a breath as his finger traced circles around my wall and up to the delicate bud, teasing it in swift motions.

"*Oh, Sawyer,*" I said, my head falling back. I couldn't help it, my eyes closed again. His fingers thrashed against my clit, and I felt my knees tremble. I didn't know how much longer I could take of this sweet torture; my entire body throbbed, building up to the release I so desperately desired.

Sawyer slid my panties off in a quick motion, discarding them on the floor next to the bed, his fingers back to my entrance. He pushed them inside of me as I held my breath, but then he stopped; my heart pounded as Sawyer's eyes met mine, never leaving my gaze as his head lowered to my core. He pressed his mouth gently into me, bringing those beautiful fantasies I'd been having to life. His beard felt satisfying between my legs, *amazing*. I shut my mouth to try to fight back the moan but lost. I let out a loud cry as my fingers intertwined in his silky hair.

"*Sawyer*," I breathed.

"Hmm…" he murmured.

"*Oh*," I cried.

He continued licking and sucking, pressing his fingers into me and I cried out again, again, and again. I felt my body hum underneath his mouth; all my control would be lost very soon if he kept continuing. His hands flitted to my breasts as his fingers rolled my nipples.

And I lost it. My body erupted with intense pleasure. I felt my legs tremble as I pushed them around his waist, my toes curling into his thighs. My head fell back as my fingers weaved more into his hair and to his shoulders. He lifted his mouth and watched as I came detached.

Sawyer slowly moved up to me, kissing each breast as his mouth found my neck, and then to my earlobe.

"I want you so badly, Abby. Can I have you?" he breathed. I nodded, unable to speak. My hands flitted to his shoulders, pulling him tighter on top of me. With his head buried into my hair, he leaned to the side of his bed and pulled out a silver package. He propped himself up as he slipped off the remainder of his clothes, freeing himself. My eyes widened as I looked down at him, standing tall. I looked back up at his face, my breathing ragged, as he ripped the plastic with his teeth. Before he slipped on the latex, he gently grabbed my hand and brought it to him.

"I want you to feel me first," he murmured huskily. I drew in a breath, biting my bottom lip as my hand discovered him, felt him. I felt my eyes harden into his stare as I gently pumped back and forth. To my satisfaction, Sawyer let his head fall back, reveling in the moment.

Sawyer grabbed my hand, kissing the top of it, before covering his perfection with latex. He pulled my waist closer to him, repositioning me underneath him. He kissed the insides of my thighs, causing another moan to escape me, before Sawyer stilled, his eyes back to mine.

"Do you want this?" Sawyer whispered to me. I nodded fiercely, clearing my throat.

"I need you to say it, Abby. Tell me you want this," he said, his eyes scorching me.

"I want this," I whispered. "I want *you*, Sawyer."

He nodded, leaning over me, bringing his mouth back to mine in a soft kiss. I wrapped my arms around his back, pulling him tighter to me. I wanted to feel his naked chest to mine. I felt my body still as his erection touched me; he lifted his lips from mine, his eyes soft, yet still burning.

And then I felt him; we were two perfect jigsaw pieces, a perfect match for the other. I whimpered as my head fell back again, savoring this delicious feeling. My head started to feel fuzzy, as if I was drunk just by his love making. Agonizingly, he pushed back and forth slowly as my body adjusted around him. I felt my fingers dig into his back as his movements quickened, his chest crushing mine.

"*Abby*," he huffed. "You feel amazing."

I moaned in response.

I met each of his thrusts and felt another whimper escape me as he wrapped his arms tightly around me, his kisses suddenly urgent as he made love to me; the moment was perfect, blissful, and I knew I wanted to experience this with him again and again.

Just as I thought I couldn't take anymore, I felt my body erupt around him again as he stilled, his heart hammering against my own.

"You are the one for me, Abigail," he whispered into my ear huskily. My entire body fluttered at his words. "It's always been you."

Sawyer

I stared up at my ceiling fan, watching it move in circular motions as I listened to Abby's breathing. I had her cradled in my arms, her head lying on my chest; she had her own arms wrapped securely around my back. You couldn't slide a piece of paper between us. I trailed soft circles on her shoulder with my fingertips as I inhaled the scent of her hair; she had a flowery smell to her that I couldn't get enough of.

Abby was quiet, too quiet for my liking. I desperately wanted to know what she was thinking. Was she regretting the moment we just shared? I was too frightened to ask, knowing that if she did, it would absolutely crush me. The way her face fell, and eyes lit with pleasure played over again in my mind and I felt my erection building again from just remembering how perfect she felt and looked underneath me.

She set the bar so high for me that I knew no one would ever come close to touching it.

I glanced over at the clock on my bedside table; it flashed nine thirty-five in red. I hoped like hell she wouldn't go home this evening. I knew she probably would though, so Remmy wouldn't wake up without her. I felt selfish for wanting her to stay with me, but I couldn't help it. I wanted to hold her all night and wake up to those pretty blues in the morning. I wanted to kiss her and make love to her again when we woke, and then make her breakfast.

It wasn't even just tomorrow morning. I knew as soon as I kissed her in my kitchen tonight, that I wanted to do this with her for the rest of my life. It sounds fucking insane, but that woman does something to me that I can't even explain. Her kisses were electrifying, her soft embrace comforting, and I knew there would be absolutely no one else that I would want. She was it for me. I even knew that back in high school.

"Abby," I whispered, "Are you asleep?"

"No," she whispered.

"Can you tell me what you are thinking?" I asked. I had to know. She let out a sigh.

"I'm thinking about how wonderful you make me feel."

"Oh?" I asked; I grinned, my body relaxing.

"Yes. Why, what are you thinking?"

"About that chocolate cake," I joked, lightening the mood. She let out a small laugh.

"Do you want me to go get you some?" she offered.

"If you're offering," I said, laughing.

Abby leaned up, exposing her bare chest to me, her lips turning into her beautiful smile. Her dimples popped out at me, and I lifted my hand to her face, rubbing the indent of her cheeks with my thumb.

"Your dimples are cute as hell," I murmured. I watched as a soft red flushed her cheeks, and her face leaned into my hand, as if she was embarrassed by my words.

"You're just saying that..." she teased, looking away.

"No, I'm not. I've always loved your smile." I watched as that radiant smile increased on her face as she shyly pulled away from me. She leaned out of my arms and already, I missed her warmth. She leaned down, arching her back to me and scooped up my tee shirt. She turned to me, her eyes playful as she slipped the t-shirt on.

"You'll be lucky to get this back," she told me.

"It looks better on you, anyway." It was the truth; seeing her in my shirt made my stomach clench with desire all over again. She rolled her eyes at me and tiptoed out of the room. I laid my head back into my folded arms as I listened to her maneuver around my kitchen.

I've never felt so alive in my entire life.

In just a few minutes, she returned with a large slice of chocolate cake on a paper plate with two forks. I cocked an eyebrow at her.

"Where's yours?"

"I'm sharing."

"What? I don't share very well."

"You'll learn," she teased. I propped myself up as she handed the plate to me. She sat next to me with her legs crossed as she took the fork and dove into the piece before me. I chuckled.

"You should have gotten your own." She closed her eyes, savoring the taste, but shook her head at me.

"I'd rather share with you."

I shook my head at her, and took a bite of the cake, the sweetness of the chocolate clouding my tastebuds. I nodded in appreciation, pointing at the cake with my fork. "Very good job, Abs."

She beamed.

We both ate in silence, taking turns digging into the cake.

"What else would you share with me?" I asked, my eyes looking down at the plate.

"What do you mean?" Abby asked, licking her fork clean; I felt my insides tug.

"What else would you share with me?" She cocked an eyebrow at me and shook her head at me.

"Not sure if I'm following, Saw."

I narrowed my eyes. "Will you share yourself with me?" Abby's eyebrows scrunched together.

"Pretty sure I just did," she said with a small giggle.

"That's not what I'm talking about," I told her, rolling my eyes, but grinning nonetheless. "Even though, that was pretty fucking amazing." I said, grinning. "But I'm not talking about that— I'm talking about *everything*, Abby. Your life, your heart, your mind, everything." I felt my heart tug in my chest as the thudding continued.

"Sawyer," she whispered, her head tilting to her side. The grin she was just bearing washed away as quickly as it had come, and I felt my stomach clench. Maybe it was too early to get everything out in the open; that's what I wanted though. I wanted her to know how I felt about her.

I wanted her to know how much I loved her.

"Like I said before, Abby. You do things to me. Things I can't explain."

"You do things to me, too, Sawyer," she whispered almost too soon though. I nearly flinched at how robotic her words sounded.

"I'm sorry if I'm coming on too strong. I probably sound like a fucking douche." I shook my head, looking down at the plate again; for some reason, I couldn't meet her eyes. "I promise, I'm not just saying this because we had sex. I'm saying this because..." I tried to search for the words and looked around my room, as if they were written on the walls before me. I sighed and looked back at her. "I've put off dating for a very long time. I always said it was because I was way too fucking busy, but that's not true. I discovered the real reason when I saw you."

My heart pounded fiercely in my chest as I watched Abby's lips part, her eyes shining brightly. I gave her the best grin I could and shrugged. That's all I could do. I hated that I sounded like a damn Hallmark card and felt my cheeks start to burn. I needed Abby to say something, anything, but she didn't. Instead, she collected the plate and fork and set it to my nightstand as I held my breath. Abby turned to me, her eyes glossy, but fierce, and she leaned into me.

Her lips pressed against mine was answer enough for now; I'll take whatever I can from her. Abby pressed her body into mine, her lips frantic against my own as her hands were back into my hair. I stripped her naked again in front of me to feel her bare chest against my own. We made love again, slowly this time. Abby's face was buried into my neck, and I listened to her sweet breaths and hums as I moved into her.

I loved this girl; I loved this girl with my entire heart. I'd give anything to keep her here with me. I knew that I wasn't just giving her a piece of me, but I was giving her my entire beating heart; hoping, praying, that she wanted it.

That she wanted *me*.

Chapter 15- *Abby*

"Mmm…" I mumbled into my pillow. My eyes were closed, just waking from a beautiful dream of Sawyer and I in the sunflower field; the sheets felt perfection wrapped around my naked body. I turned, reveling in this wonderful feeling, inhaling Sawyer's husky scent.

My eyes bolted open as I sprang upward, my eyes searching around when it hit me that I was at Sawyer's still. *Shit, shit, shit.* It wasn't my intention to sleep over. The last thing I wanted was the third degree from my mother this morning. I glanced around quickly, searching for the time, when I saw that it flashed six-thirty AM. I breathed in a sigh of relief and looked around the room for my discarded clothing. It wasn't on the floor, scattered around where I left it last night, but neatly folded on top of Sawyer's dresser. My heart squeezed.

I glanced back at the bed, wondering how I woke up alone. I tried to listen for sounds of him throughout the house, but it was silent as I tugged on yesterday's clothes. I tiptoed through his house and down the hallway. I found my purse by the door, just where I left it, and dug around inside of it searching for my phone. I grabbed it, expecting calls and texts from my mother, but I didn't have any from her. I had a missed call and text from Michael. I rolled my eyes and told myself to check it later, but the notification was taunting me, so I opened the text.

Who's really Sawyer, Abby?

"*Shit,*" I breathed. I felt my stomach lurch as I threw my phone back into the purse, running my hands through my tangled mess of hair. I closed my eyes and took a deep breath, in and out. *Everything will be fine,* I told myself. I wasn't keeping Sawyer a secret, but having Michael know his name sent eerily chills up my spine.

I got up from my crouched position, and hurriedly walked to the kitchen, expecting to see Sawyer sitting there, but he wasn't. On the counter, a hint of yellow caught my eye next to a white coffee cup.

Another single sunflower, with a brown note attached.

I went for a run. Wait for me. Love, Sawyer

My heart tugged again at his simple words, but I felt an odd twist in my stomach. The coffee pot was full, the white light blinking at me, mocking me. My body stilled as I internally swore at myself and closed my eyes. I held the green stem in my fingertips, twisting it back and forth. I had to decide. I knew what I should do, and that was to stay and wait for Sawyer, but my body started to tremble head to foot. I imagined a tall man holding my head underneath the depths of the water as my lungs burned for the much-needed air.

I nearly bolted for the front door, my heart hammering in my chest as I scooped up my purse and dug inside for the keys. I hurriedly walked to my car, unlocked it, and slid inside. My eyes glanced around, as if expecting to see Sawyer running after me. I imagined what his face would look like, puzzled and confused. I turned the ignition and reversed out of the driveway as quickly as I dared; the tires screeched a little when I hit the pavement.

Every turn I made on the way home, I imagined that Sawyer was there, running on the sidewalk and looking at me with sad eyes. Each turn I took I breathed a sigh of relief when he wasn't there; I couldn't deal with Sawyer this morning, I couldn't bear to see the hurt behind those eyes. My heart was hammering in my chest as my eyes burned. I hadn't even realized that I was crying until I pulled into the driveway. I wiped at my eyes viciously, telling myself to get a fucking grip. I saw the lights on in the house, and if I was crying, just leaving Sawyer's house, my mother would grill me to no end, and probably hurt Sawyer.

And he didn't even do anything. I was the one acting like a damn idiot. I don't know why I was crying or feeling this way; the evening I spent with Sawyer was beyond perfect. He was perfect, but that was the problem. I didn't deserve him. He was way too good. I grabbed the single flower from the passenger seat and hurriedly walked inside, wanting to escape to my room to freshen up before my mother noticed me, but she was sitting there on the steps for me, her eyes guarded as she drank me in.

"Well, well, well," my mother said. She was clutching her cup to her lips, her eyebrows up in the air as she took me in.

"Morning," I told her quietly. Mom's eyebrow cocked in the air.

"Have a fun night?"

"Remmy awake yet?" I asked, ignoring her question.

"No, still sleeping."

"Good," I said, sighing.

Mom took a sip of her coffee, her eyes examining me.

"Have you been crying?"

"No," I lied.

"Your eyes look like you have been."

"I'm just tired, Mom."

"I imagine so." She cocked an eyebrow at me again and I shook my head at her.

"Mother...."

"No judgment coming from me." Mom said, getting off the steps. She walked back to the kitchen. "Want some coffee?"

"In a bit, I'm going to shower."

"Good idea."

I rolled my eyes and hurried up the steps. I poked my head into Remmy's room first; he was sleeping soundly, his face mashed into the pillow, mouth open. He'd probably sleep another few hours. I was thankful for it this morning, I needed time to unravel and process the mental breakdown I was surely having.

I tossed my purse by my bedroom door, not even bothering to take the extra few steps to put it into my room. I crept into the bathroom, turning on the lights and went straight for the shower. I spun the dial until the water flowed out of the showerhead and watched the droplets fall with a heavy sigh. I discarded my clothing, tossing it next to the door. I avoided my gaze in the mirror, refusing to look at my spineless self. I knew the answers I was seeking were right in that mirror, and I wasn't ready to face them.

Gingerly I stepped into the shower, the hot water stinging my skin at once, but I welcomed it. Steam casted around me as the water branded my skin. I let my head fall back, letting pressure relax my tense body; I let out a sigh as I stood here with my hands on my shoulders. Finally, I closed my eyes and leaned my body onto the cold shower tile, letting the warm water blast my backside.

Flashes of yesterday evening attacked me. I saw Sawyer, nothing but Sawyer. Sawyer, leaning over me, kissing me with so much passion that I stood in the shower on wobbly knees. Sawyer, leaning over to kiss my cheek. Sawyer, running his hands through my hair with the lightest touch. Sawyer's hard grip around my waist as he filled me. Sawyer's cocky grin that set my insides burning. Sawyer, dancing with me under the lights. Sawyer, cradling me in his arms, holding me as if I might break. Sawyer, asking me to share myself with him.

Sawyer, Sawyer, Sawyer.

I leaned my forehead on the cool tile and felt the tears cascade down my cheeks. I let out a loud cry, letting the shower drown out its noise. I placed my palms on the tile before me, hitting it with my palms.

I was so angry with myself. Here, I had a wonderful guy, who welcomed me with open arms—flaws and all—and I was already running for the hills. What the hell was wrong with me? Why couldn't I just let myself enjoy this?

Because you are undeserving, I thought.

I sat down in the shower, cradling myself in my slick arms, trying like hell to hold the broken pieces of myself together. And I wept for the girl that I so desperately wanted to be.

*****

I tiptoed down the staircase, listening for signs that Remmy was awake, but I still didn't hear his little voice. If he was awake, I would have already known. He would have been pounding on the bathroom door. I had put on my leggings and a tank top, my wet hair brushing my shoulders. I didn't leave the bathroom until my face no longer looked puffy; I could not, would not, let my mother know that I was crying.

My mother still sat in her white bathrobe. She was perusing a magazine, cup still in hand. She eyed me as I walked into the kitchen, her expression smooth, unreadable. I went for the coffee pot that she had already put a dent in and poured myself a cup. I waited for the third degree to start, but she didn't say anything, and I was thankful for it. I knew if I opened my mouth about yesterday, I would probably cry again.

I filled the cup with sweetener and a dash of milk and took a drink of my coffee, my back to my mother as I stared out of the kitchen window; the drink provided the warmth I needed. I felt cold, even though my skin was still pink from the hot shower.

"Abby," my mom said finally, breaking the silence. "Are you okay?"

"Yep," I replied instantly.

"You sure? You looked…sad. Did something happen? Did you and Sawyer fight?" The lump in my throat throbbed.

"No, everything's fine, Mom," I told her.

"Well, can you explain why Sawyer is on the front porch waiting for you, if everything is fine?"

I whipped around to her, my eyes wide. "*What?*"

Mom's eyebrows raised, her eyes narrowed and scanning my face.

"He's outside, on the porch. He wouldn't come in. He said he'd wait for you outside."

I whipped my head to the front door and back to her again, my body suddenly tense.

"Okay," I whispered, but I didn't move. I felt frozen.

"Are you going out there?" she asked. "He's been waiting for like twenty minutes already. He told me not to bother you in the shower."

I bit my bottom lip, which only increased my mother's intense stare. I sighed and tiptoed throughout the house, my heart thudding louder with each step. My hand gripped the doorknob, and I felt my body freeze again; I was not ready for this with him. I had no time to prepare or to gather my thoughts. I felt my mother's stare burning into my back; I sighed and turned the doorknob.

The morning humidity clung to me as I took a step out on the porch. Sawyer was sitting in the rocking chair, the bouquet of sunflowers he had at the house, sitting on the porch table. He didn't look at me but stared out past the porch and into our small town. I could barely look at him; my cheeks were already flushing a bright red as I took a seat next to him in the next chair. As I sat down, his eyes scanned over to me, and I felt that lump harden under his intense blues. His eyes were hard, jaw tightened as he watched me.

"Hi," I said, breaking the silence. I didn't know what else to say.

"Hi," Sawyer replied.

I looked away from his intensity and started fiddling with my hands.

"You didn't wait…" Sawyer said gruffly.

"No."

He paused. "Why?"

I sighed and let my shoulders fall. "I don't know," I told him honestly, my head shaking. Hesitatingly, I looked up to meet his eyes and immediately regretted it; his face turned into stone, but he couldn't quite hide the hurt from his eyes.

"I see."

"Do you, because I don't..." I told him honestly. "I just...I don't know Sawyer. I had a wonderful evening with you. It was perfect. Then I woke up this morning...and kind of just freaked."

Sawyer nodded and looked away from me, his penetrating stare on the driveway before me. In a swift motion, he stood up and started to walk away.

"*Sawyer!*" I called, but he didn't turn around. I got up and darted down the steps, nearly tripping over the last one. I cursed at myself internally and stomped right up to him. I tried to spin Sawyer around to look at me, but his body felt like a rock.

"*What?*"

"I don't know!" I told him again, throwing my hands up in the air.

"That's just it, Abby. *You don't know.* I know how *I* feel." He pointed at his chest with his fingers. "I know that I want *you*. You're it for me, Abby. Yet, you tell me, *I don't know.*"

"That's not fair," I told him, biting my lip; I blinked furiously, willing the tears not to spill.

"You're right." He shrugged and looked away from me, his eyes narrowing, and jaw clenched tightly. I hated seeing him so angry and knowing that I was the cause of it. "It's not fair and I'm sorry; truly. It breaks my heart that you're going through this. But it's also not fair what you're doing to *me*, Abby. I told you to think about what you want, I told you I would wait for you, and yet you came to my house, we had sex, we had a wonderful evening, yet you run off the next day. You're running from your feelings, Abby because *you know* you want this just as bad as I do."

In two long strides, Sawyer closed the gap between us and placed my cheeks in his hands, his eyes freezing me into place.

"If you don't want me, tell me *now.*"

My eyes went wide as I stared into Sawyer's face; he was breathing hard, his shoulders rigid, but his grip on my face was gentle despite the anger rolling through him. I tried to pull away and tugged at his arm, angry tears wetting my cheeks; I couldn't look into his eyes anymore, it hurt my heart too much. Sawyer let go, and took a few long steps away from me, turning his back to me again.

"I'll take that as my sign," he said, calling over his shoulder.

"Sawyer, *wait*," I said, letting my shoulders fall. I felt my entire body shatter into a million pieces. He cocked his face in my direction, his back still to me and shoulders rising with each hot breath.

"Do you want pancakes?" I asked him. Even my tone sounded defeated. He turned his torso to me, his face flashing mixed emotions.

"*What?*"

"Do you want some pancakes? I'm going to make Remmy some soon." I gave him a shrug. He turned more to me, his eyes still malevolent.

"*No*, I don't want pancakes."

"Too bad," I said with a pretend sigh, "I make some mean chocolate chip pancakes." I cocked an eyebrow at him. Sawyer let out an angry growl as he rubbed his hands over his face.

"Leave it to you, to try to make humor out of this situation." He lifted his hand to the back of his neck, the corner of his lips twitching.

"Come inside," I told him quietly. "Eat with us." Sawyer hesitated, his hands on his hips and leg jiggling like mad. I could practically see the wheels spinning in his head, while he contemplated on what to do with me. I hoped he'd figure it out soon because I didn't even know what to do with myself. His face had a hard edge to it, but I saw his body fighting to relax. This was the Sawyer I was familiar with; angry enough to tell the world to kiss his ass, but big enough to keep his mouth shut. Growing up, I was the opposite. I always let my words fly.

"Abby," he said, running his hands through his hair, "I shouldn't. I can't." He put his arms up defensively. I crossed the gap between us this time and carefully placed my hands around his waist, drawing him into me.

"You're right, Saw. I ran because I'm a fucking coward, okay? Is that what you want me to say? I do want this, I want *you*, but it's just…I don't know, extremely intense, I guess. I never thought I would feel this with someone else so soon, and especially with you. You scare me, Sawyer," I confessed. I let my shoulders drop again.

Sawyer's eyes went wide and somber, his cheeks pulling into that grin that I love so much. "Abby, you've *always* scared the hell outta me."

He leaned in and brushed his lips to mine, his kiss soft and sweet. I felt my body mold into his perfection as he cradled me in his arms. He drew back, too quick for my liking, and kissed my forehead.

"As much as I would love to keep kissing you, we are directly in front of your parents' house and the last thing I want is for your dad to kick my ass," he chuckled. "How about those pancakes?"

I nodded but stepped onto my tiptoes and brushed my lips quickly to his again, needing just one more before we went inside. "Come on, then."

I grabbed Sawyer's hand and held it tightly, leading him up the path back to my front door. I don't know if I handled things correctly with Sawyer.... My insides were still twisting but watching him turn his back to me was a sight I never wanted to see and hoped to never see again. Something told me though that this wasn't going to be the last freak out moment, but I told myself, next time, I would handle it better.

I promised myself I wouldn't hurt Saw and I had to live up to that promise.

Sawyer

I have successfully turned into one of those people; the ones that keep their phone close by in hopes they'll get that phone call or text. Each time my phone pings, I dash for it, praying like mad that it's Abby, but I haven't had one single text or phone call from her this week.

And it's frustrating. Annoying. *Maddening.*

I have officially crossed into desperation mode, and I despise myself for it. I'm *not* that guy; the guy that's holding on to each breath, hoping that she would call. I have never, in my life, felt this way about another woman; let alone had a woman that *doesn't* call. This is a first for me and I hate it and honestly, feel kind of bad to all the women that I'd done this to in the past. I know I can call her, and she would be completely fine with it, but I told myself after spending last Sunday with her, that I needed to give her time. Her freak out said it all to me. She wasn't emotionally ready, and I had to give her space.

For fuck's sake, she was going through a divorce. That had to be emotionally draining, and then adding me to the mix? I wasn't helping and I could see it in her eyes that morning. What got me the most, was that I wasn't even surprised that she wasn't at my house when I returned from my run. I had that inkling that she wouldn't be there, and unfortunately, I was right. I told myself when I saw the empty bed to take it easy, but I found myself instead grabbing my keys and driving to her house. I couldn't just leave things like that, and I had to know where her head was.

Now we are in this weird limbo, and I have no fucking clue where I stand, but I knew deep inside, that I had to let her find her own way.

And I hoped like hell that it would be right to me.

I already went for my run this morning, but my body was screaming for another release. I grabbed my running shoes, tied them into place, and started running. Running has always been relaxing for me; it helps me clear my head when I have too much shit bouncing around in it. As I turned the corner, I knew that it would be harder this time to shut it off. My mind was racing about *her*.

With each heavy breath, I pushed myself harder, faster, my eyes focusing straight ahead as I pleaded with my mind to remain blank, but her beautiful blues continued to resurface; her soft skin, the way she let out a heavy sigh after we were done making love, her sensual smile, the way her back arched into me.

I sprinted faster as old memories started to play back to me; the way her eyes flashed with anger when I teased her, that pouty look she always had when I beat her on a test or a race, her eye roll when I was acting like an idiot, and the way she took my breath away when she walked down the hallway on our first day of high school. She was beautiful and even though I didn't want to admit it, I knew right then that she was going to be my undoing, and I was only fifteen.

I came to an abrupt stop on the sidewalk and leaned over; my lungs felt like they were on fire and sharp pains started stabbing my sides. I placed my hands on top of my head and started walking, taking deep slow breaths. The sun was starting to set, casting beautiful yellows and oranges on the horizon, and I knew I needed to head home before it got dark. I started walking back into the direction of home, even though heading home to a quiet house wasn't where I wanted to be.

I wanted to be with Abby and Remmy. I wanted to hear their laughter and watch Remmy bounce around the house. He rarely walked, and even when he did, he had a little leap to it. He was also always smiling; seeing that goofy grin of his, always made me feel a sense of pride towards him and he wasn't even my kid. I was growing attached, and I knew that after the summer ended, not seeing that grin or hearing his laugh was going to be hard as hell.

I broke into a light jog, anxious to get back home. I left my cell phone at home and wanted to see if Abby had called. I knew she probably hadn't, but I was still hopeful that maybe I at least had a text from her. If I didn't, I told myself that I was going to call her this time—just to check in. I wouldn't make any plans, but just to see how her week went.

I reached the corner of my street and almost came to a complete halt on the pavement; there was a car in my driveway that wasn't mine. I squinted and felt myself pick up my pace back into a sprint. It was Abby's Mom's car. My insides started to somersault as I pushed myself harder to the front of my house.

Abby was sitting on my front porch step, wearing short, faded jean shorts and a sunny yellow shirt; her hair was in one braid down her back and she had a tired smile on her face. I slowed down when I reached the driveway, trying to catch my breath and calm my heart. That feat would be almost impossible if Abby kept looking at me that way.

"Hey," I told her. "This is a surprise." In a few quick strides, I was close to her and kissed her lightly on the cheek before I sat down next to her on the step. I was a sweaty mess and hoped that she didn't mind.

"I know, I'm sorry for just dropping by," she offered me an apologetic smile. I shook my head at her, grinning.

"You never have to apologize for that. It's nice seeing you. You are always welcome here."

Abby gave me a soft smile, as she looked straight ahead. Her eyes had that distant look to them that caused my insides to squirm.

"How was your week?" I asked her. She nodded and turned back to me, placing her chin in her hand.

"Long and tiring." She sighed. "I put a lot of hours in at the daycare to help Emma and spent a lot of time with Emma afterwards. Her wedding is in a few weeks, and she had a lot of stuff that needed done. Sorry I haven't reached out to you much this week...." She gave me her soft smile and I felt the squirming start to cease.

"I figured you were busy," I told her. "I was, too, anyway." This was a lie, but I wasn't going to tell her that. "Did you want to come inside?" I asked, gesturing to the door. Abby quickly nodded and I helped her to her feet. I opened the door for her, and she slid inside, slipping off her shoes before she met the carpet. I did the same.

"Want a drink? I have beer, some of that wine left, water, and that's about it," I said with a laugh.

"A beer would be great," she replied. I nodded and grabbed two bottles of Coors Light out of the frig. I popped the tabs open and handed them to her.

Abby and I stood awkwardly in the living room with our beer; after a long moment, she turned to me, a playful grin on her face.

"How about we step outside?" she said, gesturing to the back door.

"Oh, I see, you came here for your oasis," I said. Abby laughed.

"I mean, yeah, I kind of did," she admitted, her nose scrunching. "But, I also wanted to see you too." She touched my arm lightly as she said it and I felt my skin prickle underneath.

I grabbed her free hand with mine, squeezed lightly, and led her to her oasis. When we stepped outside, I turned on the twinkling lights and watched as her face relaxed into a calming smile. She plopped down in her seat and leaned her head back, watching the lights glow above us.

"How is Emma's wedding planning coming along?" I asked her casually. I took a quick drink of my beer. Abby did the same, nodding as she did.

"It's going great. It's going to be beautiful. Emma did a wonderful job planning. I forgot how big of a workhorse she could be though. She had me up so late this week from working on everything from bouquets to decorations." She smiled. "But I'm more than happy to help her." She gave me a shrug.

"That's pretty nice of you."

"I don't mind, she's always been a good friend to me. But that's part of the reason why I wanted to drop by." She looked at me, her eyes twinkling. She bit her lip, hesitating.

"The wedding is in two weeks, and I need a date." She scrunched her nose up again with a playful grin. "Will you go with me?"

"Oh, I don't know, that's a hard time for me…" I clenched my teeth, making a face. Abby's thin eyebrow sprang upward. "Of course I'll go with you."

She relaxed her face with a smile. "Thank you, Sawyer."

"Only if you promise to dance with me," I said, raising my chin.

"As long as it's not the chicken dance." I laughed.

"The chicken dance is an iconic wedding song," I argued. "It's a must." Abby rolled her eyes and shook her head at me.

"We'll see," she said, making a face at me.

"Hey, I know that 'we'll see'. That's what you tell Remmy after he has an off the wall idea." Abby grinned sheepishly.

"Catching on, Saw."

I shook my head at her and looked up at the now darkened sky; the stars were starting to twinkle back at us, and I heard Abby let out a slow sigh.

"How's everything else going for you?" Abby looked down to me with a frown.

"You mean with Michael?" she asked. I nodded.

"I don't know; he's become silent again." She shrugged and looked away from me. "I'm starting to look for places to rent around here."

My eyes widened; this wasn't something I had expected. "For real?" She nodded, a sad smile on her face.

"Back in Florida, I don't have any kind of support. His mom is flaky, and Remmy hates going over there anyway. Michael won't be any help, so it'll just be me alone trying to juggle his school schedule and events and work. I have a great babysitter there, but she's going off to college anyways. Here, I would have my parents and Emma's daycare when I needed it. I started perusing full time jobs here, too, but I haven't had that much luck. It's hard trying to land a full time Processing job right now." She sighed. "I know it will work out as it should, but it's just kind of hard starting over."

I leaned closer to her and covered her hand with mine and gave her a gentle squeeze. "You'll figure it out, I know you will."

"Thank you," she whispered. "I know I will, but to be honest, it's exhausting."

"I'm sure it is. Let me know what I can do to help." I gave her hand another sympathetic squeeze. "For selfish reasons only, I really like that you're thinking of staying." I watched her lips tug back into her smile.

"It just seems logical. Besides, I can't bear to think of going back there." The smile disappeared from her lips as quickly as it had come; my heart constricted. She deserved so much better.

"Well, I'm here for whatever you need."

"Thank you," she said. "You're the best."

"I try."

We fell silent, drinking our beer and listening to the country music playing on the radio. Abby seemed content in her chair; she was slouched down with her knees resting on the table, her eyes closed. I watched as she stifled a yawn and I glanced at the time on my phone; it was nearing ten o'clock. I could tell she was tired, but I was frozen in my chair. I didn't want to suggest that we call it a night for fear that I would go another week without seeing her again. Abby yawned again and looked up at me.

"I'm sorry I'm such a downer tonight."

"You're fine," I told her earnestly. I tossed my empty bottle into the nearby trash can and grabbed Abby's hand again. "Should we call it?" I looked back into her pretty blues, trying to gauge a reaction from her. Her eyes sparkled again as that slow, sexy smile slipped on her lips. I narrowed my eyes in turn, my heart starting to pick up from her seductive smile.

Abby leaned out of her chair and turned to me; her eyes stuck on mine. I felt the lump in my throat harden as she slowly sat down on my lap, her fingers lifting to my head, as she softly trailed her fingers through my hair.

"Abby..." I whispered, eyes narrowing, but I felt my lips tug. "I'm still sweaty from my run."

Abby waved me off and continued stroking my hair. I leaned into her gentle touch and closed my eyes, my hand resting on her waist. This moment felt so good, so *right* and I felt my nerves tingle from her gentleness. My eyes opened wide when I felt Abby's lips brush against mine; her eyes were closed, kissing me fully. I closed my eyes, feeling her lips move against mine slowly. Perfectly.

"How about we get you cleaned up?" Abby whispered against my mouth. My eyes sprang open to see her blues piercing mine; a look of want and need flashed across her eyes, and I pulled her in tighter.

"Your wish is my command," I murmured to her, pressing my lips against her. I grabbed her legs and cradled her to my chest, holding her securely in my arms as I made my way back through the house. I crushed my lips to hers as I tried to maneuver the corners of the house.

I set her gingerly on the ground in the bathroom and noticed she was on wobbly legs; I caught her arm, steadying her. Abby's body instantly mashed against mine, her lips back on me as she tugged down on my shorts and underwear; my cock sprang to life in front of her as I watched her eyes darken. I took my own shirt off, and turned on the showerhead, letting the water warm before stepping in.

When I turned back to Abby, she was staring at me widely, her eyes taking in my nakedness; I narrowed my eyes and gave her my best smile.

"Like what you see?" I asked her, waggling my brows at her.

"*So much.*" I laughed at her and grabbed her arm, pulling her back to me. Slowly, I stripped her naked, starting with unbuttoning her shorts and removing her silky black underwear. I felt her body purr underneath my hand, as I slowly slid my finger between her folds. Her head fell back, eyes staring at me widely.

"Hell, Abby," I whispered to her, pulling her back into me. I kissed her neck and then looked back at her face. "Are you sure you want to do this?"

"It was *my* idea."

"Just checking." I raised her arms in the air before sliding off her shirt; her matching black bra cupped her attractively and my hands slid underneath the wire. I felt a soft groan slip from me as she hummed. Her pupils dilated with need as she quickly unhooked herself, letting her bra fall to our feet.

I took a long, lingering look at her. I wanted this woman, and I was about to show her exactly how bad I did. I crushed my lips back to hers, grabbing her waist and pulling her to me tightly; her bare chest felt smooth against my chest, and I could practically hear her racing heart.

With my freehand and lips still pressed to Abby's, I felt the water and decided it was good enough. We stumbled into the shower together, laughing at the way Abby clumsily stepped in. I grabbed her, securing her, before I pressed her body to the shower wall. The hot water cascaded around us as our naked bodies collided in the most complete way.

"You are so perfect," I told her. Her eyes widened and I watched her cute as hell blush appear on her cheek. I softly caressed the reddened parts, before crushing my lips back to hers.

I love you, I love you, I love you, I thought as I felt her wet skin. I kissed her neck and trailed down to her breasts as her body continued to hum.

I just hoped one day soon that I would be able to say those three words.

J. Glassburn

Abby

I'm exhausted. I'd been helping Emma with last minute wedding arrangements whenever I could this week. My fingers were constantly throbbing from the tedious work of arranging flowers and centerpieces. In my free time, I gave all my attention to Remmy. I wanted him to have a great summer, and it was ending too quickly for my liking; the calendar mocked me as the days passed by, and as each day ended, my phone buzzed with texts from Michael.

I was looking at flights back home, but not in the way that Michael thought. Our time back in Florida will be short; maybe a week, a week and a half, so Michael could spend as much time as he wanted with Remmy before school started, all while I did the daunting task of packing up our lives. I was going to leave pretty much everything to Michael. I didn't want those possessions from *our* life anyway, but I planned to pack up my personal items, clothes, jewelry, shoes, and the items Remmy wanted from his room. If Michael threw a fit about that, then so be it, I would just buy new.

I thought it would be best to have that conversation with Michael in person that I wasn't staying, and about how Remmy would be going to school in Illinois this fall. Even though I think Michael is an ass, he deserved better than me telling him over the phone.

The last few weeks Remmy and I swam, went to the local zoo, to the park, and in the evenings, we had his baseball games. The last baseball game was also approaching. As much as I was looking forward to having our evenings back, I also didn't want it to end. Watching him play a game he loved so much, made me feel so proud of how far he had come. I also loved watching Sawyer work with him; coaching him, encouraging him, and teaching him to play the game that Sawyer loves.

In the evenings, when Remmy was fast asleep, I snuck away to Sawyer's. My mom never complained; she always told me to go have fun, with that sly smile of hers. She knew not to expect me until the next morning. I always slipped back into the house before Remmy even opened his eyes. I never asked Sawyer if I could come over, but somehow, he was always expecting me, and waited for me on his front porch with a single sunflower in hand. Sunflowers, in all their beauty, were now my favorite flower.

Each night spent with Sawyer was perfect. Amazing. Out of this freakin' world. I've always found it humorous how big and tough Sawyer looked, but he always had that featherlight touch about him. He always cradled and held me with the lightest hands and when he looked at me, my entire world would zone out before me.

Sawyer Gibson was stealing my heart, one kiss at a time and finally, after all these years, I was letting him have it—not just pieces, but my whole heart.

Today was Emma's wedding day. I texted her this morning to check in on her to see how she was doing; she texted back in all caps: *FREAKING OUT. GET HERE.* I chuckled and replied that I would be there as soon as I could.

Mom and Dad had plans to take Remmy up to Chicago this weekend and they left yesterday morning. They had a weekend packed with seeing the Brookfield Zoo, Legoland, and The Aquarium. I told my mother that she was freakin' nuts to do all those things in one jammed weekend, but she waved me off and told me, 'That's what grandma's do'. She'll learn. Remmy will be a tired, grumpy little boy come Sunday morning.

"Besides, that way you can have a weekend to yourself..." Mom told me, but when I looked up at her, she was staring me down with that eyebrow in the air. I could read between the lines; I knew what she was insinuating.

I spent all day on Friday, helping her set up the venue; we didn't stop until it was time for her rehearsal dinner. She hugged me so tightly and squealed in my arms.

"I can't believe you did all this for me. Why don't you stay for the rehearsal dinner?" I gave her another squeeze.

"This is your evening with your family. You enjoy it. I'll see you in the morning."

"So, what you're saying is, you have plans with Sawyer," she said with a playful eyeroll. "Tell me all about it later." She added in a hushed whisper.

She knew me all too well. As soon as I left, I drove straight to Sawyer's and met him in the driveway; he kissed me, pulled me into his arms, and he carried me hurriedly right back into his bedroom.

Now it was the morning and the bubbly excited Emma had vanished after I received menacing texts to my ass over there as soon as I opened my eyes. Sawyer wasn't ready for me to leave though; he pulled me into his shower again and we were in there until our toes and fingers were wrinkled.

I showed up at the venue looking like a hot mess; my lips were swollen and hair damp. Emma didn't say anything but arched her perfect brow at me. I wasn't in the wedding, so my presence wasn't really needed except for emotional support. Emma was keeping her wedding small, just her sister standing with her, and her soon to be brother-in-law on the other side.

The morning passed quickly; we shared tears, laughs, and many hugs. Emma looked dazzling; her hair was elegantly pulled up from the nape of her neck and makeup on point. Her eyes were magnified magnificently, and I never knew that she had a hint of green in them until today.

We shared mimosas, chatted excitedly, and I tried to get some food into Emma's stomach. She nibbled on a few crackers, telling me that there's no way she could eat anything else. When the photographer arrived to steal Emma, I decided to leave. I hurried home and as soon as I walked into the door, I ran up the stairs to get ready, and yes, I tripped on the way up, knocking my knee hard on the stairs.

I showered again to calm my nerves; I wasn't sure why I was so nervous. I wasn't the one getting married today. When I stepped out of the shower, I turned on some music to help my mind relax.

Before I knew it, my hair was curled, and makeup done as good as I could get it. I added a little gloss to my lips before exiting the bathroom. I walked to my bedroom and stared at the dress hung in the closet. It was a short, navy dress that snugged my thighs and body, a little too tight for my comfort, but not so much that I felt I was suffocating. The dress was tightly stitched in a flower pattern; the top above my breast was loosely stitched and you could see my tanned skin. When I tried the dress on with Emma, I wasn't sure about it, but after Emma's encouraging words, I bought it, with a pair of nude heels to go with it.

I slipped into the dress, tugging it down into place and took a long look at myself in the mirror. My curves were well noticeable, and I sent a silent prayer to the Lord above me that my ass wouldn't fall out when I bent over. As I was grabbing my purse, the doorbell rang and I scurried downstairs, carefully though since I placed my feet in the heels. Before turning the doorknob, I took a long, slow breath, and closed my eyes.

I opened the door slowly, poking my head around first and felt my breath catch in my throat; Sawyer was wearing a navy suit with a white button up underneath his jacket. His hair was cut and styled into a messy, but sexy array on top of his head and his long beard I was growing accustomed to this summer, was shaved short in fine lines. I watched as his eyes popped and smiled.

"Abby," he mumbled, grabbing my hand. "Wow, you look—"

"Like I'm going to fall in these death traps?" I asked, scrunching my nose and lifting my leg. He chuckled and wrapped his arm securely around my waist and pressed his lips to my forehead.

"I will make sure you do not fall tonight. You look *stunning*, Abby Lou. I'm a lucky man."

I smiled, feeling the burn on my cheeks already. "You look pretty good yourself," I told him, and I kissed his cheek.

"Shall we?" he asked. "Or would you rather us go upstairs?" He winked. I rolled my eyes at him.

"Let's go before you seduce me with your wicked ideas."

"Probably a good idea; I am pretty good at seducing you." He waggled his brows and threw me his cocky grin which caused my heart to soar high above us.

Sawyer

Abby was a sight to be seen; as we approached the venue, I noticed many turned heads in our direction. She leaned into my side, and I watched as her cheeks slowly burned from the attention.

"Why are they staring at us?" she whispered, eyes wide.

"Because you look beautiful, of course." She rolled her eyes at me but tossed me a grateful smile.

"I don't have anything out of place?" she whispered back. "Toilet paper on my shoe? Ass hanging out?"

I glanced toward her ass, glad to have the reasoning to do so and gently patted it with my hand.

"Nope, firmly in place."

"Sawyer," she hissed, glaring.

"What? I had to check, for your sake."

The wedding was outside, and I already felt the beads of sweat on the back of my neck. The suit and jacket probably wasn't the best idea for an outdoor wedding. As soon as the wedding ceremony was over, I'd take the jacket off. I walked Abby up to the garden, white roses were seen everywhere, as we took our seats in white folding chairs. I wrapped my arm around Abby, drawing her in close to me, and watched as she tugged on the bottom of her dress.

"You look beautiful." I touched her hand and she stilled.

"It's so short," she mumbled.

"I like it. Easy access for later," I whispered into her ear. She rolled her eyes. I kissed her cheek.

We sat there for just a few minutes before the ceremony started. Emma looked beautiful coming down the aisle, but I found my attention going to the groom. His mouth fell open as soon as Emma came down, his face reddening as the tears spilled from his cheeks. My own heart prickled in my chest for the man, and I felt my arm squeeze Abby next to me a little tighter.

I glanced down at Abby as silent tears slipped down her cheeks. I dug into my pants pocket and pulled out a package of tissues; I had a feeling she would need them. She tossed me a look of appreciation and dabbed at her cheeks carefully, her eyes trained on the ceremony before us.

Emma and Dustin said their vows in shaky words, and I couldn't help but smile at the two of them. Everything about the ceremony was beautiful. The way Emma cried as Dustin vowed his love for her, the way Dustin's hands trembled as he tried to slip the ring on her finger. I know a man wasn't supposed to admit those kinds of things but watching my old childhood friend get married made me feel at peace. Emma deserved this perfect day.

The officiant declared them man and wife and I watched Emma and Dustin lean in for their kiss. Everyone clapped, including myself, but I felt my gaze turn over to Abby. She was clapping, her eyes shining with tears as she laughed. The words I spoke to her at our high school graduation popped into mind. *"I'm going to marry you someday."*

Never until this very moment, did I hope that wish would come true.

Abby

Everything about this evening was perfect. Emma looked stunning and Dustin looked at her like he was the luckiest man on earth. They were perfect for each other, in every way. I hugged Emma so tightly when it was our turn to congratulate them. Emma was crying and I gave her the tissue package that Sawyer gave me so she could wipe her eyes.

"I'm so happy you're here," Emma told me, she was positively beaming.

The reception was thankfully inside, and I followed Sawyer in for cocktail hour. He bought us a few drinks while I snuck into the bathroom to freshen up. When I returned, a young lady was chatting Sawyer up. She was, of course, blonde. He was grinning at her, and she was tilting her head, completely engrossed by him. My eyes went into daggers as I marched right up to them.

"*Hi,*" I said to the girl. I securely placed my hand in Sawyer's and watched as the woman's face fell. *That's right,* I thought.

"Hi," she replied, giving me a forced smile. I almost arched my brow but refrained.

Sawyer gave me a puzzled look, but turned to the woman in front of us. "Janet, this is my girlfriend, Abby. Abby, this is Janet."

I felt my eyes go wide at the word *girlfriend* and felt my head turn to Sawyer. He was grinning at me, his eyes somber, yet playful.

"It's nice to meet you," Janet told me kindly. "I'll chat with you both later." She tossed me a dirty look before walking away and I flashed my smile right back to her.

"I never thought that jealous Abby would be so damn cute," Sawyer whispered in my ear.

I turned to him and glared. "I'm *not* jealous."

"Then what the hell was that?" Sawyer said, chuckling.

"Not jealousy."

"Hmmm..." Sawyer said, kissing my cheek. "Alright, my Abby."

I felt my heart swell at the way he said, *'my Abby'*. I wanted to say, "You remember that," but I didn't want to ruin the moment.

"Wanna go make out in the coat closet?" Sawyer asked. I turned my head to him and laughed.

"*What?*"

"It'll pass the time," he said, wiggling his eyebrows at me. I shook my head.

"You are a bad influence."

"You gotta admit, it sounds a little appealing."

"Maybe, if the coat closet had doors, but...." I gestured to the hallway; the closet was wide open.

"Damn, maybe next wedding then."

"Next wedding?" I asked.

"Oh, didn't you know Abby? You're my forever wedding date now. Hope you like what you see." He flashed his hands in the air and I giggled.

"I *love* what I see."

"That's good because I'm yours, Abby." He leaned in and kissed close to my ear; I felt a shiver ripple through me from his hot breath. "Yours forever."

Sawyer

I've never had this much fun at a wedding before; Abby was the perfect date. We danced nearly to every song, and yes, I got her cute ass out there for the chicken dance. We laughed until we cried, when she started to do her *'moves'* as she called them, and I couldn't help but kiss her. The DJ started to play a few slow songs and I wrapped her in my arms and held her tightly against me, reveling in the way she felt.

I wasn't ready for the night to end; she felt perfect in my arms. She nuzzled right into me, her head on my chest, and I felt like I was flying high. The evening passed quickly; the DJ announced it was the last song, a fast one, and I watched as Abby busted out her moves again, her arms flailing as she shook her ass with Emma. I stood from the sides this time and I stifled my laughter many times.

After the song ended, I went up to Abby and pulled her into me. "Ready to go?" I murmured into her ear.

"Already?" she asked, breathing fast. She looked around the reception hall; many people had already left. I laughed and nodded. Her lips pulled into an adorable frown, but ran over to Emma, engulfing her in a hug. While they said their goodbyes, I grabbed my jacket, her purse and shoes, and waited by the door for her. Abby came leaping over to me a few moments later, her smile radiant as she stopped right in front of me.

"Ready!" she called. I handed her the shoes, but she shook her head. "I'll just go barefoot." She looped her arm through mine and nuzzled herself against me.

I opened my truck door for her and watched her slide in, shutting it securely in place. When I got into the truck, she was beaming over at me, a wide smile on her face.

"What now?" Abby asked, her eyes lit with excitement. I turned my head to her, eyes narrowing.

"What do you want to do?"

"Well," Abby said, tapping her chin in thought, "I have some ideas…but first, I need you to take me home so I can grab a bag."

"Do you really need a bag?" I told her, backing out of the reception hall. "You pretty much took over my bathroom already." She rolled her eyes.

"I bought something the other day and I wanted to grab it."

"What is it?"

"It's a surprise."

"Clue me in, Abby, or I'm driving your fine ass right to my house. Do you know how hard it was tonight, looking at you in that dress? I've been waiting to take it off you all evening."

"You'll like it."

"*Abby…*"

"Okay, okay, I'll give you a hint. It's something that you wear…when you are feeling…sexy."

"Something that *I* wear? Because that's nothing, Abby. No way you're getting me in a man thong."

She let out a loud musical laugh. "Not you, *me*."

"Okay…I like where this is going. Quick stop to your house, Abby. I'm giving you five minutes, tops, before I barge in and take you right there."

She rolled her eyes. "Not in my parents' house."

"Then you'd better hurry up," I said, pulling into her driveway. I put the truck in park and looked over at her. "Five min––" but I stopped talking. The bright smile she had all evening was gone. Her face looked instantly pale, eyes wide, as if she had seen a ghost. My eyebrows puzzled together as I looked at her line of vision. And my stomach dropped.

Chapter 16- *Abby*

I almost vomited right in Sawyer's truck. My stomach twisted so tightly and my chest felt as if I had a bunch of weights sitting on top of it. I cleared my throat, glancing over at Sawyer. He leaned back in his driver's seat, his arms tensed around the steering wheel as his eyes hardened into the windshield.

Michael was sitting on the patio; no, not sitting anymore, but standing, his hands jammed into his khaki pants. I could tell just from the truck he was trying to gain his composure, but the way his jaw clenched told me everything that I needed to know. I licked my lips nervously and grabbed Sawyer's arm.

"Don't get out," I told him, opening the truck door. I looked down at my bare feet as I walked, and after inhaling a large breath, I glanced up at Michael. To my relief, Sawyer stayed in the truck.

"Abby," Michael said in a clipped tone. His jaw clenched as his mouth snapped shut.

"Michael, what are you doing here?" I asked.

"Came to see my son." Michael's eyes raked over to the truck and then back at me. "Who's that?"

"None of your concern," I told him, raising my head high. "Remmy's not here. My mom took him to Chicago for the weekend. You should have called."

"Yes, because that's gotten me *so* far." He glared at me, and I felt my body still.

"I've always called you back," I told him.

"When it was convenient for you."

"We've been busy, Michael."

"I see that." He looked back at the truck. "Why don't you invite your friend out? I'd just *love* to meet him."

"That's not happening," I told him. "Michael, this is not a good time." I shook my head at him, but Michael ignored me. He marched down the stairs and I caught his arm, but he shook it out of my grasp.

"*Michael.*"

"Yeah, I would shut the hell up, Abby."

Sawyer slammed the truck door open, and I watched as his shoulders rolled; his face hardened into a stony expression, his nostrils flared, and I bit my lip. I haven't seen that look on Sawyer in years, and the hairs on my neck started to stand tall. This wasn't going to end well…not at all.

"*What did you say to her?*" Sawyer asked, cockily. He arched his brow as he met Michael in the driveway, his chest rising and falling rapidly.

"Don't worry about what I say to *my wife*," Michael said, standing tall. Michael wasn't nearly as big as Sawyer, but I knew his ego would never allow him to back down. My stomach heaved. Oh shit. Oh *shit*.

Sawyer's fists were clenched at his sides as I saw the tick in his jaw start. I've seen that tick before, and it brought fresh memories of the high school Sawyer. I froze. Sawyer let out a low laugh, cocking his head to the side as Michael crossed his arms over his chest.

"Maybe you shouldn't talk to her that way," Sawyer said, eyes glaring. He wasn't yelling, but his voice was cold as ice.

"I'll talk to her however I please."

"Yes, because *that's* gotten you far. I suggest you don't disrespect her in front of me."

"Who the fuck do you think you are?" Michael seethed, with a low laugh.

"Sawyer Gibson, nice to meet you," he said with a mocking smile. "I'm the one showing your wife how a lady is supposed to be treated."

Michael stiffened as he glared at me and I caught my breath.

"I suggest you leave before I kick your ass," Michael whispered, his tone hard.

"I don't see that happening."

"*Stop it!*" I yelled at them. I sprinted over to them and squeezed myself in between of them, my back to Sawyer. Sawyer quickly scooped me up with his arm and put me behind him.

"You've got balls touching my wife right in front of me."

"Someone's got to," Sawyer challenged. "Sure as shit ain't you. You and all this wife talk, brother. Didn't she serve you?"

"If you think I'm going to let you crawl your way into her life, you've got another thing coming. I suggest you get back into that shitty truck and go home."

Time to end this.

"*Guys*, knock it off!" I said, my heart pounding. I pushed myself back in between them, but this time faced Sawyer.

"Sawyer, go home," I told him. His eyes flashed to me, and his pained expression nearly cut me into two.

"What?" Sawyer asked. His eyes flashed so much hurt that I almost took the words back. I hesitated and took a deep breath.

"You should go," I told Sawyer softly.

"*Me?*"

"That's right, *you*," Michael said, head bobbing. I threw him a nasty glare.

"This is not helping anything right now. I'll call you tomorrow." Sawyer stood in front of me, his tense shoulders falling, and my heart literally shattered in my chest. "I'll call you tomorrow," I said again. I wanted to reach out to him and felt my arm raise, but I placed it back to my side. Sawyer nodded, licking his lips as he looked back up to Michael's stare.

"You hurt her or so much as *touch* her," Sawyer said, "I'll break you in half."

With that, Sawyer spun on his heels and darted for his truck, slamming the truck behind him. The engine roared and Sawyer peeled out of the driveway as fast as he could, all the while, staring at me with such pain in his eyes. I almost chased his truck down and begged him to stop.

"Good choice," Michael grunted from behind me.

"Fuck you, Michael." I pushed passed him and stomped to the front door. Michael followed, quick on my heels.

"Sorry I ruined your date," Michael said with humor in his voice. "Really though, you'd think you'd pick someone who had better taste in vehicles."

I turned around and faced him, my anger bubbling to the surface. "You are a despicable human being."

Michael rolled his eyes. "I've heard worse. Can we go inside? I'm exhausted."

I felt my jaw clench as I unlocked the front door and opened it. I almost slammed it in Michael's face but didn't. I threw my purse and shoes to the side.

"You look different, Abby," Michael said, watching me. "You look good."

"So glad I have your approval after all this time," I mumbled underneath my breath. "You sure you don't think I'm a fat cow?" Michael rolled his eyes.

"Looks like you've lost weight; good for you." I glared at him.

"I like your hair short, too."

"I'm sure you do; short hairstyles *are* your thing. Too bad I'm not blonde."

"Seriously, will you stop?" Michael asked.

"No. I don't know why you're here," I told him, pulling my arms over my chest. Michael's eyes saddened for a minute as he leaned against the sofa.

"I'm here because I want you back, Abby. This summer has been stupid without you. I miss you. I miss Remmy. I want you both to go home with me."

"Are you insane?" I told Michael. "Like, are you actually delusional?"

"No, I just miss you." He walked over to me and put his hands on my shoulder. My body recoiled underneath his touch.

"Michael, I told you the last time I saw you, I wanted a divorce."

"Well I don't. I think we should work this out."

"There's nothing to work out. I served you, Michael. I want out." I tried to get out of his grasp, but his hands squeezed my arms tighter to keep me in place.

"I can't let you go." His eyes tried to remain soft, but they started to have that hardened edge to him.

"Sure you can. You can sign, and we can be done with it. Did you read the papers, Michael? I'm leaving you practically everything."

"And asking me for child support."

"To help with *Remmy*. Your son."

Michael let go of me and stepped away from me, shaking his head side to side. "You have no job."

"Not true; I work part time at the daycare in town." Michael's eyebrow raised.

"Because that pays well, I'm sure."

"I'm looking Michael. This is just temporary and I'm helping an old friend."

"Like Sawyer?" He asked.

"No, *Emma*. That's where I was tonight, at her *wedding*." Michael nodded and I watched as his eyes snaked over me.

"You really do look good."

"Thank you. Are we done here? I'm tired."

"Me, too. Where do we sleep?" He bounced towards me and for a moment, he reminded me of Remmy. I turned to him, eyes glaring.

"I sleep in my room. You can sleep in Remmy's."

"*Abby*."

"Michael, you're a flippin' idiot if you think I'm letting you sleep anywhere near me. You're lucky I don't toss you out and make you find a hotel. Which, mind you, we don't have one in this town."

"God, it's so small here," Michael mumbled.

"That's the way I like it."

"Since when? You love Florida."

"Times have changed." I grabbed my purse and shoes and started to walk up the stairs, but Michael pulled me back to him.

"I'm not letting you move back here, you know. I'm not letting you take that boy states away from me."

I felt my lower lip pull into my mouth as I stared hard at him. His jaw was clenched, his eyes serious, and I felt my heart pang in my chest.

"You and I both know that you really don't care if we stay or not. You spent zero time with him when we *lived* with you. All that boy knows from you is disappointment. Here, he and I have a support system, my mom and dad, Emma's daycare. Don't make this into something it doesn't have to be."

"I work, Abby. It was hard juggling my time, but I'll do better."

"I wish I believed you, but you have so many blonde distractions, that I can't."

I spun from him and stomped up the stairs.

"You know, Hallie and I aren't together anymore." I froze on the last step and turned to him, my eyes drinking him in. "If that's the reason why you don't want to go back, you don't have to worry about it."

"I highly doubt that. You've been displaying your relationship all over Facebook. Don't think I haven't noticed."

Michael rolled his eyes at me. "I told her we were done and that I wanted to be with you. I told her it was a stupid mistake."

"Are you still going to work with her?"

"I have to, Abby. She feeds me a lot of deals. I'll set boundaries with her."

"*Whatever.*"

I spun around the corner of the hallway and slammed my bedroom door behind. Before I flopped on the bed, I locked the door.

*****

It took forever for me to fall asleep last night; I tossed and turned and when I finally succumbed to sleep, I dreamt of Sawyer. He was driving away from me on a dark path, and I was running after him, begging him to stop, but he never did. When I woke, my eyes sprang open, trying to recall yesterday evening. It started out so perfect; Sawyer and I danced the night away until the DJ stopped playing music. He held me, kissed me, and introduced me as his girlfriend. I felt so whole when I was with him.

And then it all went to hell. Literally. Michael's and Sawyer's chests were practically bumping. All I could think about was how Sawyer's eyes looked when I asked him to leave. I didn't *want* him to leave, but what other choice did I have? Michael flew in, didn't have a place to stay, and I couldn't just *leave* with Saw. Even though in my heart, that's where I wanted to be.

Before I left my bedroom, I dialed Sawyer's number. I had to speak to him, make sure he was okay, but he didn't answer. My shoulders fell as soon as I got his voicemail, but after the beep, I shakily left a message.

"Hey, Saw, it's me, um, Abby. Listen, call me when you can. I want to talk to you. See how you are." As soon as I hung up, my eyes started to burn.

I tiptoed out of my bedroom and went to the bathroom, shutting and locking the door behind me.

Sawyer

Abby called me this morning, but I wasn't ready to speak to her. Instead, I watched the phone ring, my heart pounding in my ears. On the last ring, I almost answered, but I threw the phone down on my bed instead. I listened to her voicemail three times in a row; her voice had a sad edge to it, but at least I knew she was okay. I felt a ripple of anger shortly after as I thought about how she asked me to leave. *Me.* I know my actions were ridiculous; he was still her husband after all, but I was so damn mad about it.

I knew it wasn't necessarily anger, but jealousy. It burned my entire body.

Michael was the exact person I thought him out to be, an entitled prick that thought the world shined out of his ass. I was thankful that I didn't give in to the anger and punch the lights out of him—that wouldn't have done me any favors with Abby.

I laced my running shoes and took off on a dead sprint again. The anger rolled through me, and I pushed myself harder than I ever had. I ran all over this town, different routes that I normally wouldn't take, but nothing stopped my mind from thinking about how Abby was at her house with Michael. I stayed clear from the Foster residence, knowing that if I stopped, it would be a shitshow all over again. My shirt and hair were soaked with sweat as the sun beat down on me, but it didn't faze me. I just pushed myself harder.

I took a turn, ready to head back to my house, when I saw him running towards me. I stopped abruptly, my shoes skidding fast against the sidewalk. I froze, my chest rising and falling.

Michael stopped, too, and flashed me a big smile, his eyes narrowing, taunting me to come forward.

I shook my head and ran across the street to the other side, my hands started to shake. I went into a jog, pointedly ignoring him, when I heard his footsteps come behind me. My jaw twitched as my teeth gritted together.

"You're a runner, too, huh?" Michael called behind me. "Abby sure likes her runners."

I kept my mouth snapped shut, afraid of what I might say or do.

Michael kept pace with me though and was running alongside me as I willed myself to push forward. I refused to look at him.

"You know," Michael said, breathing hard. "I should thank you. For getting Abby back to the way she was. She sure is pretty now." I closed my eyes for a moment, but when I opened them, all I saw was red.

"She's getting her figure back. She sure looked good last night. Even better when she was naked on top of me."

And then I went for him. I turned my torso toward him, red hot as I hurled myself at his waistline, ready to lay him the fuck out. We collided to the grass, and I heard Michael's breath catch as he landed on the ground with a loud thud. My arm flexed as I knocked it back, but as his eyes went wide, I stopped. In a matter of seconds, I saw a hint of Remmy's features in Michael's face. I clenched my teeth together, my jaw ticking. I willed myself to hit him, but I knew I couldn't. Remmy's tiny grinning face popped into mind, and it willed the urge away; this was his *father*. Instead, I got close to his face.

"*Don't fucking talk about her that way,*" I spat. Michael's eyes narrowed as that cocky smile of his came back into play.

"Too big of a pussy to hit me, Sawyer?" he taunted. "Do it. *Hit me.*" I stared him down, breathing rapidly as I got up from him.

"You're not worth it."

I started to walk away when Michael started laughing and I spun around, nostrils flaring. "She deserves so much better than you."

"You think you're better?" Michael laughed again; he stood up, brushing the grass off him.

"I *know* I'm better. I would never hurt her."

"Fuck you, Sawyer."

"Fuck you, too, buddy, " I yelled back.

I started to run again.

Abby

When I came downstairs to the kitchen, Michael was sitting at the kitchen island, water bottle in hand as he perused through his phone. His shirt was soaked with sweat; he must have gone for a run this morning. I noticed he had grass stains on the back of his white cotton tee, but I didn't ask how he got those. I really didn't care.

I poured myself a cup of coffee, ignoring him as I moved around the kitchen.

"I'd love a cup," Michael said.

"Great, get it yourself."

"Wow, so hostile already this morning."

I added sugar and milk to my coffee, stirring it a little too fast. The contents leaked over the cup and splashed onto the counter. I sighed and grabbed a napkin to clean it up.

"So, what do you want to do today?" Michael asked, getting up to grab a cup. I felt my eyes roll.

"Nothing with you," I mumbled underneath my breath.

"When is Remmy coming back?" I shrugged in response. "You don't know when your son is coming back? Great parenting Abby."

I clenched my teeth. "They aren't supposed to come back until later tonight. They were stopping by Legoland on their way back."

"Maybe we should drive up and meet them?" Michael offered, taking a sip of his black coffee—black just like his fucking heart.

"No."

"Well, I want to see him."

I shook my head and dialed my mom's number. She answered on the second ring.

"Morning, doll," Mom said brightly. "How are you?"

"Wonderful," I said in a flat tone. "How is Remmy doing for you?"

"Oh, he's great. He's a little tuckered out this morning, so we agreed to save Legoland for another time. We are driving back home now. Um, everything okay?"

"No," I answered, glaring at a bemused Michael. "Michael flew in, he's here."

Mom didn't say anything; all I could hear was her breathing.

"Ah," Mom finally said. "I see. When did he get in?"

"He met me on the porch last night after the wedding."

"Oh, crickets," Mom mumbled.

"Yep."

Michael gestured to the phone, but I brushed him away.

"How far are you?" I asked her, glaring at Michael.

"About two hours," Mom grumbled. I heard my dad in the background ask what's going on. "We'll hurry."

"Don't rush, Mom. Just drive safely. We'll see you when you get here."

"Okay," she hesitated. "I love you, Abby."

"Love you, too Mom."

I hung up, grabbed my phone and coffee cup, and headed out to the patio. To my dismay, Michael followed. I sat down on the patio chair, and he plopped down right next to me. I turned my chair away from him; childish, sure, but I couldn't even look at him.

"Are you going to be like this all day?"

"Yep."

"Abby, can't we just talk? Like two civil human beings?" I sighed and turned back to him.

"What could you possibly have to say?"

Michael's eyes looked into mine and I watched as his face fell. His shoulders slumped.

"I'm sorry," he whispered. "I'm sorry for everything that I did to you. What I said…was *awful*. What I did…was even worse."

And then, without hesitation, Michael cried.

I didn't know what to do or say, as I watched his shoulders hunch and the tears flowed down his cheeks. I know I was probably gawking because never in my life have I seen this man cry. Even after all the hurt he caused me, my heart went out for him. Michael looked up at me, his gray eyes glossy from his tears.

"Can you please forgive me, Abby?" His lower lip trembled as he spoke.

I let out the breath that I didn't know I was holding in and looked away from his streaming tears. It broke me watching him like this, but really, how could I forgive all the awful things he said or did?

"If not for me," Michael said, taking my hand in his. This time, I didn't pull away. "For Remmy. *Our son.* He deserves a two-parent household, Abby. Do you really want him shuffled back and forth between us? Is that what you want for him?"

I chewed on my bottom lip and brought my face back to Michael's. He wiped at his tears. No, I didn't want that for him. That's the last thing I wanted. I set my cup down, my stomach twisting too much to drink anymore. I sighed.

"No, I don't want that," I admitted.

"Can we please just work on this, Abby? Give me a month. If you're still not happy, then you can go. I'll sign the papers. Hell, I'll even give you the damn house. Just *please*, can we try? I miss you so damn much."

"Michael..." I hesitated and shook my head at him, my own eyes brimming with tears.

Michael scooted off the chair and threw his arms around me, taking me off guard. He was on knees, wrapping his large arms around my waist as he buried his head into my stomach. And he cried more.

I closed my eyes, cursing at myself internally before I tenderly laid my hands on the top of his head.

"I love you so much, Abby. Don't leave me, *please*." Michael Carter was *begging* now.

"Michael..."

"Please, Abby. You have always been my person. I can't do this without you. You and Remmy are everything to me. I see that now. I'm so sorry, Abby. Please. Forgive me. Stay with me. Come back home with me."

I rubbed Michael's back in small circles, biting my lower lip as I stared up at the blue sky. Was Michael actually telling me the truth? Could he actually be feeling…remorseful?

I didn't know. Could I really just walk away from my husband, the father of my child? Should I give him the second chance he was *begging* for? Did I owe our marriage that much?

"Abby, I love you. I missed you so much, baby. Please, *please*, give me a chance." He cried harder, his tears wetting my shirt.

I closed my eyes, my own tears now spilling from my eyes. The words sprang into mind as I weaved my fingers soothingly into Michael's hair.

I'm so sorry, Sawyer.

Chapter 17- *Sawyer*

I was a damn fool for showing up here. I already knew it as I pulled the truck into park. My leg jiggled as the truck engine roared, unsure if I should get out of the truck, or stay. I hadn't heard from Abby since the first call; she hadn't tried to call or text since. I told myself if she did, I would answer this time, but it's been radio silence from her.

And it made me feel sick.

I took a deep breath as I stared out into the busy baseball field. Henry was out on the field already practicing with the team. I eyed the field for Remmy but couldn't find him.

"Fuck it," I whispered. I turned the engine off, and stepped out of the truck, my eyes scanning the crowd of parents around the field for Abby. I looked for Abby's mom, knowing she'd probably be here, but I couldn't find her. I started walking up to the field, tossing the glove back and forth between hands, when finally, I saw them.

Abby, Michael, and Remmy were walking up to the field. Remmy was in the middle, holding each of their hands. He was talking excitedly, bouncing as he walked, his eyes never leaving his dad's. This should be a happy scene, a son walking with his family, but the stabbing in my heart froze me in my tracks as I watched them.

Michael let go of Remmy's hand and ruffled his hair, just as I have done so many times. Remmy gave him a high five, his mother a quick hug, and then darted out to the field with his team. Michael turned to Abby then and wrapped his arm around her shoulder and pulled her into him. The jealous burn hit me all over again as I watched the two of them.

Well, damn.

Abby's face turned to the side, her eyes looking around the throng of parents. She mumbled hellos to other moms as she scanned the field. I had a pretty good guess that she was looking for me.

Look at me, I pleaded. *Just look at me.*

Abby's eyes continued searching, her lips pressed into a fine line, when finally, she found me. Her eyes went wide, and then settled, giving me the answer that I needed to know. Her eyes held me into place as I watched a pained expression flash her pretty features. Slowly, she shook her head no at me.

I felt a piercing stab right into my heart as I watched her eyes grow somber. I nodded solemnly and pressed my lips together tightly. I spun around quickly and headed straight back to my truck. I knew she wouldn't follow.

As I geared the truck into reverse, I felt the hot tears sting my eyes.

Abby

My mom was standing in my bedroom, her back leaning against the wall. She was watching me pack my suitcase up in silence. Every few minutes, she let out a heavy sigh, but I pointedly ignored her. I knew she was just buzzing to lay into me. Honestly, I was too exhausted to hear it; I was emotionally drained from it all. I packed up the last of my things and zipped the suitcase tightly shut.

Mom sighed again, and I groaned.

"Do you have something you would like to say?" I asked her.

"Me? No," Mom said, shaking her head, but her eyes said otherwise.

"Just say it."

Mom pursed her lips, hesitating, and then finally, said, "You really think he's going to change?"

I groaned.

"*Mom.*"

"Abby, I just don't think this is the right choice."

"You're entitled to your own opinion," I told her. I zoomed passed her and headed towards Remmy's room; Mom was quick on my heels, her voice lowering so others wouldn't hear.

"You really think he's going to change?"

"Mom."

"I think he's just feeding you a bunch of bullshit." I spun around, my annoyance flaring.

"You would think that my mother would *encourage* me to work on my marriage."

"Not when he's a cheating liar."

I sighed again. "Mom, he asked me for a month. A *month* to work on things. What kind of person would I be if I didn't at least try?"

"*A smart one.* He's playing you, Abby. He wants you back in Florida to control you. You are foolish if you think he'll really change. Maybe he'll put in the effort for the month, but after that? You'll be right back to where you were. Crying at home *alone* while he's out screwing his way through Florida. *Like father, like son.* His dad is an awful person and his mother? *Medicated*, Abby."

"Tell me how you really feel," I said underneath my breath. I opened Remmy's suitcase and started tossing things in.

"That's my job," she said proudly.

"If you're going to just stand there, you can help me pack."

"I refuse to help." Even as she said it though, she grabbed clothes and started piling them into the suitcase. I shook my head at her. "This is a *big* mistake, Abby."

"I have to try, Mom." I threw more items into the suitcase, not even caring that they weren't perfectly arranged like I generally would. "For Remmy," I added in a lower voice.

Mom threw her hands up in the air. "Don't be the woman that stays just for the children."

"It's a good reason," I amended.

"No, it's foolish. Do you really want Remmy to grow up in a loveless home? Michael did and look where that got him. He's just like his father. Do you want Remmy to be like that?"

I couldn't take it anymore. "Alright, I'm done with this conversation Mother." I pointed at her. "You don't have to like my decision, but you need to respect it."

Mom's eyes narrowed at me, but she threw the clothes down in the suitcase. With a huff, she turned around.

"You are an adult capable of making your own choices. I'm done talking about this. But," Mom said, turning back to me, "I'm disappointed, Abby." Her words sliced my heart in half. "What you did to Sawyer is…*awful*. I feel so bad for that boy."

Shaking her head, she walked out of the room.

I fell to Remmy's bed, a scream wanting to leave my lips, but I choked it down. Instead, a fresh stream of tears fell. I clutched at my stomach, as if trying to hold myself together, but then I gave up. The pain in my heart would probably never go away.

"Me, too, Mom," I whispered to the quiet room. "*Me fucking, too.*"

Chapter 18- *Sawyer*

"Sawyer, need a Bud," Lance called over his shoulder. I dug into the icy cooler and pulled out a Bud Light can and handed it over to Lance.

Every year, Lance and I volunteer two hours of our time at the town's 'End of the Summer Bash'. Today the streets were filled with children and tonight, adults. A band was playing in the square with a large crowd around them, drinking, talking, and dancing.

This was the first time in years that I wished I hadn't signed up. I didn't want to be here with all the bubbly townsfolk; I wanted to be at home so I could feel sorry for myself in peace. Lance showed up at my house though and wouldn't let me stay at home.

"You're not acting like a fucking woman tonight. Get in the truck, *let's go*," Lance told me.

So here I am, tending the makeshift bar, which is really just two white folding tables pushed together underneath a white tent. The table behind us had coolers lined underneath with different kinds of beer and the table had an array of different kinds of liquor: Jack, Tequila, Vodka, Captain, and full of wine bottles. We weren't supposed to be drinking while we volunteered, but I had a glass tall of Jack and Coke. Lance pursed his lips at me while I poured but didn't say anything; it wasn't like I didn't pay for it. If I was stuck here for two hours, well, now it was just an hour left, I was drinking.

A line of people were on Lance's side; he was the beer guy, while I was the liquor and wine guy. Most people wanted just beer as it was cheaper, so while I didn't have a line, I helped Lance dig through the coolers. I took a quick sip of my Jack and Coke; it really was just a whole lotta Jack, not that much coke, and felt the burn sizzle down my throat. A group of young girls approached, smiling and giggly. I checked their wrists for bands, making sure they were old enough, and approached them with a smile.

"What can I get ya?" I asked, flopping my hands on the table. They giggled; I didn't know what was so damn funny, but I grinned anyway.

"Um...Rum and Coke," they spoke. "Two please."

"Seven dollars," I told them. I grabbed two cups, filled them with ice, and started to pour their drinks. They handed me their cash, exactly seven, and I handed them their cups.

"You're Sawyer, right?" one of the girls asked, flashing her white teeth.

"Sure am."

"Are you going to be here all night?" She tossed her hair from the front to the back, smiling.

I couldn't even see her face, all I saw was Abby. I sighed.

"Just for another hour."

"You should find us later," the other girl purred.

"Probably not, but thanks for stopping by." I nodded my head and turned around, flopping on the folding chair. I grabbed my Jack and Coke and took another long drink. Lance stole a glance towards me, but I ignored him.

"Sawyer," I heard a familiar voice call to me. I raised my head and saw Mya. She was wearing a jean skirt with the band's black tee shirt tied into a knot in the front, her dark hair piled on top of her head like it usually was. She smiled at me and I just nodded back.

"Funny to see the tables turned," Mya said. "Vodka on ice."

"You've got it," I said. I stood up and made her drink. "Three fifty."

Mya handed me a five. "Keep the change."

"Yes ma'am." Her hand covered my own. I looked up and met her stare.

"You seem off today."

"That's because I don't want to be here. *Come again.*" I nodded to her, clearly dismissive, but she froze, her delicate eyebrows scrunched.

"That's not like you," she said. "What's wrong?"

Lance let out a huff next to me as he maneuvered through the coolers.

"He got his heart broken," Lance called to her. He handed a patron an aluminum can and nodded at him.

I rolled my eyes. "Shut the fuck up," I mumbled underneath my breath. I sat back down and took a drink of my Jack. Mya's face fell in understanding.

"I see," Mya whispered. "Well, too bad I'm involved with a band member now, or I would have tried to make you feel better."

"Then go be with your band member." I said, not meeting her eyes. I didn't see what Mya did, but I'm sure it was colorful before she walked away.

"Dude, you're scaring off our customers."

"Unlikely," I said, draining the cup. I got up and turned to make myself another when Lance put his hand on the bottle.

"Wait until the shift is over. I don't need you getting hammered right now." I shook his hand away, staring him down, and poured the Jack into my cup. Lance's eyes narrowed at me, but he went back to the forming line. "Make sure you pay for that," Lance mumbled.

I poured a little Coke in the cup, shook out a five dollar bill out of my pocket and threw it into the cash box.

Eventually, my side started to pick up and Lance's thinned and I begrudgingly got up from my chair and did the work I had volunteered to do. A lot of the women tried to flirt with me—some of them I would have probably tried to hit on, but it wasn't in me. I felt hollow and the only thing that made me feel better was the contents in my plastic cup.

"*Well, well,*" I heard a low voice say. I looked up and felt my body freeze.

Fucking Michael.

"Other line, douchebag," I said, and I turned around, my jaw clenching. Lance's eyes peeled from the person he was helping as he watched us.

"*Sawyer,*" Lance cautioned.

"Why would I want to go to the other line when I'm getting such friendly service from you?" Michael called to me. I took a deep breath and turned around.

"What the hell do you want?" I snapped. Lance put up his hand to the next patron asking for beer and watched Michael and me intently.

"Sawyer, switch," Lance ordered, but I didn't move. I felt my shoulders roll and arms flex. Today wasn't the day for Michael to fuck with me because I *would* lay him out cold.

"Oh no, I want this fine gentleman right here to get my drinks for me," Michael said, flashing his bright teeth. "I need a Captain and Coke please and a glass of red wine. You know, for *my wife.*"

I stared at him, my jaw flexing; that familiar angry burn coursed through me, and I felt my entire body shake. I wasn't going to back down from that asshole. I looked at Lance, whose eyes were probing mine, pleading with me not to make a scene. I nodded curtly, turned around and made his Captain and Coke. Instead of pouring the red, I poured white wine and handed it over to him. "Seven dollars."

Michael looked down, his eyebrow in the air as he started laughing. "Doesn't look like you're a real good bartender, there my friend. I asked for red."

"Abby prefers white. *Trust me*," I said, nodding my head. I was acting like a cocky jerk, but with him, I didn't care.

"I'll keep that in mind when we are back in Florida tomorrow," Michael snapped.

"*Okay, okay,*" Lance interjected, pushing me back, but it took him a few times to get me to move. "I think it's time for your break, Saw."

Michael snickered and set twenty dollars on the table. "I don't need the change."

Lance looked down at the twenty and back to Michael's face. "You hurt Abby again, not only will that one kick your ass," Lance said, nodding his head to me, "But I'll be right behind him," he whispered, leaning over the table. "Now get the fuck away from my table."

Michael's eyes narrowed at Lance as his lips turned into a nasty grin. He nodded in our direction and turned around, walking back towards the band. I felt the intense urge to look for Abby, but knew it wouldn't be a good idea. Still, I craved to see that face just one more time.

"I'm out of here," I told Lance. He patted my chest, looking me straight in the eye.

"Just go *home*," Lance told me, his eyes probing mine. I could read between the lines. *Go home and don't look for her.* I nodded and turned around, leaving Lance to defend the bar all by himself.

As I walked off into the darkness, I cursed at myself for letting Michael get the better of me. This was *my* town, not his. I should have handled it better and not let the rage get the best of me. I was better than that, better than him. His cocky ass would be back in Florida before I knew it, and until then, I just needed to lay low.

I almost turned down the street towards my house when I heard a woman calling my name. My body froze as I recognized that sweet voice—*her* voice. I closed my eyes, my shoulders rigid as I tried to decide what to do. I could break into a run like a fucking child and run as fast as I could away from here. She wouldn't be able to catch me, but then again, it would have been easier if I would have driven here myself. I swore underneath my breath.

"Sawyer!" Abby called. "*Wait!*" I took a deep breath and braced myself.

Abby was running after me when she shouldn't be running at all. She wore tight blue jeans and on her feet were flip flops. Before I could call and tell her to stop, she did exactly what I expected her to and tripped.

"*Damn it, Abby,*" I cursed underneath my breath. She fell to the ground, right on her ass. In a few quick strides, I was at her side and helped her to her feet.

"Thank you," she whispered, brushing the gravel from her jeans.

"*You betcha,*" I said coldly. I turned away from her to walk home when her hand reached for my arm. "*Let go,* Abby," I whispered, my back to her.

"Not before you let me say what I have to say."

I closed my eyes and breathed in through my nose. I turned to her and crossed my arms over my chest.

The first thing I noticed was her quivering lip. The second was how sad her eyes looked; it about did me in right there. My heart jolted in my chest.

"I'm sorry if Michael said anything to you," she whispered. I kept my jaw shut.

"Sawyer…" she started.

"I don't have time for this." I turned around again, feeling my eyes sting, but her hand was back on my arm, trying to hold my body into place.

"No, please don't go," she begged. "Sawyer, I'm so, *so* sorry."

"Abby, *please.*" I spun around, my hands in the air. "Please just leave me be. Don't you get it, Abby? I can't talk to you, let alone *look* at you. It hurts way too fucking much."

Abby's body flinched at my words, and I felt the dagger go in deeper; I hated myself for talking to her this way.

"You made your decision. I accept it. Now let me be," I demanded.

"I-I just wanted to explain," She swiped at her face. "I never had the chance to talk to you about it."

"I don't want you to explain," I told her, shaking my head. "You chose Michael. I get it."

Abby's lips pursed and the tremble started again.

"*Fuck*, Abby. Just go," I said, rubbing my hands over my face. I felt the tears start to sting again, but Abby didn't move. She clutched her sides, staring at me, while the silent tears spilled from her eyes.

"I didn't mean to hurt you," she said quietly.

"I'll get over it." I breathed. I looked away from her and noticed Michael standing at the edge of the party, his eyes trained on us. "Your husband is waiting for you."

"He'll wait then," she told me automatically.

"That's great, Abby. Great way to start mending your marriage," I scoffed. "I'm done talking to you anyway."

"Well I'm *not*," Abby declared.

"What else is there to say?" I said, throwing my hands up in the air. "You want to work on your marriage. That's great, Abby. I'm happy for you."

"I'm a *horrible* person for doing what I did to you," Abby confessed. "It literally is killing me that I…I—" She was searching for the words, so I interjected.

"Led me on all summer?" I watched as she flinched.

"That's not fair."

"Maybe not, but it's the truth. I spent my entire summer with you. I got to know your son, we went and did all sorts of things together. I fell hard for you, Abby." My eyes started to burn. "You spent the last two weeks in my bed for crying out loud. I thought you and I were going to be something. But now, out of the blue, you want to work on your marriage?" I shook my head and looked away from her as a tear escaped down my face. "What's worse, is that you couldn't even *tell* me. You let me find out from seeing you guys together." I wiped at my face as another tear slid.

"Saw... I'm so sorry." She reached out to me to hug me, but I took a step back from her, shaking my head.

"This is it Abby. You and I. I wish you the best of luck in your future and I hope he treats you better this time." I nodded at her, my eyes probing her pretty blues; even as she cried, they looked stunning, and I knew I would always remember this moment. "Give the little man a hug for me," I said, my voice catching.

I turned around and as much as it killed me not to, I didn't look back.

I love you, I love you, I love you.

If only it were enough.

Abby

Michael and I sat outside, sipping coffee on the back deck. It was a beautiful morning in Illinois. Michael kept complaining that it was chilly, but I told him he was crazy. It was perfect weather, with a soft breeze and zero humidity, which was strange since it was the first of August. I had my head up, breathing in the Illinois air. This moment would have to last me for a long time. I knew in my heart it would be tough to come back.

I think my mother knew it, too; she was full of sniffles and sad smiles this morning. My mom and dad took Remmy up town for a last breakfast at the local bakery, and I'm sure they were filling him full of sugar, even though it was eight in the morning.

I set my cup down and leaned back to enjoy the moment while it lasts. I closed my eyes and listened as the birds chirped their morning hellos; the silence around here is what kills Michael. He likes the busy atmosphere of Florida, the honking cars and all the people, while I preferred this much, much more.

"You're really going to miss this, aren't you?" Michael asked, bringing me out of my stupor. He leaned over and grabbed my hand with his. I still wasn't all that forgiving towards him. Every time he touched me, I wanted to pull back, but I've been working on composing myself. If I really wanted to work this out with him, then I needed to quit jerking or flinching every time he touched me. His hands just didn't feel the same to me anymore though.

I forced a smile on my face and nodded. "Well, maybe we can come back here in a few months. Maybe for Thanksgiving?" he added.

"It's cold here around that time," I told him, without opening my eyes.

"I'll manage," Michael said. I opened my eyes.

"You'd really miss your parents' Thanksgiving party to come here?" The Carters threw a huge Thanksgiving feast every year, and each time, their guest list was always over a hundred people.

"If you wanted to," Michael shrugged, "then sure. I'm a little over all their parties anyway."

I eyed him speculatively, wondering what game he was playing; then I remembered that I was supposed to be giving him the benefit of the doubt. It was odd to me. Michael thrived in his parents' environment and every time they had a party, he was there, schmoozing his way through, while Remmy and I sat on the sides and watched.

"Hmm…" I said, closing my eyes again.

"I'm so glad you're coming home with me today," Michael said. "Thank you so much, Abby. For giving us a chance."

I forced a smile as I opened my eyes. "I'm looking forward to going home." The words felt dry coming out of my mouth.

Michael grinned and patted my knee. "I don't know how you are sitting out here. I'm grabbing a sweatshirt," he chuckled. I watched as he walked across the deck and disappeared into the house.

I closed my eyes and returned to enjoying as much as I could of the Illinois weather, when I heard a phone ping. I opened my eyes, looking around for my cell, but it couldn't be mine; mine was in the kitchen, laying on the counter. Michael's black iPhone laid on the table, the screen bright from a recent notification.

I hesitated, looking at the sliding glass door, and back to the phone. The phone pinged again with another notification. I sat upright, suddenly alert, as I looked at the phone before me.

Even from here, I could read Hallie's name.

I grabbed the phone from the table, my eyes daggers as I scooped it into my now trembling hand. I tried to put the passcode in, but it didn't work. I groaned, my eyes going back to the sliding glass door, listening hard for the sounds of Michael. My heart hammered viciously in my chest as I quickly tried another code; nothing. Last four of his social, perhaps? I tried it.

Bam. *I was in.*

I flitted to the text messages and saw Hallie's name and engrossed myself in the recent text. Two, as a matter of fact.

Hallie: Did you smooth things over?

Hallie: Are you coming back today? I need some Michael time. I know you said we would have to wait, but I don't want to. Meet me at the office this evening? I don't care if it's late.

I felt as if my eyes had lasers as I read over the last text from her. My stomach instantly heaved as a ripple of anger surged my body. I bit down on my lip, and since Michael wasn't back yet, I scrolled up to read more.

Michael: I'll be back as soon as I can. I gotta get this under control.

Hallie: Just divorce her, who cares?

Michael: My parents. They were pissed when they found out. They say it will ruin my reputation. Just know, the person I really want is you.

Hallie: You can have me any time, baby. I just don't want a relationship right now. Gotta concentrate on my career. You get it.

Michael: I plan on it. I may be quiet for a while, but just know, I'm thinking of you and how badly I want to be buried inside of you.

Hallie: ;) looking forward to it.

I stood up quickly, throwing the patio chair back from me. My entire body was shaking as my face burned. I turned to the sliding door, waiting for that fucking bastard to come out, my foot tapping as I waited. I couldn't go into my parents' house right now, in fear I would throw one of my mother's possessions right at his fucking head.

Michael walked out with a gray hoodie on; he had a full smile, about ready to say something. His mouth opened, and then the smile fell from his face as soon as his eyes flitted to the phone in my hand. He looked back up at me, swallowing hard.

"Abby, what's wrong..." he managed to say, but I took a step forward to him and pushed the cell phone into his chest. He's lucky I didn't throw the damn thing in the pool.

"*What's wrong?* What's wrong is the fact that I'm married to a disgusting scumbag, that's what's wrong. I cannot believe you!" I spun around and walked a few feet away from him by the pool's edge, trying to calm down.

"Okay, fill me in."

"I know you're not the smartest person, but even *you* should be able to solve it on your own."

I heard a groan escape from Michael, but I didn't turn around. I pinched the bridge of my nose with my fingers and closed my eyes; my hands and arms were shaking uncontrollably, and my stomach felt as if I would lose its contents very shortly.

"Abby, I can explain," Michael whispered. He approached me and laid his fingers on my shoulders, but I shook him off.

"Do *not* touch me or I swear to God, I'll kick you in your balls."

Michael sighed. "Abby, I will admit that my coming here was just to try to get you to come home with me. But when I saw you, *really* saw you, I knew I was an idiot. I haven't responded to Hallie or texted her since I've been here. I seriously have plans to go back and end it with her. *Honestly.* When I saw you, looking so beautiful in that dress, I knew I fucked up. Everything I said to you here is true. I want to work on this with *you*. I want you to come home. Please, *believe me.*"

I turned around to face Michael; his face was crumpled, shoulders sagged. His face was pleading for me to listen, but it only intensified my anger. I took a step closer to him, got into his face and whispered, "You should consider switching careers, you're a really good actor."

I walked around him, but Michael caught my arm, his face twisting.

"You're going home with me today, Abby," he demanded. "I'm still your husband and you will *obey* me."

I looked at his hand on my arm and looked up at his face, my eyes going into slits. "I suggest you get your fucking hand off me."

"What are you going to do? Call Sawyer?" Michael whispered back, his eyebrow cocking up as a nasty smile spread on his lips.

"I don't need Sawyer to fight my battles, I can fight my own. Now you better get your fucking hands off me."

Michael glared, but reluctantly dropped his hand, with that nasty smirk on his face. Without hesitation, I turned and pushed him as hard as I dared, right into the pool. He fell into the water, his head completely submerged, as I watched the splash and ripple through the pool with satisfaction.

Michael came up spluttering, his hands wailing around in the air as he tried to stand up in the pool. *"What the hell Abby?"* he shrieked. Dogs all over town could have heard that man.

"Here's what's going to happen," I told Michael, crouching down by the poolside. "You're going to fly home today. By *yourself*. You are going to *sign* the divorce papers. Remmy and I will follow in a few days. You are going to spend as much time as you possibly can with that boy while we are there. I'm going to pack up our shit and then we are moving here."

"You're not—"

"Did I say I was done talking?" I pointed at him, and Michael snapped his jaw shut, his eyes flashing as the water dripped from his hair. I gave him the sweetest smile I could muster. "We are going to set a realistic visitation schedule when we visit, and I hope to God you follow it Michael. If you don't, the only person you'll be hurting is Remmy and he deserves *so* much better than you. You are going to quit harassing me and you and I are going to be as civil as possible in front of that boy."

I stood up, my arms crossed over my chest as I turned away from him.

"Can you at least get me a damn towel?" he hissed.

"Get it yourself," I snapped.

As I walked away, I raised my hands up high and proud, flipping him the bird.

Sawyer

Football season is here, and I've never been happier for the distraction. For one thing, when I'm planning practices or working with the boys, it keeps my mind away from her. At night, when I'm home alone, I throw myself into the playbook or my lesson plans until my body and mind are both completely drained.

It doesn't stop the dreams though. When I close my eyes, all I see is her face.

Sammy texted me tonight, asking me if I would open the gym for him and I quickly agreed. We turned the music up loud as we lifted weights, doing our reps in unison. We've been in here for over an hour, and Sammy's soaked shirt told me that we should call it quits here soon. I recognized a change in Sammy over the summer; his arms were looking more defined, and I noticed as he was running the treadmill, he was keeping a better pace.

"Hey Coach," Sammy called over the music. "Do you think some time you can go with me to that auto shop you were telling me about?"

"Sure kid, anytime. I meant to do it earlier in the summer, I'm sorry."

"No problem," Sammy said quickly.

I glanced at the time and noticed it was only eight thirty. "He's probably still there, if you want to follow me and check?" I said. "Up to you."

"Alright," Sammy agreed, nodding.

Together we cleaned up the gym and Sammy followed me to Lance's shop. As expected, Lance's doors were still open, light pouring on the gravel drive. I parked the truck and waited for Sammy to pull in next to me before I got out. I couldn't see Lance, which told me he was probably in his office. I led Sammy through the shop. Sammy was slow following me, his eyes raking over the tools and the walls. I looked over at him as his eyes fell on the posters of the women and cocked a brow at him. He grinned sheepishly and looked away.

"Lance!" I called.

"In here," he grunted back.

I led Sammy to the corner of the shop; Lance's office was small, he didn't need much, but he had his desk, office phone, computer, and a tall gray filing cabinet. In the corner, was also another mini fridge that I was sure had more beer in it.

"Hey," I said to him. He didn't look up at us as we walked in; his head was bent over a tattered brown book, his face scrunched in concentration.

"Hey, what's up?"

"I got a visitor here for you," I told him. Lance looked up at us and looked at Sammy. At first, his eyes appeared confused, but then he slowly nodded, kicking back in the chair.

"Ah, Sammy, right?" Lance said, standing up. He held out his hand to him.

"Yes, sir, it's good to meet you," Sammy said, nodding. He quickly shook Lance's hand.

"Don't call me, sir. I'm Lance." Sammy nodded again quickly. I watched him swallow hard and decided to step in.

"Sammy and I were just at the gym and were talking about you. I thought we'd pop by quick so he could introduce himself," I said. Lance nodded and shoved his hands in his jean pockets, rocking back on his heels.

"Know anything about cars?" Lance asked him.

"A little."

"Are you teachable? Do you want to learn?" Lance's eyes narrowed. Sammy nodded quickly.

"He's one of the smartest kids in his class," I added. Sammy threw me an appreciative look.

"Do you play sports?" Lance asked.

"Yes, sir—I mean, Lance. I do. I play football right now." Lance nodded, clucking his tongue.

"School work and sports come first," Lance said. "After that, I'll give you some work around here. May not be what you want to do to start, more like cleaning the shop at first. As we go, I'll teach you some things."

"Okay," Sammy agreed quickly.

"Alright, I'll give you my cell. I'm here a lot so just text me when you think you can make it in. The only day I try not to work is Sunday, but if Sunday is the only day you can, we'll make it work," Lance told him. "I'll pay you depending on how you perform. Deal?"

"Yes, sir." Lance narrowed his eyes again and Sammy awkwardly smiled and added, "Lance."

Lance grinned. He gave Sammy a quick tour, which wasn't long since the shop wasn't all that big, and then Sammy told me he'd see me at practice. I nodded at him, told him to drive safe, and Lance and I stood at the garage door and watched him go.

"Kids got a nice truck," Lance grunted. I nodded.

"Yep."

Lance eyed me. "How are *you* doing?"

I shrugged. "Fine." Lance narrowed his eyes on me.

"I'm good, brother," I said, nodding, but I couldn't meet his eyes. Lance sighed and turned to the fridge.

"Let's have a beer and I'll let you share your feelings and shit."

Chapter 19- *Abby*

Remmy and I had a flight booked back to Florida in a week. I had to stay here and get Remmy registered for school, and I was desperately trying to find a rental for us. Unfortunately, it wasn't looking so hot. Houses around here moved quickly. By the time I saw an ad, it was already spoken for. My mom told me there was no rush in us leaving. Personally, I think that she liked us staying with her, but I craved my own space.

I was ready for us to start our new beginning.

I was trying like hell to avoid going into town as much as I could. I was a coward, hiding in my parents' house. Today, I didn't have an excuse though. I had to go up to the High School Commons for Remmy's school registration. I wished it wasn't in the Commons, since that was where Sawyer worked. I knew there was a good chance that I would bump into him. As I drove to the school, different scenarios popped into my head if I did run into him.

Taking a deep breath, I got out of the car and tried to add as much confidence as I possibly could to my step. I felt my eyes raking the parking lot, looking for Sawyer's truck, but I didn't see it. I breathed a sigh of relief and rushed into the school.

It looked the same to me and I felt an eerie sense of déjà vu all over again. I walked across the marble flooring, my eyes taking in the large room. White folding tables were all around the Commons, with signs directing you where to start and where to finish for registration. On the far wall was the school's trophy case and I knew my year had a trophy in there somewhere. On the walls above, were large posters of the school's current star athletes and team photos. My eyes scanned the posters, looking to see if Sawyer was up there as coach.

He was. He was standing with his football team, tall and proud, as he beamed back at the camera. I felt my chest tighten as I studied the poster further, wondering how stupid I could possibly be, to let go of a guy like that.

"Can we help you?" a lady tentatively asked me; she had short black hair and a kind face.

"Yes," I said, shaking my head. "Registration."

"What year?" she asked, kindly.

"Kindergarten."

"Okay," the lady said with a smile. "You'll want to go right to the first table." She pointed at the table that was labeled *'Elementary'*. I gave her a quick thank you, and ushered my way over, my mind focused on the task in hand.

The lady at the table handed me paperwork to fill out and a pen, gesturing to an empty table for me to complete. I nodded quickly and fell into an empty seat, deliberately choosing one that had my back to Sawyer's poster.

I let my mind sink into each question, filling out all of Remmy's information and my own. When I finally got to the last piece, I felt a weird itch wash over me and my face started to feel warm, followed by a loud clatter in the Commons.

My eyes jostled to the noise, and I watched as Sawyer scurried around, picking up the dropped football equipment. My chest instantly felt tight as I watched him, wondering if he saw me. Do I get up? Do I go over to him, or do I pretend that I didn't see him? I bit my lip. I didn't know what to do.

He must have seen me though, because his gaze met mine as soon as he had the last of the equipment in his arms and I froze. His eyes hardened, and then slowly softened as his eyebrows pulled together. I waited, sucking in a breath. *Please come talk to me*, I thought. I wanted to tell him that I wasn't leaving; I made a mistake and I was sorry, but here and now, wasn't the appropriate time. Sawyer hesitated, and just as I thought he was going to take a step forward to me, he gave me a curt nod, and spun around, turning his back to me and I watched him go.

I had the urge to get up and follow him down the hallway, but I remained seated. I was completely heart broken; this felt worse to me then when I found out Michael was cheating, and by the way Sawyer looked at me, he was, too.

It hurt so damn much knowing I was the cause of his pain.

Sawyer

Abby was at registration at the school. *Registration*? What the hell is that about? Why was she there? Why was she still in this damn town? I thought she was gone already.

How have I not heard this yet?

My mind raced as I thought of all the possible solutions. Has she changed her mind, and decided to stay? Did she talk Michael into staying here with her? Were they living here now? Hell, I didn't know how I thought about that. Seeing them through town was inevitable and I didn't think I would physically be able to see them. It would hurt way too fucking much, knowing that I was so close to having that life with them.

Or was Abby here alone?

I needed to know.

I paced in my classroom, trying to pluck the courage to go back down to the Commons. Maybe I should go back down, or corner her in the parking lot so we weren't in front of all those eyes? I wanted a private word, just in case things escalated. God only knows what she would say. She was so unpredictable.

I nodded firmly and found my feet walking back down to the Commons. My eyes darted to where Abby was sitting, but she wasn't there. I glanced around the room quickly, but she was nowhere to be seen. I started running to the parking lot, my eyes searching for her mother's blue SUV, but I couldn't see it. I ran back and forth down the sidewalk, looking for any hint of her.

My eyes located the SUV, driving down the block. I froze. Do I call her? Ask her to turn around and come talk?

I felt my pockets, trying to feel for my cell.

"*Shit*," I hissed. It must be on my desk.

I looked back at the SUV, my heart racing and begging me to start running, but she was too far. I'd never make it in time. The red brake lights flashed as she stopped at the stop sign. She turned and was out of sight.

Abby

As soon as I got into the car, I was crying. Sobbing was more accurate. I knew I shouldn't drive, but the last thing I wanted was to be seen in the parking lot crying like a fool. The town would definitely think I was an emotional wreck. I turned down the street with no destination in mind. I couldn't go back home with red, puffy eyes. I turned down the road and found myself driving out of town. My throat was on fire as the sobs continued.

I was in no position to drive, but I kept going forward, trying like hell to focus on the road in front of me, but my vision was clouded.

I had no destination in mind, but I knew what I craved—alone time.

Sawyer's sad eyes blinded me as I drove; it was all I could see. *He* was all that I could see. I was the one who made him feel that way. I was the one who put an end to our relationship when it was going so good, *so right*.

I was the one who broke his heart when all he did was care for me.

How could I do that to him? How could I have picked *Michael* over him? He was perfect, kind, and sweet, and made me feel like I was the only one that ever mattered. Michael never made me feel that way. *No one* has ever made me feel that way. Saw cared for me, and for my Remmy. And what did I do to repay him?

I broke his fucking heart.

I sobbed again as I thought about Remmy. I ruined that chance for him; a chance for Remmy to grow with someone so kind and attentive like Sawyer. He's been asking about Sawyer every day, and each time, I change the subject as best as I can. I don't know what to say to him. How do I tell my son that we can't see him anymore? That I ruined our chance? When I told him we were staying here in Illinois, he nearly leaped with excitement because he could *'spend so much time with Soy-er'*.

It was like a knife right to the gut.

I found myself turning down a different country road. Determination swept over me as I tried to recall the direction Sawyer took me on our first date to that beautiful sunflower field. It was probably a horrible mistake to go there, but it sounded like the best place for me to gather my thoughts and myself. I took a turn, but even as I was driving down the road, it didn't look right to me, but I continued, swiping at the tears as I drove. I tried to clear my throat, but the lump remained.

I took an immediate left turn; my eyes narrowing on the road in front of me. I was determined to find my way.

It felt impossible. All the country roads looked the same to me now; no houses, just corn and beanfields for miles. I groaned out loud and the urge to scream overpowered me as I hit the steering wheel with my palm.

I wanted to scream at everyone and everything. *Why* was my life so messed up? *Why* couldn't I just allow myself to be *happy*? *Why* did I break everything that I touched?

"What did I ever do to you!" I yelled out loud to no one in particular, but the words felt good coming out. I was a good person; I give, but the world keeps taking things from me. I was a good mother. I tried to be a good wife; hell, did I try to be with that man.

"Just let me find my fucking way in this world," I yelled; tears were flowing fully now as my trembling hands hit the steering wheel again. "Tell me what I'm supposed to do," I begged; my throat burned and the tears felt hot on my face.

My vision was getting way too cloudy. I knew I should pull over. I blinked, and when I opened my eyes, I screamed again, my mouth dropping. A beautiful black and white shepherd dog sprinted into the road and stopped right in the middle. My eyes widened as I clutched the wheel tighter, stomping my foot on the brake. My tires shrieked underneath and spun on the gravel road, and I tried like hell to regain control. The car swerved to the side, and I closed my wet eyes shut as I listened for the thump I desperately didn't want to hear.

My hands were rigid on the steering wheel, and I was breathing hard. I looked around slowly and put the car into park. My lower lip trembled as I tried unbuckling my seatbelt; it took me a few times to get it to snap open. I opened the door and on shaky legs I stepped out of the car, hoping and pleading that I didn't hit that dog.

The dog was upright though and cocked his head to the side as if he was confused. I let out a huff as more tears fell. I approached the dog, my shaky hand outstretched for him. He cocked his head up, sniffed in my direction, and then slowly crept towards me.

"Hi, you beautiful baby," I murmured through my tears. "You have to be careful, you sweet pup. I almost hit you."

I crouched down in the road and the dog instantly nuzzled his head into my chest. I kissed his head, stroking his soft fur, and felt for a collar, but he or she, I couldn't get a good look, wasn't wearing one. I glanced around, looking for an old farmhouse that maybe was his home, but we were surrounded by fields only. The dog licked my face happily and I let out a shaky laugh.

"You sure are sweet..." I mumbled. "Where do you live?"

The dog's ears perked as I said those words, and he jumped out of my grasp, his dirty paws leaving muddy prints on my shirt. He did a complete circle, wagging his tail excitedly before he took off in a dead sprint again.

"Oh, be careful!" I called to him; my hand stretched for him. He ran to a street sign and stopped, wagging his tail excitedly, as if I should follow him. I looked around the empty road for any sign of his owner, hoping to see a truck or a car heading this way to claim him, but the air around us was silent. He cocked his head toward me as I stared at him. Something told me that I should follow him; I don't know why, but it felt right. I glanced at my car behind me; it was parked in the middle of the road haphazardly from my abrupt stop. I got back into the car and crept the car forward slowly, careful in case the brave pup sprinted back to me. I rolled the car into park on the side and flipped my hazards on just for precaution.

My mind was telling me that I should get back in the car and go home; clearly, this wasn't exactly *safe* for a woman to be walking around like this, on a dead gravel path in the middle of nowhere by herself, but this wasn't Florida. This was home and a sense of peace washed through my chest, telling me that I had nothing to fear.

I walked towards the dog, glancing one more time, to make sure that the road was empty. I bit my lip and stopped myself right in front of the pup.

"What are you doing, sweet girl? Or are you a boy? Do you need help finding your way home? I know I sure do." I whispered to the dog. I bent my hand to pet the sweet pup, but the dog spun around quickly in a circle again, his tail wagging excitedly. I glanced around, looking to see *why* he was so happy, when my eyes looked up and noticed the green street sign.

In white bolded letters, read *SAWYER RD*.

I clapped my hand over my open mouth and gasped, a sob shaking my fallen shoulders. As if my legs could no longer take it, I fell right to my knees and slammed my hands into the earth's surface.

And I ugly cried all over again.

I cried for my destroyed marriage. Even though I was ready to move forward it still hurt that it was over.

I cried for losing my career and not knowing what the future held for me.

I cried for the time that I missed with my parents and all the memories we could have made together.

I cried for losing *myself* over the years and not knowing who I was except being a mother.

I cried for uprooting and changing Remmy's life.

And I cried for breaking Sawyer's kind, gentle heart and my own in the process.

The dog whined as he forced his way underneath my chest and tried to lift me up. I fell on my bottom and crossed my legs. The dog made his way on top of me, licking my chin before resting his head right on my heart.

I sat there for what seemed like forever, stroking the dog until the tears finally stopped. I sniffled, whispering praises to the dog for bringing me here. I looked up at the sign and read *Sawyer Rd* when my lip started to tremble again.

"Are you my sign? Did you come into my life for a reason?" I whispered to the dog, nuzzling my face into his fur. He smelled like soil and was in clear need of a bath, but I didn't mind. His warmth and sweet kisses were calming and was exactly what I needed.

"Come on then," I told the sweet pup. He bounded off me, and I headed back to the car with the sweet puppy following behind. I opened the back seat car and looked around for my mother's blanket. I laid it on the back seat for the puppy and let him climb in. In one leap, he bounded in. I closed the door and went to the driver's seat, and the dog jumped into the front seat, his tail wagging and tongue hanging out.

"Oh crickets," I mumbled underneath my breath. I envisioned little muddy paw prints over my mother's leather interior. I sighed, opened the door, and tried to sneak my way in. He leapt to the passenger seat, his tail wagging madly as I turned the key to the ignition.

I turned the key in the ignition, patted the dog's head, and did a U-turn right in the middle of the road.

I wasn't driving home though.

I was driving to Sawyer's.

Chapter 20 - *Sawyer*

I couldn't concentrate at school, even though I tried desperately to. I kept tapping my playbook with my pencil repeatedly, until finally, I gave up. I ended up packing my things in my briefcase and took off for home. I forced myself on the drive to think about the last football practice and what plays I wanted the team to improve on, making a list in my head of the next practice's structure.

I pulled into my drive and walked up to the house. As soon as I swung the door open, I felt a stab of loneliness wash over me. I sighed and dropped my briefcase by the door and headed to the kitchen for a beer. It was only five o'clock at night and I had no plans. The thought of spending the evening alone again made my heart pang in my chest.

I was so fucking tired of being alone.

I popped off the beer tab and walked back into the living room and plopped down on the sofa. I flipped through the apps, trying to find a show or movie to watch that would distract me, but nothing looked appealing to watch. I groaned, turned the TV off and stood up from the couch.

I was pacing again, back and forth in the living room.

Maybe I should just drive to the Foster's and find out for myself what was going on with Abby... but what if Michael was there? I tried to think of a reason that I could just show up there, unannounced. Abby did have some things still here. I could pack them up, and bring it over?

Even that sounded lame though.

I sighed and cursed at myself again.

I heard crunching gravel from outside and stopped pacing. I went to the front window and peaked through the curtains.

I held my breath.

I bolted to the front door and jerked it open, my eyes wide and heart hammering as I watched Abby stumble out of the car; she clearly wasn't paying attention to me, but to something else in the car. Abby closed the door carefully and looked up at my front door.

Her eyes widened as she froze in her steps; her face crumpled into a sad smile and with that fire in her eyes that I loved, she sprinted towards me.

My body moved forward, and I met her on the sidewalk as she leapt into my arms. I held her tightly to my chest, closing my eyes as I committed this moment to memory. She smelled and felt so good. I kissed the top of her head as her face pressed firmly on my chest.

"Abby," I whispered.

"Don't say anything," she said back, squeezing her arms tighter around me. "Just, don't."

I felt the tears well in my eyes as I held her tighter and stroked her beautiful hair. I never thought I would be able to hold this woman again; my heart lifted as it continued to strike in my chest. That's when I noticed a black and white dog running around us.

"Did you bring a dog?" I asked, my eyebrow raising.

"Yeah," she admitted with a little laugh.

"Is it yours?"

"No."

"Did you steal a dog, Abby?" I asked. I felt her shoulders shaking as she laughed without sound.

"No, she just kind of... found me. It's hard to explain, but really, that dog is the reason I'm here."

"Good dog," I murmured; I swept my hands through her hair.

Abby lifted her face from my chest and looked at me; her pretty blues pierced mine as they glossed over.

"I missed you so much, Sawyer," Abby whispered.

I felt my body hesitate as I scanned her stunning eyes. They were red and puffy. "Why are you here, Abby?" I said quietly.

"I just had to see you. I mean, I'm not exactly sure why I'm here, I just knew I *had* to be here," she said quickly. She gave me a sad smile. "Sawyer, it's always been *you*. I'm sorry that I am just now realizing it, but it's the tru—"

I didn't even let her finish. I leaned my head down and pressed my lips firmly to hers. Our mouths moved together in unison, slow, perfectly, before her mouth parted and we let our tongues collide. I relished the way her lips felt on mine and how she tasted. Her body instantly melted into mine as I heard the sensual hum from her throat.

I knew we had to have that talk; there were a lot of hurt emotions we needed to air out before we could move forward, but right now, that talk could wait. The only thing that mattered to me was that she was here.

I separated our lips and looked back into her blues. I rubbed my nose gently on hers, back and forth.

"Sawyer, we really should talk."

"Another time," I whispered, pressing my lips back to hers. "Right now, I just want to enjoy this."

Abby's eyes sprang with tears again as I kissed each of her dimples, her jaw, her neck, and back to her lips.

"I love you, Abby," I whispered against her jaw. "I always have."

There it was. Out in the open. Finally, I said the words I needed to say to her for so long. I pulled back and watched her face transform. Her eyes spilled a few more years before she whispered back, "I love you, Sawyer Gibson."

My heart instantly soared above us as I pulled her tightly against my chest and I buried my head back into her neck, reveling, enjoying, the way she felt with me; against all odds, my girl came back to me.

The dog ran circles around us, barking excitedly as he did.

Abby

Everything felt right in the world; the stars finally aligned in place. Emma, Sawyer, Lance, and Sammy were helping me unload boxes from my U-Haul into my new rental home. I found a place to rent a few days after my reunion with Sawyer. It wasn't a big home, one story with just two bedrooms, small bathroom, and a kitchen and a living room, but for just Remmy and I, it was perfect. We had a decent size backyard that was fenced completely. On the plus side, it already had a swing set outside and it allowed pets.

Remmy buzzed around the backyard excitedly with our new dog, Bella. When Remmy saw her, he fell in love with her and gave her the name. She instantly popped into Remmy's lap, and she's been his little follower ever since. Sawyer and I tried to find the dog's owner, but no one claimed her, and she wasn't chipped. We took her to the vet, and all was well; a little malnourished, but fine. We put ads all over town, but no one came forward. I told Remmy that a day may come where someone does, just in case, but I secretly hoped no one would.

Emma and I started unpacking boxes in the kitchen. Sammy brought a big box in with a huge grin on his face. I was starting to adore Sammy; he was so kind, and such a happy kid.

"Where would you like this?" Sammy asked.

"Um, the living room would be great. Thank you, Sammy." He nodded and set it down with the other boxes.

"Ms. Carter, are you going to the football game this Friday?" Sammy asked.

I nodded. "Sammy, you can call me Abby. Sammy grinned sheepishly. "And yes, I am. I wouldn't miss it."

"Do you think you could maybe sit with my mom? She's going, and I'd hate for her to sit by herself," Sammy asked. "She keeps to herself a lot, but I thought it would be nice if she made a few friends." He shrugged nonchalantly. My heart went out to him. He was such a nice kid.

"Of course, I would love to," I told him. Sawyer already pointed her out to me when we were walking Bella through town. She was in the bakery, cleaning up a table. "I'll look out for her."

"Thank you," he said with a grin. "I'd better get back to it."

Emma nudged me with her arm, a smile playing on her thin lips when Sammy walked away from us. "How are things with you and Sawyer?"

"Great. Perfect. *Wonderful*," I said with a dreamy sigh. Emma beamed.

"I'm glad everything is working out," she murmured. "You deserve it. And you know, you can work as many hours as you want at the daycare until you find something else. Or…" Emma said with a playful grin. I already knew where she was heading with this. "You can become my full timer."

"*Maybe*," I replied.

Sawyer and Lance came in, boxes piled on top of their arms. Sawyer set them in the living room and let out an exhausted groan.

"I thought you said you only had a few things to unload from the U-Haul. That is *not* a few things." He put his hands on his hips in a dramatic sort of way. I giggled.

"Oh hush, yes it is. I barely brought anything from Florida."

"Um, no," Sawyer said, shaking his head. "That's a lot from Florida."

"That box goes into Remmy's room," I told him, pointing to the box by his feet. He rolled his eyes at me.

"I just hate that you're unloading all of this here. I mean, it won't be long until you move in with me." Sawyer displayed his cocky grin while his eyes danced mischievously.

"Oh, you think so?" I asked, walking towards him. I wrapped my arms around his waist as he nodded determinedly.

"I know so," Sawyer said. "Don't you know, Abby, that we are made for each other?"

I heard Emma pretend to gag behind us. I giggled again as Sawyer made a face at her.

"I do know that, but that doesn't mean that we need to live with each other, Saw. I thought we said we were going to take it slow."

"I think waiting thirteen years for you is slow enough. I don't plan to wait that much longer." Sawyer nuzzled his face into my neck. "I'm not a patient man," he whispered, kissing my cheek.

"You'll have to be," I told him simply. "Nice and *slow*, Sawyer."

"I'll get you with me sooner or later," Sawyer said, kissing the tip of my nose. "I'll wait forever for you if I have to because one day, Abby Lou, I'm going to marry you."

I shook my head at him as I grinned at that gorgeous man. Hearing him say those words to me made me want to jump him right there. I leaned in and pressed my lips to his in response.

"I've found my way back to you, isn't that good enough?" I whispered. Sawyer's eyes danced, his fingers lightly caressing my cheek.

"For now."

And he pressed his lips softly back to mine.

Epilogue: Abby

Friday night football was in full swing this evening, the bright lights illuminating the field. The crowd was alive tonight, cheering and chanting for our first home game. A few cowbells rang in the air as our team got into position on the field.

Sawyer was standing on the sidelines, pacing back and forth. He looked as fine as ever this evening, with his khaki shorts, black Nike tennis shoes, and his black polo. The polo fit him perfectly, and I watched from the bleachers as his shoulders flexed. He looked down at his clipboard intently. Even from here, I could tell that he was nervous. He's been working so hard with his team, determined to take the team all the way this season.

Lance sat next to me on the silver bleachers, his leg jiggling nervously as he hunched over. His jaw was tense, as if he was a coach, too. He loved football as much as Saw did; I always wondered why he didn't try to be a coach as well. He would have been a great one.

I looked down at the sidelines and watched as my little man paced behind Sawyer, his little arms on his hips as he walked back and forth, nodding just as Sawyer was. Remmy was so excited to be able to stand on the sidelines with him; it's all he could talk about all week. He was wearing black athletic shorts that could barely be seen because of the team's football jersey he was wearing; it nearly reached his ankles. His jersey was number one, because as Sawyer had said to him, "You're my number one guy, always." I have officially become a pile of mush in Sawyer's hands. Each day with him gets better and better and I've found myself completely in love with that man.

Lance's eyes scanned the field as he looked for a certain player. I already knew who he was looking for, and when he located Sammy, he clapped with enthusiasm, his head nodding. Sammy's hard work all summer paid off; he was on the field, jumping up and down, getting amped for the game.

I rested my hand on Lance's jiggling knee for a moment. "It'll be alright," I told Lance. He eyed me from the corner of his eye, a smirk on his lips.

"I know it, I just want him to play well tonight."

"He will," I said, patting his shoulder. It was adorable watching Lance get close to Sammy. It was always 'Sammy this,' and 'Sammy that' with him these days. I loved that for Lance.

I eyed the crowd and noticed a woman walking up the steel bleachers. Her eyes looked wide, as she scanned the crowd for an empty space. She was a pretty woman; her dark brown hair was piled into a clip on the back of her head. She had a thin face, full lips, and bright green eyes, the same as Sammy's. She was wearing jean shorts and a black tee shirt with an oversized black bag slung over her shoulder.

"Jessie!" I called.

I introduced myself to her the other day at the bakery when she was working, making good on my promise to Sammy. Jessie's eyes looked over to me and I saw her shoulders relax. She gave me a tentative smile and a wave and started to walk towards us. "I saved you a seat." I told her, patting the empty space next to me.

"Thank you," she whispered. "It's a full house tonight."

"Yes, it sure is. I love that for the boys." Jessie sat down next to me, and I noticed as she fidgeted nervously with her bag, her body tense. It didn't fail my notice that Lance was practically gawking at her. I nudged him, giving him the *look*, and he sheepishly grinned and looked away from Jessie.

"Jessie, have you met Lance?" I asked her, gesturing to Lance. Jessie's green eyes looked over at Lance and her brows pulled together.

"Not officially, but I've heard of you," Jessie said quietly. She extended her hand to Lance, and he quickly took it, his eyes wide as he stared at Jessie.

"Nice to meet you," Lance told her.

"And you," Jessie whispered. She quickly removed her hand from Lance's and started fidgeting back to the strap of her bag.

"I love your boy, he's a real good kid," Lance said to her.

"He is," she agreed quietly. "But I should tell you, I don't like that he's working with you."

Lance's eyes sprang wide as his lips pulled into a half grin. I was also surprised and couldn't stop myself from looking back and forth between them.

"I didn't know that," Lance replied.

"He should be studying, working towards his goals. He wants to go to college," she said. "It's nothing personal towards you."

"Well, he and I already had that talk; he knows his schooling and sports go first."

Jessie's eyes averted over to him as she studied Lance's face. My gaze flitted between Jessie and Lance again. I couldn't help but feel that a spark just ignited, and my heart lifted at just the thought. I've always had a soft spot for Lance; him finding happiness is something I have always wanted.

"Sammy's on the field," I said, nudging Jessie with a smile. Her eyes left Lance's as she glanced over at me.

"He told me he was starting today. I thought I was going to be late."

I shook my head. "No, you're right on time."

The whistle blew as I said the words, and I watched as our kicker ran at the ball and kicked it high above the other team.

I glanced down at Remmy and Sawyer on the sidelines; my two favorite people. Sawyer stood like a statue, arms over his chest, nodding at the field. Remmy stood next to him, his little face glancing up at Sawyer every so often. He copied Sawyer's movements to a tee, his little head nodding just as Sawyer had done.

I couldn't help but grin down at my boys. My whole heart was on that field.

And I wouldn't have it any other way.

The End

J. Glassburn

The story continues…

Can Lance let himself fall in love?

Will Jessie ever allow herself to fall in love again?

Stay tuned for Book Two in the 'My Way To You' series where you will find yourself in Lance and Jessie's journey and even more to Abby and Sawyer's future.

Want to connect? Visit my website, www.jglassburn.com and join my newsletter for updates and more.

The release date for Book Two will be announced on my website as well as my other social media channels.

Follow me on Facebook @authorj.glassburn where news, updates, and more will be shared.

Thank you from the bottom of my heart for reading 'My Way To You'! I hope you enjoyed Sawyer and Abby's journey to love.

Love,

J. Glassburn

Cover designed by Ryan Palmer with Ryan Palmer Art

Follow Ryan on Facebook 'Ryan Palmer Art' to see more of his amazing talent!

Made in the USA
Monee, IL
01 November 2022